SOUL FRAUD

Book One of
The Debt Collection

SOUL FRAUD

Book One of
The Debt Collection

ANDREW GIVLER

For Mom and Dad, who taught me to read and to love stories.
Basically, this is their fault.

CHAPTER 1

They say "the Devil is in the details," but I met my first demon at the movies. Some poor sucker had to go all the way down to Georgia to sell his soul to the Devil, but I met one of his employees in an empty theater in Los Angeles, which I guess makes sense. It was my twenty-fourth birthday, and I was hiding from it. I did this by going to one of those five-dollar movie theaters that can only exist in a place where people are so obsessed with entertainment they even like the old stuff.

It was the kind of theater that only showed old films from before the world was in color, back when all sound was polluted with hisses and pops. The cushioned seats were probably older than me. They smelled of cigarettes, stale popcorn, and what I can only assume was distilled sadness. But I didn't care about any of those things. It was just a place to go to be alone. My hair was still wet from the drizzle that often accompanies the emergence of spring. Unbidden, I heard my mother's voice, echoing from my childhood: *April showers bring May flowers.* I've always thought April got the raw deal in life, something my birth month and I have in common.

I pulled the bottle of tequila I'd smuggled into the theater out from under my jacket and wrested it open. I say *smuggled*, but if I'm being honest, a place like that probably didn't care. The elderly man who was working the graveyard shift that night seemed more upset that someone bothered to show up. It meant he had to turn on the projector instead of dozing behind the popcorn machine or whatever he normally did with himself.

I took my first sip of tequila and learned an important lesson: Breathing right after drinking raw liquor burns. I coughed on the fumes stuck in my throat for a few seconds before staring at the bottle with a sense of betrayal. I'd never really drank before; it hadn't been interesting to me. But with my life firmly hanging out on the bedrock level of Rock Bottom™, I was willing to try almost anything. Every action movie I had ever watched had promised me that the miraculous adult juice was the key to a getaway of bliss. A couple glasses of scotch or a few beers with the bros, and everything was supposed to be better. Instead, it turned out alcohol kind of sucked. Whatever. So did everything else. I could have another drink.

I managed to take my second swig with a bit more dignity and settled more into my chair. I don't actually like old movies or old anything, but flashing lights and sound are good distractions from thinking, and I had a lot I didn't want to think about. Four years ago to the day, my mother and my two sisters died in a car accident. They were on their way to visit me at college for my birthday when April showers swept them off the road and into a swollen creek.

Since then, I'd flunked out of college, the love of my life—not that she knew it—got engaged to my best friend, and I basically ended up living on his couch. Which was why on tonight of all nights, I wanted to be anywhere else. Every year since the accident, my friends tried a different birthday approach. The surprise party didn't go well. The fancy dinner last year was awkward too. So this year I was hiding from them to spare us all. Maybe this tequila stuff would turn out to be a better companion.

"Hey," a voice whispered at my left elbow. With a strangled yell, I jumped in my seat. Cut me some slack, when the movie started, I was the only person in the theater, so no one should've been there to talk to me. Plus, talking while a movie is playing is a sin. I glanced over, and my jaw hit the horrific, sticky floor.

The creature sitting next to me looked about five feet tall. He had a neatly trimmed thick black beard accompanied by a comically long handlebar mustache. His bright teeth were so white that they seemed to glow as he flashed a smile in the dim theater. Two black horns curled out of his forehead and pointed inward. In his left hand, he held a pitchfork, and the end of a pointed red tail (which I assumed was his) was wrapped around the tines. Oh yeah, and his skin was a bright red, like tomato soup. I probably should have mentioned that first.

"Are you Matthew Carver?" he asked.

I nodded stupidly, too shocked to formulate a more intelligent response. Technically, most of my friends called me Matt, but I wasn't prepared to correct this thing, whatever it was.

"Great," he said with another quick smile and a rush of breath as he inhaled. "My name is Dan. I work in the Sales Department of Hell. I was hoping to take a few minutes of your time to speak with you about some of the exciting offers we currently have available. Would that be all right with you?"

I looked down at my bottle of tequila and gave it a betrayed look. This was not what I had signed up for. "Maybe I got one of those bottles with a worm or something. That's supposed to make you hallucinate or whatever, right?" I mused. The dem— No. I couldn't bring myself to even mentally call him a demon. The red horned guy sighed flamboyantly and pinched his nose between two clawed fingers.

"There's so much wrong with what you just—no. The worm isn't even used in making tequila. It's a marketing ploy to mess with stupid gringos like you who don't know better. Either way, you're thinking of wormwood and absinthe. And that stuff will mess you up."

I looked up from my bottle and shrugged at him. "I guess *you* would know, wouldn't you?"

Dan the Alleged Demon stared at me for a few seconds, his smile flickering once before freezing in place. My sarcastic jab seemed like something he was completely unprepared for. I graciously gave him a moment to collect himself. Then the moment passed, and his smile returned to life, resting easily on his face.

"Exactly," he said with a little too much gusto and a creepy wink. "But Mr. Carver, while I have you here, let me take a moment of your time to run you through the exceptional deal I can offer you right now."

I took another swig of tequila and shrugged. I had no idea what was going on, but it was a lot more entertaining than whatever old movie was playing. I had no idea who Kane was or what he was a citizen of at this point. I must have missed something.

"It's actually so simple," the demon said, his smile widening far enough that I could see that his teeth were pointy, more like a shark's than a man's. Had they been like that the whole time? I couldn't remember. "If you could have anything in the world right now, absolutely anything you wanted, what would it be?"

I'd like to blame my answer on a strong drink and a low tolerance. But I am not certain I'd drunk enough alcohol to blame it on that. Furthermore, I cannot in good conscience say that my answer would have been any different if I had been stone-cold sober.

"There's this girl," I started.

"Mm-hm, there always is," Dan agreed.

"We've been friends since freshman year of college, and I've always secretly been in love with her, but she's marrying my best friend—"

"And you wish she was with you instead?"

"Yes. No! I don't know?" I sighed. "Of course I wish that. But Connor is my best friend. I wouldn't want to…"

Dan nodded sympathetically and placed a clawed hand on my left shoulder. It emitted a strange warmth that I could feel through my jacket.

"Say no more, my friend. I understand. But I'm happy to say that we can help you with this. In fact, it's our specialty. I can offer you ten years." As he talked, his pearly whites flashed like the moon in the dim theater.

"What do you mean ten years?" I asked.

"Ten years of everything you want. You get the girl, you live out your dream life. It will be literally the best possible outcome you could have."

"Then what happens?" I asked.

His smile winked out again, a momentary flicker like a power surge to a room's light fixture. "Then you'll need to pay for your wish," he said in a somber tone. "The, uh, price for that—the ten years of bliss—is your soul." He stared at me, his enormous smile suddenly absent, and in its place was only a nervous, frozen patience, like a fisherman waiting to see if his bait had hooked me.

Now, this was my first demon sales pitch, but according to every bad TV show I've ever seen, this was the part where I was supposed to be overwhelmed by my crippling depression, desperate for one thing to go right with my wretched life. The crushing weight of this should have made Dan's deal seem worth considering.

But like I said, I've seen those TV shows. I've read those books where the characters do that. I listened to my college professor drone on about Faust. The universal takeaway from all of them is that taking the deal is a *bad* idea. Maybe it's postmodern American cynicism or something, but I wasn't even a little tempted. Which seemed odd to me, since temptation was what creatures like Dan were supposed to be the best at.

"Nah," I said, pausing to take another sip of tequila. "I'm good, thanks." My refusal appeared to hit Dan the Demon with an almost-physical force. He slumped forward in his chair and placed his head in his hands.

"I don't get it," he said into his palms. "Why am I so bad at this?" He raised his head to glance at me with a pitiful stare. "Were you even a little tempted?" he asked hopefully.

"Not really. Sorry, man," I replied. I felt strangely bad for him. Wordlessly, I offered him my bottle of tequila, which he casually accepted.

"Balls," he muttered after taking a sip. "Do you realize what you just did? I can't tempt a miserable human into changing his horrific life, but you can hand me a bottle of liquor without any setup at all. And I took it without a thought!" He pushed the bottle back to me and buried his head in his hands again. He muttered something that sounded vaguely like "Mpphgr denkin Australia."

I didn't know how to react to his pity party. We sat in awkward silence as whatever black-and-white movie continued to drone on. I had some more tequila. Part of me, the ever-present self-aware portion of my consciousness, was very aware of the fact that I was in the process of getting inebriated while hanging out with a demon at a movie theater. What would my mother say? I don't really know. No one ever taught me how to prepare for a situation like this. In all the stories I knew, people always accepted the deal. Maybe when the movie was over, we would both go our separate ways. Maybe demons actually like old movies. Maybe that's all Hell is: endless old movies. I could see that, come to think of it.

"I'm gonna do it," Dan said after a solid ten minutes of silence.

"Hmm?" I asked, trying to not seem rude.

"It's unethical, but who cares? I'm screwed either way."

I realized at this point that Dan was talking to himself. He turned away from me and pulled a briefcase, which had apparently been resting out of view, up into his lap. It was black and looked to be made of cheap faux leather with two flimsy brass clasps holding it shut. Dan held it in his lap for a moment, still closed, hesitating, like a man about to dive into frigid water. After a few seconds, he nodded to himself and opened the case. A reddish glow emerged from the inside, highlighting his face. I felt a blast of heat consistent with the theme of the night.

"Listen, Matthew, you seem like a nice guy," Dan said as he fished around inside the case. He leaned into it, his scaly red arm vanishing past his elbow, which was trippy because there wasn't enough depth to the briefcase for him to be going that deep. "But I have a quota to hit, and as you can see, that's not going well for me." He pulled his hand out, holding a stack of pages with dense printing between his claws. "There it is," he muttered. He snapped the case closed and set it aside.

"Well, I'm sorry to hear you are having such trouble, I guess?" I said. My mother had raised me to be polite. I guess that extended to demons too. She hadn't ever specified them as an exception to the politeness rule. Dan ignored me and produced a pen from somewhere. I say pen, but it was probably more accurately a quill, made with a large black feather. Maybe a raven's? I'm not really up on my quill knowledge. He licked the end with a forked red tongue and began filling out his paperwork.

I sat quietly next to him, content to watch the moving pictures and listen to the fuzzy sound without paying attention. Usually, my brain doesn't stop moving. It is always in search of something interesting. If there was the mental equivalent of a treadmill, my mind was constantly on it. That's not to imply that I'm some sort of genius astrophysicist. More like a hamster on drugs. I'm usually thinking about something dumb like dragons or laser beams. Or about that time I congratulated a woman who wasn't pregnant. But my brain had decided it was time to take a breather for once. The old thought box had kicked its shoes off and was lounging on the couch. It was a nice feeling. I was starting to see the appeal of alcohol.

"Let's see, initial here," Dan murmured to himself. "MSC, MSC, and MSC." Each time he said my initials, he made a mark on his paperwork, and I felt a weird tingling in my fingers and toes. It was a faint electric kiss, the kind you feel a millisecond before you shock yourself on a doorknob after walking on a shag rug with your socks on.

"Wait, what are you doing?"

"Matthew Steven Carver," Dan said, ignoring me and signing the bottom of a piece of paper with a flourish. But Dan didn't say my name. His mouth moved, but I heard my mother's voice. We all have a true name—anyone can call me Matthew, and I'll know that they probably want to talk to me—but when your name is said a certain way (usually by your parents), it grabs you as though someone reached through your chest and squeezed your heart with their bare hands.

I felt that same jolt, but magnetized by a thousand—no, a million times. My skin felt too tight for my body. Pins and needles flared everywhere. Not as if my leg or arm had fallen asleep, but as though every part of my being had. Dimly, I was aware of the sound of the tequila bottle shattering as I dropped it from my stunned hands. I don't know how long it was before I could think straight. It might have been five seconds or five minutes.

When I came back to myself, Dan was almost done packing away everything in his weird briefcase.

"What the hell was that?" I asked angrily. My heart was racing. I had a terrible feeling that I knew the answer. Dan froze for a second, bloodred shoulders hunched away from me. If he wasn't a demon, I'd have said he was scared of me. He turned back to face me, his glowing smile replaced with a stony expression.

"Like I said, you seem nice, but I've got a quota to hit. I'm in between a rock and a fiery place. Best of luck. I hope you enjoy your life, I really do. We will see you in about ten years."

He stood up, briefcase nowhere in sight, and turned to walk away. It was at this moment I realized he was naked. Thankfully, his lower half was covered in a dense black fur. But I was still far closer to demon butt than I ever wanted to be. I couldn't believe what was happening. This was against every rule I had ever read about in supernatural stories.

"Are you kidding me?" I asked. I leapt to my feet and glared at the retreating demon's back. This was for two reasons: partly because I was furious, but also because I wanted to get my face farther away from demon-butt altitude. It was so weird with the tail and the fur and everything. "Did you literally commit, like..." I frantically sought for a word to express what was happening. "Soul fraud?"

Dan turned to face me, his clawed hands clasped together in a nervous gesture. "For what it's worth, because I feel awful about the whole thing, I hooked you up," he said.

"You what? What does that even mean?" I shouted.

"You know, I supersized the deal. I gave you the Eddie Bauer edition. You are going to enjoy these next few years, man, don't worry." His freaky white smile returned, and he winked at me. "Trust me, you won't regret it."

"Trust you? *Trust you?* You are literally a demon who is trying to defraud me out of my soul or something, and you want me to trust you?"

Dan winced a little bit, and the smile gave up and retreated once more. "I'm sorry," he muttered again, and then (literally) turned tail and ran out of the theater.

"I am never drinking again," I muttered, looking down at the shards of glass at my feet.

CHAPTER 2

April was still showering away when I emerged from the theater. I snuck out past the dozing attendant before the movie ended. There was broken glass and tequila all over the floor, and I couldn't deal with that right now. I felt bad, but given the circumstances, not that bad.

The theater was five or six blocks from the L.A. apartment I shared with Connor. That is the trick to hiding when you don't have a car. You gotta go far enough to be annoying to find, but close enough that you can amble back home.

The rain was cool, but the night was still warm. The California heat had poured into the pavement during the day, radiating surprising warmth hours past when the sun went down. The sidewalks were mostly empty, since most people don't like to walk in the rain. It was still a few hours before midnight, and plenty of cars drove by, threatening to spray the few pedestrians as they plowed through the puddles.

I spent the first three blocks of my journey home trying to rationalize what had happened. Just because Dan the Demon told me that tequila with worms didn't give you hallucinations didn't mean he wasn't a hallucination. In fact, that sounded very much like the kind of thing a hallucination would say.

But as much as I wanted to, I couldn't convince myself that I had somehow imagined the whole thing. Even in the most vivid dreams I have ever had, there was always some sort of surreal quality to them. I couldn't feel the chair I was sitting in or couldn't read the words on a page. But there had been no snags in the fabric of reality during that scene. I had felt the crappy theater chair I was sitting in. I could read words on the screen. There had been absolutely zero clowns. As much as I might want to, I couldn't dismiss what had just happened to me as some sort of crazy fantasy.

At the same time, who even believed in demons anymore? I mean, besides old church ladies, people from third-world countries, and apparently me now. Even if I accepted that demons were real—I really had no proof that they weren't other than the fact that I didn't want them to be—then what else was real? Things like unicorns, magic, and the Tooth Fairy all became a lot more plausible.

I spent the rest of my walk home specifically trying *not* to think about demons and monsters. Which, naturally, meant I thought of nothing but. Have you ever tried to not think of something specific, like elephants in ballet tutus? It's literally impossible. Almost as bad as trying to not think about manual breathing.

At one point, the downpour increased, and I stood under a bus station awning, letting the angry sky vent a little more of its frustration. The desert and the sky don't get along as far as I can tell. Desert Dude is always hot and cranky, and when Lady Rain finally decides to visit, she isn't gentle. It feels like those of us dumb enough to live in the wasteland that is San Fernando Valley are stuck in between their eternal lovers' quarrel.

Stuck with nowhere to go, I pulled out my phone and checked it for messages. A couple from my friends wishing me well or checking in on me. None from my father. On a whim, I pulled up his contact and stared at it for a long moment before putting my phone away and walking out into the rain. It wasn't worth it. Not even for a birthday.

The floating feeling from the tequila faded on my walk. Maybe the constant drizzle and the exercise had sobered me up. Maybe there was something about being visited by a demon that lowered your blood-alcohol content. Or—and probably most likely—maybe I hadn't actually had as much as I thought.

The old four-story building that housed our apartment was one of those buildings that are probably historic but no one has ever cared enough to take care of it. A vibe that is consistent with the neighborhood of Northridge, a place I often refer to in my head as the "armpit of Los Angeles" because we are off to the side, and it smells a little funky. It's the Valley, what can I say?

The tan limestone exterior had wooden accents that were splintering and worn down from years of being exposed to the elements. The brown trim was faded and in desperate need of a new coat.

I opened the front door, which creaked in mild rebellion. Stopping at the bottom of the linoleum stairs, I tried to mentally prepare myself for the onslaught to come. You can never truly avoid some sort of birthday shenanigans with friends like mine. My hiding tonight had only delayed the inevitable. With a sigh, I started my trek up to our third-floor apartment, my wet sneakers squeaking with every step, echoing through the cavernous stairway. While not my preference for a theme song, it also sounded about right.

Our door was also pretty old, but this was one time I was okay with old. It was a big wooden monstrosity, quite heavy and thick. The kind of door that seemed like it could withstand a siege by the Mongol horde. The number for our apartment, thirty-one, was marked with two bronze digits that weren't quite the same size. I let myself in, braced for contact with human beings.

The interior of the apartment was much more modern than the outside would imply. Don't judge a book by its cover, I guess. The door led into a short hallway with a closet and a guest bathroom. The end of the hall opened into a large kitchen area that blended seamlessly with the living room. Being bachelors, Connor and I had stuck a couch and a pair of recliners in front of a TV and called it good. The walls might have once been limestone or wood, but now they were modern drywall, painted and spackled to look like every other white wall ever. A pair of doors on either side of the living room led to the two bedrooms.

"Matthew? Is that you? Connor! Matthew's here," Violet's voice called from the kitchen.

I stepped out of the hallway and did my best to smile. She was a tall girl, probably about five foot ten. Her shoulder-length blonde hair was pulled back in a ponytail, which danced vigorously as she put something away. She was wearing a red apron, which I suspect she brought with her because we didn't own any. Under the apron, she wore a white blouse. She rolled her head to the side and stared at me over her shoulder. Her eyes were a bright green and sparkled with a natural friendliness. She had a round face and a small nose that could only be described as cute by everyone, not just me.

"Hey!" she said brightly with a quick smile and a wink.

Her warmth hit me like a punch to the stomach. Part of me wished she wouldn't do things like that. Not that she was doing anything wrong, or that anything was even her fault. She couldn't help being wonderful any more than I could help noticing.

"Hey, sorry," I said. "I went and caught a movie."

"It's okay, we figured you did something like that. Happy birthday!" Another smile flashed across her face as she turned back to her work. "I baked you a cake. It's cooling in the fridge."

See, this was the kind of crap I was talking about. In an instant,

I felt like a jerk for ditching my friends. I know I complained about them a lot, but they really loved me.

"Hey, man!" Connor enthusiastically greeted me with a sideways tackle that was more hug than attack. "Happy birthday, brother." He pounded me on the back.

"Thanks, dude, I appreciate it." I hugged him back for a second before we parted. Man Code having been correctly observed, I glanced back toward Violet. She was watching us with another smile.

"You called it," she said to Connor. "Movie."

"Of course," he replied with a laugh. "Matt has one move. Totally predictable."

Connor was a bit taller than me, putting him somewhere about six feet and two inches if I had to guess. He was so skinny that he never seemed imposing, instead toeing the line to gaunt. He ate twice as much as me and never gained an ounce.

He had jet-black hair that he kept long enough to almost reach his eyes. It was cemented meticulously in place with some sort of hair product. I'll be honest, I don't know the difference between pomade and glue. The effect was that his hair always looked like a wave, mid crashing down, frozen in time. I guess chicks dig that. He had brown eyes that always seemed to be laughing at a joke no one else got.

"Oh, a package came for you a little bit ago," Connor said. He grabbed a flat manila envelope from the table and handed it to me. "Looks like it's from school."

Sure enough, the envelope, which felt stiff, like it had cardboard in it to keep documents from getting bent, was addressed to me and bore the school's branding.

"Well, they can't kick me out twice, right?" I sighed. "Maybe they realized I owe them more money somehow." I pried the metal clasp open and slid the contents of the package out into my hand. The top piece of paper was a letter addressed to me.

Mr. Matthew Carver,

It has recently come to our attention during an audit of our records that your suspension due to academic inadequacies was the result of a clerical error rather than any fault of your own. Upon further review of this situation, we have found that you have completed the requirements to graduate. Please find enclosed...

That was as far as I bothered to read. My heart racing, I threw the letter aside and looked down at the second piece of cardstock below it. My eyes frantically scanned it, and I saw the words: MATTHEW STEVEN CARVER and BACCALAUREATE DEGREE IN ENGLISH LITERATURE. I stared at my diploma for a long time. I'm not sure how long. The world wasn't making sense.

"Matt, is everything okay?" I looked up to see both Violet and Connor staring at me with worried looks. Wordlessly, I extended the cardboard backing with my diploma still resting on it. They both read it, jaws opening slowly in tandem with shock. It was adorable to watch in a sickening kind of way.

There was another round of hugs and excitement. And cake. Violet had made my favorite: yellow lemon cake with white frosting. Why is it that we describe cake flavors by color? Regardless of the descriptor, it was delicious, and for a moment, I enjoyed my birthday for the first time since... well, you know when.

But that didn't last. For the rest of the night, I had trouble relaxing. My mind was fixated on the diploma. Even if I hadn't failed the classes that they originally failed me for, I never finished my senior year. It was literally impossible for me to have graduated. But there was my diploma, as large as life, sitting on my kitchen table. In the back of my mind, I kept hearing Dan the Demon's voice over and over: *You are going to enjoy these next few years, don't worry.*

Crap.

CHAPTER 3

Sometime in the dead of night, the other shoe dropped. My subconscious wrenched me out of my dreams with all the violence of a car crash. My brain clicked into being awake, and I sat straight up in bed with a horrified gasp.

This might sound ridiculous given the day I'd had, but I hadn't been sure what was bothering me the most. It wasn't that I couldn't identify reasons I *should* be concerned—I could have written an extensive list detailing all the things I was worried about—but there was something that I hadn't thought of yet. My subconscious was more concerned with the proverbial cherry on top of my anxiety sundae.

The little alarm clock on my bedside table read 4:05 a.m., its red light casting a faint glow into my otherwise pitch-black room. I sat there for a few moments, trying to catch my breath. My heart was pounding. I was sticky with sweat, and despite my adrenaline, I felt exhausted.

None of that mattered now; I knew what was *really* bothering me. Dan hadn't been very transparent with the logistics of his scheme. But as far as I could tell, the general idea was that he'd faked my signature on a demonic deal and called it good. And what was the one thing that I had opened my big mouth about and told the demon that I wanted? I had told him that I was in love with Violet and that her relationship with Connor was the roadblock. Well, technically I had only said there "was a girl," but I had a feeling the masters of temptation could fill in the blank. Which meant Dan was going to try to break up Connor and Violet.

I couldn't let that happen. I'll admit that there were nights where I allowed myself to imagine a scenario wherein Violet and I had ended up together. Generally, it involved Connor getting very sick and tragically passing away. Then after a respectable amount of time, the two of us were brought together, having bonded through the hardship of losing him. Or something like that. Don't judge me—I was very sad.

I would never actually wish Connor dead. He was my best friend, my brother in everything but blood. And yes, I was envious of his relationship with Violet. But this wasn't some barbaric myth where one brother killed the other to be with their wife. My macabre daydreams were born out of loneliness, not malice.

Right then, I decided that no matter what, no matter how out of control this situation spiraled, I would not let it reach my friends. I would do whatever it took to keep their relationship safe. Besides, while I wanted to be loved by Violet in return, I'm not pathetic. I wanted her to love me for me. Not because some supernatural power adjusted her until she did love me. That's not love. That's creepy.

But I realized I had no idea how to prevent a supernatural attempt to break them up. I didn't know the rules of the world I had suddenly been exposed to. Everything has to have rules. Ant colonies have rules. The weather has rules. The DMV exists entirely to create and enforce rules. Dan using a contract implied there were rules in his world too.

There was also the slight detail that I wasn't exactly clear on the scientific definition of a soul, but I was absolutely certain that I didn't want to sell mine for ten measly years of fake happiness. I should get at least twenty, minimum.

I needed to get educated fast if I was going to prevent this from tail-spinning further out of control. Sleep was no longer an option for me that night, so I rolled out of bed and grabbed my laptop, figuring I might as well get started. I eased out of my door quietly, doing my best to not make noise. Violet had her own place across town, closer to where she worked, but Connor would be asleep for a few more hours.

I plopped down at the kitchen table and popped my computer open. I sat for a moment, staring at the bright screen, letting my eyes adjust. I wasn't sure where to start. I sat there for a few moments trying to figure that out. "How do I stop a demon from defrauding me of my soul?" didn't seem like a good question to get any useful answers on the internet.

As I started digging, I learned a couple of things quickly. The first was the instant you added the word "demon" to anything, you got a whole lot of wild results. And the second thing was it was impossible to tell which crazy stories were true, and which ideas were from people who didn't know what they were talking about.

Some people claimed the traditional view of demons, that they were fallen angels under the command of good old el Diablo himself. They were generally called super fancy names like Abaddon or Samael. They were most certainly never called Dan.

Other so-called experts said they were powerful dark beings and had nothing to do with angels. Some said they were angry spirits that had never found peace. One of my personal favorites said that they were the stars, and that the earth itself was an angel named Gaia. Any of those could be true. All of those could be true. I did not know enough to sort fact from fiction.

But where did one go to find the people who could help? Was there some Catholic priest who knew the truth or a Wiccan coven I could meet with? And if there was, how in the world was I supposed to find that needle in this supernatural haystack?

I gave up on my internet research with a sigh. Connor would be up soon anyway, and I didn't want to deal with him wondering why I was suddenly fascinated with demons. The best-case scenario for that was him and Violet teasing me about it forever. I certainly wasn't going to tell them the truth. Can you imagine that conversation? I snorted quietly to myself. I needed to take a different approach if I was going to get real answers.

Several hours later, after showering and breakfasting, I was on the streets. The signature April rain clouds were all gone, leaving the sun alone in the clear blue sky. And that big ball of fire seemed determined to make up for lost time from yesterday. The late-morning sun was already starting to crank up the heat, and I suspected by noon I was going to wish I wasn't doing this anymore. Everything smelled clean and washed, which would be nice while it lasted. Big cities after a heavy rain were a lot like Pigpen after a bath—surprisingly clean for a startlingly short amount of time.

I was convinced that the only chance I had of sorting facts from fantasies was to find someone I could talk to face-to-face. It's a lot easier to tell if their story is ridiculous if you can see whether their pupils are the size of dimes.

No matter my approach, I was on an epic needle-in-a-haystack hunt. Finding accurate information online was probably about as easy as finding someone who believed in the supernatural on the street. My odds might be even better on the streets, but that wasn't saying much. Like buying two lottery tickets instead of one. I still wasn't going to win. I wasn't even certain what I was looking for. But in the twelve or so hours since I had been defrauded of my soul, I had realized the internet wasn't the place to find answers. Which, in hindsight, maybe should have been obvious.

A couple blocks from our apartment, I found myself standing outside a Catholic church named St. Sebastian's. It was an old church, nestled next to tall office buildings that had shot up like weeds. But try as they might, they had not been able to strangle it out with their capitalist chokehold. It looked a little run down, like it had gone a few rounds with the Devil recently, but then, who hadn't? The beautiful brown adobe clay rose like a little dome over the one-story roof. Bright purples and deep-blue drapes hung from each of the crosses, flapping gently in the morning breeze. It gave me the impression of something that was scrappy, holding on with sheer determination as the world around it moved on.

This might seem surprising, but I was hesitant to go in there. My grandmother had been a devout Catholic, and I remembered her telling me stories of saints and miracles when I was a young boy. And you'd think, given I had had a run-in with a demon, it made sense to go directly to the opposite team for help. After all, if you're on fire, you call the Fire Department.

Perhaps the only thing I had gained from my research this morning was a healthy dose of cynicism for what a demon even was. I'd also watched entirely too much television about this kind of subject. I knew what holy water was supposed to do to demons and demonic stuff. I couldn't be certain that I wasn't carrying some sort of demon mark or had a demon riding along inside my body with me. I mean, I didn't think I did, but how could I know for certain? The chance I could burst into flames if I stepped onto the church's land was high enough to make me hesitate. I made a mental note of the church and decided I would come back later if I got desperate. Maybe.

My phone vibrated in my pocket. I pulled it out to see it was a message from Violet, asking me if I wanted to grab lunch. I started to agree, but then I caught myself, shadowy tendrils of doubt creeping into my mind. This was not at all out of the ordinary. My own misplaced, tortured emotions aside, we were all good friends. Violet and I had eaten lunch together many, many times before. Under normal circumstances, this wouldn't be cause for alarm.

But everything was tainted now. My paranoia made me look at everything in a new light. Was she asking me because *she* wanted to, or was something else making her think she did? What would happen if I went? How much of a hair trigger did something like this work on? I could go to lunch with Violet and tell her I liked her sunglasses and BAM! She dumps Connor and tries to elope with me. Dan had graduated me from college, and I hadn't even set foot on campus.

I couldn't risk it. I realized, ironically, that my fear of losing my friends was going to make me push them away. But this was only for a time, I promised myself. I was going to fix this. Then things would go back to normal. And my best friends would never even know I almost broke them up with demonic interference. On accident.

I sent her a message back, telling her I was busy but that we'd catch lunch "soon." Right after I finished wrapping up this pesky little soul fraud business. I guess I was hoping there would be some sort of cosmic undo button. All I needed to do was find the right guy who could snap his fingers or click his heels together three times and I would be fine.

I spent the next few hours wandering the streets of Northridge, looking for the right kind of weird. Don't get me wrong, Northridge is weird. But I was looking for Dan the Demon kind of weird. It was several hours past noon when my hunger overcame my need to wander, so I started looking for a place to eat.

I found one a few streets later. A squat bar jammed in between two multistory office buildings. It was a ramshackle wooden building, a little run down and grungy. Its whitewashed sides could use a painting after being scorched by the sun and scoured by the wind for many years. The sign read OLYMPUS BAR AND GRILLE, and I decided my inaugural time going to a bar should be at a place that spelled grill with an extra "e." It seemed fancy.

The inside was in much better repair than the outside. The room was a long rectangle, with a bar running the length of one side and a giant mirror behind it. At least a hundred bottles rested on shelves in front of the mirror, at least partially full of some liquid or another. There was no sign of the grille, but from the smell of greasy food, I was guessing it was in the back beyond the pair of swinging gray double doors with the little circle windows in them.

The wood that made up the floors and booths was dark with a hint of red. I don't know my different wood types on sight. It could have been cherry or redwood? Or maybe it was just stained oak. One of those sounded right. Fans hung from the ceiling, gently spinning. They shone with warm light bulbs that cast a comfortable glow around the otherwise windowless interior. It felt like a well-remodeled cave without the natural light, cozy and hidden despite being in the middle of Los Angeles.

A mountain of a bouncer came up to me and held out his hand. Confused, I stared at him for a moment before realizing he wanted to make sure I was twenty-one. Embarrassed by my pause, I passed him my ID. He checked between it and me a few times, as though he didn't believe it was real. But after a moment, he shrugged and handed it back to me.

"Grab a seat at the bar if you want to order food," he said. "No waiters during the day."

The room was crowded, which surprised me. Almost every other booth was occupied by at least one person. This must be the day-drinking crowd I had heard so much about. I didn't know a Tuesday at two p.m. would be so busy in a bar. Clearly I had a lot to learn.

The demographics of the room seemed strange to me as well. You often hear of bars being referred to as a hangout for a specific type of people: a biker dive, a hippie hangout, a millennial molehill, or something like that. The people in the room seemed to defy categorizing; some were old, some were young. Some people wore business suits and looked important. Another guy looked like he might be carrying around his cardboard house with him, but no one seemed uncomfortable with his presence.

I made my way past a line of booths toward the bar. People stopped their conversations and eyed me in silence as I passed. They must be able to tell I was new to this. Maybe there was a kind of rite of passage for rookies to a bar like this one. I had run into too many things that I didn't know in the last day. It was a little depressing. What was the point of fake-graduating from college if I didn't know how life worked?

The bar was completely empty. I took a seat toward the right on one of those classic bar stools, shiny metal legs with a black leather circular top. I felt, for a moment, like I had arrived as an adult.

The bartender wandered over. He was tall, like basketball player tall, and lean as a toothpick. He had one of those faces that seemed to look upset while at rest. A scar started on his left brow and skipped over his eye socket before continuing down his cheek. Light-blue eyes gleamed in his sunken sockets like hidden gems. He eyed me for a moment in silence.

"What do you want, dealmaker?" he growled. The words sounded reluctant, as though he had been torn about saying them at all.

"I'm sorry, what?" I asked.

"To eat, what do you want to eat?" he muttered.

"Oh, uh…" I glanced down at a menu that had been sitting on the bar, flustered by his aggressive manner. "I'll take the house burger, I guess. Can I get onion rings instead of regular fries?"

"Negotiation skills like that must have been really useful for you," he muttered.

"What was that?" I was pretty sure I had heard him. A growing knot of concern began to curl in my stomach.

"Want a drink with that?" he said in response. His dark eyes were unreadable as they stared at me. I hadn't seen him blink yet.

"I'll have a beer, thanks."

"Which one?" He stared at me.

I didn't know. I knew nothing about beer. But everyone said they were awesome with hamburgers, and I was down to find out if that was true or just another lie.

"I want to try something new. Something that would go well with a burger."

He stared at me again before nodding and turning away. I looked back over my shoulder to survey the room again. Despite what the bouncer had told me, many of the booths had food at their table. People still paused to give me dark looks from time to time. I could all but feel the pressure of half a dozen eyes on my back as I turned forward again. My nervousness kept growing. I was beginning to suspect that this grille was no ordinary grill, and that had nothing to do with the fancy "e."

The bar was weirdly quiet for how crowded it was. I could see people were talking. I could see their mouths moving, but the voices in the room remained a low buzz. As if everyone was on a television with its volume turned down as low as it could go.

The grim bartender returned with a tall glass full of a brown liquid. It had a little bit of froth on the top, which slopped over the side as he put the glass down.

"Can I ask you a question?" He kept staring, so I took that as a yes. "Is there like a membership card you are supposed to have to come here? Why are you and everyone else giving me the stink eye?"

"Don't mind Brett too much," said a voice at my elbow. "He can't help it."

A young man, probably about my age, was standing next to me. He, too, was tall and lean, with short blond hair that had been spiked by some sort of gel. He had a friendly face, his mouth curving up to the left in a permanent half smile. Warm blue eyes peeked at me over a round nose. He wore dark denim jeans and a red V-neck T-shirt that gave off a very casual air. I had spotted him earlier, sitting a few booths over with a group of other twentysomethings. They were turned around in their booth, watching our interaction silently—I wanted to say judgingly, even.

"May I sit?" he asked, pointing to the stool to my left.

With a shrug, I gestured to the stool. He pulled it out and slid onto it with ease. Brett the scowling wonder left without a word. I hoped I would still get my burger. My stomach felt like it was going to resort to cannibalism at any moment.

"My name's Alex," he said, offering his hand. He had a firm grip in his shake without feeling like he was trying to prove a point.

"I'm Matt," I replied.

"Listen," he continued, "I'm a reporter. I work for a kind of newsletter for the community. I was hoping I could interview you about your experience. We don't actually get a dealmaker's eyewitness account very often."

"Why does everyone keep calling me a dealmaker?" I

grumbled. I don't know why I bothered asking. I already knew. I had found my weird place, and my stomach had been the thing to lead me there. Man's intuition is a weird thing, I guess.

"You must be pretty fresh, huh?" he replied.

"What?"

"How long has it been since you sold your soul to a demon?" he asked.

There it was.

Hearing another person saying it out loud was weird. I guess that wasn't surprising. It was a weird situation to begin with.

"I kind of didn't," I replied. Which was technically true.

"Please," he snorted. "I can practically smell brimstone on you. You obviously did. If you know what to look for, it's pretty easy to spot."

"There was this red guy named Dan—"

"Wait, what? You sold your soul to a demon named Dan?"

"No, I didn't," I snapped. I wasn't sure I wanted to tell him the story, but I was sure I didn't like being interrupted. "He stole it. I told him I wasn't interested in any deal, and he freaked out. He signed my name on some contract and then ran away, and now I don't know what to do. I have no idea what is even happening. I only want to fix it."

Alex stared at me for a long moment, his face unreadable.

"I think you better tell me the whole story," he said quietly.

So I did. I told him all about the theater, the tequila, Dan's terrible sales tactics, and his meltdown. I told him everything I could remember down to the feeling that hit me when he forged my signature. I even told him about getting my totally real college degree in the mail.

Alex stared at me for a long time. His blue eyes flicked all over my face, looking for something, a clue to my honesty, maybe. I waited, my heart racing. Even if he didn't believe me, I'd already learned a few things. First, there was some sort of mark on me left by my "entanglement" with Dan. Also, selling your soul to a demon was something lots of people knew about. That meant maybe someone could help me get out of this mess.

"Falling Stars," Alex breathed after a few minutes. "I think you're telling the truth."

I nodded.

"Oh man, this is bad. This is bad."

"You're telling me. The demon stole my soul!" I snapped.

Alex cocked his head as if surprised by my comment. I got the sense he was worried about something else.

"You really are new. Sorry, I kind of... Wow." He took a moment to compose himself. This was not reassuring. My situation was clearly outside of the norm, even for the weirdos.

"I want to help you. Let me come along with you, document what happens. You know, the whole reporter thing. In exchange, I will teach you what you need to know about the real world."

"How do I know I can trust you?" I asked. I'd been burned once already. And even though Alex didn't have horns and a tail, I didn't know him. Alex looked around the room in a sort of sweeping gesture. The day-drinking crowd had lost their interest in me and had resumed muted conversations within their own booths.

"I do seem to be the only candidate for the position," he said quietly. "All I need is a story. This is something different, and the repercussions of it... Well, I guess we will get into that."

I had to admit he had a point. Through the miracle of hunger, I had found the needle in the haystack that I had gone looking for. Even though I wasn't completely certain what the needle wanted, that didn't mean it was worth looking for another one. Sometimes you have to play with the hand you are dealt. I was pretty deep in the hole already. What was another round?

"Okay," I said. "You have a deal. What should we do first?

Is there someone who can fix this? What is a demon anyway? I couldn't find anyone who agreed on that online. Has this happened before?"

Alex held up his hands in a placating gesture, like a crosswalk guard trying to stem the flow of traffic. "Whoa, whoa, calm down. That's quite a bit to tackle at once." He took one of his hands and rubbed them across his face. He seemed to be trying to organize his thoughts. "Okay, here's a good place to start, I think. Take every story you've ever heard, every myth and every legend. It's simpler to start with the assumption they're all real."

"Hang on," I said. "Isn't that impossible? Wouldn't some religions being real require others to not be?"

"Ah," he said with a flicker of his crooked smile. "I said real, not true."

"I'm not sure I follow."

"Just because someone or something is real does not mean they are everything they claim to be." He shrugged. "Here's an easy example: take Mars, the Roman god of war. He's real. I saw him once. Now, him existing doesn't mean that everything he says is true. He wasn't necessarily the father of the Roman people. He could easily have co-opted them and told everyone they were his. He also certainly doesn't have a monopoly on *War*." He chuckled at a joke I felt like I didn't completely get.

I took a moment to wrap my mind around this. In an odd way, it made sense. Human beings were obsessed with making themselves look like more than they were. Why should supernatural beings be any different? That sounded a lot like politicians to me.

"Okay," I said slowly, still processing this burst of information. "But in your explanation, you still called him a god. What is a god? What does that mean?"

"It means he's big and scary. He's in a weight class above

someone like you." He smiled again with what seemed to be genuine humor. "No offense."

The bartender returned with my food. He slid the hamburger unceremoniously down in front of me and left. Good thing I didn't want ketchup. After my run-in with Dan, I could stand to never see the color red again. I scooped up the burger and took a big bite. Despite all this juicy information, I was still starving.

The burger was just okay. The lettuce was a little wilted and the bun a little stale. But I guess that might be bar food. You're supposed to be too focused on your drink to notice that it sucks. Still, I had expected a little more from a grille.

"So, if everything is real, what is true?" I asked in between bites.

"You mean the answer to life, the universe, and everything else? Who knows? It's as confusing on this side of the curtain, man. It might be more, actually. The general rule of thumb is: might makes right."

I didn't like the sound of that. Alex was making me realize that my hope of a simple explanation was a bit naive. Regular life was complicated and messy. No one knew everything that was going on. Why should this be any different?

"Let me put it this way," he offered, "if you end up meeting someone powerful enough to have a legitimate claim to have created a race, a world, or the universe, I don't recommend you doubt them to their face. Most of us weren't there back when everything was jump-started. The ancient beings that might have been there all have a different story to sell. Who knows, one of them might be telling the truth."

"What about demons, then?" I asked, feeling more nervous than when I started asking questions.

"Demons are pretty true to the classic story. Way back when, there was a rebellion in Heaven. Some of the angels tried to do things their own way and were thrown out." He gave me a sidelong glance. "They are almost all completely insane and hated. People who make deals with them are not very popular either."

"So, the dirty looks…" I gestured around the bar with my left hand. He nodded.

"Imagine it's the Cold War, and you're walking around wearing a USSR bomber jacket," he replied.

"Where do I start trying to fix this?" I asked.

Alex pursed his lips thoughtfully. "I've never heard of anything like this happening before. We're going to need to do some digging. Did Dan leave you a copy of the paperwork, by any chance?"

"No, he kind of ran off with it."

"That's unfortunate," he mused. "I think I know a few things we could try. Here, let me give you my number." He reached inside his back pocket and pulled out his wallet. It was an old leather thing; the edges were cracked, and the sides were worn smooth with use. He pulled out a slightly wrinkled card on white stock.

"Alex Johnson, Freelance Reporter," I read aloud. The card also had his number and email address.

"That's me," he said with another ghost of a grin. "Give me a call in the morning. I'm going to check some things to make sure I have my facts straight. Tomorrow we can start poking at this and see if we can get any leads."

Well, shoot. The bar had been much more successful than I had expected it to be. Even if Alex wasn't able to help me, he had certainly been helpful in giving me a crash course in the real world. I still was a little unsure if I should trust him, but as he had pointed out, I didn't have a lot of options. I had promised myself I would fix this before it messed with my friends' lives. I would do anything to keep that promise.

"Sounds like a plan," I said. He offered his hand again, and I shook it.

"Talk to you soon," he promised, which for some reason I believed to be sincere, instead of what most people mean when they say it.

He left without returning to the table he had been sitting at. But as he stepped out into the sunlight, he looked back into the bar with a frown on his face.

CHAPTER 4

After parting ways with Alex, I wandered home. I hadn't realized how far I had walked until I had to go back. By the end of my forty-five-minute return hike, I was glistening with an appalling sheen of sweat.

Connor wasn't there when I got into the apartment, but Friday nights were usually date nights, so I wasn't surprised. It was a little relieving to not find him here. It meant his and Violet's lives were continuing as normal. For now.

I was in the kitchen working on dinner. I don't love to cook, but there's always been something cathartic about it for me. For some reason, I find it easy to think while I cook. I'm not a good cook, but it's the right kind of task to distract my ADHD or something.

When I say that I was "cooking," I really meant that I slapped some chicken in a pan and was making a salad. The salad was from a bag, so I'm not even sure it counts. But that was all I had left in the fridge. I hadn't bothered to go grocery shopping for a week or two. Supplies were running low.

While I worked, I kept running my conversation with Alex through my head, analyzing it from every angle I could think of, hoping to find some sort of obvious lie. But the more I thought about it, the more it made a lot of sense to me. It had been incredibly naive of me to think that a supernatural world would be rigidly structured and straightforward. That might be part of the human fascination with the supernatural. Our everyday vanilla world was so chaotic and messy. But when you read about demons or wizards, their world was often super structured. It turns out even they can't force the world to make sense and follow the rules.

And like the real world, this world was complicated. There were various groups running around that wanted different things. Necessity might give birth to invention, but greed was what lies and deception were born of. There was no reason that Zeus and Odin would get along, assuming they, too, were real. In fact, they probably both wanted to be top dog and would have good reason to lie to and about each other.

Alex had compared it to the Cold War, and I think I got what he was trying to say. Perception and fear were powerful weapons. Superpowers didn't actually like to fight very often; it was too risky to go into an all-out brawl. If Soviet Russia and the USA had nuked each other into oblivion in the sixties, neither nation would have won. So they fought with economies and policies instead of bombs, a battle to the death where both sides agreed to hold back.

But as much as it might all make sense and work logically, I didn't think this truth was good news for me. When was the last time the United Nations stopped Russia from screwing over whoever they wanted? I couldn't think of one. Admittedly, this was partially because I was pretty sure the UN was insanely ineffective and partially because I paid no attention to world politics. I hoped Alex paid more attention to his world than I did to mine.

My chicken was done. The salad was de-bagged. I dumped

it all on a plate and headed toward the little table in the center of our kitchen. My stomach gurgled with a surprising amount of excitement. Even though I had eaten a late lunch, all the walking had made me hungry. No wonder all those marathon runners were so skinny. For a moment, things were a little better. A decent meal when you are hungry can turn everything around.

I heard a key turn in the front door, and it opened. I turned to look down the entry hallway, surprised. Connor and Violet usually weren't back by six on a date night.

"Hey, Matt," a girl's voice called cheerfully. "Connor told me you are totally out of food, so I made a supply run. I figured we could cook you a real meal and watch a movie or something,"

For the second time in two days, I was dimly aware that I had dropped what I was holding. My plate smashed to the ground and shattered, sending chicken and lettuce flying all over the floor.

The girl, a tall brunette with short hair pulled back into a ponytail, gave a startled shriek at the sound. She was wearing khaki shorts and a blue button-down shirt. Her green eyes had a brightness to them that can only live in the eyes of someone who is prone to laughter. Her name was Megan. She was my sister.

You know, one of the dead ones.

"Well, that's just wasteful," she drawled, looking at the disaster at my feet. A smirk lit up her face as she looked at me. I knew that smirk. I had seen it a billion times in my life. I hated it. I loved it. I had thought I would never see it again. "I'm not cleaning that up. But I will make us a real dinner. You get to deal with ground zero." She stepped past the mess, careful to avoid the pieces of lettuce that lay everywhere. The white plastic bags in her hand rustled as she moved.

"Was that a salad from a bag?" she asked as she passed me. "Little brother, you know that's cheating, right?"

With a probably audible clunk, my brain finished its reboot. My heart was racing like a lazy student's on finals day. I think it had forgotten to beat for a few seconds and was trying to catch up.

Damage report: My chicken and bagged salad were ruined. Connor and I were down a plate. Shards of porcelain were everywhere. My sanity was almost as shattered as the plate.

"I'm mad at you, by the way," she continued, ignoring my shock. She had her grocery bags on the counter and was pulling items out. Kind of like the scene where Mary Poppins moves into the Banks' home, but without the physics-defying handbag. She paused her unpacking to glare at me.

"Uh, why... why is that?" I croaked out. My voice wasn't working properly. I was staring at her, trying to soak up the sight of her like a man lost in the desert would guzzle water. She had a strong, slightly pointy nose and a chin with a tiny dimple in the center that was awfully familiar. I saw it every day in the mirror. She definitely looked like Megan.

"You find out you actually graduated from college, and you can't pick up your phone and call your sister?" she yelled indignantly. She had a point. I definitely should have called her right away. I had just, you know, thought she was dead. There had been a funeral, a coffin, and a burial. Silly me.

I moved to the side of the fridge where we kept the broom and dustpan. I felt like a machine following its programming. There were a lot of important thoughts that I was supposed to be having right now. They all started with things like "where," "what," "how," and "why." But they all had the same answer: Dan. I couldn't even begin to process the implications of my sister being alive. What about my other sister and mother? Did this mean they were alive too? Or was Megan the only one to... come back? I was too happy to think much about any of that. Also too afraid.

"Helloooo, Earth to Space Cadet, come in Space Cadet," Megan called.

"Roger, Earth, this is Space Cadet," I responded automatically.

"Dork." She chuckled. "But that doesn't get you off the hook."

"Right, sorry. I don't know what I was thinking. It was so unexpected, you know? I didn't really have a plan."

I started sweeping the mess I had made into a pile. "But I really am sorry I didn't call."

"Hmph," she said, turning back to the counter. But after a second, she looked at me and smiled a little. "Mom would be so proud, you know. Lily too."

That answered that question. Some of my feelings must have shown on my face because she stopped what she was doing and rushed to me. Before I was even remotely emotionally prepared, my dead sister wrapped her arms around me in a fierce hug. For a second, my body locked up in surprise. I don't have a problem with hugs. But I had never thought I would see my sister again, let alone hug her. This close, I could smell her. I knew that smell; I had smelled it my whole life. She smelled like strawberries and innocence.

With her scent, it finally clicked. I think because I've never dreamt a smell. That's only something that can happen when you are awake. My sister was alive. I wrapped my arms around her as tightly as I could. My whole body shook once as I choked back a sob.

"I love you," she said emphatically. "I miss them too."

We stayed like that for a few moments. I didn't want to let go. She was here. She was real. Part of me was afraid if I let her go, she would vanish. Like a really good dream you desperately don't want to wake up from. Eventually, we let go. I returned to my sweeping, and Megan started cooking.

When she met her untimely end, Megan had been going to culinary school. I'm admittedly biased, but she was the best cook

I knew. I was thrilled beyond words to eat her food again.

"What are you making?" I asked as I dumped the last of the plate shrapnel from the dustbin into the trash. She had been quiet for several moments, working her magic on the counter. I'd seen some chicken, heard some eggs cracked, but that could still be turned into many things. Cooking has always seemed so magical to me. Two things can be made from the same five basic ingredients yet taste wildly different. It may only have been a day since I learned magic was real, but part of me always thought cooks were secretly wizards.

"Chicken parm," she replied absently. Of course she was; it was my favorite. She was wearing the apron Violet had been using yesterday. She must have left it here. "Do me a favor, now that you're a real adult. Uncork the wine and pour us some?" She tilted her head toward a bottle she had produced from her bags.

"You got it," I said. I wasn't certain that we had a corkscrew in the apartment. I checked through a few drawers without any luck.

She sighed. "Fourth one down on the left. I told you that was where I was going to put it when I gave it to you. I swear, sometimes words really do go in one ear and right out the other with you."

I checked the drawer she mentioned. There was a corkscrew in there. It was one of those Swiss army–type devices that also featured a bottle opener on the top. A shiver of dread crawled down my spine as I stared at it. Megan had never visited this apartment before the accident. That was a fact. But I could feel the cold stainless steel of an item I had never held before in my hands. I kneeled by the drawer for a long moment, staring at it. Megan seemed to have no idea she had been gone for years, and she had memories to fill them in. She had told me she talked to Connor already, and he didn't call me freaking out. Assuming they talked, that meant he had forgotten her death as well.

It was one thing to have fake memories. It was another to have fake memories that were backed up by physical evidence. Because no matter what I remembered happening, I was still holding a corkscrew that my dead sister thought she had given me, but I was certain she had not. She clearly remembered doing so, but I didn't. I remembered how things had been in my corkscrewless existence when my sister had been dead. Everyone else was crazy, not me. Right?

"Generally, it works better if you take it to the wine bottle," Megan said, her voice cutting into my dark thoughts.

"Silly me." I forced a smile. "I'm new to this." I stood up and returned to the bottle. The corkscrew, despite its mysterious origin, worked like a charm. I found a pair of wineglasses that I didn't remember owning in another cupboard. I poured some of the red liquid into each of the glasses and handed one to my undead sister. Despite my statement that I would never drink again after my run-in with Dan, I felt like this situation justified, nay, required it.

"Cheers," she said, and we clinked glasses. She took a long sip and set hers down on the counter and resumed her work. I took a tentative sip of mine. There are a whole lot of words that people throw around to describe wine, but none of them have ever made sense to me. It was wine. Wine tastes overwhelming to me, a vicious punch of something earthy. It certainly tastes nothing like grapes. I wasn't even sure I liked it. But I was all out of tequila, so it would have to do.

"Real cooking can only happen after you start drinking," Megan stated emphatically.

"Why is that?" I asked.

"Food is like a wild animal. It can sense your fear, or your anger. If you cook stressed out, your food will taste stressed out. If you cook happy"—she gestured toward her wineglass—"your food will be happy too."

"How much did Mom and Dad pay for cooking school again?"

"Listen, I know you're some sort of know-it-all college graduate now, but I'm still the authority on cooking. Trust me; it's a scientifically proven fact. You literary types wouldn't understand anyway." She gave me a firm nod and took another sip of her wine. "Come on, let's sit. We can't do anything while the oven gets hot anyway."

We dropped onto the small couch over by the television in the living room. As I've mentioned, the kitchen seamlessly blended into the living room. It was like two identical squares had been joined end to end to make two halves of a rectangle. A carpet and linoleum divide indicated which half was the living room and which was the kitchen. I know interior decorators like to call it "open concept," but personally, I think it's cheaper to build fewer walls.

"You don't fool me, by the way," Megan told me with a wicked smile as she sipped her wine. She sat with her legs curled underneath her, her blue shirt marked with a few spots of flour that had gotten around the protective shield of the apron. She was leaning back into the corner of the couch and its left arm, wedged comfortably in a way that reminded me of a cat in a box.

"Fool you about what?" I asked. I felt at a disadvantage in this conversation. It was entirely possible she might reference things I didn't recall. Like when a friend at a sleepover makes fun of you for talking in your sleep. I had no idea what my actions would be like in her memories. It was an uncomfortable feeling. If I did something or said something terrible in everyone's memories, did I still need to feel guilty for it? It didn't really matter if I should or shouldn't. If it was something stupid, I probably would anyway.

"Please. You really think I wouldn't notice how much you like Violet?" she asked. "I literally taught you how to sneak cookies from the cookie jar when you were five, and which window you could sneak out of at night without making any noise when you were fifteen. I know all of your tells."

I froze for a second. This was not a good turn. This was the kind of thing that could snowball into an avalanche. I wasn't really sure how vulnerable Violet and Connor's relationship was to demonic influence. If all it took to break them up was a nudge, then Megan could be a catalyst I couldn't stop. I needed to be more careful than a blind man in a minefield.

"Oh, yeah," I said, trying to sound as casual as I could. "She is great. She and Connor are so perfect for each other, don't you think?"

Megan stared at me for a long moment with narrowed eyes. I knew that look. She got it whenever something wasn't going her way. It meant she was running the scenario through her head again, looking for what she had missed. I took another sip of my wine and tried to look uninterested.

On the inside, my heart was racing, my skin felt a little cold and clammy. I think I had already been nervous enough over the last twenty-four hours to have stressed away a year of my life. But I supposed, thanks to the corrupt salesman, I was already down to only ten years left anyway. Or more correctly: nine years and three hundred and sixty-four days. Actually, now that I thought about it, do leap years figure into supernatural calendars? Or was that something mankind had invented? I should probably look into that.

"You're a good friend," Megan said without any other explanation. She reached over and squeezed my elbow with one of her hands. "Even if you are blushing." Something beeped in the kitchen. "Oh! The oven's ready." She hopped off the couch and trotted over to the kitchen.

I stayed on the couch and closed my eyes. It had been a long day. I wasn't sure when the last time I walked that far in one day was. The sun had not been particularly forgiving either. I probably wasn't even blushing, just a little sun-kissed. I should probably have been drinking water and not wine at that point. But I've never claimed to be a smart man. For a moment, I smiled. This felt a lot like how I'd imagined my life should be. All those late nights spent wandering the bitter hallways of "What If?" had felt exactly like this. Which, I noted as I started to nod off, was kind of chilling.

"Hey, no sleeping!" Megan yelled from the kitchen. "Here I am, toiling away to make my brother a nice meal to celebrate graduating from college, and he can't even stay awake. Some people's children, I tell you."

"I'm not sleeping," I said, snapping out of the warm, comfortable darkness.

"Sure, I've heard that one before." She laughed. "Here, come help me set the table."

I couldn't remember the last time I ate real dinner at a table. I mean, real me, anyway. For all I knew, in the fake memory land that my sister lived in, we had eaten a hundred dinners together over the last few years. But in my memory, I could think of maybe six times I had actually sat down and had dinner since Megan died.

And there wasn't any sort of special meaning to that. It wasn't on purpose. But two bachelors and the occasional girlfriend were happy enough eating on the couch watching a movie to bother going through the trouble of setting a table. Eating dinner at a table was something families did. As much as I loved my friends, I hadn't had a real family for quite some time.

We set the table after clearing off the ever-present pile of old mail and two mismatched socks. My portion of the work done, I sat down with my glass of wine and watched the wizard finish her magic. She presented me with a plate piled high with what I can only describe as edible art. Perfectly prepared linguine with a lake of red sauce in the middle. Floating on top were two chicken breasts, breaded and covered with melted mozzarella cheese. It smelled divine. Megan sat down across from me, her plate heaped almost as high as mine.

"Ah-ah-ah," she said, wagging a finger at me. "You know the rule. The chef gets the first bite."

I've never been clear if that actually is a real rule or not. Megan started talking about it after she got into cooking, but I'd never heard anyone else talk about it. It sounded like the kind of thing she would make up. My mouth was watering. This was going to be so much better than the grille's mediocre burger I had been subjected to earlier today.

With an obvious smirk on her face, Megan took her time with her first bite. Gingerly, she cut a piece of the breaded chicken and spooled it in a cocoon of spaghetti. She winked at me as she held the still-steaming bite in front of her mouth, blowing on it to cool it.

"You're a monster. I hope you know that," I said, giving her my best pouty lower lip. She laughed and finally took the bite.

"Ohmygosh," she said with her mouth full. "I must be really proud of you or something. This is perfect."

I didn't have to wait anymore. I also wasn't trying to impress anyone in the room with elegant manners. Eagerly, I hacked into the chicken with a knife and jammed a piece into my mouth. My taste buds were watering so hard, I was impressed with myself for not drooling. I closed my eyes in anticipation of that taste that would perfectly hit the spot. Everyone has a taste that is literally happiness to them. Some people love pretzels or Asian takeout or calamari. I love chicken parmesan.

But instead of a mouthful of juicy chicken, I got sawdust and sulfur. I coughed in surprise, covering my mouth to keep from spewing across the table.

"Are you okay? Is it good?" Megan asked with wide, concerned eyes. Desperately, I nodded, forcing myself to chew and swallow.

It was one of the hardest things I've ever had to do in my life, and I did it with a smile.

"Yeah, sorry," I said with a little wave of my hand. "Something tried to go down the wrong pipe."

Megan took another bite and smiled to herself, clearly proud of her work. "You know, I've always given you crap for your bad taste, little bro, but I gotta admit, on this one thing, you are definitely right."

I stared down at my plate. What had been a moderate-sized pile of wonder now seemed like a mountain of sadness. The lake of marinara was an ocean, and the breaded chicken pieces were the size of continents. I wondered if everything she made would taste good to everyone but me. Maybe I was ruined because I could see behind the curtain. I knew what had happened to her. There was no way I could tell her the truth, or truths, rather: She had been dead and came back, and her food tasted like rotten eggs. But I realized that didn't matter. I didn't care what her cooking tasted like. I had my sister back. I would gladly eat mountains of sawdust to have her back with me.

We continued our dinner in comfortable silence. She was lost in the rapture of her own cooking, which I was more than a little jealous of. I had my own thoughts to occupy me, which didn't match the pleased smile I forced onto my face.

There was no way in hell that I was going to send my sister back to... wherever she had been. That wasn't an option. But I had a sinking feeling that I couldn't shake: I wasn't sure I could accomplish all my goals. Since last night, my one plan had been to undo this situation before it messed with Connor and Violet. I would not let two of my closest friends be ruined because of me. I was still determined to do that. But I was having dinner with my recently undead sister, and that complicated things. Generally, if you demand your money back, stores don't let you keep what you paid for. If I fixed the deal, I got my soul back and protected my friends. All I had to do was let my sister die. Again.

There was a civil war brewing in my heart. My old, real family against my new adopted one. And I wasn't sure what was thicker—blood or water.

CHAPTER 5

Connor came home a few hours after Megan and I finished dinner. As I expected, he wasn't the least surprised to find her here. As far as he was concerned, it was normal for her to be alive and well. He also was happy to help himself to some leftover chicken parmesan. Normally, I'd have been furious. That stuff was worth its weight in gold to me, or more accurately, probably more than its weight. Chicken is not very heavy, but I like it a lot. He wouldn't shut up about how delicious it was and scarfed it down so fast you'd have thought he hadn't eaten anything in days.

Today, I was only jealous. Watching my friend eat my favorite food was painful. But part of me was glad he was eating it. Every bite he took meant I had less sawdust-like food to choke down later. As happy as I was that my sister was back, it tasted *awful*. He was doing me a favor, even if he didn't know it.

After she left, Connor went to bed, and I sat on the couch for hours. I stared at this one spot on the wall for so long that I'm surprised I didn't leave some sort of mark. My thoughts were full of demons and souls, the difference between something being real and something being true and wondering what Alex would show me in the morning. It was quite the party in my head.

Sometime around three or four in the morning, my mind finally gave up. Like a flooded engine eventually chokes and stalls out, my brain could no longer function. Trying to sleep while my mind runs a marathon or two is a monumental waste of time. Normally I like how I think. Some people want to call ADHD a disease or a handicap. I've never felt that way about it. It's different. It has its own strengths and weaknesses. But sometimes thinking differently than other people is helpful. It lets you see things they do not.

Handicap or not, when my thought engine finally gave up for the night, it was a relief. I crawled into bed and let the peaceful oblivion of sleep take me. I don't think I dreamed. I certainly didn't remember any dreams when I woke up. Given my life lately, I was thrilled that was the case. I had plenty of fuel for some knife-twisting nightmares. There's something about a really powerful nightmare. They hurt in a way I've never been able to quantify. Even when I can't remember what I was afraid of or what was tormenting me, I can still feel *wrong* for days. And I already felt wrong enough, thanks.

It was almost noon by the time I emerged from my room. Connor was long gone to work, like a normal adult. I felt a little guilty because I wasn't sure what my new friend Alex had meant by "morning." Eleven forty-five a.m. was still technically morning. I gave myself a pass for extenuating circumstances. I grabbed Alex's card from my wallet and punched his number into my phone. He picked up on the second ring.

"Matt?"

"Hey, sorry I'm calling you later than I thought. I had a long night," I told him.

"No worries. I've been doing some legwork to get started anyway. Want me to come and pick you up?" He didn't sound annoyed. Whether or not he was just being polite, I couldn't tell.

"Sure," I gave him my address and a few directions.

"Be there in thirty minutes," he said and hung up abruptly.

I spent the next half hour getting ready. Twenty of those minutes were spent in the shower mentally preparing myself. I'm one of those people who does their best thinking in a shower. There's something about the warmth of a hot shower and the feeling of water sluicing over me that is relaxing. Taking a shower at the start of the day is like taking the last big breath before you dive off a cliff into water far below. And I was pretty sure I was cliff-jumping today.

I was meeting up with a guy I barely knew, who was some sort of supernatural journalist, to try to figure out how to get my soul back. Maybe. Megan's unexpected arrival had thrown a monkey wrench into my plans. Part of me felt like if I got this deal thrown out and my soul back, it would be almost as if I had killed her again.

But on the other hand, part of me knew that she was already dead. Even if she was back right now, it wasn't natural. But who cared what was natural? Nature sucks. What is the natural human experience? You grow up, work constantly until your body fails you, then you die.

I'm not bitter, I swear.

Regardless of my dark logic, I felt selfish. Assuming I could even get out of this, the choice seemed like it had a good chance of being my sister's life versus my friends' happiness. Morally, that didn't sound like that difficult of a decision—someone not being happy versus someone *living*. But I couldn't get the taste of sawdust and sulfur out of my mouth. Megan was back, but part of me worried that her existence was more smoke and mirrors than truth. Alex's words haunted me still, skewing how I looked at the situation: *Everything is real, but not everything is true.*

Why would that have to stop with deities? There were humans who would lie about anything to get ahead. There was no reason that my sister being back wasn't too good to be true. Maybe her food really did taste awful, but the magic of the deal made my friends unable to see it, like it messed with their memories to fit Megan into the narrative of their lives. I was getting a headache trying to make this all make sense.

I forced myself to get out of the shower, which was harder than I want to admit. Sometimes I feel like if I stay in there forever, no problems will ever come find me. Except for pruned toes. But that's totally worth it. I grabbed a red T-shirt that had a superhero logo on it, because under the surface I'm still twelve, and a pair of khaki shorts. I almost put on a pair of sneakers, but I decided against it. I wasn't planning on doing any running today, and flip-flops are so much more comfortable.

I made it about five steps before I stopped. That felt like it was a momentous decision. It's the weirdest thing, those tiny decisions that seem like they are far more important than they really are. By merely thinking that I wasn't going to be doing any running and wearing the wrong shoes, I knew that inevitably I would need to run. I'd regret it if I didn't. With a sigh, I went back to my closet and changed into my sneakers.

Alex texted me when he got close, and I slipped out the door. Mrs. Sanchez, our ancient neighbor across the hall on our landing was also exiting her door at the same time. Mrs. Sanchez is the sweetest old lady. I've seen her every couple of days for the last year or two. She was always dressed sharply, with charcoal business slacks and a white blouse. Her white hair was done up in a bun on top of her head, and large horn-rimmed glasses gave her a sort of "no-nonsense librarian" look. Despite her slightly severe appearance, she always gave me a big smile and wink.

But today when I gave her my warmest smile, she stared at me with a face of judgment that I hadn't seen matched since the last time I saw my father.

She paused in the middle of closing her door and pushed it

back open, walking back inside her apartment. I could have sworn I heard her muttering something under her breath. Goosebumps flared up my arms, and I rubbed them absentmindedly. Her reaction reminded me of the people from the bar where I had met Alex. How crazy was that? The world of spooks might have been living across the hall from me all along.

Unsettled from my run-in with Mrs. Sanchez, I jogged down the stairs two at a time to wait for Alex outside. The Cali sun was already blazing down with fury. Sometimes the weather makes me hate this place. It was still only April, for goodness' sake. It did not need to be hot enough to fry an egg on the asphalt. It just did not.

My new accomplice pulled up in an old white minivan. The paint on the passenger side was scraped as though the van had power-slid along a wall. The rear bumper was completely missing too. I snorted as he pulled up along the sidewalk next to me. No wonder he was willing to work with me when no one else was. I opened the door and eyed the cracked leather seat.

"I guess being a reporter doesn't pay well in either reality, huh?" I asked as I sat down, closing the door behind me.

Alex was dressed like the last time I saw him—dark-washed jeans and a V-neck T-shirt. Today's was green instead of red, which was good because I would have been embarrassed if we matched. His short blond hair was still semi spiked, sort of like a half-hearted fauxhawk. He shot me a quick grin in response to my jab.

"You should see my other ride. It's a bike," he replied.

"Oh, nice, like a Harley?"

"I don't think Harley-Davidson makes mountain bikes, man," he said with another flash of a smile.

He pulled out into the street, and I realized I had gotten into a stranger's van to go somewhere I didn't know, and I hadn't even gotten any candy for it.

"So what's the plan?" I asked, feeling somehow more uncomfortable as he pulled back out into the street and began weaving through traffic.

He smiled again. It was an impish thing, full of mischief and humor. I felt myself smile back without even thinking about it.

"Okay, hear me out," he said. "We're going to summon a demon."

"Wait, that's actually a thing?" I asked. I guess I shouldn't have been surprised. But as a mere mortal who hadn't really thought all of this through, this sounded daunting. I know you can call the White House in the real world, but I probably wouldn't do it.

"Sure it is," Alex replied easily. "Or so I'm told."

"Wait, you've never done this before either?"

"Why would I? I've never had a reason to whistle up a demon before. It's usually smarter to stay out of their way. I spent last night figuring out how. I figure we can talk to whoever we get on the other end of the line and use that as a starting point."

"There isn't like a Better Business Bureau or something we can report them to?" I sighed. I was hoping this would be a little easier.

"There are some options, but we can't start with them." Alex's eyes narrowed as he watched the traffic. "We need proof. You don't want to try matching your word against theirs. Demons are surprisingly good liars."

"I don't really think that's at all surprising," I said dryly.

"Yeah, but if you expect them to be good liars and they still manage to trick you, that's a whole other level of surprising."

"Okay, how do we do it?" Maybe I should have questioned the logic of summoning a demon a little more. My last interaction with one hadn't worked out too well for me. But Alex was the expert, and it wasn't like I had any clue what I was doing.

"It's pretty similar to the movie tropes," he said. "Pentagrams, candles, etcetera. Our first stop is to hit up a hardware store for ingredients to pull this off. Then we need to find a place to summon them."

"Sweet." I was still working out how to respond to demon... stuff. When you're a kid, your mother tells you not to let your friends peer-pressure you into drinking, doing drugs, and other stuff. But she never covered what to do if an acquaintance offered to help you summon a demon. Or at least mine didn't. She completely skipped that chapter. But my mom was still dead, as far as I knew, so I couldn't ask her opinion on the matter.

We pulled to a stop at a red light behind a couple of cars. Thinking about my dead mom reminded me that Alex needed last night's update regarding my no-longer-dead sister.

"Oh, hey," I said slowly, trying to think how to explain this. "Something happened last night."

"Something else happened?" he asked, his voice rising.

"Yeah, so I had this sister, and she was sort of killed in a car accident a few years back. But last night she came over and cooked me dinner."

Alex's head turned slowly to face me, and he stared at me for what felt like an eternity, but it was probably ten seconds.

The car behind us honked, startling him back into the moment. Apparently, the light had turned green. He gassed the pedal, and we started moving.

"This is really, really bad," he said after a few moments. "Do you know how hard it is to bring someone back? Of course you don't. It's seriously hard. The Death Board has to have a majority vote in favor to approve it. You can't just clap your hands and bring them back. It takes a lot of clout to do that."

"There's something wrong with her too," I said.

"What do you mean?"

"My sister used to be an incredible cook, but last night, the dinner she made tasted like dust—to me at least. Meanwhile my roommate had some and wouldn't shut up about how delicious it was." A bitter tone crept into my voice. I had been so excited for my sister to cook for me.

A look of deep pity crossed Alex's face. I'd seen that kind of look before. Plenty of people wore it at Megan's funeral. There's something terrible about pity. When people look at me like that, it's like a mirror to despair. The writing is on their faces. When my mother and my sisters died, I couldn't process it. It took me weeks, or months, even, to feel anything other than *empty*. But every time I saw the reflection of my tragedy in the pity of some family friend's eyes, I began to sense the depths of my hell. It's easier to tell how bad you should feel when others show you how much they think you should be hurting.

"It's because you know what she is," Alex said softly.

"What do you mean, 'what she is'?" I asked, a little defensive. It was a knee-jerk reaction that I hadn't had since her death. She was still my sister, after all.

"She's dead," he replied gently. His eyes were rigidly fixed on the road now, not even glancing at me. "Your roommate doesn't know that. I wouldn't know it. But you do; that's how this kind of deal works. Art is the domain of humans, and you don't come back whole from death."

Alex's explanation confirmed what I had already been thinking. I didn't know the exact technical explanation, of course, but I'm not a complete idiot. I could guess why Connor and I had different reactions to seeing her again.

"If you come over for dinner sometime and try some of her food, will it be normal for you?" I asked.

"I'm not sure," he said. "There's not always a clear rule book on this stuff. There's a very good chance that the illusion would be ruined for me because I'm me, and I know what you've been through. A theory we can test at some point."

We rode in silence for maybe ten minutes, which I didn't mind. You learn a lot about a person by how they handle silence. Alex seemed stressed. His fingers drummed absently on the steering wheel. A small frown rested on his face like a lone rain cloud on a summer's day. He kept his eyes focused on the cars around us, but I got the sense that he was only half paying attention. Megan's return had unsettled him. I mean, I couldn't blame him. It unsettled me, and I didn't know nearly as much about this as he did.

Our first stop was a hardware store, one of those huge ones that was basically a warehouse with shopping aisles. We walked into the building, and Alex consulted his list.

"Okay, we need red paint, a brush, matches, and some candles," he said. "Then we need to swing by a supermarket, and we can do this thing."

It took us a solid twenty minutes to find everything we were looking for. I'm not a super handy guy, so maybe the fault was mine, but I've always found those kinds of stores confusing. The categories that exist in my mind for hardware are a little off. Nothing is where I expect it to be. Why are candles in "Garden Plants & Flowers" and not "Home and Living?" I don't know. Why is the caulk gun not in plumbing? I couldn't tell you. There's also some sort of weird man-card issue at play in these types of stores. No guy wants to admit they don't know how the categories work. It makes you look bad. Instead you wander around and check *everywhere* until you find what you are looking for. It's horribly inefficient, but it makes us feel better about ourselves.

We reached the checkout line, and Alex offered me the cart he was pushing.

"For this to work, you need to buy it," he said.

"What, you don't have some sort of investigative reporting budget that we can use?" I asked. As an unbelievably recent college graduate, I wasn't exactly rolling in the dough myself.

"You're going to be the one placing the call, if you will. It's important that you own all the materials we use." He grinned, blue eyes sparkling with a hint of mischief. "Also, you should know journalism is a dying occupation. It's a free paper."

I stared at him for a moment, trying to decide if he was messing with me or broke too. It didn't really matter. If I ran out of money or something, my undead sister would probably feed me. I mentally rolled my eyes. The fact that I could casually think that sentence was a perfect picture of how weird my life had gotten in the last forty-eight hours. Somehow I was certain that it would get weirder before we were done. I mean, I was buying hardware supplies to try to summon a demon. The weird was not showing any signs of slowing down.

I paid for our supplies, which didn't turn out to be more than forty bucks. The cute blonde girl at the door told me to have a good day and gave me a brilliant smile, so I had that going for me. We got back in the car and started driving.

"Okay, the last thing we need is kind of weird," Alex said.

"Man, I'm already on board with whatever it is we're going to try. Hit me."

"We're going to need some goat meat," he told me.

I don't know what I expected. Many stories of this kind of thing involved some sort of animal sacrifice. Which was gross. I didn't want to sacrifice my TV time, let alone any animals.

"You're not going to make me butcher some cute animals, are you?" I asked with a sigh.

"Nah, I don't think we have to for what we're doing. This is low-level summoning stuff from what I've researched. We don't need to do anything super fancy. There's a supermarket nearby that has goat. We need some shanks or something."

I've never eaten goat. I guess it's not that common in America, the land of grass-fed beef and lots of chicken. The supermarket Alex took us to was this little Jamaican grocery store nestled in a corner of a strip mall. Energetic steel drum music washed over us as we entered, and everything smelled of spices I wasn't familiar with.

"You again?" the woman called in a rich Jamaican accent from behind the cash register as we entered. "I thought I told you this store was for worthy people only."

"Listen, Angelia, that's so incredibly rude," Alex replied, holding up his hands. "My friend and I will only be here for a minute, okay? We just need some supplies. We will be super quick and out of your hair before you know it." He gestured around the store, which was empty. "Our money spends just as well as the pointy guys' does, and you're not exactly doing Black Friday volume of sales right now."

"Fine. Be quick. Don't make a habit out of this!" she yelled at our backs. "I don't want to see you impure pups in my shop on the regular, you hear?" Her accent made "hear" sound like "heah."

"What was that?" I whispered as we threaded through the store.

"I'm afraid prejudice doesn't only exist in the domain of mortals, my friend," he said, his tone short and clipped. I glanced at him and saw a faint flush on his face and a hard edge to his jaw.

Tons of seafood was on display in the back on ice, right next to a tank of live lobsters. The tanks always added an element of creepy to food for me. I like meat a lot. But literally choosing a specific animal to die so you can eat it feels kind of Hannibal Lectery to me. Which doesn't really make sense because he ate people. My philosophical wanderings aside, with the goat purchased, we piled back into the van and got back onto the highway.

"The last part of this trick is that we don't want to do this somewhere that leads back to you."

"What do you mean?" I asked. "Shouldn't they already know who I am?"

"Yeah, it's still not the smartest idea to summon a demon to your bedroom, even if you think it's going to play nice." He was quiet for a moment. "That also assumes the summons brings what you meant it to and not something else."

"Well, good," I said sarcastically. "I always wanted to meet Cthulhu anyway."

"So, here's my idea," he continued, ignoring my comment. "I know an empty warehouse that's a couple miles from here, closer to the airport. We can sneak in and try this there."

"I mean, it sounds like as good a plan as any," I replied. "If you were going to stab me and steal my wallet, I feel like this is a lot of effort. So, I'm game."

"Journalism doesn't pay quite that poorly." Alex laughed. "But close."

Alex's warehouse was another fifteen minutes away. I spent that time getting more nervous. It's really easy to not be worried about things in the abstract. Jumping off the high diving board at the pool looks easy from the ground. But when you're walking up to the edge, and you start to notice how far away the ground is, confidence fades fast.

There were so many unknowns for me in this. Alex had hinted at some. But what if we summoned some angry monster that ate us? What if the demons got angry that I was messing with the deal? What if it didn't work? I guess that would be more of a thematic letdown than anything else. My luck hadn't been too good lately, depending on how you looked at it. I was worried about what else could go wrong.

The warehouse Alex took me to was pretty much exactly what you would expect. Big cities always have hidden patches of industrial buildings, especially as close to the airport as we were. Planes flying low overhead on their landing approaches to LAX rattled my bones as we pulled up. Ours was one in a line of warehouses, currently empty. It was a long squat rectangle, its walls painted a dull brown that was peeling off the sheet-metal siding. The truck bay was empty but showed signs of extensive use in the past. A shipping company's vehicles surrounded one of the active warehouses farther down the street. Alex parked on the side of the road, a little beyond the warehouse. We didn't want someone driving by and stopping to see why there was a car parked at an empty building.

I grabbed the bag with the paint supplies. He got the goat meat and candles, and we walked swiftly to the building. The metal door was locked because that's what we do in big city America. We lock our doors. Alex reached into his back pocket and pulled out a pair of tools.

"Watch this," he said with a grin. He crouched by the door and inserted the picks into the lock. I don't know how long it's supposed to take to pick a basic lock. Television would have me believe it's about five seconds. That might be a bit extreme and done more for the sake of the story pacing than realism. Alex took closer to sixty seconds, but he got us in.

"You're one of those no-boundary reporters, huh?" I asked as the door closed behind us. It was entirely dark on the inside. A little light came in from some of the windows along the ceiling, and I thought I saw an exit sign across the way. Alex flipped the light on his phone, and I followed suit before following him farther in.

The giant warehouse still had shelving in rows presumably arranged by the last tenant. The floor had a light layer of dust that was largely undisturbed, like a fresh snowfall with occasional breaks in the purity for animal tracks and even rarer human footprints. I felt really exposed. Even though we were inside a building, its wide-open space made it feel like there was nowhere to hide. If someone were to walk in the door, they would see us right away.

"I actually used to have this girlfriend who was really

forgetful." Alex chuckled. "She kept locking herself out of things. So I learned how to get back into things she had locked us out of."

"I'm not sure I believe you," I said with my eyes narrowed.

He shot me another grin and continued walking forward. The light from his phone danced around as he scanned the room.

"Might as well use the center," I suggested as we hit roughly the middle of the building. "Not like there's anywhere to hide."

"Yeah, that works," Alex murmured as he kept looking around. "I was hoping there was a— A-ha!" he interrupted himself as his light landed on a push-broom leaning against the wall. He walked over and grabbed the broom. "We want to have a clean surface for the paint. Watch your eyes and mouth."

I turned away right as he began vigorously sweeping. A cloud of dust and dirt billowed from the ground, and we both coughed a few times before it was all done. After the dust settled, we had a clear patch of gray cement floor in the center of our abandoned warehouse. What better place to summon a demon? I certainly did not know of one.

"Okay, next step is a little weird," Alex said as he grabbed the paint can and started to pry it open. He paused for a moment with a wry look on his face, as if he couldn't quite believe what he was going to ask. "I need some of your blood."

"You what now?" I asked.

"I know it sounds extreme. We need to draw some stuff with the paint, obviously. But in order for you to be able to control the summoning, we need to mix your blood with the paint." He paused for a moment. "If this were a more serious summoning, it would need to be *all* your blood and no paint at all. Or," he muttered so softly I almost missed it, "the blood of a sacrifice."

"Well, that's chilling."

"Like I said at the bar, demons are not well liked for a number of reasons."

"So, the thing with my blood is more symbolic than anything else? Kind of like the goat?" I asked.

"Exactly." He reached into his back pocket and pulled out a small folding knife. He tossed it to me, still closed. "We need a dash in the paint. I've got a bandage in the bag too." He finished popping open the paint can.

The ruby red now seemed very macabre to me. Instead of associating it with fire trucks, it reminded me of blood—my blood. When I was a kid, a pigeon impaled itself on a tree in my backyard. Its blood had run down the tree, and I had never seen a red so vivid. That was all I could think of when I saw the paint.

With a sigh, I flipped the knife open. It looked clean enough. I was up to date on all my shots anyway and too far along with Alex's scheme to back out now. When they came for my soul, I didn't want the reason I was damned to be that I was afraid of getting a cut on my hand.

I gritted my teeth and pushed the edge along the middle of my left palm. It burned like a paper cut's big brother. I hissed as I felt it bite into my skin. Blood instantly welled up, and I cupped my hand, pooling my own red paint in my palm. Alex stepped aside, and I extended my hand down toward the can, turning it over and pouring my blood into the paint. The two reds didn't mix evenly. Mine was darker, earthier than the shiny red paint. I continued to bleed into the can for maybe fifteen seconds. Alex rifled around in his bag and handed me some gauze, tape, and Neosporin.

"That should do it," he said softly. He pulled a paint stirrer from the bag and began stirring my blood into the paint. I applied a ton of the antibacterial goo and wrapped my hand in several layers of gauze. The pressure relieved the stinging, but I knew I would feel that later.

Alex dipped the brush in and began painting on the floor. He created a familiar symbol, a pentagram, the five-pointed star that we all learned to draw in one motion in middle school. Next, he connected the points to form a circle and then slowly painted a larger circle around that circle with roughly a six-inch buffer between them.

"Okay, this is important," he said as he stood back from the pentagram. "This single point of the star is the bottom, not the top. Angels and demons use the same symbols often, but inverted. We don't want to cross our wires, or bad things might happen."

"I didn't actually know that about pentagrams," I said. "That makes sense why there were often people complaining about them when I was a kid, and I couldn't see it. That's a really minor difference."

"It makes sense if you think about it," Alex replied. "If people talk about Heaven, where do you think it is, up or down?"

"Up, and down for Hell," I said.

"Exactly. That's how everyone thinks of them. If demons are simply fallen angels, then we assume they are somehow lower. Whether any of that is true or not doesn't really seem to matter. It is what people believe, it is what they want us to believe."

Alex pulled out the candles. The red theme continued, as these were cinnamon-apple-scented candles enclosed in glass. We popped their tops off and tossed them to the side. The abandoned warehouse now smelled of wet paint and cinnamon, which was something of an improvement from musty and abandoned. It was practically homey now.

"Does the scent or color matter?" I asked Alex as I helped him light them. We placed one in the hollow of each point of the star.

"I mean, it's no incense, but it might," Alex said. "The color doesn't matter. These were out of season, so they were cheaper."

"Well, good. When this goes horribly wrong and we are eaten alive, at least I'll know we saved a buck in the preparation."

"Two fifty, actually," Alex replied offhandedly.

"I take it back. Totally worth it," I said as I looked at our demon-summoning apparatus. It looked like the set of a low-budget television show. Most likely it was some high school drama about a small town with mysterious history and a coven of witches.

"Last step," Alex said as he reached into the last bag and pulled out the goat and a piece of wood. "Here's what you need to do: Place the wood in the center, meat on top. Then get out of both the circles. Whatever you do, don't go into the circles. As long as they are intact, whatever we summon can't cross them and get to us."

"Okay, stay outside the circles. Got it." I accepted the raw goat and freed it from its packaging with my good hand. I didn't want raw meat anywhere near my open wound. I tucked the wood under my arm. "How am I supposed to light this, by the way?"

"You don't. They will."

Nervous, I stepped over the wet ring and leaned toward the center of the star. I fished the wood from under my arm and placed it down inside the center area of the star. My hands shaking with adrenaline, I placed the goat shank in the center. The second it was on the wood, I threw myself from the ring like a cat fleeing a vacuum cleaner.

I landed outside the ring and stared. Alex pointed toward the bottom point of the star, and I moved to stand below it. He took a few steps farther back to give me room and switched his phone's light off. That was okay; he had helped me get this far. This part I needed to do for myself.

"Repeat after me," he said in a low voice.

I nodded and followed his lead in some babble that I could only assume was Latin. It had a couple "omnibuses" and the word "daemonium," which frankly sounded like pandering to me. I have no idea what most of it meant. I could have been placing an order at Wendy's. But as I repeated Alex's foreign words, the candles all burst into flame of their own accord, which made me almost poop of my own accord. But I kept speaking the ominous summoning words as my new friend told me to.

After we finished, I rocked on the balls of my feet, waiting for something to happen. The room was silent as we waited with bated breath for a demon to appear. Only the five candles illuminated the dark warehouse.

A minute went by. Then two. My tension faded. Clearly, this was a bust. I turned to Alex with a questioning look. He shrugged, looking as disappointed as I felt.

A red spark appeared from within the center of the star. It landed on the wood and goat and burst into an inferno. The scent of cooking meat was delicious, and my stomach rumbled. Maybe I needed to try goat sometime.

The fire grew into a pillar almost as tall as me. I could feel its heat coming from the center of the star, but it felt muted, distant, like there was a wall between us. The heat built and pulsed. Suddenly the fire vanished with an *oomph* as it imploded. The wood and meat were gone. Instead, standing where they had been was a woman with fiery-red hair and eyes of darkness.

CHAPTER 6

The woman standing in the middle of the ring was beautiful. Though, frankly, this description falls so short of capturing her beauty that it's insulting. Her red mane flowed down to the small of her back in thick waves. A short curl of hair hung to the side and danced teasingly on her right cheek. Her skin was dusky, like a college student's at the end of spring break. Long legs were sealed in black boots that went up to her knees. Dark wash jeans clung to her in a way any woman would be jealous of. A tight red tank top similarly made sure that anyone looking was aware she had a body of the gods. If she had been a celebrity and not a demon, *Vanity Fair*'s cover would never *not* be her. The Webster's dictionary entry for beauty should just be a picture of her face.

But for all her stunning looks, there was an edge of danger to her. Her solid black eyes were unsettling. Either her sclera was the same color as her pupil, or she had giant ones, like some sort of cave dwelling creature. They flicked around the room, taking in her surroundings. Her gaze fell onto our red-painted demon-summoning apparatus, and she stared at it for a few seconds. If she had been a human being, I would have said she was surprised.

I wondered if she was some sort of succubus. They were supposed to be super-sexy demons, right?

Distantly, I heard Alex breathlessly swear, "Starfall," which was quite possibly the lamest curse of all time.

That was not promising. She looked up at the sound of Alex's comment, and her black eyes bored into mine with such intensity that I took a very big step back. And then I took another one just for good measure.

"Why have you summoned me here, mortal?" she demanded. Her voice was deep and rich. It made me think of great women I had only read stories about, like Cleopatra and Helen of Troy. I responded with the first thing on my mind.

"Are you a succubus?" I asked. I might have heard Alex gasp behind me. That was probably some sort of demonic faux pas. You can't just ask someone if they're a succubus. Her shadowy eyes stared at me, unreadable. It felt like she was trying to bore into my mind with her sheer presence of will. I wasn't sure if she could even do that, but the headache I was getting sure felt like she might be able to. If this was what a demon was like while contained in a magical circle, then I was very grateful she was stuck on the other side of some still-wet paint. It made me feel a little safer as her black eyes stared at me. It had never occurred to me that Nietzsche's line about staring into the abyss had been meant so literally. Who knows, maybe he summoned a demon too.

"Sorry, this is my first time calling," I said, breaking the silence. "Well, kind of. I met a demon the other day, and he tried to make me a deal. But he came to me. I didn't have to make a call—"

"Why are you here, whelp?" she interrupted, voice haughty and cool like a frigid wind that cuts through the thickest of winter coats.

I hesitated, unsure why she was interrupting my explanation

with the question that I was already trying to answer. Some people are rude like that.

"I'm only here to observe," Alex said from behind me. I glanced back, and he had extended both hands, palms forward in a placating gesture. As if to show her he meant no harm. "My friend here needed some help getting in contact with you all after his incident, and I was trying to help."

"So you helped him summon *me?*" she asked.

"This was an accident," Alex said. "I was told this ritual would only call the front desk. I apologize very much for the disturbance."

The demon glanced down at our handiwork on the floor again. For a brief second, a puzzled frown crossed her face. I wondered if she was also confused on how she got here. I cleared my throat, not as an impatient gesture, but because some dust from the sweeping was still in the air, and I was trying not to cough.

That switched her raptor gaze back to me. Her red mane swayed to frame her face as she glared at me. This time I was prepared and didn't retreat. Much.

She seemed to be the opposite of Dan, full of power, strength, and confidence. And she didn't have a stupid tail.

"Like I was saying," I continued as if her interruption had only been a little rude. (Instead of a lot rude, which it was.) "One of your demons approached me about a deal."

"And let me guess," she said with a sigh, interrupting me yet again, "now you have buyer's remorse, and you're hoping we have a return policy. We don't. A deal is a deal, so be grateful for what you got. Now release me, mortal, before I grow *displeased.*" She glanced down at our pentagram and circle again, and a small smile crossed her lips, which increased her sex appeal by an exponential amount. "I must say, the cinnamon candles are a nice touch. Makes a girl feel welcome."

"So that's the thing," I said. "I didn't make a deal. But your, uh, sales representative, I guess? He forged my signature on the contract and ran off. I didn't make a deal. I don't want a deal. I just want my life back."

The demon froze at my words. And I don't mean that she stopped moving like it's a normal thing. This was some next-level freaky demon stillness. It was like for a moment she was in absolute zero. She didn't blink. Her clothes didn't shift. Even her hair stopped swaying. It lasted only a couple of heartbeats. Then she was back to normal. Her black eyes went back to Alex for a moment and then back to me, like a predator sizing up the animals at a water hole.

"May I see your contract?" she asked in a poisonously sweet tone. I was already pretty sure the construct of blood and paint was reducing her ability to affect me, as well as containing her. But even on the other side of the magic wall, my heart skipped at the allure promised in her voice. It was a potent blend of forbidden fruit, carnal desires, and need all tied into some sort of sensual pretzel knot.

"I… I don't have a girlfr— I don't have it." English was hard after that blast of desire. "The demon that forged my signature ran off with it."

She frowned at me slightly and sighed, shrugging her shoulders, a motion that was frankly dangerous to watch. She glanced at the blood–paint mixture on the floor again and smacked her lips a few times, like a reptile tasting the air.

"Matthew Steven Carver?" she asked after a moment.

"Yeah, that's me." I shivered. That was too creepy.

The demoness gestured with her right hand, and a large stack of paper appeared in her hands. It looked like the contract Dan had shown me in the theater, so basically a large stack of papers. Casually, she began perusing it, midnight eyes darting across the page. She turned the page and froze again. It only lasted a second, and then she was back to normal. As she turned more and more pages, her eyes began to dart faster. She finished the many-page document in record time. She dropped it to the ground at her feet. Her right hand slowly curled into a fist. It was the first non-sexy thing I had seen her do. There was something about it that was pure menace. But still in a hot kind of way.

"Matthew," she said in a crisp, businesslike tone, "I believe I have entertained your complaints more than enough. You must be quite the negotiator to have struck such a deal. But you have reached the limits of what you can bargain for. I suggest that you enjoy it while you can. Now release me."

"You're not listening to me," I protested. My heart was pounding, and I could feel my face turning red. This wasn't fair. "I didn't *make* a deal. I don't even know what the deal is!"

"I'm done playing with you, Matthew Carver," she hissed. There was no hint of pleasantness or allure in her features anymore, only anger. "Release me now, or I shall get angry."

"Yeah, but you're stuck in there until I let you go, demon wench," I snapped.

Alex whimpered behind me. I didn't care. I had this demon trapped, and I was going to make sure that she listened to me. After all, how tough could she be if a little bit of paint and blood was all it took to lock her in place? I was not impressed.

"You're going to stay there until you listen and help me fix this!"

She threw back her head and laughed. It was not a pleasant sound. It also wasn't a Disneyesque Maleficent cackle or some other caricature. She did not use "muahahaha" for her laugh track. Her laugh was loud and piercing, like the cry of an eagle. Suddenly I felt like an idiot. You know, modus operandi for my life.

"You have no idea who I am, do you?" She chuckled in amusement. "Your friend does. That's why he looks like he's trying not to pee his pants." Her black eyes bored into mine. "I don't think you have the cajones either—you're ignorant. One last warning, mortal, as a courtesy, since you are a client. Release. Me. Now."

"Make me," I snapped. Her words had struck home under my skin. I was seeing red, and it wasn't just her hair. My blood was rushing. I could hear it in my ears, feel it underneath my skin.

She didn't bother to respond. Her glare said enough. She clenched both hands now and lowered them to her waist. Her eyes still locked with mine, she flexed slightly, and a maelstrom erupted inside the center of the pentagram.

Fire pulsed out from her in all directions. It slammed into the lines of the star, and for a second, it held. The fire faded, only to be replaced with another wave that struck like a hammer blow. I could feel the heat, muted by the protection of the circle but still warm. Another hammer blow of flame struck the magical walls, then another. The room no longer smelled of cinnamon and paint, but sulfur and what I had to assume was brimstone.

"Matt, we've got to go," Alex yelled over the windstorm of fury that was coming from our binding. "I don't think the paint can hold her."

"She has to listen," I yelled. "It's holding her."

Another fire wave struck, and there was a ringing like a gong. The red paint on the star crisped and burned. The candles were flung out in all directions like an exploding star. I heard the glass shatter as they smashed on the cement floor.

The inner circle and star were completely black now. Only the outer ring remained intact. The waves of fire had ceased. The demon stood there, still staring with those nightmare eyes. Casually, she stepped out of the star and inner ring and began pacing along the line of the larger circle.

"Do you really think this can hold me?" she asked, mocking

laughter in her voice. "Me. Lilith. I, who remember when mankind was living in caves. I, who have slain angels and eaten their flesh. Do you think you can contain me with some *blood and paint?*" Her voice rose into a shriek, and the flames erupted inside the circle again, slamming into our last barrier.

I panicked. I don't know what made me do it. I think I saw it in a movie once. I threw out both my arms and shrieked "THE POWER OF CHRIST COMPELS YOU!" at the top of my lungs.

The flames vanished, and Lilith almost flinched. It looked almost reflexive, like an abused dog when her master moves suddenly. She stared at me for a second before the mocking laughter returned.

"You do not have the power of the White God." She laughed, gasping for air. She bent over, resting her hands on her knees. "You are a long way from His help. After all, you *sold your soul to a demon.*" Her laughter pierced me. Now I really felt like I was alone in this.

"Matt," Alex's voice cut urgently through the demon's laughter. "We need to go. Now." He wore an expression of extreme concern on his face. Was that sweat beading on his forehead?

Lilith's laughter stopped abruptly. I turned back to find her smiling at me. It was not a pleasant smile. More like how Tom the cat smiled at Jerry the mouse in those old cartoon episodes. I did not like it one bit.

"Uh, can't we just send her back?" I asked him.

"Normally you do that by blowing out the candles," he said softly.

Lilith's smile grew even larger. She looked like the human version of the Cheshire cat. Desperate, I looked around the room for the destroyed candles. I saw no points of light in the darkness. They must have blown out when her flames sent them flying across the room.

"Oh no," she taunted in a falsely sweet voice. "Did I break something?"

"Okay," I said, trying to sound calmer than I felt, like I was desperately trying to plunge a rising toilet. "What do we do now?" We were both speaking in hushed tones, and I was doing my best to not make any sudden movements. Sort of like what you're supposed to do if a wild dog corners you. Don't startle it or it might attack. And I had a feeling that if she started attacking again, she could get to us quickly.

"Indeed," she mocked. "What ever will you do?" Apparently, being a demoness also comes with excellent hearing. She raised a single finger and tapped on the invisible wall that was projected upward from the circle on the ground. It sounded hollow, like someone tapping on the glass of a cage at the zoo. She moved her finger a few inches to the left and tapped again. Another six inches and another tap. She cocked her head at that one and tapped in the same spot again. She drew her finger back into a fist and slammed it into that spot with all the driving force of a pile driver.

There was a faint cracking sound, like a tray of ice cubes being loosened. A red glow surrounded her hand for a split second, and she pulled it back quickly, shaking it as if it was hot. The smell of sulfur and brimstone once again came from the circle.

Imagine diving off the coast of Africa with the great white sharks, sitting safely inside iron bars, watching those apex predators circle you, confident in your security. Then one of those monsters starts tearing the cage to shreds like it's made of rotten plywood instead of metal. That warm feeling around your hips? When all your courage suddenly decides to exit your bladder? Listen, I don't need to go into more detail. You get it.

"Hear me out," Alex said softly, his eyes still locked on Lilith. "We run."

"You cannot run from me," she taunted. "I will feast on your flesh and bathe in your blood. I will drink the marrow from your bones. I—"

"Yeah," I whispered to Alex under her violent monologue. "Running sounds good to me."

I turned and sprinted through the dark warehouse as fast as I could go. Behind me, I heard Lilith's voice rise to an irritated shriek. There was another *whump* and a loud cracking as she smashed into the magical circle's barrier again.

Alex was running by my side. I could hear him breathing as we raced toward the exit. The door was ahead, framed where light leaked through its imperfect sealing. Alex passed me and rammed into the door with his shoulder, not even bothering to break stride.

The door exploded outward, slamming into the wall with a heavy crash. I followed him out the exit, fear lending me the strength to be far more fleet of foot than I would be normally. Like two startled deer, we galloped to Alex's minivan and dove in.

Alex had his key in the ignition before I was even fully in my seat. The van roared to life, and Alex floored the gas. We pulled onto the street, cheap tires squealing. I looked in my passenger mirror at the warehouse behind us, straining for any glimpse of Lilith. I'm not sure what I expected, maybe a flurry of bats or something, but that's not what I got. Not even kind of. Instead, the entire building burst into flames. It was not a gradual combustion. One second, the building was a normal not-on-fire warehouse. Then it was all fire, as if it were the head of a match that had been struck.

The door we had fled out of was still open, waving in the intense heat from the flames. For a moment, I thought I saw a figure framed in the inferno, looking out after us. But then we peeled around the corner and left that little section of Hell behind.

I turned to Alex and looked at him for a moment. He was

breathing quickly, eyes wide with the same adrenaline rush that I was coming down from. He kept shifting his hands on the steering wheel, squeezing the outer ring so hard that his knuckles were turning white.

"So," I said in between gasps, "I'm no expert. But I think we might have made things worse?"

Alex looked at me for a moment. In his eyes, I could see how desperately he wanted to communicate his fear to me, but he didn't know how. He was speechless.

"Yeah," he managed after a few seconds. "We made it worse."

CHAPTER 7

W ho in the *hell* was that?" I asked Alex several blocks later. We were on the highway now, swimming along in the school of midday traffic. Nervous, I glanced in the passenger-side mirror to check behind us. I saw no signs of an angry demoness in pursuit of our minivan. My heart was still racing from the rush of almost being toasted alive.

"Her name is Lilith," Alex said softly. His usual smile was nowhere to be seen. Both hands clung to the steering wheel like a drowning man to a piece of driftwood. He was completely different from his usual cheerful self. "She's a super bigwig in Hell. If you think of demons as employees in some kind of evil corporation, she'd be something like a vice president." He looked over at me for the first time, and his blue eyes were dim and watery. He looked defeated. "She's also having an affair with the boss."

"Oh," I said, trying to follow the analogy. "*Oh.*"

"Yeah," he said flatly.

"So she and Sat—"

"Yes," he interrupted me. "You get it."

"How was she able to get out of our circle?" I asked.

"Our setup was never designed for something like her. That was the equivalent of trying to keep a tiger contained in a plastic bag. We're lucky it held her that long."

We rode in silence for a few moments while I tried to wrap my brain around the enormity of everything that had happened. My life over the last few days felt like an avalanche. All it took was one snowflake rolling down the top of a mountain, and before I knew it, my life was being carried away like an unfortunate ski resort. In the last seventy-two hours, I had managed to lose my soul, start a demonic plot to break up two of my best friends, resurrect one of my dead sisters, and make an enemy out of an important demon. I'm not sure I could have ruined my life better if I had been trying to.

"How did we accidentally summon the super-scary demon lady, Alex?" I asked. Part of me was feeling a bit more cynical toward my reporter "friend." He was the one who had provided the summoning ritual, after all. Although I didn't really have any insights into what he might gain by helping me upset such a powerful figure.

"I don't know," he said somberly. "Maybe we messed something up with the summoning. I followed the instructions I was given, though. And it's not like they were particularly hard."

"That's a bit of an understatement, man," I said dryly. "There were like two circles and a star. That's at least kindergarten level of instruction."

"Yeah, there's not a whole lot to get wrong."

We rode in silence for a few more minutes. There was something unsettling about the whole situation. I mean, aside from the obvious part. There was something I was missing. My subconscious mind was struggling to communicate to my conscious mind what that was exactly.

"I don't suppose," I said slowly, trying to tease the thought into the light, "that whoever gave you the instructions secretly hates you and would enjoy you getting eaten by a very powerful demon?"

"I've been wondering that myself," Alex said grimly. His hands seemed to grip the steering wheel even tighter. I realized that he was shaking. It was subtle, like minor tremors in a placid pond. Surprised, I looked at him again. This time I really looked, forcing my mind to calm down and actually think. Alex wasn't afraid or sad. No, the stillness in his eyes and the knuckle-whitening grip of his hands weren't the aftereffects of fear. He was enraged. He was desperately trying to tamp it down, to turn it off. For some reason, I thought of Bruce Banner from *The Incredible Hulk*, trying to keep from going green.

"She recognized you," I said slowly.

Alex said nothing. His lips compressed into a tighter, flatter line.

"What did she call you?" I tried to think back. "A… whelp?" My mouth soured a little as I thought about the meanings of the word whelp. I had been too occupied with my own agenda to think about what Lilith had meant when she spoke to Alex in the warehouse. "Alex, why did she call you a child?" I asked. My voice took on a harsh edge without a conscious thought. "Are you a demon?"

"No!" The vehemence in Alex's response echoed the rage I still saw in his posture. "Not really," he said more softly.

"What do you mean *not really*?"

"It's complicated…" he replied. He seemed to be searching for something to say.

"Well, you better explain it to me quick," I snapped. My own anger was starting to rise. I had trusted Alex, only to find out he wasn't as clean as he made himself out to be.

"I'm not a demon," he said emphatically. "I have no affiliation to Hell, or their kind. I've never met Lilith before, and I did not know that would happen." He hesitated for a second, like he was about to jump into cold water. "I swear to you that I am speaking the truth. A second time, I give my oath that I am not a scion of Hell. Thrice, I swear that my words are true." He spoke the words formally, his voice heavy with tradition.

It reminded me of a fairy tale for some reason. My instincts told me that the repetition meant more to Alex than I knew. Alex glanced over at me, his eyes no longer dancing with his anger. They were quiet, intense pools of blue.

"I'm not a demon," he repeated slowly. "But one of my great-great-grandfathers was."

"What?" My question exploded out of my mouth before I even finished processing what he said. I was completely floored by this revelation. How would that even work? I didn't even know if demons had all the necessary biological, uh, "attachments," let's say, to... well, you know. I mean, Lilith had certainly looked the part of a woman, but so do mannequins in department stores.

"It doesn't happen much anymore," he said hesitantly. "But back in the olden days, when..." He paused again, struggling to formulate his words. "It wasn't unheard of for a demon to, you know, have his way with a human."

"So you *are* a demon, then," I said, my voice still burning with my anger.

"No," he whispered once. He sounded sad, almost broken. Not defiant and defensive. "Think of it like this: Do you know your family's genealogy? Like how people will say 'I'm twenty-five percent German' or they're 'mostly Irish'?"

I nodded slowly. Like many Americans, I'm a giant European mutt when it comes to my bloodline, but I was familiar with the conversation. Everyone has that one friend who is way too into their heritage and won't stop bringing it up at every party.

"Well, the child of that union is half demon and half human. They're something quite different from me. I'm about one-thirty-second demon," he said simply. "The inhumanity breeds out over generations, like any other bloodline."

I took a minute to absorb that information. In theory, it made sense, if the offspring—it felt weird to apply the term "baby" to some sort of half-human hybrid—but if the offspring of a human and a demon was half of each, and then it in turn reproduced with a human, the baby would be seventy-five percent human. I tried to do some quick math in my head, but genetics is kind of tricky, and I'm a literature guy, not a math guy.

"So, you're, what, three or four generations removed from a demon?" I asked.

He shook his head slowly. "The math is a bit more complicated than that," he explained. "You're assuming that there was no more contamination in my ancestry. My kind was seen as abominations when the world was more savage. They often intermarried. I'm closer to ten or eleven generations removed from a true demon, I think."

"Wait, your *kind*? There were a lot of people like you?" I asked. "What are you called?"

"Names are tricky things." Alex smiled softly for the first time since we left the burning warehouse. We were comfortably out of reach of the demon for now, and it was easy to feel like things were returning to normal. As normal as a conversation about inhuman offspring can be, at any rate. The steady flow of traffic was calming both of us, I think. "The Europeans called us fairies, but the Greeks and the Romans called us demigods. I must admit I kind of liked that one. The oldest name I know of is the Nephilim."

"Wait, demigods? Isn't that like Hercules and Achilles?" I asked excitedly, for a moment forgetting anything serious. I mean *come on*, that was cool.

"Absolutely," he said, his own excitement bleeding into his voice as he began to relax. "Although from what I've heard, they both were kind of awful."

I had about a thousand questions running through my head. How many Nephilim were there? What was the name of the demon he was descended from? I sat there sorting through my pile of questions, trying to decide which one to ask first, kind of like an overwhelmed child on Christmas.

Seeing my face, Alex laughed out loud. I glanced at him and saw his eyes were back to their normal brilliant blue. The tension from our near-inferno experience was fading with my excitement.

"Dude," I said with a stupidly large grin on my face, "this is so cool."

"I think so too," he admitted with a laugh. "Once you get past the demon bit, it's pretty sweet."

"How old are you?" I asked. That seemed like a stupid question. Alex looked like he could be my older brother, at least age-wise. He was maybe twenty-four or twenty-five. But a couple of things he had said bothered me. He arched an offended eyebrow in my direction. "You said that this was an old practice," I explained, "but even if you're ten generations away from a demon, that's only two hundred years, maybe three hundred…"

"You are a quick study." Alex chuckled. "Yes, I am older than I look. Even someone like me, who is far more man than monster, still receives some benefits. They also fade with the bloodline. I remember the Civil War, if that helps."

"Holy crap," I breathed. While I don't have the actual dates of the Civil War memorized, it was solidly in the 1800s. No one still alive today was from those times. As far as the average person knew anyway, I supposed.

"So, can you, like, punch through walls or throw fireballs?" I asked.

"No," he said, his smile fading a bit. "Achilles was, at best guess, somewhere between a quarter and a third demonic. His grandfather was a demon. He had a lot more juice than I do. I'm a little stronger, I'm a little faster than I should be, and I can live a long time. But I'm nothing like that." As he spoke, I pictured him bolting out of the warehouse with me, the ease at which he passed me and the power that he had used to slam the door open.

"That's too bad," I said, trying to sound sympathetic. "It would probably be fun to have that much of the hot sauce."

"I wouldn't wish to be Achilles for all the gold in the world," he said immediately.

I shot him a surprised glance. The youthful part of me felt like anyone who wished they didn't have superpowers was fundamentally incorrect.

"You don't know enough to grasp this yet," he explained in response to my look. "But the less human you are..." He shivered a bit. "I count myself lucky to have what I do. The more demon blood you have in your veins, the less control you have. Achilles was a quarter, and his bloodlust was insatiable. He killed and killed." He shook his head, eyes distant again. I don't know what he was seeing, but it was not pleasant. "The full Nephilim are even worse." He glanced at me again. "I'm very grateful to not have been born a monster. Free will requires you to have a soul. I like mine very much."

Okay, that's fair. I nodded slightly, not sure how to respond to that. I guess everything has a cost, even superpowers. That sucked. My curiosity about Nephilim was not satiated in the slightest, but the somber tone reminded me that we had some big things to deal with now.

"So, what do we do next?" I asked. "Since talking to Hell didn't really work out so well for us."

"Well..." Alex glanced at me. "I don't suppose you're willing to let this go and take the deal?" he asked grimly.

"Of course not," I said, thinking of my lost soul and the mess that this deal had already stirred up. "It's not like it can get much worse from here." Alex didn't respond to that right away. I got the sense he might have disagreed with me but decided not to push it.

"I think we need help," he said finally. "I know someone who might be able to guide us. But I need a little time to set up a meeting with him. He doesn't usually talk to people who are so... mortal."

"Got it," I said with a mock salute. "I'll take a shower before we meet. Who is this guy?"

"I have to get his permission before I tell you," Alex said, shaking his head.

"You're serious?" I asked.

He nodded.

"Is he going to know that you told me or something?"

Alex shrugged. "Probably not, but it's not worth the risk. He is very... particular. You will understand after you meet him. I don't know how to explain it in a way that would make sense to you."

"Aren't you supposed to be some sort of writer?" I grumbled. "Isn't that your job, to describe things with words?"

"Yes." Alex laughed. "But writing is about communicating shared experiences and telling stories that everyone already knows. A well-written story is something anyone who has been alive for a few years can connect with. You are basically a baby in life experience with some of this stuff. Trust me when I say, you've never met anyone like him."

"Fine," I sighed, slightly annoyed. My natural curiosity was an impatient creature at best. I didn't like waiting for answers. I mean, I guess most people don't, but it particularly bothers me. My brain latches onto little things, questions I don't have the answers to, and ruminates on them endlessly. It's annoying.

"How long until we can meet with your mystery man?" I narrowed my eyes. "Or not-man, I suppose."

"If he agrees, we can probably talk to him tomorrow. I can

drop you off at your place and then go speak with him."

"Do we have that much time?" I asked. I don't know why, but I felt like there was a big hourglass behind me slowly draining away. The smaller the amount of sand left in the top glass, the larger the amount of stress I felt.

"Relax," Alex said pointedly. "We have literally a decade to fix this. They can't take your soul until after that. And rushing things is only going to put us in more danger." He glanced away from the street to look me in the eyes. "That's on me too. But we can't afford another bad situation like we had today."

I closed my eyes and leaned back into the seat. Deep down, I knew Alex was right. I didn't know his side of the world nearly as well as he did, but lawsuits weren't resolved in a single day in the mundane world either. There was no way this was a one-day fix. Besides, I'd already managed to make an enemy out of one super-powerful being today. No need to go for a twofer.

"Yeah, you're right," I said after a moment. "I suppose we've got a day or two to spare. But what if Lilith comes looking for me?"

"She already has you in the contract. All she has to do is wait, and she will eventually get her hands on you."

I tried not to gulp audibly. Assuming selling your soul to Hell worked like the fire and brimstone Baptist preachers on TV made it sound like, an eternity hanging out with Lilith was not on my bucket list.

"Especially if the contract really is a fake. They're not going to want to make a scene around you."

"I thought you believed me," I said, feeling a little stung. I was surprised that his doubt hurt my feelings. I guess I was already starting to think of Alex as a friend. Summoning a demon together is kind of a bonding experience.

"I do. Sorry, that was poorly phrased. There are people who tend to take notice when Hell decides to personally screw someone over," he said slowly. "The last thing they would want to do is draw eyes to you that might discover the truth and use it against them."

"Why don't we find these powers and tell them the truth ourselves?" I asked.

"Just because they don't like Hell doesn't mean they'll like you. This isn't the classic 'enemy of my enemy is my friend' kind of situation. It's more like 'the enemy of my enemy is a pawn I can use to get what I want, and I won't hesitate to sacrifice him for my goals' kind of thing."

"Okay, yeah, never mind," I said. "Let's not do that."

"Besides, you should be safe inside your home," he said. "Or at least safer."

"I know this. Is it a threshold thing?" I asked, feeling happy that there was one fact I didn't have to be taught.

"Very good." Alex smiled. "Homes are places of human dominion. If a human makes their life somewhere, it's difficult for inhuman creatures to enter it or to find it." He glanced at me. "Like everything else that's a fuzzy line, though, lots of Nephilim stronger than me wouldn't be the least bit inconvenienced."

I nodded, a little chilled by the thought. In stories, the idea of a threshold was often kind of a catch-all wall. Nothing that goes bump in the night could come through. But still, I'd take what I could get. I'd rather not have Lilith letting herself into my apartment anytime soon.

"Don't worry about me," I said with conviction. "I've got no problem sitting inside all day. It's practically a hobby of mine."

"Good," he said seriously. "I don't think you are in any immediate danger, but—"

"But better safe than sorry," I finished for him.

"Exactly."

CHAPTER 8

Forty minutes later, Alex dropped me back off at my apartment. It was mid-afternoon, and I hurried inside. I don't know if I've mentioned it yet, but it's hot in Los Angeles. I didn't want to spend even one more minute outside than I had to. In the daylight, the faded paint and old wood of my apartment building looked even trashier than usual. It was the kind of place that made you wonder about how easy it was to pass building inspections.

I made my way up the stairs to my door without seeing anyone, my steps echoing loudly as I made my way to the second floor. I was still trying to figure out everything that had happened to me.

But the scope of that was something else entirely. It's hard to go from zero to one hundred no matter how you measure it. We're proud of vehicles we've designed that can do it in a few seconds. But human beings aren't machines. In fact, we tell the members of our species that are more machinelike than the rest of us that something is wrong with them.

It was easy enough to accept the premise that "demons are real." Cool, okay, got it. But what did that *mean*? Why are they real? There were so many implications wrapped into that. Of course, there were the big-picture questions that humanity had been arguing about for as long as we'd existed. The classic things like "Where did we come from?" "Where are we going?" And so on.

But there was more to it than those two questions. What did it mean that mankind wasn't the apex predator that we thought we were? At least on land. I give sharks the top spot in the ocean. They're literally torpedoes with teeth. I can't compete with that.

What did it mean that there were demigods and other things that were operating on another level from humans? There was a common assumption by people in first-world countries that they were safe. Even if you lived in a heavy crime area like a bad neighborhood of Detroit, or some backwater country town with scary, inbred rednecks, you were still "safe." We as a species had conquered the planet. The only real scary thing left was us. We spent all our time wondering if Russia was going to invade some place or if China was going to pick a fight with us. We didn't worry if Lilith and her scary sugar daddy were upset with us. Not anymore.

So there were all these questions rattling around in my brain as my mind tried to rebuild my basic understanding of how the world worked. But an even bigger question eclipsed all of those thoughts. It was a simple, selfish one. One that everyone had at one point or another in his or her life, I think: *Why me?* Was I picked at random to have my life completely screwed over? If not, what did I do to deserve this? I wasn't Mother Theresa or the Dalai Lama, but I didn't feel like I deserved this.

In short, I was feeling sorry for myself. I don't feel like that's completely unreasonable. I was frazzled; the adrenaline rush of earlier had left me feeling empty physically, on top of the emotional drain I was already suffering from. The last three days,

I had basically been going at one hundred percent steam the whole time. I needed a break.

Connor would still be at work, and I was completely okay with that. I was looking forward to being by myself for a little while, to get a chance to collect my thoughts and rebuild my existential framework of life in general. You know, little things.

I paused at my front door to fish the key out of my pocket. However, when I inserted it into the lock, I found the deadbolt was already open. If the paint job on the outside of the building didn't give it away, our neighborhood wasn't the kind of place where you left the house with the door unlocked. Someone was home.

I stood there for a moment with my key still in the lock. I didn't want to deal with anyone right now. All I wanted was to lie in my bed and stare at the wall. But what was I going to do, turn around and walk away from my own apartment? With a sigh, I put my key back in my pocket and opened the door.

I didn't announce myself, hoping to sneak past whoever was there and lock myself in my room. The shades in the apartment were all drawn, and the lights were off. I wondered if Connor had come home for lunch and left without locking the door. Relieved that we weren't robbed, and that I had some alone time, I walked to my room and opened my bedroom door to find two girls on my bed.

Violet sat cross-legged at the head of the bed, her eyes red and puffy. She was sniffling and had a box of tissues in between her crisscrossed knees. A small mountain of used tissues was piled next to her. Megan was lying on her stomach next her, doing her best to look comforting. I made eye contact with her, and she gave me a small, sad frown.

"Hey, guys," I said slowly as I placed my keys on my dresser. "Um, what's going on?" I slid my feet out of my sneakers without unlacing them. My feet immediately rejoiced at being freed from their oppressively warm prisons. I peeled my socks off and wiggled my toes while Violet tried to compose herself. At least that felt good. I had a bad feeling that my day wasn't about to get any better.

"Violet and Connor had a fight," Megan informed me with a knowing glance. Violet sniffled again, burying her face in a wadded-up tissue. Well, great, the gears on this part of the machine were starting to turn too. I had known it would only be a matter of time.

I won't pretend to be good at understanding women. I struggle to understand what makes them cry or what makes them angry. They often react to things in a way that does not make sense to me as a man. My sister once called me an "emotional idiot," and I think that was both hurtful and accurate.

In the years I had known her, I had never seen Violet cry. Real crying, I mean. I seem to recall that she teared up in a few movies, but that doesn't count. On top of that, Connor and Violet didn't fight. I'd barely ever even seen them argue. This all smelled a little like brimstone to me.

Slowly, I sat down on a corner of my bed, next to my sister. I took my time, trying to stall and figure out what to do next. On a bright and clear day a week ago, before my life got more complicated, I wouldn't have known how to react to this situation. Now it felt like I was suddenly in the middle of a minefield. I wasn't sure where I could step without blowing everything up.

"Where's Connor now?" I asked.

Megan shot me a frustrated look. Trust a big sister to let you know when you've said something dumb.

"I don't kno-ooow," Violet sobbed. "He ju-just left. He was so mad. I've never seen him like that." Again, that smelled wrong to me. Connor was very level. He didn't even get mad at me for breaking all those dishes I kept dropping.

"What happened?" I asked, looking at Megan for a hint of

what I should be doing. She kind of shrugged in response. I couldn't tell if she was also mad at me or if she didn't know what was going on either.

"We were having lunch here," she began, "and working on plans for the wedding."

That surprised me. Connor and Violet were engaged and therefore "planning" on getting married, but they were both a little lazy. Maybe lazy wasn't the right word. But they both sort of seemed to feel like the big hurdle was *agreeing* to marry each other, rather than actually doing it. They had been engaged for at least six months or so, and this was only the second wedding planning meeting I had heard about.

"Wedding planning can be stressful," I said, trying to find something reassuring to say. Not that I knew anything about wedding planning. But I'd seen people fight about it on a sitcom once. "I'm sure that once everyone calms down—"

"I told him I didn't want you to be his best man," she interrupted me with a sob.

"I... Oh." That took me by surprise. I had been assuming that if this fight was somehow triggered by Dan's stupid deal, then it wouldn't be Violet actively trying to cut me out of the wedding party. For a moment, I felt better. Maybe this was normal life. But on the other hand, if it was only real-life emotions, my feelings were going to be a little hurt. Until yesterday, Violet and Connor had been the only living people I cared to call family. Yes, Megan was back, but I was still trying to figure out exactly how I felt about that. Violet not wanting me to be in the wedding party was like finding out I wasn't invited to family Christmas anymore. It stung.

"If that's what you want, I can step out," I said slowly. "I don't want to be something you guys are fighting about. If it would make it easier, I can be sick that day or something." I shot Megan another desperate look for help. She made one of those faces people make behind the back of someone who is being crazy. Her lips pulled down on one side, and her eyes widened. It was oddly reassuring that this didn't make any sense to her either.

"No, Matt, no," Violet said with the breathless speech of someone still holding back tears. "Of course I want you to be in our wedding. You are a part of our family, no matter what," she said emphatically. She raised her puffy green eyes up to meet mine. Wet mascara slithered down her red cheeks like dirty icicles. Her blonde hair had a ton of wild strands pointing in every direction. She looked like an adorable mad scientist who had narrowly avoided being struck by lightning. "I thought we had agreed to use our siblings."

Oh, that made sense. Connor had a younger sister named Sarah who was still in high school. Violet had an older brother who I had not met, and honestly had kind of forgotten about.

"Listen, I totally get that," I told Violet. I was starting to feel much better. This whole day had me looking for demonic finger puppets lurking in every shadow. I could help smooth this out, get everyone off my bed, and take a freaking nap. With a little luck, I could save today, or at least what was left of it. "I can talk to Connor when he gets back. I have no problem with being a groomsman and letting your brother be the best man. There's no reason to get all worked up about this."

"But that's the problem," she sobbed again. "This is a simple, small thing. If we can't even work through something this simple without a huge fight, how are we ever going to live the rest of our lives together?"

Uh-oh. Danger, Matthew Carver, danger. This had somehow gotten into very scary territory very quickly. I needed to do something to turn this ship around, and fast.

"I wouldn't worry too much about that," Megan chimed in to save the day. "Everyone has these kinds of arguments. The trick is learning how to work through them. You guys *never* argue. I don't think I've ever heard of it happening, like even once."

"Me neither," I chimed in, eager to be the backup crew.

"The point being," Megan continued, "that you guys don't have a lot of practice with working through disagreements yet. And even if this one was a little… explosive, that doesn't mean you both don't still love each other, right?"

Wordlessly, Violet nodded, a small smile flashing across her face, cutting through the tears. Megan sat up and put an arm around her shoulders comfortingly.

"I tell you what. Let's make you some tea. I'll whip up some dinner. I guarantee you that Connor will come to the same realization that you did." She shot me a meaningful look over Violet's head, which told me that was going to be my responsibility. "And then you guys can talk it out, and we will all have a nice evening and good food. How does that sound?"

"That sounds nice, I guess," Violet said in a small voice.

"Come," Megan said, patting the bed next to her. "Let's get up. We'll give Matthew back his bedroom and get this all sorted out."

With a final sniff, Violet scooted off my bed, doing her best to herd her flock of used tissues into her arms. She missed a few, but as she shuffle-walked out of the room with Megan, I decided not to press the issue. I was getting what I wanted anyway. No point in being greedy.

Megan shot me one last pointed look behind Violet's back as she closed the door. It said, *Fix your friend, right now.* Which was fair. It sounded like Connor had overreacted a tad, maybe even a smidge. But that kind of didn't surprise me. Connor was very protective of me, especially since my family's accident. Even though we are the same age, he has an older-brother complex. It might be the fact that he was the oldest child in his family, so that was the only way he knew how to relate to a sibling-type relationship. I'm a middle child myself, so who knows. But I could see him getting flustered in this conversation, torn between wanting to protect me and trying to make Violet happy. I could make this quite easy for him.

I grabbed my phone and shot him a message, letting him know to come back for dinner and that I was fine with being a groomsman. With a contented sigh, I tossed my phone onto my pillow and flopped down onto my bed.

Boom, disaster averted.

It felt good to have dodged at least one bullet today. As I lay there, tired and drained, I knew that I wasn't going to be able to actually take a nap. There were too many other things to think about. The first thing I had to acknowledge was that Alex was right. I had a decade to fix this. Well, technically a little less. But if I kept trying to keep moving at this breakneck speed, I was going to die before my ten years were up.

Assuming I could die. Did my ten years guarantee me life until the end of them? I doubted it. That seemed like the kind of thing that would be in the fine print of the stupid contract, if I ever got to read it. But me dying early would allow them to collect sooner; I couldn't see that being something they would give away.

The point being: We needed to slow things down. Do proper research before summoning any more demons. I needed to start sleeping again. This whole thing was turning into a marathon, not a sprint.

A big part of me wanted to find Dan and wrap my hands around his little red neck. I wasn't even sure if that would do anything. For all I knew, I might burn my hands. But it might make me feel better, and that was a start.

CHAPTER 9

I dozed off for a minute. My dreams were intense and disturbing, I think. When I woke up to the sound of someone knocking on my door, I couldn't remember what they were about. But I was uneasy. It's like how the monster in monster movies is scary at the beginning of the film because you don't know what it looks like yet. It's the fear of the unknown or some fancy term like that.

Don't look at me, I only fake-graduated from college.

"Matt, dinner's ready," Megan called from the other side of the door. A little forcefully too, I might add. It flashed me back to my childhood and bossy older sisters. I was grateful to feel that irritation in my life again. No matter how weird it was, I was very happy to have my sister back. Even if I wasn't sure exactly how that was going to play out.

"Okay," I mumbled, trying to ditch my sleep inertia. I'll be there in a second." My stomach rumbled helpfully, reminding me that I had neglected to eat a proper lunch and had thematically sacrificed a goat instead. This was not nearly as filling as eating the food, despite what you may have heard.

I rolled out of bed with a groan and shambled to my door. I

grabbed my phone and saw I had a response from Connor. He was on his way home and had sent that a while ago. I guessed we'd be seeing him in the next few minutes, assuming traffic wasn't worse than usual.

The rest of the apartment smelled amazing. My mouth started watering at the rich scent of fresh bread and other delicious smells that I couldn't quite place. My stomach began doing jumping jacks for joy. Then I remembered it was all going to taste like ash and sulfur to me. Good thing I was hungry enough to eat rocks. At least this would be easier to chew.

"Look who's finally awake," Megan called from the counter where she was finishing tossing some sort of salad. She had that half-teasing, half-accusing tone that sisters do so well.

Still shaking off my grogginess, I grunted in response and grabbed a chair at the table. Violet set a full glass of water at my place and at the seat next to me and smiled. Her face was cleaned of all its ruined makeup, and she no longer looked like she had been sobbing her brains out in my bed. I smiled back at her and took a sip of my water. The two of them continued their conversation about the last step of dinner. I tuned them out to stare at the food.

The table was loaded down with what must qualify as at least half a banquet. Fresh bread had been sliced and sat in a fancy basket with a towel. I didn't even know we owned a breadbasket, but I was not going to complain. Well, given the circumstances, I might complain a little. A large bowl held a steaming pile of mashed potatoes decorated with chives and what looked like bits of bacon. As I took in the fantastic sight, Megan slid a bowl full of Caesar salad onto the table as well. The grand centerpiece of the table was a pile of beautiful steaks. These had been pan-seared to perfection. Just like the other night, it smelled like a meal worth dying for. I had a desperate hope that the sulfur-flavored meal was a fluke.

My stomach's lust was interrupted by the sound of the apartment door opening. Violet and Megan grew quiet, and the room's relaxed feel vanished. Violet made her way down the entry hallway to where Connor had to be lurking. I could hear them talking in low tones for a few moments but could not make out what they were saying. Megan and I exchanged helpless looks, like two friends of a patient sitting in the waiting room while their loved one is in surgery.

A minute went by, probably a lot less, actually. It felt that way because it was awkward. Violet and Connor emerged, holding hands and wearing embarrassed smiles. Megan and I both made vomiting sounds to let them know everything was back to normal. Connor was wearing a sharp gray business suit that was probably custom tailored. His black hair was immaculate, per usual. Working in finance seemed exhausting to me. From how hard you have to work to look good enough to actually go to work, let alone the actual job. I was more of a business-casual kind of guy myself. I never felt like myself when I was wearing a suit.

"Dinner's ready, lovebirds," I said dryly, gesturing at the table. "I'm hungry, so hurry up."

"Give me thirty seconds to change," Connor said, heading for his room.

"One Mississippi, two Mississippi, three Mississippi," I called after him. He made a rude hand gesture over his shoulder as he walked away.

Man-to-man relationships are a funny thing. That interaction meant we were cool. No further discussion was needed on today's drama. I was grateful for that.

True to his word, Connor was back in a very short amount of time, wearing a pair of khaki shorts and a fancy polo. Everyone joined me in sitting around our little square table, and we could finally eat. Regardless of how it would taste, I was starving, and the smell was doing nothing to help me wait any longer.

After the initial flurry of activity that starts a dinner, passing around different dishes and serving food, I was staring down at a mountain of food on my plate. A large steak was surrounded by creamy mashed potatoes, a still-warm slice of bread, and a small patch of the salad. Still apprehensive about the taste, I shoveled a forkful of the potatoes and a bite of steak into my mouth with gusto.

I guess scientifically speaking, the taste was fascinating. It's remarkable how precise the taint of Megan's... situation was. Because both Megan and Violet had worked on dinner, only some of the food was awful. The steak was clearly Megan. It was seared to perfection. Not to say that Violet wasn't a good cook, but she wasn't a trained chef like my sister. The mashed potatoes on the other hand, were delicious. My senses were assaulted with the sharp taste of sulfur and ash from the steak, and the smooth taste of good mashed potatoes. It was really weird. But the potatoes helped smooth the steak down. I think Marry Poppins would have been proud.

"Mmm, this steak is *so* good," Connor said through a mouthful.

"Megan did the steak," Violet said, confirming my suspicions.

"Did you do the potatoes?" I asked. "Because they also are delicious."

Violet beamed at me and nodded from across the table. Everyone focused on their food for a minute. I alternated bites between completely normal food and a blend. I kept a nervous eye on my ration of mashed potatoes and hoped I had enough to last.

It turned out the salad was also edible, which might be the only time I've ever uttered that sentence in my life. The bread, however, not so much. Which is so unfair. I knew it was store bought, but apparently if Megan even cut the bread, it was going to be ruined.

"So, Matt, what were you up to today?" Violet asked as the gorging began to slow down. "We didn't see you home at lunch."

"Oh," I said, quick on my feet as ever. Indeed, what *had* I been doing that day? Obviously, I couldn't tell them the truth, for so, so many reasons. So many. But I didn't want to lie to them. Already I could feel the pressure of all the secrets I had accumulated in less than three days, making me feel distant from them.

Secrets have a way of doing that, even innocent ones. They burrow like worms, eating out the meat of a relationship until there's nothing left but a husk. I was sitting at a table with a dead girl who wasn't dead. Everyone else at the table knew she was dead too, or at least had known that at some point. But they had been made to forget. That alone was a pretty big scoop of secret, and I didn't want to add some white-lie sprinkles to the top of my sundae of deceit.

"I had to try to make some returns," I said after a moment of thought. "There was a mix-up when I went out the other night, and I somehow ended up with something that was pretty expensive."

"I hate returning things," Connor said sympathetically. "They always make it such a pain to figure out how to do it. Half the time, if I end up with something I didn't want, I find myself thinking, 'Whatever, I'll probably use this anyway,' and I end up keeping it."

"I think that's the general idea, doofus," Violet said teasingly around a mouthful of steak.

"Yeah, way to give in to the system, Connor," Megan chimed in.

Connor shrugged and happily took another bite from his

plate. At this point, I was no longer starving, and each bite was getting harder to eat. Watching the three of them enjoy their food made me want to kill them. But then I would have no friends, so I decided to suffer for their sakes. I forced myself to clean my plate, eating every bite. I'm not sure why, really. I think it was as penance to myself. This was my fault, or at least partially so. The least I could do was eat my dead sister's food and make her happy.

After dinner was over, Violet and Megan went and sat on the couch. They said something about the people who cooked dinner not having to clean up after, which was hard to argue with. That was how Connor and I ended up next to each other, with him washing the dishes and me drying.

I hate washing dishes. There's something about the slimy feel of soap and discarded food that gives me the shivers just thinking about touching it. As a child, I frequently traded my dishwashing turns to my sisters in exchange for double the chore load. Tonight, I agreed to take the garbage out to the dumpster if I got to dry.

"Hey, man, thanks," Connor said to me quietly as I stepped in to take the first dish he scrubbed.

"Of course," I said, equally as soft. The kitchen opened straight into the living room, and while Violet and Megan appeared to be watching some reality show, you can never be too safe around girlfriends and sisters. "I'm happy to help things go smoothly. Don't worry about it at all. We're good."

He nodded and scrubbed away at a plate for a few moments. I finished drying a serving bowl and set it on the counter to be put away. I'd probably need to ask one of the girls where it had been before. It may have been our apartment, but Heaven help us if we were to put things back in a new place.

"I wanted to tell you, by the way," he continued in that same tone, "that I'm really proud of you for getting your degree.

I always thought you got kind of screwed over by the system with… everything that happened, but I'm glad you really carried through with it. I always believed in you, man."

"Thanks," I said, feeling a little wave of shame. While Connor was not wrong—I did get kind of screwed over by the system—I still hadn't earned my degree. It wasn't something that I had buckled down and gotten for myself. You could make the argument that I did deserve it, after everything that had happened to me. But Connor thought I had earned it, and I wasn't sure I could honestly say I had.

"I guess now I need to find myself some sort of big-boy job," I said with a laugh.

"That reminds me, my firm is looking to hire some guys for the marketing department. They need some more writers for their blog," Connor said. "I could put in a good word for you with the manager of that department."

I wrinkled my nose at him in distaste.

"You are such a tortured artist." He laughed. "Come on, man, words are words, and you're good with them. Plus, finance money is pretty good. That's the best part of getting a big-boy job, dude. Suddenly being free to do real things, buy real stuff. You don't have to eat ramen or buy clothes from cheap stores anymore." He handed me a clean plate, still dripping wet. "Being an adult is awesome."

"You may be the only person in our age bracket to think that," I said with a laugh. "I appreciate the offer, I really do. Let me think about it. I'm still trying to mentally process the change, if that makes sense. After all, I didn't think I had a college degree to use to find a real job until very recently."

"That's fair," Connor said, handing me another plate. "But let me know soon. It'd be awesome to be coworkers."

I was tempted. But I couldn't lose focus on fixing my

"situation" with my soul and everything else that was spiraling out of control. On the other hand, this problem probably wasn't going away tomorrow, and I was going to need money to pay bills and eat. You know, the little things.

We finished the rest of the dishes in silence, each lost in our own thoughts. When we finished, Connor wandered over to the living room to join the girls. I pulled out the full bag of trash in the kitchen and tied it up. Our dumpster was in a little alley alongside the left of the building if you were looking at it from the street. It was an evil-looking alley, narrow and overgrown with weeds, but that was where the trash went, so I had to go there too.

I trotted down the stairs and out the front door of the building, letting it close heavily behind me. Whistling softly to myself, I walked down the alley and opened up the dumpster. Despite the fact that everything in my life was out of control, I was in a good mood. I had good friends and family. Some people don't even have that much. My soul—which was probably a different thing than what Dan had stolen from me—felt whole. I tossed the trash in and let the lid slam closed. Everything was going to be okay.

I didn't see what hit me as I turned from the dumpster. One moment I was alone and able to breathe. The next, something hard slammed into my stomach, making me huff all my air out in an instant. I slammed into the side of the metal dumpster with a crash and slid to the ground, simultaneously gasping for air and unable to breathe any in.

Dan the Demon stood above my crumpled form, still as red and ridiculous as ever. His face was mottled with rage, and the baseball bat he held in his left clawed hand answered the question of what had hit me. Two slightly taller figures lurked behind him, wearing gray hoodies that obscured their faces from view and dark baggy jeans. Black gloves covered their hands so none of their flesh was visible. I could make out a pair of horns peeking out of the closer one's hood.

"You've ruined everything," Dan hissed, and raised the bat again.

CHAPTER 10

Wa-wait," I managed to gasp out, holding a hand out toward Dan.

The demon ignored me and slammed the bat into my stomach again. I had no breath to scream with, otherwise, trust me, I would have let out a doozy. Dimly, the part of my brain that loves to remind me that I am an idiot flashed back to my conversation with Alex and the safety of staying inside my apartment. Oops. So much for that.

"I gave you so much," Dan shouted, raising the bat again. His cheesy salesman's grin was nowhere to be seen today. This time, instead of slamming it down on me, he took his anger out on the side of the apartment building. The bat bounced off the wall with a dull thud. His pointed tail curled spastically behind him in time with his shallow breaths. "All you had to do was shut up and take the gift. That's it! But no, what do you do? You stupid, mortal human! You go and start complaining that having the world's best life wasn't good enough. You had to start getting people asking questions."

I was guessing that my conversation with Lilith earlier today might have had some repercussions. It's funny, it hadn't occurred to me that Dan wasn't operating in an aboveboard capacity with Hell. He had obviously faked my signature and committed some sort of fraud, but I hadn't thought too much about whether or not his bosses might be upset about that. I mean, Hell wasn't exactly highly rated by the Better Business Bureau, at least as far as I knew. It's kind of like getting screwed over by the cable company. You're not sure if it's the representative or the company that's really out to get you. Could be both. Lilith had certainly looked a little surprised when I told her I hadn't actually agreed to the deal. And given Dan's rather batty reaction to my conversation with Lilith, I got the sense he maybe wasn't supposed to do that. What happens to a low-ranking demon when he gets caught doing too much evil by his superiors? Do they give him a Demon of the Month award or force him to work in one of the really crappy circles?

"Didn't mean to," I gasped, still trying to regain the breath that had been knocked out of me. I peered up at the short demon thing. It struck me how different he was from Lilith. She had been tall and elegant, a literal picture of artistic perfection. Dan, on the other hand, was a caricature of the human perception of demons, some last remnant from old Saturday morning cartoons. Even lying at his feet, looking up at his fire-engine-red skin and curled horns, he seemed small. I knew he was only about five feet tall, but it wasn't just his physical height. His presence was small, like a thimble compared to a football stadium. It wasn't the same thing in size or kind.

"I was only trying to get more information," I wheezed. "You didn't even give me a copy of the contract. We thought we were calling the front desk or the customer service line. Didn't know she would answer."

"What do you mean 'we'?" Dan asked, his voice rising in pitch. So, whoever his source had been, they had left out Alex.

I couldn't think of a reason that could be at the moment. But I tried to make a mental note of it to investigate later. You know, assuming that Dan didn't bash my head in and scatter my brains all over the pavement.

"Some crackpot dude I met at a bar," I said. "You know I know nothing about this freaky supernatural world. I was confused and scared. He told me he could help."

"Where is he now?" Dan demanded.

"No idea. He ran off after Lilith almost killed us," I replied. "I'm not actually sure he expected his ritual thing to work. I think he was hoping to con me out of fifty bucks."

Dan was silent for a moment, apparently weighing his options. Absentmindedly, he tapped the bat against the side of the building a few times. His two goons, still obscured by their hoodies and human clothes, continued to stand behind him, silent and completely still. Why in the world would Dan need bodyguards from me? I was assuming that was what they were for anyway. They had that sort of brute-muscle-henchman kind of vibe to them.

"I tried to go easy on you," he said after a long moment, his mind apparently made up. "Yeah, I did. I hooked you up. And this is how you repay me?" He looked down at me, hefting the bat again. "I tried to do this the right way, but you've left me no choice." He sounded more like he was trying to convince himself than me.

"Dan, wait!" I said, holding my hands up again. "Think this through, man. People are already asking questions, right? I don't claim to be an expert in any of this, but I imagine if you kill me right now, I don't end up in a good place, right?"

He stared at me silently, the baseball bat still raised above his head.

"Won't it make people *more* suspicious if the guy you sold a deal to ends up dead the next day?" I asked.

His furry black eyebrows moved together, like two gross caterpillars making out.

"If you kill me now, there's not much incentive for me to keep my mouth shut on the other side."

The two goons behind him stirred uncomfortably at my words. I tried to sound tougher than I felt, which is pretty hard when you're still out of breath.

"Face it, buddy, as mad as you might be at me, this is your mess. Just take the deal back, and we can call it square. I won't press charges."

Dan lowered the bat with a dejected sigh. I could tell some of my words hit their mark. It was significantly easier than reasoning with Lilith had been.

"Well, that's great," Dan muttered to himself. "'You won't press charges. How very agreeable of you." He looked back at me, and my eyes met his solid black ones.

Random thought: Are they still called eyes if they don't actually seem to have any irises or other eye parts? Dan's eyes were more like two puddles of ink than actual eyeballs, a darkness that occupied the space inside his skull and was only visible through those two holes.

"I can't let you go, Matt," he said after a minute. "I need you too much for that." Dan was quiet for another moment. "But you're right. I can't kill you either." With a casual flick, he tossed the baseball bat to the ground like a piece of litter. "We need to find a way to work together for mutual benefit in this situation." His too-wide smile flickered across his face as he spoke.

That made me mad. Now that I wasn't worried that I was going to be bludgeoned to death in the next thirty seconds, and was able to breathe again, I had enough brainpower to focus on being angry. Wincing slightly, I pulled myself to my feet, bracing myself on the apartment building wall to help me stand up. I towered over Dan by a good foot. Even his two hoodied goons were only my height.

I glared down at the diminutive little demon and felt something snap. Everything I had been through in the last couple days had been building up inside of me like a volcano. Everything in my life had been put in jeopardy because of his actions. And now the catalyst of all my trouble stood before me, smiling that same smarmy smile he wore when he had stolen my soul.

Not breaking eye contact, I crouched down slowly and picked up the bat he had dropped. His smile drooped as I stood back up and slowly raised the bat. His silent goons tensed slightly, and one took a half step closer to Dan, but the shorter demon raised a hand to stop him.

"Come on, Matthew," he said admonishingly. "Surely you know that you can't kill us with a bat. Put that down, and let's discuss this like reasonable gentlemen."

"I figured," I said, showing him a grin full of teeth and setting my grip on the bat with both hands. "But as you just figured out yourself, you can't kill me either."

I whipped the bat in a horizontal swing, aiming at his stupid horned head like I was trying to hit a game-winning home run. It connected, boosting him up off of his feet and slamming him into the building. His two goons immediately stepped forward to grab me. I jabbed at the left one's hooded face with the end of the bat, forcing him to take a step back, then danced backward and took a swing at the second demon. He took the blow on his shoulder and staggered a few steps to his left. Dan started to climb to his feet, and I slammed him back to the ground with a blow to the base of his skull.

I don't claim to know anything about hand-to-hand combat or how to fight several people at the same time, but a baseball bat doesn't require a doctorate or even a real college degree to use effectively. Just smash everything you don't like with it, and you'll do just fine. I had enough anger-fueled strength to compensate for a lack of technique. The shock and fear triggered by their ambush had faded. All that was left in its place were the embers of rage already spent, right on the cusp of reigniting into a full-blown raging fire intent on consuming everything around it. And in the moment right before I took the first swing, they burst to life again.

While these demons may be immortal, able to defy time and all manner of things we mortals believe to be inevitable, they were still under the jurisdiction of the laws of Sir Isaac Newton. And in this case, my baseball bat was all the unstoppable force needed to knock these objects into motion.

I continued to back down the alley a few steps, swiping at the closest demon. After a few swings, Dan stepped between me and his goons.

"Enough," he said. I hit him in the face as hard as I could. This time he was ready. He rocked on his feet, and his head spun to the side with the blow, but he didn't fall over. The bat shattered on his face, sending pieces flying through the alley like shrapnel. I looked down at the broken bat, feeling vaguely betrayed. Dan stared at me, a bored expression on his face.

With a sigh, I tossed the broken remains to the cracked asphalt.

"Was that therapeutic for you?" he asked dryly. "Do you feel better now? I don't even have a headache, Matt. That did literally nothing except waste both of our time."

"That makes me feel a bit better, actually," I said. "You seem like a guy who probably has something he needs to do with his time right now. Me? I was just taking out the trash." I made a broad sweeping gesture that took in the three demons and the dumpster. I felt a little cool after that one.

Dan frowned a little, like he wasn't sure how to respond to that. "The point is," he said, apparently deciding to ignore my wit, "is that the deal isn't going anywhere. I can't kill you, and you can't kill me. So we had better start figuring out a way to work together."

While I couldn't kill Dan with a baseball bat, I wasn't sure that the same wouldn't be true for Alex's mystery friend. He might know a more effective approach. But I didn't want to tip my hand to him, so I decided to play along.

"Fine," I snapped after a moment's pause. "What do you want from me?"

"I want you to stop rattling the cages. Trust me, you don't want some of those people looking into this. It wouldn't end well—for you or me."

"I don't think I can do that, Dan," I said calmly.

His face fell a little. It was like he had thought we were making progress only to have it snatched away at the last moment.

"The way I see it," I continued, "I'm screwed either way. Whether it gets me tomorrow or ten years from now, I end up in the same place."

"A little less," he said absentmindedly. He barely seemed to be listening to me. If he had had pupils, I would have said they were unfocused, giving the wall behind me a thousand-yard stare.

"Whatever. If I sit here and wait, you get away scot-free with your 'soul fraud,' and Bad Things happen to me with capital letters and everything. Besides, my whole life is fake, and it sucks, so I don't even get to reap the benefits."

Dan's head shot up at that, and he gave me an incredulous look. "Black Abyss! You are a greedy mortal. I gave you everything," he said. "What could you possibly be missing?"

"You ever see *The Matrix*?" I asked half sarcastically. He shook his horned head slowly. "Never mind," I muttered. "The point is, Bad Things might *not* happen to me if I fight you on this. That's better odds than I have now."

"Balls," Dan muttered to himself, which was as amusing as it had been when he did it in the theater, for the record. He turned away from me and started pacing. "You realize," he said, stopping after a moment and looking at me, "that it's not only you, right? If need be, your family and friends can and will be dragged into this."

"You're kidding, right?" I asked with a snort. "You already involved them when you started this whole mess."

He frowned and resumed pacing. It was almost comical. I glanced at one of the guard demons and arched an eyebrow questioningly. I could have sworn he half shrugged back at me, a slight raising of his shoulders. Silent and evil he might be, but apparently, he was also confused by Dan's antics.

"You are really bad at this," I said after a good thirty seconds of watching Dan pace.

"Not helpful," he said in a singsong voice and did not stop pacing.

I was starting to wonder what everyone back in my apartment was thinking. At this point, I had been gone almost fifteen minutes. I wasn't sure how I was going to explain how taking out the trash had kept me busy this long. In fact, I didn't want to wait any longer. Dan no longer had anything to offer me, and we both knew it.

"Tell you what," I said, bringing the pacing Dan to a pause. He looked at me with an expression of defeat. "I'm going to go back inside now. You keep pacing it out. Feel free to use my alleyway if you like. I don't really care. If you think of some sort of mutually beneficial, super-sweet combo deal, you know where to find me."

A little nervous about how they might react, I stepped past Dan, but neither he nor his goons made any moves to stop me. I turned around and tossed my tiny life-wrecker a wink. "See you around, Dan," I said as cheerfully as I could. I went back in the front door of my building without looking back. The moment

I was out of sight of the three of them, I sprinted up the stairs as fast as my bruised body would go. I didn't stop running until I was in the safety of my apartment, where the demons couldn't get me. Hopefully.

CHAPTER 11

I must have looked like a cartoon character as I burst into my apartment and slammed the door shut behind me. For a moment, I leaned back against the closed door, my left hand gingerly probing my increasingly tender stomach. I was going to have a gnarly bruise by tomorrow. Maybe a cracked rib too. I wasn't really sure what those felt like. It's a thing that I hear happens to people who get hit like I did. People always say you'll know if you break your arm or that breaking your femur is the most painful thing that can happen to you. But it seems like people can hang out with cracked ribs and never even notice until a doctor mentions that it's not in the right place.

Basically, I was in pain and was pretty sure it was going to get worse. But I wasn't sure what the pain I was feeling meant in terms of physical damage yet. Yet another thing I owed the strange creature that was Dan the Demon.

No one seemed to have noticed I was gone for so long. I could still hear the TV blaring in the living room. I steeled myself, not wanting them to notice I was in pain. That would lead to a lot of questions that I didn't have answers for. Well, I had answers, but none that any of them would believe. After pausing to catch my breath and let my heart rate resume its normally scheduled beating, I pushed myself off the door and wandered into the living room.

It was a scene from my nightmares. The television, which was still loudly broadcasting, was wildly skewed, caught from falling to the floor by the edge of one of the couches. The window it had sat in front of was shattered, glass spread all over the room like gleaming daggers. Bright dots of blood were all over the carpet. There wasn't enough blood to look like someone had had an artery cut and bled out, but my guess was the glass had been the source of a thousand tiny cuts.

Violet and Connor lay on the floor in the living room, bound efficiently back to back. Their mouths were covered in duct tape, but I didn't need to hear their moans through the gags to read the screams of terror reflected in both their eyes. Both were cut and bleeding. Megan was nowhere to be seen.

Shock robbed me of my common sense for a moment, and I didn't know where to start. After a brief pause, I rushed to their side and dropped to a crouch. My bruised body complained a bit, but I ignored it. Desperate, my fingers started trying to untie the knots that bound my two friends. But the cords were so tight my fingers couldn't find any purchase. Whether their struggling had tightened them or their attackers were some sort of super Boy Scouts, I couldn't figure out how to loosen them.

Both of my friends were trying to shout at me through their gags, but I couldn't understand them. My mind was racing at a million miles an hour. How hard was it to untie knots? I was going to kill Dan. I didn't know how, but I would find a way. Had this whole thing been a distraction to keep me away? Their muffled screams grew louder. Irritated, I looked from the knots into Violet's wide, panic-filled eyes.

"Hang on a second!" I shouted, feeling frustrated and

helpless. "I'm trying to figure out how to get you out. Give me a second, okay?"

Something was wrong. They both were screaming, almost hysterical. A chill rose up my back. It started at the bottom of my spine and shot all the way up to my neck at the speed of lightning.

They weren't freaking out about being tied up. Violet wasn't looking at me, begging me to get her free. No, she was looking behind me. They both were trying to warn me. Something was behind me. Somehow, I knew it had to be *something* and not *someone*. The panic in their eyes told me there wasn't a normal burglar behind me. It was an I've-seen-a-monster-for-the-first-time sort of terror.

I tried to subtly glance around our ruined apartment for something I could use as a weapon. A long shard of glass, like a two-dimensional icicle, lay near Connor's feet. Gingerly, I reached out and held it in my hand, being careful to not cut myself. There was no way I could grip the piece of glass hard enough to stab anyone without slicing my own hand, but if whatever was behind me was as terrifying as my friends' faces indicated, a cut hand might be worth a chance to kill it.

Slowly, I rose to my feet, gripping my blade that cut both ways. I turned to look back into the kitchen, which I hadn't spared a glance at as I raced to my friends' aid. My heart wasn't racing. This was like the third dangerous situation I had been in today. My adrenaline was all used up, apparently. Or maybe I was already getting used to the danger. Instead of the monumental amount of fear I expected, there was only emptiness, a void of emotion or distractions. All the random thoughts and other crap that normally went spiraling through my head were gone. There was only one thought instead of many: *Protect your friends.*

A tall figure stood in the middle of the kitchen. And when I say tall, I mean it was *really* tall, like NBA center tall, easily seven feet in height. The table had been knocked over and slammed off into one of the cabinets to make room for it. It wore a black cloak, which billowed and pooled around its feet. Like most of the supernatural creatures I had met so far, it kept its skin covered—except for the doglike snout protruding from its hood.

Although the snout looked canine, it was hairless, with leathery blue-gray skin covering it. A pair of large fangs poked out of either side of its lips, which were only mildly threatening. Its mouth quivered as it panted slightly, like a dog that has exerted itself.

For a heartbeat, we stared at each other as I tried to decide what to do next. I had been ready for another demon. That was really the breadth of my supernatural experience so far. I didn't know what this was exactly, but it was something new. Or at least, it was new to me. It might be *very* old for all I knew. But while I was trying to come up with a better plan than "stab him with a piece of glass," I got the sense it wasn't nearly as intimidated by me as I was by it. It gave off an aura of savagery that I might expect if I came face-to-face with a grizzly bear in my living room.

But its posture was all wrong for a rampaging beast. It wasn't coiled, ready to pounce. No growls rumbled out of its throat. It stood tall and calm, more like a statue than a dog-person-thing. I didn't get the sense that this thing was trying to decide what to do with me—it was waiting for something.

"Can I help you?" I asked after coming to that conclusion. I wasn't even sure that it could speak. Dog mouths and tongues aren't really designed to be able to articulate complicated speech patterns as far as I know.

"Do not look for her," the thing said. It had a deep voice, a bass so low it could probably rattle the tabletops. There was a growling edge to it, like someone speaking through gritted teeth. "My master bids me to urge you: do not look for her if you wish to spare her pain."

Megan. He had to be talking about Megan.

"What have you done with my sister, dog?" I snarled. My right hand unconsciously tightened on the shard of glass. It hurt, but I didn't care. I took a step forward, doing my best to be menacing. The creature growled. It was a savage sound, that sounded like it belonged to the primeval sire of the modern-day junkyard Rottweiler. The implied threat in his growl drew me up short. As much as I might want to fight him, my chances of bringing a seven-foot dog-man into submission with a glass shard were not great.

"Do. Not. Look for her," he repeated in that deep voice. "You will only make things worse for her." With a wordless growl, he dropped to all fours and leapt forward. Instinctively, I flinched away, to my shame. My heart and body jolted as the terror I hadn't felt yet came crashing down on me like a tsunami.

Cognitively, there's no doubt in my mind that I would fight and even die for most of my friends. To the rational portion of my brain that makes the big overarching life decisions, that's a simple choice.

The spirit may be willing, but the body had not been conditioned to that concept. I didn't have a lot of experience getting into fights with human beings. Which is a little surprising, given how much I'm prone to running my mouth. And your brain can have all the combative intentions in the world, but when a giant monster leaps right at you, your body listens to your instincts instead.

The beast continued its lunge past me and beyond my tied-up friends. It leapt through the broken window without even hesitating at the ledge. A dull thud sounded as he landed in the alley below and was gone. I stared at the broken window for a second, afraid he might decide to leap back in and kill us all. But a muffled cry from Violet snapped my attention back to my bound friends.

I ran back to them and carefully, ever so carefully managed to cut the knots with my improvised glass blade. I freed Violet's hands first. Not for any other reason but because that was how I was raised. My mother always told me if two of my friends were tied up by monsters, when it was time to free them, help the lady first. Or maybe it was something about pulling the chair out for women at the dinner table. I don't really remember the whole lesson too well.

The instant her hands were free, she started to tear at the duct tape over her mouth with a frantic need. I couldn't blame her. Being so constricted, unable to move or even speak while a monster was present sounded horrifying. I shuddered at the thought of feeling so helpless. I let her do that, afraid to try to free her legs with my glass while she flailed around.

Next, I cut Connor's hands free. His dark eyes were calmer than Violet's had been. With his hands free, he, too, began to work on his tape gag. I sat back on the floor with my head in my hands, trying to calm my racing heart.

"Matt, Matt," Violet gasped as soon as her mouth was free to speak. "They took Megan."

"What the hell were those things?" Connor demanded a few seconds later, after he was free to speak. "Did you see that? It looked like some sort of werewolf."

I knew without looking they both were staring at me. Their gazes were so heavy I could feel them putting pressure on my skin. Megan was gone. This was not fair. I had lost her once already. She had died, for Pete's sake! I had only started to come to terms with having her back. I couldn't go through a second funeral for her. I didn't think I could take it.

"I'm calling the police," Connor said after a moment. He had freed his legs and went to grab his phone.

Everything was a blur after that. I sat on the glass-strewn floor and stared at my feet. Dimly, I heard Connor calling the police, his frantic voice reporting that something terrible had happened in our apartment. After he placed the call, he and Violet continued to talk, discussing what they had seen. But I couldn't focus on it. I couldn't actually make out what they were saying. Their voices were muted, as though they were speaking from the other side of a wall of Jell-O.

My shoulders sagged under a tremendous amount of guilt. Because of me, Megan had died the first time. Because of me, she had come back from wherever she had gone. And now, because of me again, she had been taken. Apparently being a relative of mine could cause a two hundred percent mortality rate.

A loud, authoritative knock snapped my head up for the first time in a long time. I don't actually know how long it took the authorities to respond to Connor's call. Left to my own devices, I might have sat in shock for hours. Violet opened the door, and a handful of police officers with crisp black uniforms and shiny golden badges entered.

In the blink of an eye, the officers swept us out of our warzone of an apartment so they could investigate the scene. Two detectives—judging from the cheap suits they were wearing—walked us down the stairs of the building. As we passed, a group of people were going up, carrying cameras and lab equipment. It was like a bad crime TV episode happening in my apartment live.

They took us out of the front of the building and to a big black SUV parked by the curb. They opened the side doors and let us sit in the car. Connor and Violet slid into the middle row; I sat in the passenger's seat. The officers stood outside of the car on the curb and pulled out their notepads to take down our information.

The male detective was probably in his late forties. He was big, the kind of big that's neither fat nor muscular but a strange blend of both. Despite a beer belly, he could probably also bench press me. He wore a dark-gray suit with a white shirt underneath it. He had a tough grizzled face, but he had a kind voice as he spoke.

The Latina woman was shorter, with jet-black hair that fell to her shoulders. Her blue jacket noticeably bulged under the shoulder where her weapon was holstered. She had dark-brown eyes that were sharp with intelligence as she stared at us. I got the sense that these two were very good at what they did.

"Okay, everyone, I know you've just been through a crazy incident," the man started. "I understand how hard it can be to focus after something like that. But we need your help to try to figure out exactly what happened here, so we can help your missing friend, okay? My name is Detective Jones. This is my partner, Detective Rodgers. Believe me when I tell you that we will be doing everything we can to find the monsters that did this."

Silently, we all nodded in response.

"Let's start with you, young lady," he said, moving on past his introduction. "What's your name?"

"Violet Moore," she replied in a small voice. I think she, too, was feeling the horror of what had happened rushing in to fill the vacuum that adrenaline had left.

"Okay, Violet," he said, still kindly. "What happened here?"

"We had just finished dinner, and Connor and I were watching TV—"

"Which one of you is Connor?" Jones interrupted.

"I am," Connor said from the back seat.

"And you are the one who placed the call to dispatch?" the detective asked.

Connor must have nodded.

"Okay, sorry, honey," Jones said to Violet. He somehow managed to say that in a way that wasn't patronizing. A certain timbre of his voice made it sound more genuine than it ever has for anyone who isn't a Southern grandmother.

"We were watching TV," she continued, "when suddenly some people burst in through the window."

"The window?" Detective Rodgers asked sharply. Her voice was not nearly as kind, instead it was brisk and professional, like a creek in September. "You're on the third floor." The incredulity in her tone was almost tangible.

"I don't know how they did it. I didn't have time to see," Violet said defensively. "There was a crash, and then glass was everywhere, and they were attacking us. There were three of them, I think."

"Can you describe them?" Rodgers asked, furiously scribbling on her notepad.

"Not really. They all wore black clothes, like a robe or a cloak or something, and their faces…" She hesitated.

"They had, like, these werewolf or dog masks or something," Connor finished for her.

I almost gasped in surprise. My friends may have seen some sort of evil monster, but they didn't know it. That wasn't a category in their brain that they could fit the knowledge in. Instead of realizing what they saw, they rationalized it away. A couple of days ago, I probably would have done the same thing. I was silently grateful that Violet had gone first. My story would have made me sound like a raving lunatic.

"They tied Connor and me up," Violet resumed her narration. "Then two of them grabbed Megan and took her away out the window."

"And this is Megan… Carver?" Jones said, checking his notes. "Sister of Matthew Carver, which I'm guessing is you?"

I nodded, not trusting myself to speak.

"Where is your sister currently employed, Matthew?" he asked, turning to me.

"Uh," I said, caught off guard. Crap! I had no idea. My sister hadn't really been around that long. I wasn't sure where she lived or where she worked. But maybe, a flash of intuition told me, it didn't matter what I said. Maybe the same perk of the deal that brought her back wouldn't let me be wrong with what I said.

"She is a sous chef for Martinelli's," Connor supplied for me before I had a chance to say anything.

"Yeah," I said, nodding. "Sorry, I'm still a bit shaken up."

"That's quite all right," the friendly detective said. "You've been through a lot today. If I could, I'd let you all sit and rest, but time is not on our side. Where were you while all of this was taking place, Matthew?"

Double crap! I was pretty sure that the correct answer to this question wasn't "I was having a throwdown with a trio of demons by the dumpster, Officer." But the best lies are ones with a little bit of truth in them.

"I left to take the trash out after dinner," I explained, doing my best to make sincere eye contact with Jones's reflective aviators. "I guess I stumbled on the thugs when I went into the alley. One of them chased me. He caught me and held me down in the alley. Maybe he didn't know who I was or something, but he let me go after another one came and found him. I ran back to the apartment for help, and that's when I found them."

"And the one still waiting in the apartment," Violet added.

"Yeah, he said…" My voice broke, and I looked down. "He said not to look for Megan, if I wanted to spare her pain. Then he jumped out the window."

The detectives were silent for a moment as they wrote down some more notes. A field tech of some sort, wearing white latex gloves, came out the front door and approached the two detectives. She spoke to the pair in low tones and motioned for them to follow her back inside. Rodgers went inside.

"Okay, that's enough for right now," Jones said, turning back to us. "You guys stay here. We're going to want to run through the story again just to make sure we didn't miss anything." He turned his friendly gaze back to look at me. "Don't you worry, son. We're going to find her," he promised.

I wished I found that reassuring. But these guys had no idea what they were getting into.

"Don't worry, Matt," Connor said from behind me as we were left sitting in the police vehicle. He reached up from the back seat and gave my left shoulder a squeeze. "Nothing is going to happen to Megan, okay? She's going to be fine."

I nodded numbly. I might have found it easier to have some hope if something hadn't already happened to her in her first life.

CHAPTER 12

The police finished up sometime around midnight. Violet left after, too shaken up to stay at the scene, and by "scene," I meant our apartment. The detectives gifted us with a lot of unhelpful statistics about how important the first twenty-four hours are to rescuing the victim. They left a patrol car sitting outside to keep an eye on the place. The best thing we could do now, they told us, was wait. Let the professionals do their job.

Connor and I spent an hour or two trying to restore our apartment back to some sense of normalcy. We swept the linoleum and vacuumed the carpet over and over and over again. Extricating all the shattered glass felt akin to trying to get all the mines out of West Germany after World War II—exhausting, a waste of time, and a little bloody.

I threw myself into the work with a desperate need. I poured 110 percent of my will and focus into getting every shard of glass. If I threw every single ounce of brainpower I had into this, then I couldn't think about anything else. We worked in silence. Connor was either working through his own baggage from tonight or he could sense that I didn't want to talk. Either way, I was grateful for the silence. It let me focus on not thinking. Over focusing is practically impossible if someone is pulling you out of it every five seconds with conversation. After an hour, we had done all that we could. The glass was all gone.

Just like my sister.

We covered the gaping hole where the window used to be with a blue plastic tarp one of the officers had given us from his car. But occasional tugs of April's light breeze left no illusion that the window behind the tarp was gone.

Just like my sister.

The kitchen table had been broken in two. It was cheap. We had bought it during our junior year of college at some garage sale for like ten or fifteen bucks. Connor had cleaned the kitchen, and even the pieces were gone.

Just like my sister.

I didn't make a conscious decision to punch a wall. In the movies, the handsome male protagonist stares at the wall for a few seconds, giving it a steely gaze that lets the sheetrock know what's coming. I don't think I gave the wall or myself any warning. Dan the Demon came into *my* home and messed with *my* family. He ruined *my* life and thought he was going to get away with it.

One instant, I was looking at all the emptiness in my home and seeing it reflected in the emptiness of my life. The next, Connor was grabbing me to stop me from trying to beat the wall of our living room to death. Tears were streaming down my face and the skin on my knuckles had cracked. I'd left a couple of red smudges on the wall already.

"Matt, Matt, stop!" His voice got through to me, and I stopped fighting him to get at that wall. It probably looked like one of those classic bar-fight-that-almost-happened scenes, but instead of two drunk guys, it was me and some drywall.

"Listen, man," he said as he wrapped me into a comforting bro-hug, "I know this is hard. I don't know what to do either.

I feel as helpless as you. But she's going to be all right, okay? I know it."

"You don't understand," I muttered thickly, absently wiping at my tear-stained face with a free hand. My rage had abated a bit. Maybe some of it had bled out of my fist and onto the wall. "This is my fault," I said, breaking free of his embrace. He let me go without any resistance.

"What are you talking about?" he asked incredulously. "You had nothing to do with this. This is random."

"Come on!" I shouted. Oh, there was that anger again. It wasn't gone; it had only been taking a break. "Open your mind, Connor. You're too smart for this. You saw those guys. They weren't wearing werewolf masks. That was his *face*. You saw it move when he talked. It was flesh, not plastic. That thing wasn't human."

"Matt," Connor said in a voice that was too calm. It's the kind of calm you use to talk to confused old people or small children. "I think you're excited. It was a crazy thing that we went through today. Adrenaline and fear can make it seem like—"

"She was dead! You don't remember it because she's not dead anymore, of course, but she was. You were there. You hugged me by her grave."

"What?" Connor asked. His features, normally intent and focused, were slack with confusion. His dark eyes looked at me uncertainly, as though I might be a wild animal.

"I killed her once then, and now I get to have her death on me again!" I was aware that I wasn't making any sense. I didn't care. Whatever mental lid I had been keeping on my weird life events had ruptured like Mount Saint Helens's crater.

"Megan wasn't in the car accident!" Connor yelled slowly as if he were speaking to someone a little thick in the head. "She was here tonight, you saw her." He shook his head as if to clear his thoughts. "Besides," he said in a softer tone, "your mother's car accident wasn't your fault. It wasn't anyone's fault. It was an accident. That's what the word means."

And there it was. The part of the story that I don't like to tell anyone about. The story behind the accident that killed a confusing number of my family. Besides all of it. You see, my freshman year hadn't been going great. I had a bad case of being homesick and wanted to see my family on my birthday. When the rains started, my father told my mom that the trip might be too dangerous. But I knew another route that would "totally be fine in the rain, Mom."

"Yeah, well, tell that to my father," I muttered bitterly. We hadn't spoken since the funeral. The last words we had exchanged were while standing in front of Megan's grave. He had looked me in the eyes and said "goodbye." We had both taken that literally.

My outburst gave me a sudden sickening thought. I had been asking myself why I had been targeted. Why had a demon come to me to try to buy my soul in the first place? It occurred to me that a person who was selfish enough to risk his family's life because he was lonely was probably pretty high up on Hell's call list.

"All we can do is wait," Connor said after a long pause.

I guess he decided my psychotic ramblings weren't worth interacting with. I couldn't really blame him. If I was on the opposite side of the fence and had not seen what I had seen over the last few days, I'd probably think I was crazy too. To be honest, I wasn't one hundred percent certain of my own sanity.

"I have to do something," I said. "I need to make a phone call."

"Who are you gonna call?" he asked.

We stared at each other for a second. I didn't say "Ghostbusters" like he expected me to. His face sagged a little, as if my refusal to tell a joke reinforced the nightmare we were living in.

"I have a friend who might be able to help," I told him.

"How? By getting in the professionals' way? Matt, we don't want to mess with this. What if something goes wrong?"

As far as I was concerned, something was already going wrong. The police were doing everything by the book, looking for normal kidnappers with normal motives. But my sister had been taken by monsters, and I didn't mean that as a metaphor. Unless the entire PD was secretly aware of the, let's call it *broader*, world around us, I didn't think they had a prayer of saving her. I needed to rustle up some support from the land of the spooky if I was going to save my sister. I could still make this right.

"It's okay, his brother is a whaddaya call it. Private eye. He's a professional too," I lied. Kind of. "It would be relieving to get a second opinion, you know? I want some reassurance that we're doing everything we can. Nothing too crazy here, I promise." That was probably a promise I wasn't going to be able to keep if the last couple days were any indication. I crossed my left pointer and middle fingers to make my conscience feel a little better.

"If you think it will help you feel better..." Connor said reluctantly. "It probably can't hurt."

"Totally," I said. I whipped out my phone and called Alex. The line rang several times before it occurred to me that my phone wasn't safe to have a weird conversation on right now. The police probably shouldn't have a record of me saying insane, impossible things while they were conducting a manhunt for my missing sister. I needed to get a little creative. To get my point across to Alex without sounding too weird.

"Hey, Matt," Alex's voice greeted me distantly as he answered his phone. It sounded like the phone's receiver was not quite lined up with his mouth. "Now is not a great time, actually."

"I'm sorry, man," I replied, trying to sound as anxious as possible. "This is an emergency."

"Is everything all right?" he asked, his voice growing sharp as he adjusted the phone's positioning.

"Not in the slightest," I told him. "I don't want to tell you about it over the phone. Can you get here ASAP, and I'll tell you then?"

"Yeah, I'll head right over." Genuine worry flooded through Alex's voice. I may have only known the guy a few days, but I really did feel like he was being honest with me.

"Oh," I added, trying to sound as nonchalant as possible, as though this were a normal request, "bring your brother too. We might need his help with some of the cleanup."

Alex didn't respond for a second. I think my request caught him off guard. Whoever his super demigod friend was, I bet people usually went to him, not the other way around.

"That big of a mess, huh?" he said after a bit.

"You have no idea," I told him.

"Yeah, I'll see if he can come. He might have to work…" Alex was a quick study. He may not have known what was going on, but he had transitioned into speaking in code with me effortlessly. Granted, it wasn't a super complicated code, but he stepped into the role flawlessly. A lot of people might not have made the conversation sound so believable.

"I'll text you when we're on our way," he said, and hung up abruptly.

I lowered the phone and looked over at Connor, who had dropped onto one of the couches, and his eyes were starting to droop.

"Hey." I waved at him to get his attention. He jerked a hair, startled from the edge of sleep. "Go to bed." I gave him my best reassuring smile, which, given the situation, was probably mediocre at best. But this was perfect. He had already risen above and beyond the call of friendship tonight. He needed some sleep, and I needed the freedom to talk to my weird compatriots without having to force some clunky code. I wanted clear answers from them.

"What about your friend?" he asked sleepily.

"They're going to come later, but you're falling asleep. I'm okay, really. That phone call already made me feel better. Made me feel a little less helpless."

"Okay," he said slowly, rising to his feet like an old movie zombie. "Come get me if you need me, okay? I'm gonna take a power nap."

"Absolutely," I lied.

CHAPTER 13

Alex didn't text me for over an hour. I spent that time on an emotional roller-coaster. I paced wildly around my apartment, manically waving my arms, imagining what I would do to my sister's kidnappers when I found them.

Next, I slumped dejectedly on my couch, certain that I would never see my sister again—again. Then I picked up one of the pillows she had been holding before to my nose, desperate to smell her one last time. All I got was a little hint of floral and a dash of sulfur. Even the scent she left behind was tainted.

Eventually my body couldn't keep up with the frantic pace I had been keeping, and I dozed off on the couch. My slumber was free from dreams, which I counted as a blessing. Given the nightmares I had been through in the waking world today, I didn't want to see how my brain could twist them to make them even more exciting.

My phone buzzed in my pocket. I gasped as I was pulled from sleep's dark, peaceful embrace. The process of waking up is a surprisingly accurate measure of how close your life is to rock bottom. For some people, the ones with everything clicking exactly as it should be, waking up is the worst thing that happens to them in a day. Because sleep is amazing. It's mornings that are evil. It doesn't matter if you're rich or poor, fat or Mr. Universe. Sleep is the lesser equalizer after death. We all get to enjoy it, and it eventually finds us all. Waking up is a shared pain for all of us. Even those freakish morning people.

You know that your life has plummeted as low as it can go when waking up is the best part of your day. Horrific nightmares excluded, sleep is the escape from our torments. When you're asleep, your mind isn't as free to remind you every second that everything is terrible.

There's a moment, one glorious half second of freedom when you first wake up. It's like your subconscious has to finish booting up before it can run through the list and make sure you're up to date on why you're miserable. It happens somewhere between your consciousness kicking back in and that first opening of your eyelids. In that heartbeat, nothing can bring you down. You are just a human being waking up; you don't know your name, where you are, or the total of your bank account. But right about the time your eyes focus and take in your surroundings, those little reminders come flooding back in. It's like a micro dose of hope, just to have it taken away again.

Oh yeah, my friends' futures are in jeopardy because of me.

Oh yeah, my soul has been stolen.

Oh yeah, my sister has been kidnapped.

That nagging litany never goes away. It's always there. Even if you manage to find something to distract yourself for a brief while, it will always bubble back to the surface, tainting *everything*. Fear isn't the only mind-killer. Anxiety will do as good a job.

My situation now firmly back in my mind, I looked down at my phone. I apparently slept through Alex texting me that he was on his way. His newest message simply said *Here. Come down, please.* My phone also informed me that it was after three in the morning. I groaned as I rolled off the couch and got to my feet. However long I had conked out for hadn't been enough to start a deep REM cycle, so I wasn't groggy, just exhausted.

I made my way down the stairs, a faint glimmer of hope starting to kindle in my chest. Hopefully Alex would have his friend with him, and we could start to get to the bottom of this.

His white minivan, the ever-faithful steed, was parked at the curb in front of my apartment. My little spark of hope dwindled as I saw the passenger seat was empty. I guess he couldn't get his reinforcements to come.

Alex motioned for me to get in from the driver's seat. I opened the door and slid in next to him.

"Hey," I said, unsure of where to start.

"What happened?" Alex asked urgently, concern etched into his features. The lightning smile was nowhere to be seen now.

"A moment, if you don't mind," a rich voice said from behind me. I jumped a little and turned to face the other person in the car. I use the term "person" loosely. The same way I would use the term "boat" to describe the *Titanic*. He was tall. I couldn't judge exactly while he was seated, but I knew he'd easily have a couple of inches on my six feet. Everything about him was long. His arms and legs had a lean length to them, like a champion swimmer. His fingers were long and elegant. I could practically see them comfortably dancing on a piano's keys. He had jet-black hair cropped short in a classic military cut, high and tight.

He wore dark wash jeans and a black leather jacket open in the front. Underneath that was a gray T-shirt. It wasn't cold enough for a jacket, which meant it was either for style or necessity. He looked like the type who might ride a motorcycle.

His eyes were the unsettling part. I could barely make them out in the dim light provided from a nearby streetlight, but they reflected oddly, in a way that reminded me of a cat's eyes. I got the unsettling feeling that he could see me perfectly in the dark.

This, then, was one of the greater Nephilim Alex had told

me about. Someone who had more demonic blood running in their veins, warping their bodies. Even more than his impressive physical appearance, there was an aura to him that I couldn't put my finger on. It was like the calm before a summer thunderstorm, a crystal stillness that promised big things to come. Lilith had been scary in her flamboyance; she had made a show of her power and wasn't afraid to wave it in front of my nose. There was an eerie calm to him, which made me almost more afraid. Or it would have, if I hadn't decided to stop being afraid.

"It's not that I don't trust you, Alex," he continued in an even voice. "But I must insist on a test to prove he's as you say."

"Uh, what do I need to do?" I asked.

"It's simple," he said, his eyes still dancing strangely in the light. He turned away from me and grabbed something from the bench seat next to him and handed it to me. It was a legal-sized notepad and a pen. "Write a poem, nothing too complex. A few lines will do."

I stared at him for a second, trying to decide if he was serious. His tone was too even, not quite robotic for me to be able to tell if he was sarcastic or not. He motioned for me to proceed.

I paused, placing the pen on the first line of the page, desperately trying to recall a poem from my college lit classes.

There once was a man from Nantucket...

"Ah, no," he interrupted me smoothly. "I don't wish for you to recycle a poem. Make me one."

I glanced at Alex for confirmation. He nodded slowly and mouthed *later* to me at the same time. I shrugged and looked back at the stranger. This must be some sort of weird supernatural hazing ritual. I bowed my head and closed my eyes, trying to drown out the distractions around me.

There is a demon named Dan,
Of whom I'm not a fan,
But I'm desperate for a plan,

Which is why I'm in Alex's van.

"That will be sufficient," the stranger interrupted me. "Although your meter is sloppy and your style nonexistent, I am satisfied."

"What are you, my American Lit 303 professor?" I grumbled, handing him back his notepad and pen. "Poetry isn't my thing, okay? I'm more of a prose guy."

"Matt, this is Orion. Orion, this is Matthew Carver. He's my friend I was telling you about."

"Orion, huh? That's a cool name. Named after the constellation?" I asked as I offered him my hand. He seemed surprised by my question, hesitating for an instant too long before clasping my hand in a disgustingly loose grip. There's almost nothing worse than a loose-handed handshake. I got the impression this Orion guy didn't go to meet-and-greets very often.

"Yes," he said slowly. "Just like the constellation. Alex has told me a little about your situation. But I need to hear it from you. From the beginning."

I glanced again at Alex, who gave me an encouraging nod. At this point, I figured what did I have left to lose?

I told him everything: meeting Dan at the movie theater, having my soul stolen, my sudden college graduation, my undead sister, and our summoning of Lilith. His head came up sharply at that story.

"Describe for me what you did to summon her," he said. His voice had lost a hint of its even keel, revealing a glimmer of iron beneath it.

"Uh, we painted a circle around a pentagram with paint mixed with a little of my blood, with some scented candles in the points. Then we put pre-butchered goat in the center on a piece of wood, said some words, and poof, there she was."

Orion shifted in his seat, the first major movement he had

made since I got in the car. He motioned for me to continue.

"Dan came back tonight and kidnapped my sister," I said, skipping ahead to tonight's events.

"What?" Alex gasped. "How do you know it was him?"

"I took the trash out to the alley after dinner," I said, gesturing out the window of the van. "He and two goons in hoodies were waiting for me. He was screaming about a summoning. Lilith had gotten people asking questions and getting him in trouble."

"How does your sister figure into this?" Orion asked.

"It was a distraction. While I was downstairs, he sent some monsters. I don't know what they were. The one I saw kind of looked like a werewolf."

They exchanged concerned glances.

"They smashed in through one of the windows and tied up Violet and Connor before taking off with Megan. One of them was waiting for me when I went upstairs. It told me not to look for her if I wanted to spare her pain."

"That makes no sense," Alex said. "Dan can't take your sister from you. Not without violating the terms of your contract."

"Yes, because he's seemed super worried about legal proceedings so far in my interactions with him," I replied sarcastically.

"This is different," Alex replied, shaking his head. "Those contracts are binding in a pretty serious way. Souls aren't traded around like gumballs. It's literally impossible for him to double back on a deal. Lie about you being in one, maybe, but this doesn't fit."

"Matthew," Orion interjected from the backseat. "Would you permit me to take a look inside your apartment? Alex is correct—something does not add up here. And if your story is true, I will act. I do not tolerate monsters in my city."

There was a hardness to his tone that was unsettling. I think I understood then why Alex had been nervous about bringing him in.

"Yeah, sure, let's go," I said, opening my door. "We cleaned up a bit of the mess. I hope that didn't ruin the crime scene or anything."

Orion gave me a small smile, one that, if it wasn't so even, I would have said looked a tad condescending. I decided not to worry about it. I was, after all, only human.

I led them up the stairs of my apartment building and to my front door. As I had guessed, Orion was taller than me. If he was less than six and half feet tall, it was only barely. Quietly, trying to not disturb Connor, I opened the door and stepped inside.

"A moment, Matthew," Orion said, pausing at the door. He and Alex had both stopped short of coming in. "It will be much easier for me to do my work if you invite me in. Otherwise, I'll have to leave a lot of my… help at the door."

I hesitated for a second and glanced at Alex, who shrugged as if to say it wasn't that big of a deal. This was a moment where fact and fiction blended. Every spooky supernatural TV show has some sort of variation on the theme of how monsters must be invited in. How many times have you seen some vampire standing on a threshold, with quick wit and a quicker tongue, trying to trick his way into some future victim's home? And his dark eyes, which I could see clearly now, were less than comforting. A memory tickled at the back of my mind, but I couldn't think of where I had seen eyes like those before. At this point, I didn't have a lot to lose, so why the hell not?

"Please," I said, stepping back from the door and gesturing with my arm into the hallway of my apartment. "Please do come in, Orion." A faint twitch at the corner of his mouth made me wonder if he had almost smiled. I eyed Alex with an arched eyebrow. "Do you need an invite too, or are you his plus one?"

"I mean, technically, not really," he said with a good-natured shrug. "But if you don't mind, it itches a little bit." I might have heard Orion snort quietly to himself as he passed me.

I followed the two Nephilim into my living room and watched as they surveyed the scene. Aside from the missing furniture and tarp over the window, there wasn't a whole lot to see anymore. There was a gaping emptiness in the room to me. But that may have had more to do with the fact that I knew how it looked yesterday rather than anything more sinister.

Orion looked around the room slowly, taking in the scene like an artist visiting the Met. His hands were on his hips, flaring his black leather jacket out. He held that pose for at least a minute, as Alex and I stood behind him and watched. Visual survey complete, he leaned forward slightly and sniffed loudly. It sounded like a sound you might imagine coming from a disapproving butler, or someone dying of ragweed allergies. He turned his head toward the kitchen and sniffed again. He padded toward the kitchen, where the monster had been waiting for me. A third sniff, and he was standing right on the spot. He crouched down and stared at the floor intently, looking at something I couldn't see.

"One of them stood here for a while," he murmured, not turning back to look at me.

"Yes, that's where the one that was waiting for me was standing when I got back up here," I supplied.

"Come here, Alex." Orion waved with his hand.

Alex trotted to the taller man's side. My brain supplied me with a Hallmarkesque vision of an older dog training a young pup to hunt, and I had to keep a small chuckle to myself. I didn't think it would be good for my health to laugh at those two. I probably would at some point anyway, though. Let's be honest—I know who I am.

"Do you smell that?" Orion asked Alex, looking at him intently.

Alex leaned over the section of my kitchen linoleum and

sniffed loudly too. His face was strange, like he couldn't believe he was actually doing it. He sniffed a few more times.

"I got nothing," he said. He sounded frustrated. Or maybe disappointed?

"Ghoul," Orion said with a sigh, shaking his head. He rose from his crouch. "That is why you are shunned," he said dismissively to my friend.

"What's a ghoul?" I asked. I made a mental note to ask Alex about the other part of that sentence later. "I mean I know the term ghoulish, but I wasn't aware it was an actual creature."

"They're Arabian," Orion replied to me dispassionately. "They don't come up in a lot of the myths that get told around here." He moved over a few inches in the room and sniffed again, peering at something I couldn't see. "They're creatures of the underworld, connected to death. They love to dig up graves to eat the dead."

"Kind of with weird, hairless skin and a dog snout?" I asked quietly.

"That's them," Alex replied.

"I can sense your sister's presence here," Orion mused after a moment. "There's a particular taint left behind by someone like her." He paused for a moment as if some part of his brain was struggling with a concept just out of its grasp. "No offense."

"But what would they want with my sister? She's not exactly dead."

"She's not exactly alive either. Dying leaves its mark; it changes things. To creatures like a ghoul, your sister stands out like an unusual vintage of wine. People that have come back again are extremely rare. There are all sorts of things that would find her fascinating."

I shivered at his explanation. There's a certain kind of savagery that doesn't occur to a person who lives in modern society. Eating dead people and fascination with the undead makes sense, I guess. Objectively, it also makes sense that there is something that does those things. But it's not something that I would have thought of, because that's freaking weird.

"What will they do to her?" I asked, dreading the response. Whatever part of my imagination that fed my nightmares was kicked into overdrive. A litany of unspeakable ideas paraded before my mind's eye. I shook my head to clear it.

"It's hard to say, exactly," Orion said, standing up and turning to face me. "Ghouls are kind of stupid creatures. They're often used as simple soldiers. But they also are scavengers, and they prey on targets they think are vulnerable." He strode across the living room and to the window, peeling the tarp back a little to peer out. "The question is: Which happened here?"

"Well, does your magical greyhound nose work out in the wild? Can we track them or something?" I was getting annoyed at his lack of answers. If someone could give me one straightforward answer, I would literally have given them all the money I had. Granted, that wasn't exactly a big bounty.

"Matt, what's going on?" Connor asked, shambling back into the living room from his bedroom. His eyes were squinting against the light, and he was wearing a white T-shirt and a pair of boxers with ducks on them.

"This is my friend Alex, the one I was telling you about," I told him. "This is his brother, the private detective."

"Great-great-uncle," Orion mused absentmindedly, staring at me with a laser focus. His expression was unreadable, but that seemed consistent with his character. I got the sense he was studying me, like I was a wild animal that he couldn't predict. I was too busy processing the ancestry comment. Connor was apparently groggy enough that he missed it. I did some quick mental math. Given that Alex was unnaturally old already, and Orion was his great-great-uncle with several generations on top of that, he must be at least... super old. I should have been a mathematician.

"Okay, do you need me?" Connor asked. He seemed to be having trouble keeping his eyes open.

"No, man, we're good. Sorry we woke you. Get some rest."

He gave me a groggy salute and went back into his room, shutting the door behind him. Well, that was one awkward element to this conversation removed. The last thing I needed was to try to explain Alex's and Orion's origin stories. I had enough of a taste of how that conversation would go earlier tonight.

"So, do we start knocking on doors?" I asked sarcastically. "What can we do?"

Orion crouched down and peered at the carpet in my living room. After a second of scanning, he reached down and plucked something from the floor. He held it up, and I took it from him, turning it over on my palm. It was a short white hair, like the bristle of a pig.

"Ghouls are not completely hairless," he said.

"How the hell did you spot this?" I asked. "A team of lab techs with fancy black lights worked this room over and didn't see it." I handed it back to him, worried I might lose track of the tiny hair in the palm of my hand.

Orion ignored my question and looked down at his hand. "Magic will allow us to follow the ghoul. The hair still considers itself a part of him. It still shares a connection with the ghoul, and with a little coaxing, will gladly lead us to him."

Whoa, there it was. The "M" word. I had begun to wonder if that one was ever going to come up. During my supernatural renaissance, I had been exposed to things that did not fit into the traditional twenty-first-century theory of "how the world works," as believed by mankind. Or at least "educated" mankind. I had performed a demon-summoning ritual. I had fireballs thrown at my person. But I hadn't actually heard anyone use the word "magic" or proclaim themselves to be a wizard.

"You can do magic? Are you a wizard?"

"Fah, no, Matt of the Many Questions. I cannot be a wizard. But magic is much like a branch of your science. Can you split an atom?"

"Obviously not."

"And yet, you can combine cola and Mentos to explode a soda container." He chuckled to himself and shook his head like an adult does at the antics of a child. "Similarly," he continued, "I cannot split atoms. I have neither the training nor the ability, but I can cause a few reactions."

"Will this lead you to the specific ghoul?" I asked. "Or just the nearest one?"

"The very one who left a hair in this apartment," he said solemnly.

"Of course, ghouls are hardly pack creatures," Alex interjected with a small sigh. "There's a very real chance that if we find this ghoul, he'll have already parted ways with the others."

"You are correct," Orion said, walking toward my kitchen. "Please get my bag from the van, Alex. I'll need some of the materials to prepare the spell."

A flicker of something passed across Alex's face for a moment. I'm not quite sure what I saw. Resentment, perhaps? Frustration at being ignored? There was more to their dynamic than I fully understood, even if they were related. Part of me didn't like this Orion guy. Alex may have only been a friend for a few days, but in some ways, he was my only friend right now. Connor, Violet, and Megan were my family. But he was the only friend who could understand the world I was dealing with. That'll help a friendship go from stranger to best friend real fast.

Alex left the apartment without an audible complaint to fetch Orion's stuff. He continued into my kitchen, the little monster hair still pinched between thumb and forefinger. He pulled open one of the drawers in the counter and started rifling through my utensils.

"Orion?" I asked him after a moment of silence. "What do we do if Alex is right, and the ghouls have split up? What if this one isn't with my sister anymore?" I tried to keep hopelessness from sneaking into my voice, but it was a futile effort. It crept in like the shadows that invade corners of your home in the late afternoon. Orion, the half-demon, half-human creature, turned and fixed me with a stare that made me feel like I shouldn't be breathing.

"If that's the case, then that ghoul will tell me everything we need to know to find your sister, before his deeds catch up with him," he said as calmly as if he were ordering a pizza delivery over the phone. A shiver ran up and down my spine as I stared back into his dark, unknowable eyes. I realized why they looked familiar.

Lilith's eyes had been just as full of the abyss.

CHAPTER 14

Alex returned with a black duffel bag slung over his shoulder. Orion helped himself to a Ziploc bag from my drawers and stood by the counter. He accepted the bag from Alex and placed it at his feet with a dull thud. He slipped the tiny hair into the bag and placed it on the counter.

He dropped to a crouch and unzipped the long zipper down the middle of his bag. The hilt of a sword poked out, as well as some other dark objects of clothing I couldn't identify.

Orion rifled around in his bag for a bit, producing a tackle box like you might get at any sports store. He popped it open, and it revealed several tiers of shelves stuffed with powders and leaves instead of fishing lures and twine.

I glanced up at Alex, who came and sat on the couch next to me, as Orion continued his work. This may sound odd, but I wasn't that curious about the specifics of what he was doing. I knew I should have been, but merely learning that magic was a thing was enough to sate my curiosity for the moment. Plus, I was realizing that asking Orion questions was pretty pointless. His answers only gave me more questions. Talking to Alex was a much better use of my time.

"Great-great uncle?" I asked him below my breath as we sat.

He shook his head and spoke at a normal volume. "He can hear you," he said in a defeated tone.

Orion didn't react to either of us talking and continued his work. There was a machinelike quality to him. He reminded me of a movie depiction of artificial intelligence. He could see humanity, analyze it, imitate it, and even interact with it. But he couldn't quite reproduce it. Lilith had been obviously inhuman, despite her physical appearance. Orion was not obviously anything, except different. I guess that made sense, since most demigods of myth and legend were sort of tortured souls. They didn't fit in with either of the two worlds they straddled. I wondered how that tension trickled down to someone like Alex, still straddling two worlds, but without as much balance. He was, after all, more demi and less god than Orion. Would that make it easier or harder for him? From the frown on his face and the tone of his voice, I was guessing the latter.

It was obvious that I wasn't going to get more out of Alex now. I resolved to press him later to fill me in on what I wasn't understanding. Like the poem thing. That one was still weird to me.

I watched as Orion selected a couple items from his tackle box. First, he dropped a couple of dried leaves, which were a starved sort of brown, into the bag with the hair, crumbling them as he did. Even across the room, I could smell a faint herbal scent coming from them. Next, he dropped a little of what looked like sea salt into the bag. Then he angled the bag and wiggled it, so all the contents were grouped in one of the corners of the bag instead of scattering across the bottom.

Finally, he pulled a military-looking flip knife from his bag, and it sprang open with a startling click. It wasn't ornate, a simple black plastic and dark steel. It had the look of a tool that was made to cut and didn't really care what it looked like while it did so, as long as it got the job done.

Without hesitation, he flicked the edge across his left thumb. Immediately, a bright-red drop welled up on his thumb. He stuck his hand inside the bag and dripped the blood on the contents in the corner for a second. Then he pulled his hand out and sucked on his thumb, which was the most human thing I had seen him do. He pulled his thumb out of his mouth, and no more blood welled up on the wound. In fact, from where I was sitting, I couldn't even tell he had ever been cut. A shiver worked its way down my spine. This was getting too metal for me.

I remember as a child, I had a blackhead stuck just beneath the skin on my cheek. I endured its discomfort and humiliation for months because I wasn't willing to prick it with a needle to get it out. Pain is something that defines the human experience. Eating the wrong food can give us pain. Sitting the wrong way for too long can give us pain. Someone who heals like that couldn't possibly process life the same way we do.

Orion sealed the top of the bag, squeezing all the air out as he did so. He held his left hand out, palm up, and placed the bag flat on it. He closed his eyes and murmured a phrase in a language I didn't know. I was guessing Latin, partly because thematically it would make sense, and also, I heard a couple "ums" in there, which is pretty characteristic of some of the Masses I attended with my grandmother as a child.

I realized I was holding my breath as he spoke the words. I had never seen magic before. I was ready for a burst of smoke, a magic trail of glowing dust, some sort of showy click that would let us know we were on the trail. I mean, computers ding at you when they want your attention. Why not magic too?

I didn't get any flashy special effects. The VFX budget was apparently low for this scene. The bag in his hand began to turn of its own volition. It rotated about ninety degrees, until the corner with all the stuff in it was pointing the other way. Orion pointed a finger in that direction. I understood. The bag had been turned into a makeshift compass. The corner with the hair and junk in it would point not at the North Star, but at the ghoul.

"Our prey is that way," he announced confidently. He glanced back at Alex. "Grab my bag; you drive. This will only last for forty-five minutes or so." Without another word, he strode to the door of my apartment and left.

Alex quickly gathered the black duffel bag, shoving the tackle box back in and zipping it closed. He had to lean on the sword hilt a bit to get it to go back down, but he got it in without too much trouble. His face was expressionless, and he was clearly working hard to keep it that way. I didn't press him. He had come up big for me tonight; the least I could do was give him some space while he played super caddie.

I followed Alex down the stairs and to his white minivan. Orion was already seated in the passenger's seat, eyes locked on the bag held in his palm. As I approached the van, his eyes snapped up and locked on me.

"What are you doing?" he asked.

"Getting in the back seat?" I replied.

"You cannot come with us. It's bad enough that I bring him." He jerked his head at Alex. "I cannot bend on this further."

"They took my sister," I began. Orion held up his other hand to try to stop me. But I had momentum going; there was no stopping this train. "And no offense, but I don't know you. You two are the only people even looking for her, and one of you is a total stranger."

"Be that as it may—" Orion began.

"I'm not asking your permission," I snapped at him. "Think of it this way: You're not allowing me to come. I'm exercising my free right as an American citizen to take a ride in my friend's car. George Washington died for that specific freedom. Look it up."

"We are on a limited time schedule, Matthew," Orion told me.

Again, I wasn't inclined to let him finish. If you let someone finish an argument, then they get to make a point you have to interact with. As far as I was concerned, there was no point that would convince me to stay behind. I was going to help find my sister.

"Then why are you wasting it arguing with me?" I asked. I slid open the back door of the van and hopped in. "Let's go find us some ghouls."

Orion was deathly silent for a moment. Silent like an empty church sanctuary is silent, or maybe more like a graveyard is silent at midnight. I wasn't sure which. Then he sighed, and Alex began to pull out of his parking spot.

"It's your funeral, I suppose," Orion muttered to the silent car.

"Yeah, it is," I replied hotly. Which might be a contender for one of the worst comebacks of all time. We'd have to wait for awards season to find out.

As we pulled out into the early-morning streets, it occurred to me that I really wasn't sure what I was doing. The nice supernatural man had offered me an extremely easy out. I could have avoided more danger and taken a nap. Who knows, when I woke up, Megan might have been back at home. As tempting as that should have been, it really wasn't at all. If this was me a week ago, I probably would have taken the offer. But now, I was tired of not being able to help anyone. I was tired of not being able to control my life. I was tired of hurting the people I cared about. I was going to do something about it, come Hell or high water. Or I would get eaten by a ghoul. One of the two. My tombstone could read: HERE LIES MATT, AT LEAST HE TRIED. ONCE.

We took the 405, leaving Northridge, and headed south. We rode in silence on streets that were almost as quiet as the three of us in the car. Los Angeles is a metropolis, so even at three o'clock in the morning, there are always some vehicles on the major streets, but we made good time, unhindered by the devastating traffic that the city is famous for.

LA is really a ton of small neighborhoods and cities smashed together, spilling on top of each other like a preschooler's fingerpainting project. Some idiot found gold in California way back when, and people have been shoving their way into the city ever since. We were cruising along the edge of Van Nuys— one the only places in the Valley worse than Northridge—when Orion spoke.

"Take this exit," he said, pointing up ahead.

I shifted in my seat, leaning forward to peer over his shoulder. The baggie in his hands had begun to turn as we continued to travel north, turning gradually to the right, locked on something we were passing. My heart rate immediately doubled. This was it. We were almost there.

Hang on, I thought loudly, hoping Megan might hear it. Or maybe it was a prayer, I don't know. I wasn't even sure if my prayers could reach anyone right now, or if having your soul in the hands of Hell caused them to get caught in some sort of divine spam filter.

We exited the highway and began driving through the old crumbling homes of Van Nuys. The homes in this area were mostly ranch style, left over from when LA was affordable to live in.

We rarely saw another moving vehicle as we moved past darkened homes where innocent people slept, unaware of the bumping that was going on in the night. I wished I could go back to that. Dealing with the supernatural ruins your sleep schedule.

Orion navigated us through the maze of the neighborhood as we narrowed down the location of the ghoul. It took another ten minutes of tense back-and-forth driving as we hunted. The only way to make sure we weren't wasting our time and not going far enough was to deliberately overshoot. Once the arrow cranked back from where we had come, we'd turn ninety degrees toward it and repeat the process. It was like a slowly closing snare trying to sneak up on some unsuspecting rodent.

I started to worry about time. Orion had said that the spell would only last for about forty-five minutes, and there wasn't any sort of range indicator on this spell. But the bag was moving much more responsively when we took turns than it had been when we started. We had to be getting close now.

"Pull over here," Orion said a few moments later, as we turned onto a street called Elm for the second time in less than five minutes.

Alex complied with the command, pulling over to park in the street in front of a darkened home. My heart continued pounding so loud I was surprised they couldn't hear it. Although, given Alex's warning about Orion's hearing back at my apartment, maybe he could.

"It's one of these houses on the right," Orion said after we parked. "We'll go on foot." He turned to look back at me as Alex turned off the battle van. "Are you still insisting on coming with us? You can wait for us here."

"No way." I shook my head. "If my sister might be in there, I'm coming."

"Very well," he replied with a strange look in his eyes. "I cannot deny you your right to choose."

"I cannot deny you your right to choose," I muttered under my breath with a little sneer as I mimicked him.

Orion didn't bother to respond, instead he reached across me to the seat on my left and grabbed his black duffel bag and pulled it into his lap. I heard the violent sound of the zipper being opened, and we waited in relative silence as Orion searched through his bag.

"Here," he said, turning back to me. He handed me a black pistol and two spare clips heavy with rounds. A third was already locked in place. My heart skipped a beat as I accepted them. I was very aware of the weight of the gun as I put it in my lap and stared at it. I'd shot guns before, but only ever at gun ranges at inanimate objects. And the kinds of guns we shot back then were simple guns meant for sport, like .22 caliber rifles.

This gun felt nothing like them. The black pistol was compact and sleek, made mostly of metal. This was a weapon made to fight, and I was holding it with the intention of fighting. Somehow the cold steel brought that home to me. It wasn't possible for me to be more nervous, but my brain certainly tried.

"Do you know how to shoot?" he asked me after turning back to his bag.

"Yeah, I've been to ranges and stuff a bunch of times."

Orion grunted noncommittally. "Don't hesitate. If you need to shoot something, shoot it. Line it up and squeeze the trigger. There will be no time for you to be sure. Just shoot."

"Isn't that, like, the opposite of what they teach in gun safety courses?" I asked.

"Yes," he told me, opening the passenger door. "This isn't safe."

I slid the side door of the van open and joined Orion and Alex outside. Orion had pulled several large items from his bag. He was carrying some sort of assault rifle, which had a collapsing stock to fit inside the bag. Across one of his shoulders, he had looped a belt with spare clips and a couple of things that looked suspiciously like grenades and maybe even a flashbang.

Do you ever suddenly get the feeling something isn't going to end well? Because I was certainly getting that vibe as I watched a demigod load an assault rifle on the sidewalk of a suburb.

He leaned back into the car and pulled out the sword, whose

hilt I had seen peeking out of the bag in my apartment. It was a long sword, although I don't know the technical specifications of whether or not it was an actual longsword. But if the plain black leather sheath was to be believed, the blade was probably about four feet long. The hilt was like what you might expect from any medieval Hollywood movie, made of a silvery metal with grooves molded for a grip. The grip below was wrapped in the same black leather that the scabbard was made from. Overall, the sword seemed like it was designed for function rather than being ornate, which matched Orion's aesthetic to a T.

The only exception was the pommel, which had a large red stone set in it that I refused to believe was a ruby. Simply because a ruby that size had no business being on a sword and not in a museum behind a thousand security lasers. The deep red of the stone danced slightly in the dim light from Alex's van, and then winked out as Orion shut the door.

He swung the sword over his shoulder, with the strap running opposite his bandolier. The hilt with its giant red eye peeked over his right shoulder, ready for a right-handed draw.

Wordlessly, Orion stepped away from the car and started to walk down the block, the enchanted plastic baggie still held in his left hand. Alex and I followed. My friend had produced a pistol from somewhere in the car and held it with both hands, keeping the muzzle aimed at the ground. I figured he probably knew what to do at least a little more than I did and copied his pose as best I could.

I was glad the odds of people looking outside their living room windows was low at three in the morning, as we followed a six-foot-six warrior of legend, collectively armed with enough weaponry to make Rambo hesitate to mess with us, through a residential neighborhood of Los Angeles, California.

We were about halfway down the block from the van when Orion drew up short. "By the Abyss!" he swore. With a contemptuous flick, he tossed the Ziploc bag aside, and it drifted down to the sidewalk.

"The spell died, didn't it?" I asked, voicing my fears.

He nodded, peering up the street with his now-free hand on his hip. I got the sense he was trying to make up his mind about something.

"Please tell me you know which one we need to go to."

"It's either this one." He pointed at the closest house on our right. It was a small ranch house. The roof was dark gray with slate shingles. A single red sedan was parked in the driveway, and a young tree had been planted in the front yard. It looked like a great home to grow up in, all things considered. "Or it's that one." He gestured to the next house down the street.

That house didn't look like any more of a villain hideout than the first had. It was a two-story red-brick home with black shutters hanging by the windows. The roof looked to be made of the same shingles. It had a pair of vehicles in the driveway, a sweet little white sports car and a blue minivan that looked much nicer and newer than Alex's. Basically, there was a distinct lack of evil lair clues from either of their exteriors.

"So what do we do now?" I asked.

"What do you suggest?" Orion asked, turning to address Alex.

"We have to check both of them," he replied.

"We're going to barge into some suburban home and hope it's the one filled with monsters?" I asked.

"You did say you would do anything to get your sister back," Orion pointed out. "In one of these homes is probably a nice family, safely asleep in their beds. In the other, the family is probably long since dead and eaten. And the only clue to finding your sister is there."

His cold words sent a shiver down my spine. I hadn't thought about what might have happened to the family that lived in the home that the ghouls had moved into.

Both houses looked lived in. Not that they were in bad shape, but they weren't Stepford houses, manicured to the point of not being real. I doubted that ghouls bothered to mow and water the lawn. Nervously, I adjusted my hands on the gun. Its deadly weight helped keep me grounded. I was here for my sister, to rescue her no matter what. I wasn't going to think about the pieces of a family I might find when we went inside.

"Let's do it," I said, hoping I didn't sound as worried as I felt. The result was my words came out harsh and forcefully. The two Nephilim turned to regard me with a hint of surprise. I tried not to be too offended. But after a second, Orion nodded.

"Follow me," he said. We crossed the lawn of the ranch home. Orion led us to the side of the house, where a white gate opened into the backyard. We crept through the pitch-black side yard, avoiding a motley collection of potted plants and bushes until we came to a door. Orion moved silently. I did my best to be stealthy behind him, but I kept kicking things I couldn't see.

I didn't even hear him brush a single plant or hear his footsteps crunch down on the grass. I wondered if this was a small taste of how Lewis and Clark had felt following Sacagawea through the wilderness. Granted, I was pretty confident that Orion's vision was much more suited to the dark than mine.

The door was the type you see on every home you've ever been in. It was made of wood, with a bright brassy doorknob. Above the knob was a matching metal bulb for a deadbolt. Orion examined the door for a moment before stepping back to brace himself, presumably to kick it down.

"Wait," hissed Alex, sliding in between the huge Nephilim and the door. "I got this." He crouched down and produced his lock-picking tools. After a few tense moments scratching at the deadbolt's lock, there was a click that sounded like thunder in the dead silence of the night. Alex immediately drew back, pocketing his picks. Orion stepped forward, turning the knob and easing the door open. He held his assault rifle in his right hand. Despite the weapon seeming to be designed to be held with two hands, he had no trouble handling it with just the one.

Once again, I adjusted the grip on my gun and suddenly remembered that I was about to commit several crimes. If this was the family home, this was probably something like armed robbery, or some kind of felony with the word "assault" in it. It seemed my new supernatural life was dragging me into all sorts of trouble.

No alarm went off. I wasn't sure if that was a good or bad sign. It could be that this was a nice-enough neighborhood that people didn't bother to set their alarms. Or that the people were dead, and the ghouls didn't know how.

Orion waved for me to go in first. I adjusted the grip on my pistol and nodded. Slowly, I stepped into the room, trying to watch every direction at once for an ambush. An impatient hiss behind me made me spin to look at him. He stood impatiently at the doorway and gave me a motion to do something. Oh! Of course. He needed to be invited in. I guess I counted because I was human, even if I didn't technically live there. I mouthed *Come in* to him, trying to make sure it was obvious. He rolled his eyes but did so.

I followed Orion into a dark kitchen. It was a square room with an island in the middle to give it extra counter space. On the far side of the room, the microwave blinked the time in green numbers: 3:23 a.m. I was aware of Alex entering softly behind me, and he closed the door behind him. That bothered me a little. Wouldn't that slow us down if we needed to get out fast? I glanced at the big rifle and sword Orion was carrying. Maybe we weren't the ones he was expecting to want to run.

The kitchen opened to a long hallway that branched off to our left and right. Orion hesitated at the crossroads for a moment before waving for us to follow him to the right. It was a few steps until we emerged in the front living room. A dining room table was in one half, with dim outlines of couches sitting in front of a big bay window that looked out onto the street.

Suddenly something furry rubbed on my leg. I jumped what felt like fifteen feet in the air, my hands automatically swinging the gun to point at what was my feet. Orion's left hand snaked out lightning quick and caught my wrist before I started blazing away.

"It's a cat," he whispered in a reprimanding tone.

I barely heard him over the rush of blood in my ears. It was like waking up to find a spider on your face, times a million. Sure enough, a black cat wound its way in between my legs, purring up a storm. After a moment, it grew bored of me and wandered off down the hallway, deeper into the house.

"We can leave," Orion said quietly. "The ghoul is not in this home."

We filed back out the side door. Alex even locked it behind us so that the family would never know the intrusion that happened that night. Well, unless they could speak cat.

Moving swiftly, we passed over the front lawn to the next house. From the outside, the red brick looked no more sinister than it had when we first pulled up. But now, armed with the knowledge that a monster was hiding inside, my mind made it a house of evil. The black shutters now seemed a pointed sign rather than a normal design. Of course the ghoul was in the house with the black trim. Why did we even bother checking the other one?

"We go in the front on this one," Orion said. "Ghouls have powerful hearing. There's no point risking them hearing you picking the lock. We know it's in there. Stay behind me and keep your eyes open. He'll try to run; they're more like jackals than wolves. We'll need to cut it off."

"You sure this is the one?" Alex voiced the question that had been in my head too as we approached the front door.

"Are you doubting me, young one?" Orion asked. There was a tone in his voice, an edge that had not been there before. "You doubt my knowledge of a hunt?"

"Just checking," Alex replied meekly.

Orion grunted. Grasping his assault rifle by the barrel in his left hand, he took two aggressive strides toward the front door and kicked the door smack dab in the middle with his right boot.

I'm not sure what I expected. In movies, when an action hero kicks a door, the frame splinters a bit and the door swings open. I think that's how it is basically supposed to work. Instead, Orion's kick smashed the door, ripping the hinges out of the wall with sheer force. The door fell inward with a smash and landed flat on the ground, except for the slight angle from the doorknob poking up. My eyebrows shot up as my jaw dropped. I knew he was supposed to be stronger than a mortal man, but that was ridiculous.

Before the door had even finished falling, Orion had his assault rifle back in his hands, the stock firmly pressed to his shoulder, and his cheek resting against the side of the rifle as he sighted down the barrel. Without hesitation, he moved forward into the house, stepping over the fallen door. He was tense, like a coiled cobra ready to strike.

Alex and I traded glances for a moment after Orion surged into the house. With a tiny sigh, he flipped the safety on his weapon with a hefty click. I felt around and found the one on mine too. Together, we entered the house. The wood of the door groaned a little as we stepped on it, but my footing was steady.

Orion took the lead, going down the hallway the front door opened into. He was moving slowly, one gliding step at a time, like you might if you were trying to sneak up on some forest creature. It struck me a little as wasted effort. There's not much point to being a silent hunter after smashing your way through a tree in the forest.

The hallway was pitch black. I could barely make out the shape of Alex and Orion ahead of me. A low-pitched canine whine sounded to my right. Immediately, Orion twitched and opened fire with his rifle. The bursts of the automatic rifle lit up the hallway like a violent disco ball. After a few bursts of firing, he stopped and moved forward aggressively.

"Watch the door!" he hissed and dashed out of the hallway to the right in pursuit of the sound. I barely heard him over the ringing in my ears.

"YYeah, watch the door!" Alex passed the command back to me and dashed after our juggernaut companion. This left me all alone in a dark house as the final barrier to a monster that was desperately trying to escape. Me. Little old human me. The one with the least experience with any of this Dungeons *or* Dragons stuff. The mortal who couldn't see in the dark in the best of circumstances and was now night-blinded by the bursts of gunfire. Hindsight being twenty-twenty, it probably wasn't the greatest plan to give me that responsibility.

Faintly, I heard another keening whine, immediately punctuated by another burst of gunfire, and this time I thought I heard a yelp of pain. Then there was silence. So much for the next-door neighbors getting to keep their illusion of safety.

The silence stretched on. Fifteen seconds, then thirty, then a full minute. I stood in the doorway, nervously adjusting the grip of my sweaty palms on the handle of my gun. Any second now, Alex or Orion would come and let me know to stand down. That last round of gunfire had done the trick... Any second now.

The dark shadows of the hallway seemed to creep toward me like a thousand evil fingers hunting for me. I gulped and shifted my grip on my gun. My eyes darted around, trying to spot a monster lurking in the inky darkness.

Suddenly I realized the night was no longer silent. There was a faint breathing, more of a panting, like a dog after a brisk jog. Instantly tense, I raised my pistol and pointed it into the shadows of the hall.

"Guys?" I called, fear adding a crack to my voice. "I think it's here!"

With a cry that was something between a bark and a roar, a shadow lunged from the back end of the hall. I fired without even making the conscious decision to do so. My shot rang out with a burst of light and sound, briefly illuminating the night like a strike of lightning. The gun bucked in my hand, and I did my best to ride the recoil and keep the muzzle aimed at the deadly shadow.

In that first flash of light, I saw the gray hairless skin it had. I fired again and saw what big teeth it had, opened and ready to attack. It was only a few feet away and coming with all the speed of a bullet train. I fired a third time, and it let out an angry howl. There was a thud as it smashed to the ground.

My eyes danced with spots of light as my pupils struggled to catch up with the return of absolute darkness. The ghoul growled, and I heard it shifting, trying to rise to its feet. Before it could, Orion and Alex burst back into the hall from within the house. I heard a meaty *thwack* as Orion smashed down on the monster with the butt of his rifle.

"Well done, Matthew," he said. He sounded almost approving. "You just bagged your first ghoul."

CHAPTER 15

We didn't pause to celebrate our catch. We didn't take one of those classic hunting photos with me crouching next to the still form of the ghoul, holding its head up to be admired. Granted, that might be mostly because this one wasn't dead. The not-so-distant sound of police sirens was not very conducive to taking our time either.

Orion snapped into action. "Alex, you and Matt get the ghoul in the van. I'll sweep the house to make sure we didn't miss anything. We leave in thirty seconds. Move!"

Alex handed me his pistol, its barrel still cold to the touch. I took it as he bent down to the still form of the ghoul. With a grunt, he pulled the creature up and slung it over his right shoulder. He staggered slightly as he straightened. I made a move to help, but he waved me off.

"Get the van door open," he grunted. "I'll need to put him down fast."

I nodded and took the lead as we fast-walked past the front of the two houses we had broken into. No new lights were on in the first house, but I wondered if they had been the ones who called the cops. With the amount of noise we had made, it was more likely *everyone* had called them.

I was moving too fast to be thinking about how I felt. I had just shot something. Granted, this wasn't like my dad had taken me hunting and made me shoot Bambi's mom. I had shot a monster, not a peaceful forest creature. But still, I had been in combat. That wasn't something that was going to go away. I was no longer a virgin to violence. I didn't really have an opinion on that yet. I did know that I didn't want to get busted for having shot up a residential neighborhood late at night. Or having to explain a giant dog-monster that I was helping kidnap. The sooner we got out of here, the better.

I got to the van a few paces ahead of the grunting Alex. I slid the side door open and stepped back to give him room.

"Lower the seat so I can throw him in the back," he grunted as he approached.

I found the lever at the bottom of the seat and folded it down. My friend dumped the ghoul in with no measure of grace. Once the beast was in, Alex grabbed a bag of plastic zip ties, eerily similar to what had been used on my friends earlier this evening. Moving quickly, he bound the ghoul's hands and feet. I liked the poetry of that.

"Time to go," Orion said, running up the sidewalk behind us. "The sirens are less than three minutes away." It did seem like they were a little louder. But my hearing was only the plain old vanilla kind, so what did I know?

We piled into the van, and Alex peeled out into the street. Orion took his seat behind me, riding with the ghoul, which was exactly where I wanted him to be if that thing woke up.

"Turn right here," Orion called at the first intersection. "Left," he said at the next.

Alex followed his directions without question. We made several more turns, seemingly at random. By my mediocre sense of direction, I thought we were actually heading deeper into the suburbs.

"Pull over here on the street and turn off the car and lights," he commanded a few moments later. We parked on another darkened street, in front of a similarly dark house. Objectively, there wasn't much difference between this street and the one we had shot up. We sat in the van in silence. I was still struggling to catch my breath and slow my heart rate down, but my two spooky compatriots seemed fine. Like they hadn't just been throwing down with a monster and breaking into sleeping people's homes. That was something that they probably had more experience with than I did.

"What are we waiting for?" I asked after a few tense moments.

Before Orion had a chance to respond, four LAPD cruisers shot through the intersection ahead of us at ninety miles an hour. Their lights and sirens blared as they blasted by. My poor heart skipped about seventeen beats. I was certain this was it. Those cars knew where we were, and they were circling us. One of those troopers would see us parked a few yards away, and it'd be all over. I'd go to jail and be a felon for the rest of my life.

Or those poor police officers might get in a fight with Orion, and I suspected that wouldn't go well for them. They were doing their job, but Orion wasn't someone who fit in their world. I suspected it would take more than 9mm pistols and tasers to take him down. It was my fault he was unleashed in this mess. I didn't want whatever might happen to the officers who got in his way on my conscience.

But my fears were unfounded. None of the cars even slowed; they all raced toward the scene of the crime. I guess that was Orion's plan. He didn't want us to meet the cavalry, riding in the other direction like a bat out of Hell. This early in the morning, there weren't a lot of cars on the street for us to hide ourselves in the herd.

"We good?" Alex asked after the squad had passed by.

"Not yet," Orion replied calmly from the back. A moment later, another group of cars shot by.

"Go now," he said. "Slowly, like a normal citizen who happens to be out at almost four in the morning."

We drove in tense silence for a few moments. Another pod of police vehicles swarmed by us at one point, but they paid our minivan no mind.

"Was there anything else in the house?" I asked Orion, turning in my seat to glance back at him. I could barely make out his outline in the dark car, like a brooding statue.

"The bodies of the residents," he replied darkly. His voice was... strange. It was almost unnaturally calm, like Siri or any other computer that tries to talk to us. But at the same time, the placid nature felt like a veneer. Like a perfectly calm sea with a hurricane on the horizon.

"Were they okay?" I asked, even though he'd said "bodies."

"No."

At that moment, the ghoul apparently woke up. A surprised growl came from the back seat, and I heard it trying to move. There was a sharp crack, and the ghoul whined pitifully. Orion snarled like a dog, and the beast fell silent.

"Do you speak Ghoul?" I asked.

"Yes," he told me in the same rigid tone.

"Where are we going?" Alex cut into my questioning impatiently.

"We need somewhere to question the dog," Orion replied. "Somewhere quiet, where we won't be disturbed." The ghoul let out another whine but stayed still.

"I know where to go," I said. "There's not going to be anyone at the warehouse, Alex."

"You mean the one we burned down?" Alex asked, sounding slightly incredulous.

"I mean, *we* didn't burn anything down, as far as I know. But yes, it is probably still closed for investigation or something. And no one is going to be doing that at this ungodly hour."

"Makes sense," Alex replied after a moment. Orion grunted, which I took to be agreement. Alex abruptly changed lanes to head toward the warehouse. "Let's get this over with," he said grimly.

It took about thirty minutes to get back to where we had summoned Lilith. If it hadn't been so abominably early in the morning, it probably would have taken at least forty-five. There are some perks to being up when no one else is—no traffic is one of them.

The warehouse had definitely seen better days. We had sped out of there as Lilith was beginning her rampage, and while I had expected it to be crisped, the burnt-out husk that greeted us exceeded my imagination's wildest dreams by an order of magnitude.

All of the windows had been blown out. The roof had collapsed in several places. The concrete walls had a gaping hole that didn't seem like something a fire would cause. With a second look, I realized it appeared to have been smashed outward by something exiting the building. Which was both terrifying and somehow not surprising. The whole building was charred and black, despite being made of a lot of nonflammable material. I shivered once again at how close we had come to dying earlier today.

"Let's get this filth inside," Orion snarled as we parked. The surreal tranquility of his voice was cracking, the hurricane getting closer. A big part of me didn't want to be there to see it arrive. But I was committed to rescuing my sister. I couldn't back out now.

Orion dragged the ghoul out of the back of the van and walked him toward the warehouse. Orion still had his sword and assault rifle slung over his shoulder, like some avatar of violence.

The creature came quietly, with Orion's viselike grip on his arm, like a bailiff walking a criminal to see the judge.

Alex and I followed, with me carrying Orion's bag this time. We paused to duck under some plastic yellow tape surrounding the scene which boldly said: POLICE LINE – DO NOT CROSS. We did anyway. The cops were already looking for us elsewhere in town. Why not add to the charges?

The bag was heavier than I expected. But I guess when you are casually super strong, you don't notice how much crap you jam into your go-bag.

"You're carrying the bag from now on," I puffed at Alex as we approached the building. "I don't know why you're making the normal guy do the heavy lifting."

"Hey, I carried the ghoul to the van," he countered. "The way I see it, it's your turn to be the caddie."

"You're the superhuman here. You've got great power. Therefore"—I gestured at the heavy duffel bag slung over my shoulder—"great responsibility."

"Yeah, okay, Uncle Ben." He snorted at me and sped up his pace.

I muttered a curse and did my best to keep up. The door that we had raced out of to escape from the rampaging Lilith was no longer there. It appeared to have been blown completely off its hinges. Which was impressive since it had been made of metal and was very heavy. Much heavier than a residential door anyway. Not that it was a contest, but let's be real: it kind of was.

The interior of the warehouse was pitch black. Even the fire exit signs had been burnt. Alex and Orion continued in without hesitation.

"Stupid super humans and their night vision." I sighed.

"There should be a flashlight in the bag," Orion called from ahead of me.

I grunted and fished around until I found the zipper at my side. I opened the bag and stuck my hand in tentatively. There had been a sword in here earlier, so who knew what other sharp things might be waiting for me? The last thing I wanted to do was take an ER trip with a ghoul and two Nephilim to get a tetanus shot. I rooted around in the bag, still being careful, for a few seconds before I found the light. It was one of those big black flashlights made of metal that cops sometimes use as a double for a nightstick. I clicked it on, and a brilliant beam shot out into the warehouse.

I know they use candles as a measurement of power for flashlights, which to me is kind of stupid, but we still use horsepower as a measurement for cars even though I don't really know what a single horse's power looks like. Anyway, this flashlight was easily worth several million candles. I brought forth the light of high noon wherever I shone the light through the destroyed building.

"The power of the sun... in the palm of my hand," I said in my best villain impression. My two companions were silent. I guess it was work time, not fun time.

The interior of the warehouse was as desolate as the outside. All that remained of the shelves were warped, twisted pieces of metal that might have passed for some sort of modern-art sculpture that a millionaire would be proud to own if it had been in a gallery instead of an arson scene. Everything reeked, equal parts char and rotten eggs. Sulfur seemed to be a bit of a theme with demonic work, I was noticing.

After a moment of sweeping my lighthouse of a flashlight's beam, I located the remains of the painted circle we had tried to use to contain Lilith. A chill settled down my spine as I stared at it. The inside of the circle, where the star had been painted, was crisp and black. The cement floor was extra crispy there, like a piece of toast left in a toaster set to ten. The red paint was still barely visible, cracked and dried as if it had been there a hundred years instead of a day.

Orion noticed where my light was shining and led the ghoul over to it. He shoved the creature to the ground and squatted down to look at the remains of our handiwork. He peered at it for a long moment, settling into that uncanny stillness that seemed to indicate he was deep in thought.

"Troubling," was all he said after a long moment and turned away from our destroyed demon ring. "We will investigate that later," he proclaimed to me, anticipating my questions. "For now, we should deal with the monster at hand." He walked over to me and took the bag from my shoulder.

The ghoul, for its part, seemed to take waiting on the floor, bound and helpless, with a fair amount of patience. If that were me, I'd be struggling, snarling, trying to do something to get away. Maybe that was not the nature of ghouls, maybe they were braver souls than me. Or maybe, I thought with a glance at Orion, the ghoul knew there wasn't any point in trying to get away from his captor.

Orion dropped his bag next to the dog-monster and pulled out a medium-sized box. Inside the box were several metal spikes and a rubber mallet. Orion began to whistle softly, a tune that seemed familiar to me, but I couldn't place it.

He walked over to the ruined concrete floor within the circle and knelt. Still whistling, he drove one of the spikes into the ground with several powerful strokes of the mallet. Blackened concrete chips flew up and away with each blow, but when he tested the spike with his hands, it remained firmly in the ground. Orion cheerfully continued his work, driving three more spikes into the cement to form a square.

That done, he turned to the ghoul and snipped the plastic zip tie with a knife. I braced myself, ready for the ghoul to lunge at us, but again it offered no resistance. With a new zip tie, Orion bound each of the creature's feet and hands to a stake, stretching him spread-eagle on the ground. When that was finished, he rose, and I got my first good look at a ghoul as I shone my beam of starlight on it.

The gray-blue ghoul was silent as it lay there. It had broad, thick shoulders and abs to die for if you didn't mind a few fleas. Its black eyes gleamed in the reflection of my light, and I couldn't help but notice what big teeth it had. It was like someone had crossed those hairless Egyptian cats with human and dog DNA and then added a dash of monster.

Its wrinkled hairless skin and absolute nakedness robbed it of any sort of humanity. The beast looked more like one of those old rescue greyhounds than a terrifying creature capable of violence and terror. On its right shoulder, a small hole oozed dark black blood. I assumed that was a souvenir from my gunshot. It didn't seem to be bothering the ghoul any more than the zip ties were. My shot probably did little more than catch it off guard and stun it for a moment.

"You know who I am," Orion said, that dangerously still tone present again. He addressed the ghoul in English for what I assume was Alex's and my own benefit. The ghoul was silent and still. Orion sighed slightly and turned to his bag once more. He pulled out a wicked-looking knife, curved like a small scimitar, like a lot of Middle Eastern knives I'd seen in movies. He pulled the blade from its sheath, and it was clearly older than I had thought. A bronze blade flashed dimly in the reflection of my powerful flashlight.

"Please answer me when I address you," he said.

After a moment's pause, the ghoul growled a short response.

"In English," Orion corrected him immediately.

"I know you," the ghoul said in a grudging reply. His voice had that same deep quality that I had heard in my apartment. I could feel it reverberating in my chest.

"You were part of the group that kidnapped a girl from this man's home this evening, were you not?" Orion continued.

"Yes," came another grudging answer.

"I see. Where did you take the girl?"

"Gave her to Master's human servants," he rumbled.

I felt the small ray of hope in my chest diminish at its words. If Megan had been delivered somewhere, this ghoul might not be able to lead us to her. She might already be out of our reach.

"And who is your master?" Orion pressed.

The ghoul did not answer this time.

"Tell me who your master is," Orion repeated, his voice the distant rumble of an approaching storm. The ghoul remained silent.

"You know what I will do to you, dog," he said after a moment of stony silence. "I found what you left behind of the family that lived in the home we took you from. I know the justice you deserve. If you tell me what I want to know, I will make the punctuation mark on your life a period instead of an exclamation mark."

I didn't know exactly what that might look like, but from the ghoul's slight twitch, I think he got his point across fine.

"My, my," a female voice cut through Orion's threats with amused ease. "I've heard that criminals always return to the scene of the crime, but this is a tad ridiculous." The voice was haughty and strong, like the darkest of red wines, but it sent chills down my spine for another reason.

Lilith, vice president of Hell, emerged from the darkness of the warehouse, stepping into the light of my super flashlight without squinting against the brightness. All of us, even the prone ghoul, turned our heads to stare at her, a pack of moths distracted by a porchlight.

Her black eyes reflected the light like dark gemstones. She was wearing the same outfit that I had seen her in last, while I was fleeing this exact burning building. Even though black leather boots, dark jeans, and a red tank top are not particularly fine pieces of clothing, I suddenly felt underdressed in her presence.

"Hello, boys," she said cheerfully. "I do appreciate an attentive audience." She took a few steps around the edge of the pool of light, peering down at the bound ghoul. "Getting into even more trouble today, I see?"

Fear, my good friend after the last few days, immediately moved back into my heart and occupied the rooms it had previously vacated after the excitement of our neighborhood assault had faded. I glanced at Alex to see if he was giving me the "run" cue again. I promised myself that this time I'd listen the first time he said it. He stood on the opposite side of Orion with his arms crossed. His bright blue eyes met mine, and he nodded his head ever so slightly toward Orion. I took that to mean something like "let the adults talk" and nodded back my understanding. That seemed like a good plan.

"And now you've gone and dragged the poor, tormented Hunter into your mess." She smiled at Orion with a dazzling flash of white teeth. It was somehow both flirtatious and predatory, which fit on her mood board. She was a sensual great white shark. "Nephew," she said, dipping her head at Orion but never quite breaking eye contact with him, "have you forgotten your manners?"

Orion didn't actually move as far as I could tell. His feet certainly didn't shift, nor did his hands move from his sides. But there was a sense of shifting from him. All that coiled, dangerous energy that had been focused on the ghoul had found a new target.

Lilith noticed it as well. She blinked once, a long, slow movement that seemed deliberate. It was like she was giving him a second to change his mind before she officially noticed his tone. Off the top of my head, I could only think of two reasons why she might do that. The first was that Orion was not someone she hated. She was offering him a chance out of some sort of affection. Maybe she didn't want him to get in trouble. She had referred to him as "nephew." I didn't like the idea of Lilith and Orion being pals. But Alex had called him a great-great-uncle. Given their blood, the familial reference seemed more social terminology than them being actual relatives.

The second option was on the opposite side of the spectrum: she was hoping he would change his mind because she was afraid of him.

"It seems you have," she hissed after another handful of heartbeats had passed and Orion remained silent. Her pleasant, flirtatious voice was gone. All I saw now was the venomous character who had burst from the circle on the very floor we were standing on. "Very well. I've been saying that someone needed to remind you of your place for centuries. I didn't think I would be lucky enough to get to do it."

Orion remained still during her rant. His focus was so palpable, he might as well have pointed a gun at Lilith's head. Except I doubted a gun would hurt her even as little as my shot had hurt the ghoul. Lilith's beautifully manicured hands—with gold-painted fingernails, for the record—curled into talons, and she took one step toward Orion.

His reaction was immediate, but at the same time languid and almost disinterested, like the cool kid in high school who doesn't want to be seen taking too many notes in class. He raised his right hand above his shoulder, mere inches from the hilt of his sword. The red stone in the hilt pulsed once, brightly, with a light of its own.

Lilith stared at the hilt as if noticing it for the first time. She waited for a moment too long for it to be smooth, but her hands dropped to her sides, and her posture went immediately back to playful.

"You're quite right, nephew," she said brightly as if Orion had spoken aloud. "We can have a conversation in a civil manner. It seems your manners are not as lost as some have claimed."

Orion didn't speak, but his hand went back down to his side. My heart thudded against my chest, and I wiped a sweaty palm on my jeans. I was not sure about all the intricacies of what I had just been a part of, but I think I finally understood a little better what it must have been like to live through the Cold War.

"To business, then?" she asked but moved on without waiting for an answer. "You are aware, I assume, that your compatriots committed a sizable offense against me right here in this very room?"

"We didn't insult you on purpose," I protested. "That was supposed to summon a receptionist, not you."

"Regardless, you did summon me, little manling," she replied smoothly. "And let me assure you, jamming someone like me into something like that is most unpleasant. It's like inviting a houseguest and giving them a closet and a sleeping bag."

"What do you want from us, then?" Alex asked calmly, cutting me off from launching into a tirade about soul stealing and how, as far as I was concerned, she could be insulted until the sun imploded. I eyed him with a rueful glance. His approach was probably better suited to keeping the peace.

"His sister's kidnapping is not just a tragedy for you," Lilith replied, locking her gaze on my friend. Her focus reminded me of a T-Rex from *Jurassic Park*—based on movement. "It is also a personal insult." She smiled faintly, but it was less pleasant and more predator than usual. "And unlike yours, it is very deliberate."

"So you *want* us to rescue my sister?" I asked incredulously.

Her raptor gaze swept to me, locking on a new target. "Quite," she said flatly. "However, I require that you perhaps handle the rescue a bit more *definitively* than you would otherwise."

"No survivors," Orion filled in the blank for me.

"Burn and salt their organization like the Romans did to Carthage," Lilith said cheerfully.

I wondered if her ever-changing tone was an aspect of her personality or a sign of some sort of nervousness. She wasn't making eye contact with Orion, I noticed. Rather, she was staring at the hilt of his sword.

"And if we do what we were, more or less, going to do anyway, you'll give me my soul back?" I asked hopefully.

"Oh, my dearie, you are too cute. You have insulted me personally. Doing this task will be a personal favor to me to balance the scales between us. But I can't allow my own personal feelings to interfere with the operations of business."

Of course, it had been foolish to even think that getting out would be that simple. At this point, you'd think I'd have gotten the hint. There are no free outs.

"So hypothetically, let's say we don't do this," I said, putting my bargaining hat on. "You might be feeling very wrathful toward me, but what can you do? If you don't let me out of the deal, then you're sort of bound to let me have the greatest life ever. You can't touch me."

My speech killed the flirtatious glint in Lilith's expression with each word. She started to take a step toward me, her black eyes full of malice, before she caught herself. She drew back quickly, brushing one of her red tresses back over her shoulder in a casual motion to try to hide the awkwardness of it. Her gaze flicked back over to Orion and his sword hilt once more. It might have been my imagination, but I thought the handle glowed again, if only for a second.

"You're correct, of course," she said harshly, dividing her attention between me and Orion's hilt. "But there are always loopholes, little man. Maybe I'll pay a visit to some of your other family members. Maybe I'll wait for years till you forget to be afraid. Then one day, I'll kill every person you saw on some

Tuesday. Your friend Alex isn't protected under the same aegis. I can still keep the word of my employer but destroy him piece by piece."

Crap, I hadn't thought of that. I glanced at Alex, who might have looked a shade paler but otherwise showed no emotion on his face. As much as I didn't want to do work for Lilith, I wasn't going to leave my friend hanging. Besides, these people *had* kidnapped my sister, just in case we had forgotten that part. That fact really killed my moral compass when I tried to point it at this issue, I realized. I really didn't care what happened to the kidnappers; they'd get what was coming to them.

That raised a question about my own psyche. Had I always been this dark? Three days out of the civilized world, and I was ready to kill some people who had kidnapped my sister without nearly enough hesitation. Had I simply never tapped into my Hyde side, or was I being twisted? Everyone around me was being messed with. Hell, my sister didn't remember being dead. Was I still me? I'd have to do some soul searching (yes, I see it) about this later.

"Fine," I snapped. "What do you want us to do?"

"Your sister is in the hands of an organization called the Lazarus Group," Lilith told us.

Orion grunted slightly in recognition. The ghoul let out a whine that reminded me of a skittish dog hearing a far-off thunderstorm.

"You've heard of them?" I asked Orion.

"They're human scientists who've found their ways to do more primeval things."

"Yes, they love to stick their noses in places they aren't suited for or welcome to," agreed Lilith. "They're obsessed with death, or rather, with stopping it."

"That doesn't seem so bad," I said slowly, feeling a little confused.

"That's because you don't know what they would be willing to do to your sister for the sake of science," Lilith said flatly.

Images of every evil scientist's lab I'd ever seen on television flashed before my eyes, full of biting drills, whirring saw blades, and burning needles. That didn't make me more afraid or more concerned for my sister's well-being. While I suspected she might not be able to die, I knew she could still feel pain. That made me angry.

"Do you know where we can find them?" I asked.

"They have a laboratory set up near the Air Force base," she replied promptly. The ghoul whined again. She reached into one of the pockets of her tight jeans and pulled out a scrap of paper. "This should give you the address," she stated, holding it out expectantly.

After a moment's pause, I took a step toward her to take the piece of paper. Orion stopped me in my tracks with a restraining arm across my chest.

"Never accept gifts from a demon, Matthew," he said in a tone like ice.

Right. I probably should have known that lesson, considering.

"You're no fun," Lilith shot back across the several-feet gap. "Here, I relinquish any claim on this measly scrap of paper." She tossed it, and we all watched as it fluttered like a dying moth to the concrete floor between us.

Orion remained still, with his arm holding me back. Through our contact, I could feel a humming tension in his body. If he were a spring, he would be coiled up as tightly as he could possibly be, desperate to burst forward at the slightest release.

"Black Abyss," she swore after another moment had passed. She took several deliberate steps backward, away from the scrap of paper, before Orion lowered his arm. Two long strides ate up the distance to the paper. He bent down and scooped it up in one motion, stuffing it into one of his pockets as he stepped back to where he had been standing originally.

"You are all kinds of broken inside, aren't you, halfling?" Lilith said, her black eyes dancing with amusement. "Straddling two worlds, not able to be a human or a demon. It must be so hard for you," she crooned.

Orion's hand crept toward the hilt of his sword again.

Lilith took note with widened eyes, but her smile grew even more wicked. "Don't you boys have a kidnapped sister to go rescue?"

Orion turned away from her, and Alex and I followed the big guy's lead. I caught a glimpse of his black eyes, which were a terrible sight to behold. Whatever buttons Lilith had been pressing had hit home.

"Leave the ghoul," Lilith called after us. "Someone should keep me company."

The ghoul whined again. Without slowing down, Orion pulled the curved knife from under his jacket and stabbed it down into the ghoul's neck. Viscous black blood gurgled from its throat, and it began to seize.

"Find your own," Alex called cheerfully as we left.

I thought I heard her sigh.

CHAPTER 16

As we piled back into Alex's van for what felt like the umpteen millionth time that day, I couldn't help but feel a newfound sympathy for pinballs. They spend their lives bouncing around, being whacked and sent wildly spinning in a new direction. That's pretty much all I had been doing for the last few days, running from one crisis to another.

"Does anyone else think that this is kind of dumb?" I asked as we drove.

Orion passed the scrap of paper that he had extricated from Lilith up to Alex. As it passed me, I got a whiff of something flowery. Not quite perfume, something more than that. It was like the overly sweet scent of a flower trying to lure a bee in to pollinate. And even though I knew what it was, I still found myself wishing I could smell it one more time after the scent faded.

"Like, oh hey, I'm some random guy that a demon decided to personally screw over, then my sister comes back to life, is kidnapped by a group of mad scientists that happens to have upset the same bigwig demon I have annoyed, and now suddenly it's my job to destroy these scientists?"

No one had any clever response to my complaints.

Alex started up the trusty old van, and we were back on the road. I took a second to appreciate the fact that no one had stopped to even discuss if we were going to look for my sister now; everyone assumed we were. My new friends might be strange, but they were good half-people.

"My big question is: Who hates you this much?" Alex asked.

"Well, we did a good job making sure Lilith does like half a day ago," I said dryly. "You might have forgotten. Lots of fire, threats, and running. Ring any bells?"

"I meant before that, doofus." He chuckled.

"I saw the circle you two used," Orion volunteered. "You were correct—it should not have summoned a demon like her."

"She certainly looked surprised to be there when she popped through."

"This just in," Alex said, "demons are really good at acting. Which is really a civilized word for lying."

"You're saying this is all a play," I said slowly.

"It is highly likely that this started before the demon came to you in the theater," Orion said. "Demons are master schemers. They exercise as much care and precision as a spider when they lay their traps."

"So the big questions are..." I started counting on my fingers. "Why me? And why would Hell want to use me to destroy Lazarus?"

I already had some theories about why Dan had come to me to try to buy my soul. If the death of my family had proven anything, it was that I might be selfish enough to go for it. But I wasn't really keen on discussing that little portion of my history with these two. Connor knew, and my father knew. But that was the end of the living portion of that list.

"You are thinking about demons and Hell a little too

monolithically, Matthew," Orion commented, pulling me from my dark thoughts.

"What do you mean, Mr. SAT Prep?" I asked.

"You are familiar, I assume, with the story of how demons became demons and ceased to be angels?" he asked.

"Uh, kinda," I said, trying to think back to my grandmother's Sunday School lessons. "Didn't Sat—the Devil want to be God, basically?"

"A simpler explanation would be that he had problems with authority, but you are close enough. However, it is not as though he was the only Fallen with that particular character trait. They all have their own plans and power plays. He is the most vicious and cunning of them all."

"Every kid thinks he might be President someday before they grow up," offered Alex.

"Demons are the same way, but they never grow up." Orion's voice was somber. I remembered Alex's comment about Achilles when he had first been explaining the Nephilim to me.

Human beings change. We talk about how we don't change, but we do all the time. When I was a child, I didn't brush my teeth regularly because I hated the taste of toothpaste. Now I brush all the time, but I still hate the taste. I grew up and realized I hated dental bills even more. From what Alex had told me, people like Orion didn't have that much freedom. It was like being an eternally self-aware Peter Pan.

I wondered if Orion's slightly rigid nature wasn't him being aloof, but more indicative of the line he had to walk. Like an addict white-knuckle-gripping sobriety as he battles his inner demons, Orion had to do the same with his own nature. I remembered what the anger in his voice had sounded like when we took the ghoul from the home. There was a terribleness to it that I hadn't been able to place. A depth to him that I couldn't begin to understand.

"So, we're just going to walk right in there and smash the place up?" Alex asked softly. "That's going to cause all sorts of drama."

"We don't have much of a choice. Regardless of how she came to be back among the living, Matt's sister is an innocent victim. We cannot leave her as a prisoner in the hands of Lazarus."

"Plus, Lilith is sort of demanding that we go into this."

"We are maybe damned if we do, definitely if we do not," Orion replied soberly. "At least this way, we have a chance."

"Hey, man, you don't have to do this. You know that, right?" I asked. "You just met me tonight, and I'm super grateful for everything you've done for my sister already. But I can't ask you to walk into something like this. It's too much. You can step out here, and Alex and I will try to figure something out."

"I cannot," he said stiffly.

"No, I'm serious. The stakes are crazy high. Megan wouldn't want this on her conscience."

"I. Cannot. These actions will not go unpunished in my city," Orion repeated, forcefully cutting off any of my further protests.

I turned back to eye him curiously. But he didn't offer anything more after his proclamation. His black eyes ignored me, looking out the side window of the van at the empty roads. An uncomfortable silence settled over the car. It was so oppressive I could almost feel its weight on my shoulders.

"Okay, fine," I said, turning back to the front. My conscience was mostly satisfied. I had tried to give him an out. He wouldn't take it, for whatever reason. I was sure there was an explanation with some weird philosophical muttering about free will. Whatever, I told myself. It wasn't my fault. And truth be told, I was more than a little relieved to not be attempting this without Orion.

"So, we roll up on the address and do a smash and grab?" I asked. "Or what's the plan?"

"How full is the gasoline container I smell?" Orion asked Alex in response.

"Probably more than half," my friend replied instantly. "It's got a couple gallons in it."

"That's probably enough," Orion said. "No, Matt, Lilith has tasked us to destroy, not just rescue your sister. If we die to the Lazarus Group, then she wins. Even if we manage to hurt them, she still wins."

"And she's made sure that we must still pick this fight, because of both my sister and her ability to claim a personal insult," I finished for him. "If we weren't so screwed, I'd be kind of impressed. Makes the hacks in DC seem kind of amateur."

Both Nephilim snorted at the same time. I decided to not follow that rabbit trail for the time being.

"So what are you thinking?" I asked Orion again. "We check the place, then torch it?"

"Basically," he said with a grunt. "We don't have the stuff to make a bomb in any reasonable amount of time, and fire is... effective."

"I hope this isn't rude," I said slowly, "but I've been doing some math in my head. And there are three of us. Now, Orion, I know you're kind of extra tough, so I'm willing to bump us up to a metaphorical party of five. But I'm guessing that a company calling itself the Lazarus Group also has at least one or two more people than that. Are we going to have a prayer with only the three of us? I'm not even a Musketeer, whatever that means."

"The Alamo only had about a hundred men in it, and they held off all of Santa Ana's army," Alex pointed out cheerfully.

"And then they *died*."

"Fine," sighed Alex. "Let's try it this way: Think of some of the demigod myths that you've heard. Legends of warriors like Achilles, Prometheus, and Hercules. We've got one of their peers in the back seat. Then ask your question again."

"I suppose that's fair," I replied, feeling a little chastised. "But what if they've got a bunch of Nephilim as, like, security guards or something?"

"Fah, impure puppies," snarled Orion. "No *real* Nephilim would be working at such a place. If there are any of our cousins here, they will be no problem."

I blinked in surprise at the disgust in his voice. Once more, a tense silence settled in the car after his response. I wondered how that made Alex feel. It was probably like overhearing Michael Jordan making fun of your dribbling skills. Or seeing Michael Phelps laughing at your backstroke.

"No offense," Orion said after a few awkward moments. It seemed the source of the awkwardness had finally occurred to the emotional brick wall that was Orion.

"None taken," replied Alex graciously. I glanced at him and saw a tightness around his blue eyes. The comments had stung, even if he was smart enough to not make a big deal out of it. But it defused the situation. You could feel the tension leak out of air so fast I think my ears popped.

"The blood has thinned out a lot over generations," Alex explained to me. "There isn't any new demon blood entering the gene pool anymore. So unless you take two demigods and breed them, their offspring will always be a little less, an echo of the generation before. A lot of the originals aren't around anymore either. Spoiler alert, but Achilles dies at the end of *The Iliad*."

"So demons stopped breeding with humans?" I asked, surprised. "Why?"

"Generational repercussions," Orion said stiffly from the back seat. "The child of such a union is without fail a monster. But the monster's child is less likely to be one, and the grandchild even less so. Each monster they created spawned a line of a thousand humans who are stronger, faster, and more resistant to demons than they would be otherwise."

"Ah, so they literally weren't getting enough buck for their bang," I mused.

"You get the gist of it," Alex agreed.

My mind felt full, like it had eaten a five-course meal. The supernatural side of things was so intricate. It made me miss video games with simple plots. It's much easier to follow when the big purple guy is the only villain who wants to be powerful and rule everything. To be fair, I suppose that was Lilith's motivation too; she was just one of many bad guys (and gals).

"Um, it occurs to me we should also look for like a manifest or something," I pointed out. "Anything that might tell us more Lazarus Group locations we can burn, or where my sister is if she isn't here. Lilith gave this one, but what if it was a freebie? We might be on our own to find the rest."

It bothered me a little how easily I said that sentence. I was currently in a car on my way to burn down some sort of laboratory. And that was largely in part because a demoness had told me to do it. I'm pretty sure that saying sentences like that is how people end up in psych wards. And I wasn't planning on burning down only the one lab. Oh no, I was going to burn down as many as it took. They had kidnapped my sister and were probably going to do horrible things to her. I'd burn down their whole company if that was what it took.

But still, the ease with which my conscience accepted what we were going to do bothered me. Or maybe it would be better to say the absence of me being bothered bothered me. Humans really can get used to anything.

Maybe it was because I had already burned down one warehouse in the last twenty-four hours that a second building didn't seem like that big of a deal. They always say your first arson is the hardest.

"Good point," Alex chimed in. "The less we have to rely on her to give us anything, the better."

"Step one, we scope the place out, make sure my sister isn't there. Step two, we snoop for any clues to where else we are going to need to hit. Then, step three, we torch the place," I said, ticking each point off on my fingers as I listed them. "Sound like a plan to you guys?"

"It's less a plan and more like guidelines, but it should work," Orion said seriously from the back of the van. His observation didn't help me feel any less stressed. But I got the feeling positive encouragement wasn't one of his strong suits.

CHAPTER 17

The sun was already beginning to peek its fiery little head above the horizon as we made our way back onto the highway in Alex's white minivan. After some discussion, we decided we needed to lie low for a bit. Whatever raid we were going to attempt on the Lazarus laboratory would have to wait for the cover of night. Confident as Orion might be, even he wasn't bold enough to charge in during broad daylight. I reluctantly agreed, desperate to get Megan back, but even my desperate self could see the wisdom in the Nephilim's words.

Orion had us drop him off at a public parking lot. He walked quickly to a sleek black motorcycle and swung his leg over it before glancing at Alex and me, perched like a knight on his noble steed.

"Stay together and keep your head down," he instructed. "We'll meet tonight at dusk." Without another word, his bike roared to life, and he shot out into the street like an arrow. He wasn't wearing a helmet, but I guessed that wasn't as essential to someone like him. He was a lot less fragile than the rest of us.

Alex offered to let me hang out at his house, and I gladly accepted. I couldn't bear the thought of sitting in my apartment with its broken window and breaking relationships right now. My anxiety was already running on overdrive.

Alex's home was somehow even more run-down than mine. He rented some brick house in the suburbs not far from me. His building could have used some paint, and at least one of the shutters on his windows was hanging on by a thread. By the time he parked in the driveway, the sun was fully above the horizon, its judgmental gaze bearing down on me for staying up all night. I felt like I was dying of thirst.

We dragged ourselves through the front door, and I plopped down on the first chair I saw like an exhausted puppy after a walk. The inside of the home was exactly what I expected it to be. It wasn't dirty, but it was messy. Books, comics, and various papers covered every surface in sight. Movie posters from many different decades hung on most of the walls, from a black-and-white *Three Stooges* poster to a modern superhero film; his taste seemed to span the breadth of cinema. Which made sense since this was the bachelor pad of a man who had been alive for at least two centuries.

Alex made it a few steps farther before he threw himself onto an old red couch that was probably older than me, landing on top of a stack of magazines and comics. Unlike the Princess and the Pea, he didn't even seem to notice. Maybe if the princess spent more time running from demons, she would have been able to sleep no matter how many vegetables were under her mattress. Except, you know, for the nightmares.

"Sorry I'm taking your bed," Alex said, starting out of the exhausted silence we had settled into. He leapt off the couch and began scooping up the various reading materials scattered everywhere. He looked around, arms full of pulpy literature, before shrugging and dumping the whole of several people's life's work in a pile on the floor at the foot of the couch. Granted, there wasn't a free counter or table in sight.

"I'm sure I have a blanket somewhere," he mumbled, looking around.

"Don't worry about it," I groaned as I struggled to free myself of the chair's grave-like grasp. "If Santa Claus himself showed up in your living room, I don't think I could keep from falling asleep right now."

"Be careful what you wish for," Alex muttered as he gestured for me to take the couch and started walking toward the hallway farther into the house. "Don't wake me up unless the house is on fire," he called over his shoulder. "Although, honestly, even then, use your judgment."

I tried to come up with a clever reply, but as I lay down on the battered red cushion of the couch, my brain turned out the lights.

I woke up hours later to a sunbeam stabbing me in the eye with burning glee. My body ached, and it felt like I had slept on several rocks instead of a cushioned couch. I groaned as I sat up slowly, my body protesting every movement my muscles made.

It was after noon, and the sun had apparently scampered its way across the sky to a point right where it could shine through Alex's drawn blinds and into my eyes specifically. The giant ball of fire was literally several hundred thousand times larger than our entire planet, but it sure seemed to have a vendetta against little old me personally. It really felt like the sun should pick on someone its own size.

My phone had several missed calls and messages from Violet and Connor, checking in to make sure I was okay. I mean, I wasn't, if we're being honest, but physically, I was fine. I sent them a little white lie and tossed my phone on the couch with an irritated grunt.

"Morning," Alex muttered, emerging from the hallway that I

assumed led to his bedroom. But for all I knew about Nephilim, it could be his coffinroom. He was wearing a fresh pair of jeans and a red long-sleeve shirt. His blond hair was spiked in every direction, like he was about to get struck by lightning, and he seemed much more chipper than he had been a few hours ago.

"You're up early."

"Couldn't sleep with you making all that noise," he replied, tapping his slightly pointed ears. "I may not be able to kick doors off their hinges, but my hearing is pretty good."

"Oh, sorry," I replied, feeling guilty. "I didn't mean to be a nuisance." As an enemy of the evil Morning State, I would never want to make someone wake up. Waking was on my Top Five List of Least Favorite Things, right in between papercuts and people who put the toilet paper on upside down.

"Don't worry about it," he said, giving me a grin. "I usually only sleep for about five or six hours anyway, another one of the perks. Want some coffee?"

I grunted my yes, no longer feeling bad. I'd never been more jealous of a superpower in my entire life. He walked into the kitchen, and from the sound of it, began drumming on every single pot and pan he owned.

I hate morning people.

"I don't really cook," Alex chatted from the kitchen. From the disarray of his apartment, I thought that was probably a good thing. "But we can order a pizza or something when you're awake."

He brought me instant coffee in a mug with cartoon characters on it. I accepted it with a nod and resisted the urge to sip it. The mug gave off heat like the California sidewalks at noon. I'm guessing superhumans don't burn the roof of their mouths on hot drinks either.

"I gotta work on a few things. Let me know when you get hungry," Alex said and popped over to sit at his kitchen table, shoving some papers to the side and unearthing a laptop like some modern archeologist. I set my boiling-hot mug down on the coffee table and leaned back into the couch. It was going to be a long day.

I don't know if you've ever planned to perform an illegal assault on a corporation that was holding your sister ransom before, but sitting on your hands to wait for the sun to set makes you feel so powerless. Time is not a problem that can be worked on or expedited. I could not speed it up. No matter what I did, it would still be seven or eight hours until the sun went down, effectively an eternity. Add a roommate who is clacking away at a keyboard while you stare at a wall, and it's a quick descent into madness.

"What are you writing?" I complained after an hour or so of clickety silence. My coffee had finally cooled down to a temperature fit for mortal human consumption, and I was capable of actual interaction.

"Remember how I told you I was sort of a reporter?" Alex asked, his fingers not slowing down at all.

Now that he mentioned it, I did recall that vaguely. In all the nonstop adrenaline of the last few days, it had slipped my mind.

"Yeah, what's the deal with that? Do you write for some supernatural newspaper? *The Heavenly Times*? Or maybe *The Fairy Post*?"

Alex paused his typing to shoot me a flat glare. "When you're done making up names based off of the two newspapers you've heard of, let me know."

"Hang on, I got one more. Can't forget *Supernatural Today*!" I cried triumphantly.

Alex rolled his eyes, but his lips twitched in a slight smile. "That one's not terrible," he said, turning back to his computer. "But no, there aren't any official news sources like that. We still tell stories the old ways."

"I don't know what 'old ways' means to you," I said. "That could literally be cave paintings or pagers. Give me some context."

"We tell stories," he said. "We collect the myths and preserve them. Like Homer, like Dante, like Chaucer, and so many more."

"So instead of a reporter, you're more like a freelance… poet? bard?" I narrowed my eyes. "Minstrel?"

"Something like all of the above," Alex said with a laugh, leaning back in his chair and running a hand through his wild hair. "I've known for a long time that I was never going to be strong enough to get my own myth. You've seen a glimpse of the difference between me and Orion." He looked away as he said that, frowning slightly.

"But I've always been good with words. You don't need to be bigger or stronger to be good at them. When I was a kid, I wanted to be in a myth, but when I got older, I realized maybe I could be the one to tell them."

"Is that why you decided to help me?" I asked. "To write my myth?"

"Let's be honest," he said with a laugh. "This is Orion's myth, and we're just living in it."

I thought about the tall inhuman man staring down a demoness last night, and I had to admit that he had a point.

"Hey, Orion's pretty awesome, I'm not going to lie. But I had a demon literally steal my soul." I spread my hands. "I think that qualifies me for at least a leading role."

"Fine. You can be the damsel in distress."

I laughed. "That seems fair."

"But to answer your question, yes, and also no." He shrugged, not meeting my eyes. "You needed help, and I couldn't let you wander through this alone. But I also knew that if you were telling the truth, it would be a good story."

I appreciated his honesty. He had said as much at the bar when we had met, but now, having more context, I understood his reasonings for helping better. Even if he thought there was something to gain out of helping me, I believed him that he would have helped me anyway. It was who he was.

"Well, I hope this story has a good ending," I said with a sarcastic chuckle. "In the meantime, how about ordering your protagonist some pizza?"

CHAPTER 18

Orion roared up to Alex's on his motorcycle a few hours after the sun set. We loaded up Alex's trusty white van with an entire armory of weapons and tools and set off to cause mayhem.

The address Lilith gave us wasn't a secret laboratory. It wasn't a nondescript warehouse with boring beige-colored walls. The Lazarus Group Galahad Laboratory had a giant glowing sign in its parking lot smack dab in the middle of Century City, which seemed ironic. A simple internet search would have given us their address. If I owned a phone book, I probably could have looked them up in there too.

The building was a modern-looking structure that was at least five stories tall. It had a slight curve, like it was about to be bent into a horseshoe. The front of the building held huge arched windows supported by steel beams that revealed a large atrium. The walls were a bright-red clay peppered with windows that led into people's offices or whatever else they had.

It was the kind of building that would be shown in a television commercial to convince you that science was here to make the future great. Looking at the building for the first time made me feel a little more hesitant about burning it down. I mean, warehouses were one thing, but this was practically art.

"Are you sure a couple gallons of gasoline is going to be enough to burn this place down?" I asked Alex.

"Arson's easy," he said, far too calmly. "The trick is knowing where to start the fire."

We drove past a bright sign that was still lit up for the entrance to the parking lot. It read GALAHAD LABORATORY – NOBLE SCIENCE FOR ALL! in big letters. Above the logo was an emblem of two scrolls crossed behind what looked like some sort of chalice. To be completely honest, it was a little forgettable as far as modern logos go. Maybe their budget wasn't heavily focused on PR.

"Park on the street a block over," Orion ordered as we drove by.

"I suppose parking in the lot of the building we're going to burn down is a bit blatant, isn't it?" I remarked.

"I'm certain they'll figure out our identities soon enough," Orion replied. "But no point in making it too easy."

Following his directions, Alex parked on the side of the street about a block down from the lab alongside a strip mall. Most of its stores were dark. The only exception being a laundromat, but I didn't see anyone inside. As soon as we parked, Orion started moving.

"Let's go," he ordered. "We need to get in and out quickly. We may have already been spotted."

In what had become a practiced move, we poured out of Alex's van. Orion slung his sword over his shoulder and brazenly carried his assault rifle in his hands. Alex passed me the same black pistol I had taken the ghoul down with and a couple extra clips.

"Leave the bag," Orion told me as I started to grab it.

I nodded and held my gun awkwardly in my hands, waiting for the two of them to be ready. I'm that guy who struggles with knowing what to do with his hands in social situations. Suddenly my hands felt wrong in every position I put them in.

Obviously, I'm not used to holding a weapon and standing on the sidewalk in "public." That extra tension only made it worse. I kept my finger off the trigger because that was what every gun safety course teaches you first. And I kept the muzzle pointed at the ground. But every pose felt like I was being too cavalier or like I was a dumb kid pretending he was in a spy movie.

It was a relief to my psyche when the other two were ready. Being on the move kept me from being free to think too much. When you're actively focused on not dying, it's hard to have time to worry if you look stupid or not.

Our terrific trio moved back up the block, walking on the far side of the sidewalk from the road to try to avoid the light as much as possible. But that seemed like too little, too late. There's no subtle way to walk down a neighborhood street carrying as much firepower as we were. Don't even get me started on the sword. I still wasn't entirely sure why Orion carried it around. He hadn't bothered to draw it even once that I had seen. Although Lilith had seemed genuinely concerned about it, so I guess that was something.

Even though we were no longer standing still, my brain wasn't letting up on the negative thoughts. This really was a terrible plan. As Orion had pointed out, it wasn't really a plan at all. According to all my "research," (which was mostly movies) we were supposed to scope the place out, find some blueprints online, and then have a nerd on a headset telling us where we needed to go and how to navigate any obstacles that we might encounter. But nobody panic! We had a sword, so we should be fine.

We broke off from the sidewalk and cut across the parking lot to approach the complex from behind. I followed Orion and Alex through the middle of a row of empty parking spaces. The lights that illuminated the lot were in the flower-bed medians that cars would pull up to. The spheres of their illumination didn't quite touch, so by walking exactly down the middle in between the two sets of lines, we managed to remain shrouded in darkness.

There was something surreal about walking at a building with the intent to pillage and destroy it. I felt like I should be hugging every wall possible and humming some sort of theme song.

None of us spoke as we approached. The only sound was the gasoline sloshing with every step Alex took. I don't know if the other two were thinking the same distracted thoughts that I was. My guess was Orion wasn't. He seemed like the stiff, on-task kind of guy, laser-beam focus and all that. He was a pro and had been doing this for a long time.

Alex I wasn't so sure about. He obviously had more experience than me with… basically everything. I mean, the man was several hundred years old. But at the same time, he clearly didn't have the respect of Orion or his community at large. Some of that appeared to be a dint of birth. He didn't have enough demon juice humming in his veins to make him cool. As knowledgeable as he was, he didn't feel like as much of a soldier to me as Orion did. If the spectrum of badass super soldiers went from me to Orion, I felt like Alex was closer to my side of the spectrum.

On the one hand, that was nice, because it made me feel a little less worthless. I had brought the ghoul down, after all. While I suspected that was more luck than anything else, I couldn't help but feel that this would be a lot easier if we had like eleventeen more Orions, each with their own spooky sword.

From the back, the building's slight curve was away from us. There wasn't a giant glass atrium either. It looked much more informal, like an everyday employee entrance. A metal door with a blinking gray pad next to the handle, presumably for a keycard or something like that, waited for us right off of the parking lot. I found myself wishing we did have that nerd to hack us in.

We grouped around the rightmost door, right in the vision of a security camera. Belatedly, I wondered if we should have worn ski masks or something. But it was too late now, I guess. Alex crouched down and investigated the door handle for a moment.

"It's an electric lock," he said quickly. "There's not really anything for me to pick."

Orion nodded as if that was what he had been expecting. Calmly, he raised a booted foot and gave the door a hearty kick. The door shook, and a noticeable dent appeared in the middle like it had just been smashed by a battering ram. However, it didn't pop off the wall like the wooden residential door had yesterday. This was an industrial-strength door, made of sterner stuff.

Several more supernatural kicks from Orion drove the door inward with a fearsome crash and the scream of tortured metal. After a few more, the entire locking mechanism ripped free of the frame and swung inward with the door, deadbolt still firmly in place. A shower of sparks flew as wires and electronics were ripped apart.

The three of us stood for a moment at the doorway, straining our ears to hear anything in the silence. I heard nothing: no alarms sounded, no security guards shouted, and no dogs barked. It was as silent as a grave in the interior of the Galahad lab.

"There's no way no one heard that, right?" I asked. "We could kick in another one if we need to. There's probably still someone asleep on this block."

"Oh, I'm sure they did," replied Orion as he entered the building, assault rifle at the ready. "We'll just have to not let that stop us."

"Great," Alex muttered to me as he followed our fearless leader into the building. The gasoline sloshed in time with his steps.

I wondered for a moment if Orion had forgotten how much more vulnerable his sidekicks were. I suppose when you're Superman, there's not a lot of difference between kicking over an anthill and kicking your way into a mad scientist's lab. Although, given how angry he had sounded when we found the massacred family, I wondered if he just didn't care about consequences when he was on the hunt.

I was the last to enter the building, which made sense. Of the three of us, I was the least experienced, had the poorest senses, and was by far the weakest. If I had tried to kick that door in, all that would have happened was I'd probably have gotten a bruise. The back of the line was the safest place for me.

The interior of the building was as nice as the exterior had promised. The floors were marble and shone with polished perfection. The walls were a light clinical gray with a red band about a foot in width that ran parallel to the floor at head height. As we passed a couple of hallways, I noticed the color of the band changed down different hallways, leading me to suspect it was some sort of categorical device and not cosmetic. The ceiling was made of the spackled white tiles that can be found in every professional building ever made. That kind of amused me. Despite its fancy exterior wanting you to think of this place as something special, when you investigated the details, it was the same as everywhere else.

The lights were all on, but that didn't strike me as odd. This kind of place seemed like the sort of office that didn't ever truly sleep; it was just emptier at night.

There was definitely a lack of flammable materials. A sprinkler system was installed in the ceiling at regular intervals. I began to doubt that a single can of gasoline was really going to be enough to start an inferno that would burn this building to the ground, despite Alex's reassurances. But I guess that was phase three of our guidelines anyway.

"What are we looking for?" I whispered as we passed a few hallways without turning. We were in a section full of cubicles and offices. Maybe there would be something useful there.

"A map," Orion said from the front. "They've got to have one in the lobby for visitors."

The hallway we had entered was a straight shot into the large glass-encased atrium that was the lobby of the building. Several tall marble pillars spread evenly around the room held the dome up like miniature versions of Atlas. We moved down it swiftly, not hearing any movement. Which, given our unstealthy entrance, was very suspicious.

A number of sleek modern chairs made of red leather and stainless steel were gathered around a glass table on one side of the room. A giant desk made of the same materials took up the right side, where a legion of secretaries and administrators must work from.

"Ah-ha," Alex called, pointing to a map diagram on the wall.

"You are here," I read helpfully, pointing at the big red star in the lobby. According to the map, the main floor was for administrative offices. Then on the wings were conference rooms and an area for consulting. The next few floors were broken up into multiple office sections, with a gap where the bubble of glass from the lobby extended up and cut through it. Each section was color coded, which explained the different wall stripes I had seen coming in. The colors were all different types of specific clinics. I scanned the list; it seemed like they were all different types of cancer, nasty things like prostate, ovarian, and liver were listed, as well as some fancier words I didn't know the meaning of. But they sounded serious.

Suddenly I felt a little guilty. "Wait, this is a cancer treatment facility?" I asked. I had been on board to burn down an evil scientist's lair. Especially one full of bad guys who deserved what they got for kidnapping my sister. But this, this was different. Even if no one got hurt here tonight, how many people were depending on this place for treatment? Would destroying this place still inadvertently claim the lives of innocent people?

"It's a front," Orion grunted, "an end for them to justify their means. Any good that is done here is tainted and outweighed by the atrocities that they commit."

"Wait," Alex told me, cutting off my follow-up questions. "I'm sure you'll see."

"This map won't have everything on it," Orion said, staring at the wall. "This is what they want tourists to know about."

"Not a whole lot of room to hide things," I commented, looking at the map. "They've got everything laid out on both floors."

"Basement?" Alex suggested.

"Basement," Orion agreed.

"Basement?" I asked, a little slow on the uptake.

"There's no way it's on the map," Alex explained cheerfully. "If I had a secret lab for evil things, that's where I'd hide it anyway."

"Oh," I said, feeling a little dumb. That was kind of obvious. "Unless one of these clinics is mislabeled or something."

"Nah," Alex said. "You think they're going to keep monsters so close to where people might see or hear them?"

"I suppose not."

"Everyone spread out," Orion ordered. "Look for a door going down. We don't have long before the cavalry arrives."

We split up, following his orders. I moved at a brisk power walk, trying to move quickly without tiring myself out. I didn't want to get caught here if we could avoid it. I figured it was a safe bet that the cops weren't going to be the ones responding to whatever alarms we might have triggered. Which made me wonder: Who was coming? It was a question that I didn't really *need* to have answered, but I had a bad feeling that I was going to find out soon.

I worked back the way we had come, down the long hallway with the red stripe. There was a large sign that directed me to a stairwell, so I opened that to check it out. There was a staircase going up to the second floor, but none going down. That could mean there wasn't a basement, but I supposed having a public access stairwell would ruin the secrecy of a hidden basement.

I returned to the hallway and continued retracing our steps. I hadn't noticed anything particularly out of the ordinary on our way in, but that seemed like the point. I stopped to check a janitor's closet, peering suspiciously at mops and cleaning chemicals. No secret entrance hidden there.

Then I found something almost out of the ordinary. A second janitor's closet was in the hall, right by the back entrance that Orion had aggressively convinced to let us in. The door was a plain white industrial door with absolutely no other markings. But when I grabbed its handle, this one was locked.

The other janitor's closet hadn't been locked. Maybe it was supposed to be. Maybe the janitorial staff kept the dangerous chemicals in this one. Or maybe, just maybe, this was the secret entrance to an evil lab. It kind of made sense. It was right by a back door, so it would be easy to move things in and out without walking them through the whole building. And no, it didn't have a lot of fancy locks or a keypad, but if you have a *secret* lab, maybe you don't need them. After all, who is even going to look for a secret basement in Los Angeles, California? Basements aren't really a thing out here—too many earthquakes. The only reason we had thought of it was because a demoness told us that there was more to this place than met the eye. Most people don't have that kind of intelligence source. It was probably worth checking out.

"Hey!" I shouted back up the hall. "I might have something."

The two Nephilim came at a jog, weapons at the ready. Their super hearing made it easy to get their attention at a distance.

"We really should invest in some headsets if we're going to make a habit out of this," I grumbled to no one in particular.

"What is it?" Alex asked as they drew up next to me.

"This closet door is locked," I trailed off, my explanation sounding stupid to my own ears.

"So?"

"None of the other closets like this are." I shrugged. "It's right by the back door too, easy to move stuff in and out without a lot of attention."

Orion grunted and nodded his head at the lock. Alex crouched down by the door and dug out his pick set from his back pocket.

"Did you guys find anything promising?" I asked as he got to work.

Orion shook his head and stared down at Alex, his attention clearly focused on something.

"How much more time do you think we have to look?"

"Be silent," Orion snapped at me.

I took an involuntary step back. Orion is scary, okay?

"I'm trying to listen for sirens."

Man, I knew his hearing was good, but I didn't know it was that good. Sirens are meant to be heard from far away, but this was a little ridiculous. We were inside an industrial building, for goodness' sake. After a moment of tense silence, he shook his head and started looking around again.

"Nothing," he said. I wondered if that worried him as much as it did me.

"Got it!" Alex said as the lock clicked. The door swung open to reveal a second door. This one was a metal vault door, complete with a slot to swipe security cards. A single red light burned above the reader, like a glaring eye denying us entry.

"Well, the good news is you probably did find it," Alex said slowly as we stared at it for a moment.

"Can you kick that door down?" I asked Orion. "Alex and I could kick it a few times too. You know, to be helpful."

"We don't have to." Alex sounded a little pleased with himself.

He held up a black plastic keycard with a green lanyard dangling from it. "Some employee left this sitting on his desk."

"Well, that was certainly helpful of them," Orion said dryly.

"There's no way," I said as Orion stepped toward the door. "The guy probably doesn't even have clearance to anything cool, so he wasn't worried about leaving it out."

Alex slid the card into the reader and swiped it downward in one smooth motion. The red light winked green at us, and with a loud click, the bolt retracted.

CHAPTER 19

Alex and I exchanged surprised glances. Orion didn't seem fazed. I think he expected that he could make it work armed only with his force of will. To his credit, so far it was working.

Orion pulled on the door handle, and it swung open with a hydraulic hiss. Air whistled in around us. I think the room might have been vacuum sealed to prevent air from escaping. I'd read they do that with labs that experiment with diseases and airborne pathogens. Also known as: places I am thrilled to be walking into without a hazmat suit.

We followed Orion down a flight of concrete stairs. The door closed behind us, and I felt the air flow die as the room sealed. My ears popped as the air in the room pressurized. The stairwell was completely bare, simple concrete stairs with a bare metal rail and bright lights. A second door, as big and metallic as the first, was waiting for us at the bottom. Orion swiped the card again, and we repeated the process. Once more, air whistled past us into the next room. I wasn't sure if the stairwell was meant to be an airlock or a security hurdle. Maybe both.

Once we were through the door, we found ourselves in what I can only describe as exactly what comes to mind when you think of a mad scientist's lair. The hallway led straight ahead, past a row of two dozen or more glass cages on either side that looked like something out of *Planet of the Apes*. Everything was a pristine, sterile white: the floor, the walls of the cages, the ceiling, and the lights. The front of each cage was a clear Plexiglas material, which let us peer in and see their prisoners. The floors of each cell were sloped slightly toward a large metal drain in the center, presumably for waste, which was super gross.

The first set of cages featured a pair of ghouls. I recognized them by their blue hairless skin and canine jowls. They wandered their kennels like restless dogs. They did not react to our passing, which made me wonder if they could see out of the glass or if it was one-directional.

I didn't have the knowledge to identify many of the things that we saw in cages we passed. Some things were familiar, like a creature with the body of a man and the head of a bull. While I was pretty sure it was a minotaur, I couldn't be one hundred percent sure because its head was entirely on fire, and I didn't remember that from Theseus's tale. The bright red and yellow flames didn't seem to be consuming it or causing it any distress. It had an iron collar around its throat and chains going in every direction, firmly anchored to the walls, locking it into the center of the cage.

I passed armored carapaces and furry quadrupeds without being able to categorize them. Whatever the cells were for, they were certainly packed.

One prisoner at the end of the row looked more man than beast. He had shaggy black hair that seemed in danger of blocking his view as he looked downward. But he still had an unsettling quality to him. His movements were too graceful. He sat in the back corner of his cell, in a pair of white pants and a shirt, casually thumbing his way through a book. However, if he was really reading the book at the speed he was turning the pages, he was certainly not human. A stack of books, all bent slightly, were scattered off to the side like forgotten trash. He was the only prisoner I had seen who had anything in his cell with him.

As we passed, his eyes flicked up and locked on us, despite the one-way glass. They were golden, like ripe wheat fields. Lilith and Orion had eyes that were solid black, making it impossible to tell if they actually had pupils or not. However, it was clear this individual didn't. Golden orbs peered at us curiously for a moment, but the pages of his book never ceased turning.

"Interesting," he said in a musical tone that emerged from his glass cage through a speaker set at the door. "I don't think you are supposed to be here."

I started to stop, surprised to be addressed when every other creature hadn't noticed us.

"Don't," Orion growled, jerking me back into motion.

"Oh, come on," the prisoner said petulantly. "You're here to cause mischief, anyway. Why not let me out to add to the fun?"

As curious as I was, I was also very nervous. This seemed like as deep into the lion's den as you could get. And if the big boss said not to stop and talk to the strange monsters, you bet your life that I was going to listen, just this once.

"I'll see you later," the stranger called from his cell as we passed through the row of cages. His promise made me shiver.

The hall opened into a large room that was even more unpleasant. Everything was the same sterile white, except now with chrome accents. A large slab sat in the middle of the room, like they use in crime shows for autopsies. Pristine tools with jagged edges or sharp needles were laid out, waiting for their next victim. The entire room stank of bleach.

The sight of this torture chamber reinforced my fear that Megan was probably sitting in a cell like we had just passed, waiting to be taken to a room much like this. There she would be sliced and diced, cut and bled and tested in every way imaginable.

And because of the curse placed on her by Dan, because of me, she wouldn't even be able to die to escape. Trapped, forced to endure torture beyond what any human being should be able to withstand.

I thought that I was angry before we got here. But the feeling that now washed over me like a crimson wave would be insulted to be compared to the minor frustration I had been feeling. It was like comparing an ant to the entire expanse of the color red. Not alike in form or function.

My perception of time became jittery, as though it was under the effects of a strobe light on a dance floor. I was losing little gaps of time in the steps that I was taking. One flicker I was entering the room, the next I was holding a tray of expensive surgical tools over my head as I flung them at a wall. A third had me flipping the entire medical cart. During each flicker, I rained destruction on the room. I smashed glass cabinets and threw every beaker I could get my hands on. I would tear this building down brick by brick. I would destroy it with my bare hands. That was only what I would do to the building. The people who worked in this lab would—

A slap across my face snapped me back into real time. Orion had me pinned high against a wall, feet dangling with the palm of his hand pressed against my chest. His black eyes stared into mine like the inverse of an eighteen-wheeler's high beams. My breath was ragged, and I could feel my blood rushing through my veins like whitewater rapids. The expression on the stoic demigod's face was hard to read. It could have been sympathetic. Or annoyed.

"Matthew, control yourself," he admonished firmly. "We're wasting time." He held me there for another moment as I panted, struggling to catch both my breath and my sanity.

"I'm good," I wheezed, failing to fully catch either.

He nodded once and let me go. I slid down the wall several

inches until my feet connected with the floor and took a moment to survey the damage I had wreaked on the lab. The room was trashed. Every loose object had been thrown, every piece of glass had been smashed. Apparently, I'm an efficient vandalizer when I want to be. Savage satisfaction rose from the depths of my sternum. It might be a small gesture, to destroy a single lab's worth of tools owned by a multimillion-dollar company. I knew it would barely register on their budget sheet. But it did help me feel a little better.

Several doors branched off the back of the butchery room. Inside we found a couple of small offices with computers. Alex promptly sat down at one and started clicking around.

"This has got to be our freebie," he commented after a few moments.

"What do you mean?" I asked, snooping through a bookshelf. I picked up an annoyingly mundane photograph of a balding, overweight white man posing with his young son and a tiny fish he had caught. It disturbed me to think that someone who worked down here could have a life out there, in my world.

"Security has gotten really lax around here," he replied with a fierce grin. "People leaving keycards at their desk, not locking their computers when they go home. This place is a secret, but casually so. I don't think they were worried about people like us."

"But after tonight..." I said, realizing where he was going with this.

"They'll step up their game a lot," he finished.

"Well, if you find a file labeled 'Evil Plan,' make sure to grab a copy," I muttered, tossing the picture against the wall so that the glass in the frame shattered. Alex shot me a concerned look but didn't comment.

Feeling useless, I wandered back into the room I had destroyed. My gun was lying on the floor, dropped and forgotten when I had gone on my little rampage. Feeling a little embarrassed, I scooped it up. The cold metal felt reassuring against my hand. Its chill felt like a dog trying to cheer up its master. *Don't worry*, it seemed to promise, *cold retribution is coming*. The furious fire in my stomach liked that promise.

Orion was through the opposite door, which led to some sort of chemical lab. A pair of bright yellow hazmat suits hung by the door, but he hadn't bothered. A little chloric acid to the lungs probably wasn't going to spoil his day anyway. Not feeling quite so bold, I hesitated by the doorway. He glanced at me and shook his head with a slight shrug. As if to say, *I don't know what any of this stuff does anyway.* I made a mental note to add a reformed evil scientist, along with the hacker nerd, to our future team job postings. Our group was strong on muscle and self-deprecating senses of humor, but not much else, it seemed.

Unable to help search either of the rooms, I wandered back the way we had come, looking for anything we might have missed. At least, that's what I told myself. I was most certainly *not* planning on going back to talk to the golden-eyed, dark-haired book reader. That would be a bad plan. However, there really wasn't much left in one piece for me to investigate in the butchery room. Someone had gone and smashed everything to bits. That only left the hallway to check out. I wasn't going for my own curiosity, mind you. I was just doing my part to help out.

The golden-eyed creature wasn't reading his books anymore. He stood patiently at the edge of his cell, apparently waiting for me. He smiled when I came into view, his teeth very white and ever so slightly sharp looking.

"I thought you might have a change of heart," he said brightly, as though he were thrilled to see me. "I'm pretty sure the controls to the cell are on that wall over there." He pointed to a panel of switches behind me. I glanced over at them for a second before turning back to him. I knew I wasn't going to let him out, at least not without checking with Orion first.

"Uh, okay, good to know," I said slowly. "Listen, we're looking for my sister. Have you seen her? She would have been brought in tonight. She's human, a little shorter than me, with short brown hair and green eyes?"

The golden-eyed creature studied me for a moment, like a surgeon before making his first incision. "Are you offering to bargain for such knowledge?" he asked softly. Something *dark* flashed in his brilliant gold eyes. I'm only a little stupid, and I might still be new to this monster gig, but one rule had really seemed to stick out so far: *Don't make deals you don't understand.*

"I said no such thing, friend," I replied. I spread my hands before me in a half-hearted shrug. "I was merely checking to see if you had any information you would be willing to volunteer."

"Silly manling," he said, chuckling. "No knowledge is free." As he spoke, somehow he began to hum at the same time. It was a low baritone tune, gentle and smooth, like a warm bath. My consciousness slipped easily into the flow of the tune. It was like I was suddenly exhausted and desperate for sleep. My brain lacked the energy to press forward and make new thoughts of its own. It was content to sit there and listen to other people's thoughts.

"Now," the creature said in a whiny tone, still humming, "don't you think that it's absolutely criminal for me, your new friend, to be trapped in this boring old cage?"

You know, I had to admit he had a point. The cage was quite boring, and he seemed awfully nice. He made some of the nicest music I had ever heard. I could tell that he was extremely talented. He deserved to be free to spread his talents to the world. It was a bit of a struggle in my relaxed state, but I managed to nod a little. As I did, a wave of excitement and pleasure rushed through me, like the first sip of warm apple cider on a crisp autumn afternoon.

"I'm so glad we agree," he purred. "Why don't you go take a

look at that control panel and see if you can't open the door for me?"

Once again, I marveled at what a great idea that was. I was ecstatic to be a part of setting this beautiful creature free in the world.

I was jolted out of my sleepy thoughts as a large hand slapped down on the glass barrier, right in front of my face. The resounding crack made both me and Golden Eyes jump. He stopped humming, and my ability to form a thought of my own returned like a hard reboot of a computer.

"What the hell?" I muttered. "His singing wasn't even that good."

Orion was standing behind me, his abyssal eyes staring into the golden ones on the other side. I turned to look, and in a flash, I switched from dopey to concerned. He looked furious. Had I made him that mad? Jaw clenched, Orion raised the hand that had slapped the glass and pointed one index finger at the prisoner. "Watch yourself," he growled in a furious whisper.

The hummer visibly paled and took a step back. "Yes, of course, Hunter. I'm sorry," he murmured, casting a demure glance down to the floor. He had the good grace to look a little ashamed of himself. "Bad habits got the better of me, I am afraid."

"Did they bring in any more prisoners tonight?" Orion barked, apparently satisfied with the apology.

"Oh my." A lightning-fast grin appeared on the prisoner's face. "Do *you* wish to bargain with me, O Mighty One?" It wasn't clear to me if the title was a mocking one or not.

"Yes," Orion said in the same steely tones. I thought I heard his teeth grinding as he clenched his jaw. "Here is my offer: tell me what I want to know, and you get to keep the door in between us."

"But that's—" he began, obviously confused. He stopped as he recognized the threat in Orion's words. "Come now," he protested. "You can't blame me for a harmless trick! All I wanted to do was get out of here before it is my turn with the sawing and bone breaking. I only sang to the mortal a little bit."

"This mortal is under my protection," Orion stated calmly. "If I were so inclined, I could choose to be offended by your 'trick.'"

The singer's eyes went wide, and his jaw dropped in shock. "You'd begin hunting my people again, over a misunderstanding with a mortal?" He gasped. "He didn't even *die*. The peace has lasted over three centuries!"

Orion shrugged. "Tell me what I want to know, and you won't have to explain to your Court what broke our peace."

"Fine, you barbarian," the prisoner spat vindictively. "Let's get this over with."

"Did they bring in new prisoners tonight?" Orion repeated.

"They did, but whatever she was, it wasn't human," he said. "His description"—he nodded at me—"sounded right, but she smelled wrong. I've never smelled so much sulfur on a mortal. Even more than him."

Orion and I traded glances. That sounded like Megan. She hadn't ever actually met any of my super friends, but the ghouls had been able to find her. It made sense that she would feel different to non-mortals.

"Where did they take her?" I asked, feeling that spark of hope and excitement kindle again. The prisoner glanced at Orion as if to ask if he had to answer the question. Orion simply stared at him.

"They took her into the Pain Room." He sighed. "I don't think they did much in there. I truly have no stomach for that kind of thing. I much prefer my poetry and songs. They're far less… visceral, I suppose."

That rage I had felt in the lab reared its fiery-red head again. But this time I was ready for it. I grabbed it with my subconscious and wrestled it down. I would save it for the right time, I promised it, soon, but not quite yet.

"Where did they take her?" Orion pushed.

"They did not keep her here long. After they were done, they wheeled her back out on a gurney. The poor thing was unconscious and a little pale, but otherwise she looked okay, I suppose. I wouldn't really know how to judge mortal well-being from such a cursory glance."

"How long ago?"

"Not too long, I think I read the entire *Iliad* and most of *The Merchant of Venice* in between her departure and your arrival. An hour at the most."

I resisted the urge to scream. It seemed like we were always one step behind in every phase. We found the ghoul after it had already dropped her off, and now we found where he had taken her right after she had left.

"Guys, I got something!" Alex called from back in the offices. Without a word, Orion and I turned and hustled back toward him.

"You're welcome," Golden Eyes called sulkily after us. Even his petulant tone was somehow still melodious. It made me think of an overcast Seattle sky, just before the rain, but I couldn't tell you why. I've never even been there.

We made it about half of the way to Alex when the lights went out. The brilliant fluorescent bulbs that shone down on the lab all cut out at the same time. It wasn't only the lights; the entire room was suddenly silent, as even the refrigeration units stopped humming. For a moment, I panicked. It was absolute dark in the basement. No city-mandated EXIT signs lit up; no outside light peeked in from windows. I couldn't see my hand in front of my face.

"Demonspawn!" Alex swore. "I lost it!" There was a loud thud as he punched the desk.

A pair of flashlight beams appeared as Alex and Orion both produced powerful flashlights. I guess they both deserved an Armed Invasion merit badge for coming prepared. I hadn't thought to procure one from Orion's bag of many wonders before we started.

"Here." Orion passed me his light. I knew he could see much better in the dark than me. I held the light in my left hand to keep the pistol firmly gripped in my right. Dimly, I could hear the creatures locked up in the cages moving restlessly. Maybe they were as nervous as we were.

"So, hey, human, about letting me out?" our prisoner friend called nervously from the hall. "I think I'm okay with taking my chances with the Hunter being upset with me."

Before any of us had a chance to respond, there was a loud, heavy click that echoed many times in short succession from the hallway. I heard a faint hiss as the cage doors started to swing open.

"Oh. You know what, never mind," he called.

CHAPTER 20

Okay, quick recap: We're currently trapped in some sort of mad scientist's lab, underground and without power. My super friends and I were locked in there with a bunch of things that go bump in the night, and all of their cell doors just opened. Most of them were probably not the biggest fan of Orion, or humanity in general. I was also sure that waiting outside the lab was an unknown number of bad guys ready to take us out if by some miracle we survived the gauntlet that they had thrown us into.

The best part? This wasn't even the most dangerous situation I had been in recently. If we're being technically correct, this wasn't even the most dangerous situation I'd been in the last twenty-four hours.

"Hey, listen," the melodious voice of the prisoner we had interrogated called from the cages. "Hypothetically speaking, if the cages were to have been unlocked and a big showdown was about to go down, what would happen if I simply stayed in my cell? I'm, um, asking for a friend."

"Listen to me," snarled Orion. His voice rang forth with the fury that I had heard when he interrogated the ghoul. This was

Orion on the edge of battle, I realized. This was Orion struggling with his personal demons, trying to walk the line between warrior and monster. At the sound of his challenge, the growls and shuffling sounds from the hall fell silent. Even monsters know when a storm is coming, apparently. "If you remain in your cells and let us pass, no harm will come to you by our hand. I swear this to you all."

"Got it. I'll let my, uh, friend know," Golden Eyes called back.

The cells were completely silent for a few agonizing seconds. It seemed like Orion's threat would do the trick. But my life never gets to be that easy. It was my bad luck versus Orion's alpha male status, and only one of us could win.

We heard the footsteps first, as they trudged toward us. Heavy thuds, like the Tyrannosaurus rex's approach in *Jurassic Park*. Despite the horrific darkness, the monster was easy to see as it stepped into the hallway. Again, I don't know everything about minotaurs, but I'm fairly certain the standard edition doesn't come with a demonic-looking fiery head. Maybe Theseus only had to battle a runt in the labyrinth under Knossos. Lucky us, we got the luxury edition.

I hadn't really processed it when this thing had been chained in its cell, but it was massive. Like I think he could have dunked on a regulation basketball hoop without even standing on his tip-hooves. The glowing fiery aura that surrounded its bull head was high enough that I had to tilt my head to make eye contact with its malicious bovine eyes. The glow given off by its flaming head was dimmer than I would have expected it to be. I could barely make out the tops of its NFL linebacker shoulders in the glow before the shadow consumed the rest of it.

I adjusted my grip on the pistol, feeling a tad ridiculous. I may have been able to knock a ghoul down with a wild bullet, but I didn't think this guy was going to go down that easily. But hey, of all the monsters in the hallway, at least we could see this one in the dark—gotta look for the silver linings in life.

The minotaur gave us a once-over, sizing us up in a predatory way that made me feel uncomfortable. Apparently, it wasn't too impressed with what it saw. It snorted once and lowered its horns slightly in something akin to a fencer's salute. "Big talk," it rumbled. Then it charged.

What happened next was remarkably like a Spanish bullfight, except with three people crammed into a tiny science lab instead of having a large coliseum's worth of space to work with, and not one of us had a stylish red cape.

The three of us scattered in a way that would make bowling pins jealous. The beams of my flashlight and Alex's waved frantically as we dove away from the fleshy freight train that was rushing at us at full steam. Despite being so massive, the minotaur's acceleration was incredible. It blasted across the room, not bothering to stop when pesky things like walls got in its way. It smashed through the wall to the office Alex had been investigating like it was a gingerbread house.

It came to a halt on the other side of the wreckage, fiery head still visible in the perfect dark. It shook its head once and snorted. Then its eyes locked right on me. *Gulp.* In a brilliant move, I turned off my flashlight. But it was about five seconds too late. Bull Flame had me in its sights.

The behemoth lowered its head and charged at where I had been. I threw myself up and over the metallic operating table to dodge its furious rush. As fast as it was, it was still subject to the laws of physics, and its turning radius was crap.

The minotaur's burning head smashed into the white drywall of the torture room. There were no offices for it to burst into on the other side of that wall, so there was a heavy thud as it collided with something hard. Maybe a metal support beam or a piece of the foundation. Whatever it hit, it didn't faze it in the slightest.

It extricated himself from the dent it had made in the solid wall, swinging its head around, looking for us. Its vision didn't seem to excel in the dark. Maybe the fire messed with the dilation of its pupils. It paused for a moment, inhaling in short, sharp sniffs.

With a rage-filled roar that echoed painfully in the contained space, it dashed across the room diagonally. I heard Alex grunt as he dove to the side, out of harm's reach. This wasn't going to work. Eventually, someone was going to mess up their dodge and get flattened like a roadkill pancake.

I glanced over my shoulder and could just make out the edge of the entry hallway from the dim glow of the minotaur's fire. Without any power, there was no way we were going to get that security door open and escape. But that gave me an idea.

"Hey, Goldy," I whispered.

"What?" he stage-whispered back to me.

The minotaur had finished pulling itself out of the wall again and turned its baleful gaze toward the sound of my voice.

"Is your cell door open?"

"Yeah, why?"

I turned my flashlight on and pointed it right in the minotaur's eyes. It recoiled for a moment, squinting against the beam of light. Then with a bellow, it lowered his horns and shot right at me.

I'll be honest, my heart skipped a beat at the sight of that monstrosity racing toward me with all the fury of a tornado. I spun on my heel and sprinted the few steps into the hallway. I put my hand on the left cell wall, feeling for the gap where the door would be.

I could hear the monster's footsteps behind me, getting closer with each thud. With a scream, equal parts desperation and terror, I threw the flashlight down the alley toward the exit and threw myself into the open doorway to Golden Eyes's cell.

I barely made it out of the way. The enraged minotaur went flying by like a subway train hurtling past a station. I felt the wind of its passing as I narrowly avoided being trampled. I'm not sure if it couldn't stop or didn't care to. Maybe it was too stupid to realize I wasn't ahead of it anymore, but the minotaur plowed through the security door we had used to get into the lab.

Cement shattered, and a huge portion of the wall gave way as it burst out into the stairwell. Light poured in from the outside room, and there were startled shouts as whoever had been waiting out there suddenly had an enraged minotaur to deal with. Gunfire rang out in the hallway, followed by another enraged bellow from the beast.

Golden Eyes and I exchanged glances as if to say, *Did that just happen?* His eyes glinted brightly from the light pouring in from the minotaur's exit hole.

"Matthew!" Orion shouted from the darkness. "Time to go."

"See you around, I guess," I said to my cellmate, and sprinted back out into the hallway. More gunfire and screams echoed from the stairwell, reminding me we weren't out of the woods yet.

"We still got to burn this place down!" I yelled as I regrouped with my friends.

"I think the living wrecking ball we unleashed will more than take care of that for us," Alex remarked dryly. He gently jabbed the grip of my pistol into my abdomen since I couldn't see it. "You dropped this, by the way."

"Thanks," I said, taking it from him. The whole building shook with a heavy thud as the minotaur smashed into a wall somewhere else in the stairwell.

"They weren't expecting it to get out," Orion said. "I bet they don't have anything with them to take it down."

"They're the ones who let it out in the first place!" I protested.

"The minotaur race has never been made up of the wisest of creatures," he told me. "The infamous one probably could have smashed his way out of Minos's lair. It never occurred to it to try."

"Can we focus, please?" Alex interjected, his voice tight with stress. "We're stuck in a dead end, and we have a distraction right now, but who knows how long it will last."

Orion grunted in agreement and started down the hall, toward the hole. Apparently, the rest of the monsters remembered his threats because we passed through the gauntlet unmolested.

He paused at the edge of the stairwell and listened for a second. Apparently satisfied with what his super senses told him, he stepped out into the light, assault rifle at the ready. Alex and I followed suit, pistols gripped with white knuckles. I'd shot one monster already, but I was pretty sure these were regular people on the other side. I wasn't sure if firefights with other mortals was something I was mentally ready for yet.

The dull roar and sound of gunfire had faded farther into the building. They were muted enough that I was guessing the minotaur had gotten onto the main floor. The bright light of the stairwell was blinding as I stepped out of the almost-perfect dark. I had to squint to give my pupils time to adjust. Orion and Alex didn't seem at all bothered by the sudden change in light. Jerks.

The stairs were deserted. Whatever group had been waiting for us had been scattered by the burning minotaur. As we climbed the stairs, it became obvious that dealing with the beast in this narrow space was even less fun than our experience had been. Several guards wearing black tactical gear lay crumpled. Or maybe smashed was a more accurate term. One groaned pitifully as we walked past him, his right knee turned in a way that it should never have gone. He made no move to interfere with us. I think he was so delusional with pain that he never even noticed us.

Two more bodies lay completely silent, and from the way they were pulverized and leaking viscous red blood, I doubted that would change. My feet stopped at the body of one of the guards. He was young, maybe a couple years older than me. He looked human, or at least human adjacent, like Alex and Orion. He was dead too. There was no question. You don't come back from having your chest smashed that thin.

My eyes wouldn't look away from his face. I tried to tell them to, but they wouldn't listen to me. His face was slack now, almost peaceful except for the rivulet of blood running out of one corner of his mouth. His eyes were closed. He didn't look evil or like he deserved to die. He looked more like a guy you invite over to your place to watch sports and drink beer. I suddenly felt sick.

"Matt," Alex called gently, his voice trying to lead me away from my first dead body. I wanted to turn and look at him, to let him tell me that it was okay. But my eyes were caught in the gravity well of the guard's placid, normal face. I couldn't pull them away. I wondered if my family had looked that peaceful in death before the river got to them.

"Matthew!" Orion called sharply.

My head snapped up, and I looked at my two friends waiting at the top of the stairs.

"These men are the ones who let the minotaur loose in the first place. This is their own deeds being visited back on them. This is what they wanted to happen to us."

A small cough came from behind us. Orion's black gaze turned from me, and his rifle snapped up to cover the sound. I had been freed from the dead man's pull. I didn't let myself look back. With my slower, mortal reflexes, I turned, raising my own pistol to point the same way as Orion. Some of my confusion had faded away with Orion's words. In fact, now I was feeling a little upset myself.

Golden Eyes had stepped free of the dark prison and was looking around at the carnage with wide eyes. Both of his hands were clasped to his chest, and he looked decidedly uncomfortable.

He reminded me of a tiptoeing teenager trying to sneak out more than a dangerous immortal.

"Oh, don't mind me," he said frantically, raising his hands slightly as all our weapons pointed down at him. "I thought I'd, you know, let myself on out after you all."

We stared at him for a moment. I waited for Orion to say something. I didn't even know what Goldy was. That made it hard for me to make any judgment calls on this situation. If he was a demon or some sort of kid-eating monster, I'd be happy to throw him back in his cell. But he had helped me dodge a living freight train, so I figured I owed him.

"Orion, he did kind of help us get out," I pointed out. "What's the harm in letting him go his own way?"

"Fine," Orion growled. "But stay out of our way." His rifle creaked as he lowered it. "Come, Matthew, we're wasting time."

Meekly, I followed orders, studiously keeping my eyes off the bodies as we ascended from the basement of nightmares.

At the top of the stairs was another minotaur-sized hole, where the beast had exited into the rest of the facility. The heavy metal door that we had entered through originally rested on the far wall of the hallway. The minotaur had apparently lifted the entire frame out of the wall.

Two more guards were waiting at the entrance. These were hale and hearty. Both had snub-nosed submachine guns gripped firmly in their hands. But they weren't paying any attention to the stairwell. Their gazes were focused in the direction of the glass lobby, where more gunfire and roars were coming from. I couldn't blame them; I'd be doing the same thing in their situation. Apparently, the minotaur wasn't planning on going back to his cell anytime soon. Another huge thud shook the walls, and I realized Orion was right. We *had* let loose the ultimate wrecking ball on this building. Lilith would have to be satisfied with that.

The two soldiers had no clue what hit them. Orion broke into a sprint and was on them before they had processed the gentle pads of his footsteps. A vicious backhanded slap spun the first guard to the side. She rebounded off a wall and slammed into the carpeted floor with a grunt.

Before she had even finished rebounding, Orion was on the second guard like an octopus. The Nephilim's arms slithered around him and clamped down on his neck in a nasty choke hold. The guard's face turned red quickly as he gasped for air, desperately clawing at Orion's grip.

The first guard was game. All of the bodies we had seen were clearly in good shape and used to real fighting. This wasn't a collection of Rent-A-Cop employees. She bounced up, submachine gun in hand and ready to fire. She got a bead on Orion, who simply threw his hostage at her like a bowling ball.

The guards collided and were sent flying. As the woman fell, she triggered a burst of gunfire that blasted up one of the walls and chewed at the acoustic tiling of the ceiling. Before either of them could get up, Orion was on top of them. Holding his assault rifle like a club, he bashed them both with the stock several times until they stopped moving.

The whole thing took less than ten seconds. He turned to watch as Alex and I trotted up the final few stairs to join him, guns held uselessly in our hands. I had barely had time to process the fight, let alone try to contribute.

A roar interrupted any plans that we might have tried to make. Apparently, the minotaur wasn't satisfied with the violence options presented to it by the guards it was currently playing with. The sound of the guardswoman's uncontrolled fire had drawn its attention. The beast entered the long hallway like an eighteen-wheeler at highway speed. Its fiery aura seemed to be glowing even redder, and its cow face was twisted in cartoonish rage. Which would have been hilarious if it wasn't so darn terrifying.

"Split up!" Orion commanded as our bovine nemesis bore down on us.

I sprinted across the hallway, running perpendicular to the minotaur. This hallway had been marked with a green stripe on the wall and led into a sea of cubicles.

I heard a sickening crunch and a scream as the guards Orion had worked so hard to incapacitate were trampled by the beast. My concern for my enemies was quickly forgotten as I felt the wall tremble. A glance over my shoulder showed me that the minotaur had smashed through the corner of the wall, unable to turn after me smoothly. Its big, dark eyes were fixed on me with a murderous fury. Although it had been shot a lot, it looked no worse for wear. It bobbed its head once at me, exactly like a bull. Then it charged again.

"How the hell did Theseus kill one of you with just a sword?" I yelled back at my pursuer. He didn't respond. Minotaurs were not huge on witty banter, it seemed.

I needed to do something different and fast. There was another intersection in the cubicles coming up ahead. I'm no Usain Bolt, and if we're being honest, I didn't love even *his* chances in a straightaway against this thing. But if there's one thing that video games and books have taught me, it's that big bosses never corner well.

I may not be supernatural, but sheer terror lent my feet some wings. I sprinted down the row of cubicles, aiming for the first intersection, and hung a right, heading back toward the front of the building, where the big lobby was. As I went, I looked desperately for a place to hide, but it was all cubicles as far as the eye could see.

A few seconds behind me, I heard a horrendous screech as the minotaur smashed through a cubicle, trying to take the turn at breakneck speed. At least physics was still on my side—for now. There was nowhere to hide. My only option was to keep running. Maybe it would tire out or something? I glanced back dubiously at the monstrous freight train still chasing me. That seemed unlikely.

Twenty yards ahead was another intersection in the cubicles. I took a left this time, using whatever gas I had left in my reserves. If I could get enough space between us, maybe I could duck into a cubicle and hope its sense of smell was obscured by all the fire. Maybe everything smelled like propane to it or something.

I took a left at the next intersection, my breath coming in ragged gasps, but my deep desire to not die helped my body overcome its fundamental need for oxygen. The next intersection, I took a right, then another left. How big was this maze of cubicles? I was totally lost.

I knew I wasn't going to be able to keep this up. The minotaur seemed implacable, an untiring force. I could hear it behind me, chugging along like a steam engine, eating up the distance between us.

Another left at a cubicle crossway, and I seized my chance. I threw myself into the second cubicle on my right. Completely exhausted, I lay on the floor, too spent to move. My pursuer rounded the corner, smashing into the other side of the cubicle row as it tried to make the turn. Its heavy footfalls continued down the hallway, oblivious to my hiding place. I lay still, struggling to keep my breathing quiet.

After a few seconds, everything was silent. It was gone. With a sigh, I rolled onto my back and closed my eyes. I still needed to figure out how to get back to Alex and Orion and escape. But this was progress. I just needed a moment to rest before I went back into the fight. If my death was coming, it was going to have to wait until I caught my breath.

I'm not sure how long I lay on the floor of some lab tech's cubicle. It was at least several minutes. I clearly don't work out as much as I should. As I lay there, closer to death than

I'd have liked, I noticed how boring the office space was. The cubicle section was carpeted, unlike the main hallway. The carpet fibers were rough and dug into my back and smelled faintly of industrial-grade shampoo. The cubicle walls were made of the same gray-colored fabric as the carpet, with black metal frames. I guess cubicles weren't really supposed to be fancy. My life might suck, but at least I didn't spend forty hours a week in this hellish landscape.

Slowly, I eased myself into a sitting position. My legs felt like Jell-O, even my bones were too tired to hold me up. But I still had work to do. It took all of my strength of will to get my legs to support me, and I groaned as I rose to my feet. Now all I had to do was wander through the cubicle maze until I figured out how to get out. Maybe Orion had beaten up all the other guards by now, so I wouldn't be asked to do any more physical labor tonight. If I could limp my way to the getaway minivan and take a nap, that would be great. I glanced at the desk as I regained my feet. A nameplate read MELINDA SPARROW, and there were several framed pictures of different cats. "Thanks for letting me crash, Melinda, babe," I said as I turned. "I'll call you or something."

It was right about then that I learned that minotaurs are huge jerks.

I made it two steps out of my cubicle hidey-hole before the beast let out a small snort, like the bestial version of a snotty rich lady's deliberate cough. Slowly, I turned my head to my right to stare at it. Apparently, they can also be super quiet when they want to be. My horned nemesis appeared to have doubled back on me without me hearing anything.

We stared at each other, five yards apart for a moment, like two Wild West gunfighters from a John Wayne movie. He was part cow, and I was a boy with a gun, so the genre almost fit.

"This office ain't big enough for the two of us," I drawled, or tried to. My tongue was dry with fear. It took me a try or two to get the sentence started, but I got it done. It seemed like this was where it would finally end. I had had a good run, both literally and metaphorically, I suppose. I survived almost three whole days in the supernatural world. Vaguely, I wondered what would happen to Megan after I died. Would she get sent back or still be stuck here? Given her current circumstances, I wasn't sure which was worse.

The minotaur wasn't big on gloating. Without a word, it lowered his flaming horned head and charged. The movement was so fast and fluid that it startled me. In my panic, I dropped my gun on the floor. I had just enough time to look down at it in despair and back up at the meat truck hurtling at me. The beast was upon me, horns ready to gore. There was no time to get my gun or dodge, so my instincts did the stupidest thing that they could possibly think of.

I ran right at it.

I reached forward with both hands into the fiery aura of its flaming head. I think my plan was to grab both horns and vault myself over his charge. That seemed doable—if my name was Neo and I was in *The Matrix*. My hands met the fire, and I braced for an inferno of pain. But there was none. Instead, it kind of tickled as my hands sank in deeper.

My hands clasped his huge horns. My legs were gathered like coiled springs, ready to leap. But the second I closed my grip on the minotaur, something went wrong. The beast dropped to the floor like deadweight, as though something had knocked its legs out from under it. As it fell, it dragged my hands down as I leapt. The result was I ended up flipping over the minotaur and slamming down onto it with my back as it slid across the floor, ripping up the carpet as it went. It felt like I had been riding a bicycle at a high speed, and then only used the brake on the front wheel, sending me flipping right over the handlebars.

My landing knocked some of my freshly regained breath back

out. Which wasn't the worst thing that could have happened. A part of me was glad to not be breathing while lying on top of it. The minotaur's scent was far from a fresh field of daisies.

Groaning, I let go of its horns and brought my hands up in front of my face to check on them. Even though I hadn't felt any heat, I was afraid to see they had been burnt to a crisp.

But they weren't burnt.

They were *burning.*

The fiery-red aura that had surrounded the minotaur's head now danced around both of my hands. I screamed in surprise and shook my hands, trying to shake the fiery goop off. But no matter how hard I flapped them around, the flames clung to them like a cloud of gnats. Waving my hands around didn't seem to affect the flames at all. They didn't flare up like a match when getting force-fed more oxygen, which made me wonder what exactly they were using for fuel.

I could feel the burn a little now that I was thinking about it. Not with the high temperature of a fire but the cool burn of too much spearmint gum. It was almost a minty, refreshing feeling.

Desperate, I shoved my hands under my armpits, trying to smother the fire. That just tickled a bit. The fires continued to burn, but my clothes did not. "What the hell is happening to me?" I shouted. I scrambled off the minotaur.

It lay on the floor, tranquil as an empty pond. The fiery nimbus around its head was gone, having apparently transferred to my hands. I couldn't tell if it was unconscious or dead, but I didn't think it was getting back up anytime soon.

I looked from the still form of the mythical beast to my burning-yet-not-burning hands and back again. Whatever this was, it didn't seem to be killing me this very moment, so that was a plus. But now I was going to have to ask Orion and Alex to help me with yet another problem.

CHAPTER 21

I left the minotaur and my gun lying on the floor. Whatever was going on with my hands wasn't normal fire, but I was too much of a chicken to hold live ammunition with my flaming hands. I wandered aimlessly down the pathways, lost in the cubicle labyrinth. Since all the surfaces were the same monotonous colors, they all kind of blended together. My distracted brain was struggling to keep track of the turns I was taking. And there hadn't been any hot Greek princesses waiting to give me balls of string at the entrance to this labyrinth either, so this myth crossover episode really sucked.

Occasionally I would hear bursts of gunfire, which helped me roughly choose a path. Granted, I had no idea who was shooting at whom. And even better, I didn't have a gun to participate in the shootout if I did manage to find it. But I figured it was a safe guess that where there was violence, Orion was likely to be nearby. That was kind of his shtick.

I passed an intersection of cubicles that had clearly been smashed by the minotaur chasing me and used that to figure out which way I had come from. I wish I had thought of that earlier, when I had started my wandering. But in my defense, I had a big distraction on my hands—literally.

Back on the path of destruction my formerly fiery opponent and I had caused on our way into the office space, I moved to a jog. My friends were more than capable, but that didn't stop me from feeling like I should be helping. I suppose that's some sort of complex ingrained in me by my parents. There's always more I could be doing to help. I can't sit by and watch other people work. It hurts me on a very deep level.

Feeling guilty, I rounded my last corner of cubicles and exited into the main hallway that we had spent so much time in already. A steady burst of gunfire erupted from my left, toward the lobby. The other shots had been brief bursts, like people playing a deadly game of Whac-A-Mole. But this continued, building like a roaring wave into a full-on shootout. That had to be my friends' work.

I turned and sprinted up the hall toward the battle, flaming hands swinging. The thin, professional carpet and striped walls flashed by as I dug deep to find any last drops of energy.

I was out of time for planning. I came to the end of the hallway and paused, peering into the large lobby. Alex and Orion were crouched behind the giant metal-and-glass desk to the right of the hallway. Alex's head was down, and he was panting. Call me selfish, but that made me feel a little better about needing to take a breather a few moments ago. Even the super boys were doing it.

Bullet holes scored the surface of the desk, and shattered glass was everywhere. As I watched, Orion rose to a crouch, supporting his assault rifle on the top of the desk. He fired quickly, three controlled bursts across the room to where their assailants hid. His face was an impassive mask, like the statue of Lady Justice, who's probably a cousin of his or something. There was no fear or anger on his face, only focus. He took his shots and dropped back behind the desk as a roar of bullets retaliated.

To my left, armed guards swarmed like a legion of ants. They crouched behind pieces of furniture and peered around the marble support pillars in the room. They were everywhere, I realized with dismay. There was no way we were getting out the front of the building. And if there were this many in front of us, how many were already on our flanks coming to surround us completely?

They wore the same black uniforms that the others we had seen had, but they were loaded for war. Each of the more than a dozen guards wore a balaclava and a helmet with a golden hand emblazoned on both sides. They also were carrying more tactical gear than the ones we had encountered. This was some sort of heavy response unit that had my friends pinned down.

Orion's shots hit one guard, and the force of the impacts spun the unfortunate soldier away from the pillar he had been hiding behind. He lay on the floor, not moving. One of the guard's compatriots dropped to the floor and pulled him to safety by his boots. There were no red streaks left behind on the tile. These guys were probably wearing Kevlar vests. Or, I thought, using my brain for once, a science lab that merges magic and science might have Magic Kevlar. That made too much sense.

The guards fired a steady stream of bullets into the desk to suppress Alex and Orion, but they didn't seem overly eager to rush their position. Another tactical thought popped into my head. *They're trying to bait us into using all our ammo.* It stood to reason that even if every person was carrying as many bullets as they physically could, a dozen plus would have more than two. All they had to do was bait my friends into shooting all their bullets, then it was an easy matter to finish them. I couldn't let that happen. But I wasn't sure how I could stop it either.

I hung back from the entrance of the hallway, trying to avoid being noticed. Both sides were so caught up in their firefight that they weren't paying much attention to their surroundings. That was lucky for me. If I was spotted, there wasn't a giant metal desk nearby for me to take cover behind. Killing me would be as easy as shooting a Matt in a hallway.

Time was running out. Either we were going to run out of firepower or we'd get completely surrounded. I needed to come up with a solution to get them out quickly. We've already covered my lack of equipment—I didn't even have a gun. Nervously, I licked my lips and looked down at my fiery palms. The flames continued to dance around my digits as they had around the head of the minotaur. They ignored regular movements and seemed to react to a breeze I could not see or feel.

"All right, magic fire hands," I muttered. "I'm going to need you to earn your keep now." The flames ignored me, which didn't fill me with any confidence. I was *so* about to get shot and die.

Cautiously, I edged up a little in the hallway so I could get a good view of some of the guards. This was it. I couldn't believe this was my plan. I was either going to die an idiot or probably still die but maybe look kind of cool. Slowly, I raised my right hand and lined it up with an unsuspecting guard, palm open.

Nothing happened.

More gunfire ripped between the two groups. Alex popped off a few shots from behind the desk, and my nervousness grew. We were running out of time. Who knew how many bullets they had left? This had better work, or we were screwed. My heart was pounding, and my breath was still short.

"Pew-pew," I whispered. Still no dice. I closed my hand to do a finger gun and cocked it to an imaginary recoil. I threw an invisible baseball and tried rocking out. Nothing happened. I started to feel like an idiot as I tried every hand combination I could think of.

I spent a solid minute out of everyone's notice, waving my fiery hands and muttering to myself to no effect. And yet, there was something there, an instinct perhaps, buried just beneath the surface. It was like learning to roll a quarter across my fingertips or how to shuffle like a Vegas dealer. I was doing it wrong, but by doing so, my mind was beginning to grasp how to do it right. A sudden confidence settled over me, calming my nerves and evening out my breathing. Then, from the depths of my mind, it came to me. I knew what to do, I realized. It was so simple!

I raised my right hand, flames and all, palm facing outward like I had in my first attempt. I focused inward like I do when I'm having a conversation with myself or ranting to my bathroom mirror. But now it felt like there was a new guest in the internal conversation, another set of ears ready to listen, ready to act.

"Burn," I whispered to that new set of ears. And oh boy, did it ever listen.

Flames separated themselves from the aura surrounding my hand and blasted toward the unlucky guard. The fire coalesced into a sphere the size of a tennis ball and shot toward him like a pro's serve. The aura around my hand did not appear to have shrunk at all, which directly ignored at least one law of thermodynamics. But what do I know? I didn't even really graduate from college; a demon helped me do that.

The ball of fire hit the guard square in the chest with a liquid splash. He flew backward like the ball had actually been fired out of a cannon. I'm not sure how fire behaves normally when you throw it around. In fact, I'm pretty sure you can't toss it around like the old pigskin with your pops. Even if you could, I don't think fire has weight to it. It shouldn't have been able to do that. But this was *magic* fire, so it gets its own rules.

I clenched my still-burning fist and smiled in triumph. This was awesome. Every young boy wants to be able to set things on fire with his mind. I was just lucky enough to get to.

Then the screaming started. The burning guard shrieked, writhing on the floor in agony as the hungry fire ate at him. A smell of melting plastic, burning cloth, and charring meat filled the air. A second guard rushed to the aid of his compatriot, trying to beat the flames out with gloved hands. But my voracious fire wasn't content with one victim. Its hungry flames leapt onto the second guard rather than be dimmed at all. A moment later, they were both rolling on the tile, their screams joining in horrible harmony as they burned.

The entire gunfight screeched to a halt as all the combatants turned to stare at the burning guards. The black-shrouded guards stood with their weapons lowered, cover and firefight forgotten. Dimly, I noticed Alex and Orion rise from behind their desk to get a better look as well. The screams of the two guards continued for a moment. They may have been burning, but we were frozen, unsure how to act. Eventually they fell silent, but the smoke drifting up for their corpses still gave a sort of silent complaint of agony.

Maybe little boys and their hopeless dreams of being able to shoot fireballs from their hands are much luckier than they ever know, I thought, looking down at my hands and feeling more than a little ill. Sometimes having your dreams come true was the worst possible outcome. One by one, the guards turned from their crispy compatriots to look at me. Shock was fading like the last hints of night's darkness at sunrise. Anger would come next. I decided to not waste the time given to me during their metamorphosis.

There was a pillar to my right less than five yards from the exit of my hallway, which would put me closer to the desk. I dashed for it, mentally bracing for the impact of hot lead that would send me sprawling. But no such whammy came.

"Kill him," a voice ordered, cold and emotionless. The stormtroopers may not have been expecting a guy throwing fireballs from his hands to burn them down, but they were quick on a solution to the problem.

Bullets whizzed past me as I took the last few steps to get the pillar between me and them. A section of marble on the floor to my left shattered as a bullet skipped off it, showering me with rocky shrapnel. I slammed into the pillar at full speed, turning to press my back against it. I hadn't been willing to slow down my approach and give them more time to shoot at me.

The pillar shuddered against my back as bullets pounded into the other side, their hungry lead teeth looking for a bite of me. My lack of a plan was coming back to bite me.

Farther to the right, Alex and Orion opened up on the guards again. It turned out that my presence had been accidentally useful. The guards were now stuck in a crossfire of their own. To shoot at me, they had to turn and present their sides to the desk. Some were safe, hidden by a sibling of the pillar I was using for cover, but most were caught in the open.

As my friends opened fire and distracted my would-be killers, the shaking of my pillar slowed down. I risked a peek. A couple bullets came whizzing by, but it was nothing like the ferocity of the lead storm I had been subjected to a moment ago. This distraction meant I was now free to act.

I peeked out again, my left hand at the ready. This time I gave a mental command to the flames, and launched a handful (heh) of fireballs before ducking back. I didn't get to see where they landed, but I didn't hear any more screams. I had mixed feelings about that—glad to not be a killer, but also, I didn't want to die.

I switched hands and sides—I'm more of a righty, anyway—leaning out and sending another blast toward a guard who was across the room shooting at my friends. I saw it hit home before I ducked back behind my marble bullet sponge.

My pillar began to shudder more intensely again, as the guards' focus turned back to me like a malevolent force. I almost felt bad for them. I might have suddenly been able to shoot fireballs from my hands, but that did not even begin to close the gap in deadliness between myself and Orion. I was the bait, not the Hunter.

Out of the corner of my eye, I saw the big Nephilim leap over the desk in one smooth movement. His rifle, which must have been out of ammo, was left lying on top of the desk. The hilt of his sword peeked over his right shoulder, but he didn't draw it, even now.

His expression was calm; no trace of fear or anger dared show on his face. But his black eyes danced with something primal. The eyes of a predator finally holding nothing back.

In a heartbeat, I knew my job. If I was the distraction, I couldn't waste time gawking. I had to keep up the pyrotechnics. I had to buy him time to get close to them, maybe get another gun from one of the guards. *Okay, then,* I thought, *time to see what these magic hands can really do.*

I leaned back out toward the gunmen with both hands extended. This time I gave my fiery passenger a new command: *burn it all.*

Flames leapt from my hands, and this time I thought I did see the aura around them shrink a little. Instead of burning balls, a single bar of fire shot out of my hands. Three feet long and at least a foot wide, and it burned with a white-hot heat that I felt as it blasted away from me.

The bolt hurtled toward the pillar across the lobby from me and slammed straight into it. But this being a fire with something like a mind of its own, it simply parted and flowed around the marble like a pair of vicious snakes hunting their prey. It left blackened scorch marks in the wakes of its trail. Distantly, I heard another horrified scream.

Feeling a little bolder, I stepped out from behind the pillar and blasted another lance at a guard. This time the flames around my hands definitely shrunk. The bolt hit the floor and slid across it, setting furniture ablaze and leaving more scorched marble in its wake, like burnout tracks from a pair of old tires.

To my left, a guard leaned around a pillar, peering down the barrel of a rifle pointed directly at me. I spun, crying out to my inner fire as I did. A sheet of fire leapt from my hands like a wave as I turned, its flames hungry to devour everything in its path.

A rush of exhaustion hit me as though I had just run three marathons back to back and then competed in the Tour de France—without performance-enhancing drugs. The fire around my hands winked out like a blown-out candle. The world began to fade to black, first in the corners, slowly spreading toward the center like a drawstring bag being closed over the world. The marble floor was cool and refreshing against my cheek as I collapsed against it. I needed a quick little nap if everyone wouldn't mind not murdering me for a bit.

CHAPTER 22

Headache – noun - head·ache - \'hed-,āk : a word used to explain the idea of having pain inside your head. A descriptor that was so woefully inadequate for what I was feeling. It's like trying to use the word "cough" to describe black lung disease. I was not in pain. I was pain.

My eyes tore themselves open, an action that felt like an incredible act of violence. Sleep cement released its sealing grip on my eyelids as readily as a two-year-old lets go of a dangling pair of shiny earrings. Light invaded my irises, impossibly magnifying the pain I was feeling. I noticed in the heartbeat before I was blinded by my old friend the sun that I was lying in my own bed.

I tried to open my mouth, but my lips felt like they were vacuum sealed. I was dry, as dehydrated as a trout that had spent a day on the floor of some redneck's canoe. I managed a groan as I started to shift from the fetal position I was curled into. Muscles down my back and legs spasmed in sharp protest. I let out another groan of pain as my body rebelled from my commands to move. I guess that was what I got for not going to the gym regularly before my life became an action movie. And from my limited experience, it was going to get worse. The day after the day after your first workout was always the worst for soreness.

How had I gotten back to my bed? As my brain finished its boot-up process, I began to remember what I had been doing. Visions of minotaurs, gunfights, and flaming hands came pouring back into my head. Panicked, I opened my eyes and managed to force my hands into my vision. They looked normal, no dancing flames or hint of char. Suspicious, I raised them to my head and gave them a sniff, but there was no smoke.

I sat up in bed, still wearing the same clothes I had on last night. That was okay with me. I wasn't super keen on the thought of Alex or Orion undressing my unconscious self. But also, I'm the kind of guy who keeps his shirt on while changing his pants in a locker room.

I dug into my jeans pocket, looking for my phone, stifling another groan as my shoulders protested. Seriously, how out of shape was I? This was embarrassing. The time read just before noon the next day, and I had a message waiting from Alex.

That's one way to bring down the house. Get some rest. We need to talk once you wake up. Not sure about the hand thingy.

I dropped the phone on my lap and lay back into my pile of pillows, perfectly content to lie still. I started to review the events of last night more in depth. Had we really broken into some mad scientist's lab and ended up running from a bunch of monsters before getting into a firefight with their private army? The bruises on my body seemed to confirm that we had. In the heat of the moment, it had all seemed so… logical. But in the light of a new day, it seemed like something someone else had done. And I wasn't even ready to talk about my Edward Flamehands adventure.

"Matt, are you up?" My bedroom door creaked open, and Violet poked her head in. Her blonde hair wasn't held back today, and it fell to her shoulders. Her green eyes were concerned but brightened when she saw me awake. "Heya, Sleepy," she said with a cheerful smile, pushing my door farther open and walking in.

"Hello," I mumbled, my lips still not completely limbered up. "What are you doing here?" I asked. "Shouldn't you be at work?"

"I took the day off," she said, sounding a little hurt. "Connor had something he had to go in for. But I wasn't going to leave you alone while... Meg..."

Oh, right, I had been so caught up in reviewing the play-by-play of last night that I had forgotten the match that had lit the powder keg. Shame and fear welled up from whatever part of my gut my conscience lurks in to sink their barbed hooks in me. Some of that pain must have shown in my face because Violet was at my side in an instant.

"Matt, I'm so sorry," she breathed, wrapping me in a hug. Then I cried.

I know it's some sort of machismo stereotype that men don't cry, but I really don't. I can count on one hand the number of times that I've broken down in tears in the last ten years. Pretty much all of them were funerals or weddings. But I had reached a boiling point with everything that had happened to me over the last few days. My tears were a cocktail of all the frustration, anger, sadness, and defeat I had felt since Dan the Demon had ambushed me in a lonely theater on my birthday. So much had happened in such a short time, and even if it wasn't my fault, my life would never be the same again.

The bed shifted as Violet sat down next to me, keeping her arms wrapped around me as I bawled into her shoulder. I was doing what my sisters had taught me was called an "ugly cry." I was red faced, slightly congested, and manufacturing enough tears to drown an ant colony.

I'm not sure how long we stayed there, but I cried until nothing else came out. Then I kept shaking, going through the mourning equivalent of having dry heaves. Violet held me the whole time, patient as a therapist, with one arm wrapped around my shoulders. Her other hand rubbed a spot in between my shoulder blades in a sympathetic circular pattern.

Eventually the sadness attack faded, and I calmed myself down. I stopped crying. The sniffles faded, and my face no longer felt hot. I was going to be okay. I had friends who loved me. I had allies who would protect me. I would get my sister back. I would get my soul back.

Violet must have read in my body language that I had regained the use of my mental faculties. She stopped pulling me to her as tightly and slid down into a comfortable sprawl next to me. Her left arm went over my shoulders, and she rested her head on my shoulder. Her hair smelled of happiness and flowers.

I felt like I was forgetting something. When I was a boy, my parents always scolded me for not writing down to-do lists all the time. I was prone to forgetting tasks without them. I never did learn to write things down. See, to-do lists don't help people who are too forgetful to remember they have to-do lists. Instead, I had developed a tick, a mental litany of reciting everything I had to do in an endless loop until I could strike it from my list.

Right now, the list went: buy milk, rescue sister, regain soul, and figure out what that nagging feeling that there was something else I had been worried about was. But for the life of me I couldn't recall—

Violet snuggled closer to me, head still resting on my shoulder. Well, now it was more like my chest.

Oh crap.

In my moment of self-pity and stress, I had forgotten something. Suddenly, I remembered what item four on my list was: *Keep Connor and Violet together at all costs.*

"What's wrong?" she asked in a sleepy voice, her eyes closed as she rested on me.

"Noth-nothing," I said, trying to keep the panic from my tone, "just a little shiver."

"Well, get back under the covers, then, silly," she said, reaching down to grab where I had thrown my blanket off. She pulled it back to cover us both, somehow snuggling even closer to me as she did. "There," she said with a note of pride. "Is that better?"

"Yeah," I managed after a couple tries. Her head was resting on the right side of my chest, and I was grateful that the human heart is housed on the left side of the body. I didn't want that thing pounding away right in her ear.

I mean *technically* there wasn't anything wrong here. Violet, Connor, and I were all super close. They were like a second family to me. While Violet had never curled up in my bed with me before, it wasn't like we had huge personal space bubbles. My sister had also not been kidnapped before, so there was a legitimate reason for her to offer extra comfort in a purely friend-like manner.

I also didn't know for sure that Dan's deal would try to make Violet *leave* Connor for me. I only knew that we had discussed it, kind of. My paranoia was in overdrive, and I was overthinking things that normally wouldn't bother me in the slightest. Would normal, non-brainwashed Violet do this to comfort me, her sort-of-honorary sibling? Maybe. There was no way to be sure.

It wasn't as though she had wandered in wearing nothing but wispy bits of lace, with smoldering eyes. That would be a much more definitive answer to the question. But so far, my experience with demons told me they didn't really operate on the obviously evil side of the scale whenever possible. They loved to dwell in the gray. After all, wasn't the best way to boil a frog to turn the heat up slowly?

We lay there for a while in uncomfortable silence. Well, I was uncomfortable. She looked positively snug as a bug in a rug.

I have always had a problem with silence in a social setting. I'm perfectly fine being silent on my own, but I've always felt that when I'm in the presence of another human being, it's my job to say something. That if I'm sitting there mute, I'm somehow failing to contribute to society. In my brain, the social aspect of society primarily exists to banish the silence from our lives. Or maybe I feel like people will only like me if I'm entertaining. Now that I think about it, it's probably a little bit of both.

But in this situation, I wasn't worried about being entertaining. I was trying to figure out a diplomatic way to get myself out of the bed. I didn't want to hurt her feelings. Whether they were honest or manipulated, I knew she was genuinely trying to be kind.

You see, Violet can't help but be kind. She's like one of those girls from the nursery tale, who are made of sugar, spice, and everything nice. And while my illegitimate education taught me that they're actually mostly made of water, carbon, and something called DNA, I wasn't convinced that was the entire list of ingredients. Maybe Violet was special, but her innate kindness was something I had always loved about her.

Lucky for me, I was saved by the bell, literally. Our doorbell rang, a *bing-bong* echoing throughout the small apartment. Violet began extricating herself from the covers.

"You rest," she commanded. "I'll get the door." She padded across my room, opening the door to go out to the living area.

I took this as an opportunity to get out of dodge. I threw my covers off and swung out of bed, my muscles again protesting the movement. In that moment, I promised myself I would never take working out for granted again. As soon as this was sorted out, I was going to get a gym membership. I stumbled into my bathroom and flicked on the lights.

My own reflection glared back at me in the mirror of the medicine cabinet above my sink. I had to look twice at the strange face that appeared in front of me.

My blue eyes were sunken, surrounded by dark rings of exhaustion. There was a glint to them that I did not recognize, something a little wild that sent an involuntary shiver running down my spine. A scabbed-over scratch ran from above my left eye diagonally down to my right cheek. I think I had gotten that while dodging the minotaur's charge in the lab. My skin was a little pale, behind the three-day-old stubble that was growing on my cheeks, but that was not long enough to hide the dimple in my chin that I shared with Meg.

I forced myself to open the medicine cabinet, swinging the mirror and the face of that familiar stranger out of my sight. What had happened to me over the last few days? I grabbed a bottle of ibuprofen and popped two in my mouth. I hadn't eaten in hours, but I had a headache now, and my brain didn't care about my stomach's lining when my head felt like this.

"Matt?" Violet called from the living room as she knocked on my door. "Matt, it's the police. They want to talk to you." Her voice sounded a bit nervous.

My heart skipped a beat at her words. Did they know something about Meg? Had they found her without our supernatural assistance? Or, my paranoia wondered, did they know what I had been up to last night?

"I'll be right there," I called, turning on the faucet and scooping some water to swallow my pills. I had a feeling that my headache was only going to get worse. I turned off the faucet and splashed the water off my hands into the sink. I don't have a hand towel, because I'm a single guy with his own bathroom.

My feet felt leaden, and every step was a struggle, like the long walk to my parents' room to be punished as a child. I was already on the defensive, I realized, and that would not do. *Play the part. You are worried about your sister,* I coached myself. I glanced at the broken window, covered with only a tarp, and debated trying to escape out of it. But I wasn't a ghoul, and I was pretty sure all I'd accomplish was breaking my legs if I jumped out of our third-story window.

I found my center as I approached the doorway. A slightly nervous smile, which I didn't have to fake at all, and I figured a hint of eagerness should do the trick. Violet was standing at the door with the two detectives who had interviewed us last night. Detective Jones was as imposing as ever. He was a couple inches over six feet tall, and his clean-shaven head and bulk gave him the impression of being both an unstoppable force and an immovable object all rolled into one. His mirrored aviators peeked out of a black suit-jacket pocket. Detective Rodgers stood at his side, wearing a gray jacket and slacks over a white shirt. Her golden police shield glinted from her belt. But it was her eyes that I found troubling. The sharp brown orbs watched me like a hawk. Her look set the alarm bells off in my head again and made my breath catch in my throat.

I might have a lot of naive trust for people in uniforms, but it turns out that trust goes out the window quickly when you're guilty of at least several crimes. Mentally, I ticked them off: breaking and entering, dangerous actions with a firearm that I didn't have a license for, another set of breaking and entering, some sort of possible manslaughter charges. My stomach lurched at that thought. I guess I hadn't really processed that yet. More fun to deal with later. Oh, also, arson was probably on that list.

"Detectives, have you found my sister?" I asked.

"Not yet, I'm afraid, Mr. Carver," Jones told me. "We actually had a few more questions to ask you, if you don't mind."

"Of course," I said, trying to force enthusiasm through a dry mouth. "Please come in. We will tell you anything we can." I was now grateful that Violet had hung out with me. She could help fill in some blanks that my memory did not have the answers for.

"Actually, I think it would be better if we did this at the station," Jones said calmly.

"Oh?" I asked, feeling whatever center I had found before this conversation starting to slip from my grasp. "Sure, whatever you think is best. We'd be happy to come down and meet with you." I glanced at Violet, who nodded in agreement. I could see my nervousness reflected in her green eyes.

"We only need to speak with you," Rodgers stated. Both of them were as cool as cucumbers, like cats watching something mildly interesting.

"In fact, why don't we give you a ride?" Jones said mildly.

"Am I in trouble or something, Detectives?" I asked, hating that I voiced my nervousness. My fear had gotten completely out of control. It was steering the ship now.

"Not at all, Mr. Carver," Rodgers said. But the tone of her voice sounded like she was really saying "Not yet" instead.

"We need your help filling in some holes in our investigation," Jones added.

Oh boy. Maybe I hadn't been saved by the bell. That would have been too easy. And if I'd learned one thing this week, it was that I don't get to have nice things.

"Sure, okay." I glanced down at my bare feet, grateful for a chance to excuse myself. "Is it all right if I go grab some shoes and stuff before we go?"

"By all means," Rodgers told me in that same voice. She was the dangerous one, I decided. Jones might be all muscled and imposing, but she was the brains. I needed to be very, very careful around her.

"Great!" I said, trying to sound enthusiastic and helpful instead of terrified. "I'll be right back. Just a sec." I turned and jogged to my room, showing them all the hustle that an eager brother might show to help find his missing sister.

I popped into my room and looked around desperately for

my phone. It was still on my bed, doing its best to get lost in the sheets. Like all electronics, it is contractually bound to try to hide during times when you're likely to need it the most.

I grabbed the phone and shot Alex a message, letting him know that the cops were here, and I was being taken in for questioning. I dropped it into my pocket, looking around my room for anything else I might need.

My shoes were on the floor. I slid them on and tied the laces with practiced movements. I glanced with sadness at my flip-flops lying in the corner of the room. I realized that I didn't think I would ever get to wear a pair of sandals ever again. Hell, if things kept going the way they were, I might switch to wearing nothing but combat boots for the rest of my life, just to be prepared.

Hurriedly, I swapped my jeans for a different pair. They weren't clean either, having been lying in a crumpled pile on the bottom of my closet for who knew how long. Months, probably. I make no claims about being a responsible adult or even fully housebroken. I switched my shirt for a black T-shirt of one of my friend's now-defunct garage bands, the Chronic Jugglers. I tossed the clothes I had been wearing into the back of my closet. They smelled fine to me, but I didn't know what kind of magic residue or carpet fibers they might be able to find on me, so I figured it was better to not wear evidence of a crime scene to the police department.

Keys and wallet deposited into their appropriate pockets, I came back out of my room, moving as quickly as my fear would let me. The detectives were waiting by the door where I had left them. Violet stood inside the doorframe with her arms crossed, looking worried. I gave her a quick grin to reassure her.

Not that I felt very reassured, but she looked like the end of the world was coming, and that was not helping me stay calm. Not at all. She gave me a small smile back, which helped, I guess.

"Okay, Detectives," I said. "Let's do this. Are you sure you want to drive? I could follow you in my roommate's car, so you don't have to give me a ride back."

"It's not a problem," Jones replied with a smile that was probably meant to be reassuring but showed a few too many teeth. "We're happy to make sure you get where you need to go."

"Fine by me," I lied, motioning for them to lead the way. "After you."

I followed the detectives out of my apartment, past the baleful watch of my neighbor Mrs. Sanchez from her open door. Her white hair was up in its usual bun; today she was wearing a blue blouse and a black skirt. Always dressed to the nines, that Mrs. Sanchez.

I was pretty convinced that her sudden change in attitude toward me was Dan's fault. The look she gave me as I left with the police said that she hoped I was finally getting what I deserved. In some ways, she might be getting her wish.

The car they drove was an unmarked black police cruiser. Not a classic-movie-era Crown Vic, but one of the Chargers that LAPD had secured for themselves. Like all unmarked police cars, there was a quality to it that was unmistakably not civilian. It felt rigid and stiff, even though it was a car inspired by the legacy of muscle cars. As I got closer, I realized the metal-and-plastic wall sealing the back seat off from the front was certainly part of it.

"You'll have to hop in the back seat," Jones said apologetically. "It's the rules." As though that was supposed to make me feel better. It did not.

He popped open the back door and held it open for me. I looked into the cavernous back seat. This felt like a momentous occasion. Up there with your first drink, first cigarette, and first kiss. Once you've taken a ride in the perp side of a police car, you can't undo that. It's a part of you forever.

"Problem?" Rodgers asked from the driver's door, watching me.

"Nope, I've just never ridden in a cop car before," I said honestly.

"Don't worry about it," Jones said with a chuckle. "You get over it pretty quick."

For some reason, his joke helped me get going. Maybe I was reading too much into their serious expressions. This was, after all, a very serious situation. Maybe they were really focused on getting my sister back and being professional. Maybe I was letting my guilty conscience read into things.

I slid into the back seat, which was covered with some sort of thick plastic lacquer that crinkled like my grandmother's couch as it absorbed my weight. I supposed that made sense. Probably all sorts of gross things get on the seats of police cars. Making them be easy to hose down is probably a necessity. My nose wrinkled as I tried to sniff for something off-putting. All I detected was the faint hint of bleach. Still, it was pretty gross.

There did not appear to be any seatbelts for me to use, which struck me as humorous, since not wearing a seatbelt is a ticketable offense. Maybe that was the trap. We'd drive a few blocks, then I'd get a ticket for failing to buckle up.

The barrier between us was solid metal that ran from the floor up and stopped below the headrest of the front seats. From the edge of the metal to the ceiling was a fitted piece of Plexiglas that would allow the officers in front to keep their eyes on their prisoner and make sure he wasn't up to any funny business. It was, essentially, a jail cell on the go. Not that I've been in one of those either, but with the way my day was panning out, it seemed like I had a good chance of breaking that streak too.

CHAPTER 23

From the air, the city of LA is an expansive grid that spreads as far as the eye can see in every direction. The city is laid out like a chess grand master's wet dream. The desert land is as flat as a table, and the city sprawls across the top of it eagerly. In some ways, Los Angeles is the city equivalent of getting a row to yourself on a long flight, compared to a dense urban area like Manhattan. There's plenty of room to stretch out your legs between the seats.

On the ground, in the midst of the grid, it's pretty easy to get around once you learn how it works. There are a few major interstate highways that intersect in the heart of the city. Branching off those major arteries are the distributing veins, the infamous 101 and the 10, that let you circle an area before entering the capillaries that are the streets of the grid. Navigating in LA isn't the hard part, it's squeezing yourself through intersections that were never meant to accommodate this many people that's the trick.

The Northridge Police Station was not that far from my apartment, so we stayed on the grid, moving in slower traffic, from stoplight to stoplight. The two detectives up front were silent, which could have been their nature—or a tactic to let me stew. My paranoia had a definite opinion on which it was.

I set my gaze out of the passenger-side window and pretended that I was fascinated by the world passing by. It was a little after noon, and the lunch hour traffic wasn't that interesting. It was all people in suits rushing back to their cubicles or construction workers in dusty trucks heading back to their build sites.

I was more worried about making eye contact with the sharp female detective in the driver's seat. Her brown eyes had a piercing quality to them, and every time she gazed into mine, I felt like I gave up another one of my secrets.

It took at least twenty minutes to get to the station, thanks to traffic. The station itself was a compound of several modern-looking buildings. Each was several stories tall, made of blocky rectangles with a white stone exterior. They all had that government building chic feel, equal parts fortress and trying to not look like a fortress. The whole compound took up almost an entire block of the grid.

We drove past the public parking area and pulled through an open wrought-iron gate and into the employee parking lot, which was surrounded by a concrete wall.

Rodgers parked us in a row with several other unmarked police cars, and she and Jones clambered out. My doors did not open from the inside, which made a lot of sense. Jones opened the rear passenger-side door, his large aviators back on his face. I made eye contact with my reflection for a moment before I had to glance away, I could see my own nerves screaming at me in his mirrored gaze.

Rodgers led the way toward the closest of the fortress buildings. Jones followed a step behind me, all but clamping a meaty hand on my arm to keep me from making a run for it. A sign on the side of the building read NORTHRIDGE POLICE DEPARTMENT: CRIMINAL INVESTIGATIONS. I just hoped they were investigating criminals other than me.

The double glass doors bore the emblem for LAPD pasted on in white decals. It was, believe it or not, the outline of a fiery bird rising into the sky. I guess when that's the name of your city, you kind of have to go with it.

This is it, I thought as I stepped through the doors, following Rodgers's lead. I knew I might not see the outside ever again. Which was kind of melodramatic, I know. I think they have to let prisoners go outside to exercise sometimes, so I at least had that to look forward to. I cast one last glance back over my shoulder at the brightly shining sun and the quickly heating mesa that we lived on. I really hoped I got the chance to appreciate hating the outdoors again.

The inside of the police department was exactly what I expected it to be. It might be the fact that the most accurate part of crime shows are the sets. A small lobby with uniformed officers behind the desk instead of secretaries continued over into a large open room jam packed with desks. Men and women in suits, wearing detective shields on their belts or around their necks, were moving around the office with purpose. The desks were a uniform brown particle board not much nicer than the one I used in college. The carpet was a charcoal gray that had clearly been walked or rolled on for many years. Defined paths had been carved by the heavy traffic, like miniature Oregon Trails.

There was a hum to the room that felt electric. When I was a kid, the scenes of those detective shows showed the police department always bustling with activity—phones ringing off the hook, people running around pulling files or interrogating criminals—were the part that made me almost want to be a cop. It seemed like the life of a detective was never boring, and that appealed to me. All the gunfights and chasing criminals were a plus to my young mind.

Rodgers stopped by the front and spoke to one of the officers sitting behind the desk. Jones and I stopped a few feet back, and I missed the conversation as I took in the whole room. The young woman glanced at something at her computer for a moment, checking some information. She had dark curly hair that fell to her shoulders, where it struck a contrast to her pristine blue uniform.

"Room 3 is open," she said to us after a moment of searching on her computer.

"Thanks, Cara," Jones replied. "Mr. Carver, this way, please."

Jones led us along the left side of the building, through a door I hadn't noticed while I had been surveying the pit. The long windowless hallway seemed to run the length of the building. The walls were made of heavy cement bricks painted a fluorescent blue. Every twenty feet or so, there was a pair of numbered doors. We passed the first set and stopped at the next pair. Rodgers opened the door marked *3* and ushered me inside.

The room was practically a caricature of an interrogation set from TV. A plain metal table sat squarely in the center of the room. Three metal chairs sat around it, two on one side, and a lone chair on the other. A giant mirror took up most of the far wall, and looking at it made my skin crawl. How many technicians and special agents were lurking behind that wall, ready to evaluate my every move?

"Please, Matt... Can I call you Matt, or do you prefer Matthew? Have a seat." Rodgers gestured at the solitary chair, the one facing the mirrored wall. What a coincidence that it was set up like that. What a coincidence indeed.

"Matt is fine. My mother only called me Matthew when I was in trouble," I said, sliding into my assigned chair. Jones and Rodgers sat down across from me, which I appreciated. Jones was like the human version of the Great Wall of China, and he blocked most of the mirror from my line of sight. Even if there was no one behind the glass, having a mirror in your field of view is mesmerizing. I don't think I'm a particularly vain person, but even at a gym, I find myself staring into my own eyes at times. I think I'm fascinated by trying to see what everyone else sees when they look at me. I only get the view from behind the curtain, so to speak.

"Okay, Matt," Rodgers said, accepting a manila folder from Jones. Don't ask me where he produced it from, maybe he's a magician. I didn't take Rodgers's deliberate use of my not-in-trouble-name seriously. "We just want to go over some more details about your sister, and from last night." The sharp-eyed detective scanned the pages before her.

"After we left your residence two nights ago, did you do anything else?" Jones asked as she continued reading.

That surprised me, since I thought he was going to be the quiet, imposing cop. Also, this was a terrible question for us to start with. Lucky for me, I was an English major. I've been making up stories since before I could speak the language properly.

"I wasn't able to sleep," I said, starting with the easy stuff. The trick with a good story is figuring out how much of the real world to dump into it. Or if you're a cynic, a good lie has just enough of the truth in it to hold up an initial assessment. "You know, too much adrenaline and stress about the kidnapping. I couldn't stand being in the apartment anymore. So I called a friend and went to his place. He and his roommate hung out with me until I passed out on the couch."

There was a lull in the conversation as they digested this information.

I looked at Jones. "Why do you ask?"

"Your friend will corroborate your story?" Rodgers asked, ignoring my question. "What's his name?"

"Alex." I hesitated for a second. Crap, what was his last name? He had told me when I first met him, but that felt like an eternity ago. It was something with a "B" in it. My mind raced with possibilities: Bates, Basket, Boots, Byres, Barnes. Wait, that was it!

"Barnes," I said.

Jones took the lead again. "Matt, are you aware that there was an incident of breaking and entering caused by individuals matching your descriptions that night?"

"What descriptions?" I asked before stopping to think. "Oh, you mean"—I gestured at my face—"the weird dog masks."

"There was a break-in in a residential area in Van Nuys last night. One of the eyewitnesses said that three people exited the home dragging a fourth individual who was wearing one of those masks. This was after officers staking out your apartment reported you leaving with a pair of individuals."

My heart skipped a beat at that piece of news. Even Orion hadn't noticed them watching over us. Good thing I had told the truth about leaving—kind of.

"Did they see my sister?" I asked in earnest. Obviously, I knew the answer. I was there, following Alex as he dragged the ghoul out of the home. But I wasn't going to say that. That would be silly.

"Hours after that incident, a body was discovered at the scene of an arson investigation," Rodgers continued. "The body was tied down to the floor and had been stabbed in the heart. It matches the description of the individual taken from the home in Van Nuys."

"So, wearing the mask?" I asked, feeling more nervous now. The detectives were good at their job. They were connecting the dots on related incidents a lot faster than I thought they would. A lot faster than I probably would in their shoes. I mean, I suppose the clues were obvious, but still. It's a big city, easy to lose track of a few details.

These two were dangerous, I realized, and not in a villainous kind of way. They were dangerous because they were good at their jobs. But they were getting too close to something that was way out of their league. The things that go bump in the night don't care how good of a mortal detective you might be. They'll stomp over anything that gets in their way.

"We're still waiting on the autopsy report to properly identify exactly what was found," Rodgers said, finally answering one of my questions. She looked uncomfortable as she did. I didn't blame her in the slightest. My first encounter with a ghoul had been strange, and I had a better idea of what I was looking at. I could only imagine the mental gymnastics that the forensic techs and detectives were going through to try to explain what they had found and figure out how it fit into their world.

"'What'? Are you saying it wasn't a person?" I asked, cocking my head to the side. My perceptiveness seemed to unnerve them.

"We're not at liberty to discuss everything with you, Matthew," Rodgers said coolly. "Your job is just to help us fill in the blanks. Let us worry about what we found."

Interesting. It seemed even dangerous Rodgers had some pressure points. I did my best to look innocent and meet her brown eyes. That might have been a mistake, as hers narrowed even further.

Don't get cocky, kid, I told myself. There was still a long way to go if I was going to get to see the outside again. But my nerves had settled a bit. Anticipation has always been more terrorizing than anything else for me. Now that the game was afoot, I was too focused to waste time being scared. Somewhere in the back of my mind, a quiet voice was screaming about how screwed we— the collective we, that is—were. But my consciousness ignored it. There was work to be done.

"Then, earlier this morning," Jones continued, diverting my attention back to him, "there was a break-in at the Galahad lab near the Air Force base. Three individuals entered the building, got into a fight with some of the security there, and then burned the building to the ground."

My eyes widened at that one. They both noticed it, but I was too busy being shocked to be mad at myself for reacting to that. Burned it to the ground? I thought about the fireballs that I had been throwing around before I blacked out. It had clearly packed more punch than regular fire, but I hadn't expected it to be quite that potent. Alex's message to me this morning made more sense now.

"Burned to the ground?" I said, trying to act nonchalant in front of the two predators. "That's pretty extreme, isn't it?"

Rodgers pulled a photo from her folder and slid it across the table to me without a word. I recognized the lab, but only because of some of the metal support beams that had held up the glass dome of the lobby were still standing. They were twisted and warped, but the skeleton of the building was recognizable if you squinted a bit.

Fire had gutted the building. It looked like even some of the marble and stone had melted. The second story had completely collapsed. All that remained of the evil scientist's lair was a pile of slag and rubble. After a moment of reflection, I realized I didn't feel too bad about that.

"Wow," I said after looking at the picture for a moment. "That doesn't seem like the type of building that would burn down in just any fire." They both stared at me, silent and wary, like two guard dogs. "This is super interesting and all," I continued, "but where does my sister fit in with all of this?"

"The witnesses of the break-in at Van Nuys reported seeing the perps fleeing the scene in a white van," Jones said. "The description is a match for the van our officers saw you get into with two individuals shortly before the break-in."

"You plus two other individuals makes three." Rodgers ticked off on her fingers. "Both you and these other incidents reported encounters with an unusual individual, with the same type of vehicle seen at both scenes. I'm afraid the math is not in your favor on coincidences, Matthew."

"Well, there's only one white van in LA, so I guess that makes sense," I replied sarcastically.

"I think you know what's actually going on with your sister," Jones said in an almost-gentle tone. "I think you and some buddies got mixed up in something and got over your head. What is it? Drugs? Gambling? Couldn't pay your debts, so they took your sister? Son, we can only help her if you help us do so."

I froze for a moment, shocked at how accurate but also how wrong his guess was.

Then the door to the interrogation room swung open, and a melodious voice interjected. "Not another word."

"Who the hell are you?" Jones asked.

I knew who it was before I even turned to look. Since his escape, Goldy had changed clothes. He wore an immaculate black pinstripe suit with a glossy golden pocket square and tie for accents. A brown leather suitcase was in his left hand, the golden buckles shined to perfection. His black hair was still shaggy but swept around in a casually artful manner that could only be deliberate.

His solid-gold eyes were gone, replaced with mortal eyes that could almost blend in with us, except that his irises were still the color of a wheat field ready for harvest. They twinkled with mischief, and he winked at me. He strode into the room boldly, his movements graceful and fluid, like a master figure skater. He gave off the appearance of someone who had grown up with a trust fund bigger than the GDP of some countries.

"I am Mr. Carver's lawyer, and he will not be continuing this interrogation without my presence," he told the two slack-jawed detectives calmly. He glanced around at the three chairs, which were all occupied. "Do you mind?" he asked, pointing at Jones's seat. The mountainous detective stood up with only a moment's hesitation. Goldy grabbed the chair and pulled it around to my side.

"You called your lawyer?" Rodgers asked me with a suspicious glare.

"My client informed me of the situation with his sister when we spoke last night," Goldy replied before I could stammer out a confused response. "When I tried to get a hold of him this morning, I learned that he had been taken here for questioning."

"Do you have some sort of identification?" Jones asked, still sounding suspicious, and a little upset that he had given up his chair so readily. I didn't blame him, though. Golden Eyes had that effect on people.

"Here's my card," my self-appointed supernatural lawyer said, plucking something from the inside of his blazer's pocket. He handed the gray card to Rodgers with a winning smile plastered on his face. The gold-embossed lettering read:

ROBIN GOODFELLOW

ATTORNEY-AT-LAW

SEEMLY LAW AND ASSOCIATES

Rodgers took the card and read it with a frown on her face. She turned it so Jones could also peer at it over her shoulder. The big man loomed over the table now, his arms crossed. I found myself wishing Goldy—or Robin, apparently—had taken her chair instead. I don't care if that's not very gentlemanly of me. Having a grumpy detective towering over you like Godzilla was unsettling.

"Now, then, what are you going to charge my client with at this time?" Robin asked. His eyes might still have been sparkling, but his tone was all business.

"Nothing yet," Rodgers said, leaning back in her chair. "We were just discussing the remarkable coincidences that would imply that your client had a bit of a busy night."

"Let me get this straight," Robin said, his voice changing. It was the opposite of his normal melody. Where before there was grace and class, now there was a hint of anger and power. "My client undergoes a traumatic experience, wherein he is attacked by unknown assailants and his sister is kidnapped. Within forty-eight hours, the two lead detectives on the case haul him into an interrogation room and question him without the opportunity for counsel. And this is done to try to intimidate him and connect him to what, exactly?"

With each word, Jones's and Rodgers's faces grew redder and redder. I wasn't sure if it was from embarrassment or anger, but my lawyer's words were definitely pushing buttons. They both stared at him impassively. Robin waited, hands clasped and a small smile on his lips.

"Ah, I see," he said after a moment. "You don't even know. You're out of ideas and trails to follow, so your only plan is to harass the brother of the kidnapping victim? Does your captain know you're doing this, I wonder?"

"Your client was seen entering a vehicle that matched the description of one fleeing another crime scene—"

"Do the license plates match?" Robin asked. His question was again greeted with silence. I knew they did, but I was guessing their witness couldn't confirm that. "Detectives, I don't wish to waste your time. I'm certain that my client would rather you spent your time looking for his sister instead of shaking him down."

I nodded eagerly. I did want that, or at least the part of that where they left me alone. That seemed like a good part.

"So, charge my client or let him go."

"We can hold him for twenty-four hours without filing charges," Rodgers said, her tone growing more aggressive as the surprise began to fade.

"Yes, you certainly can." Robin's voice now had a singsong quality to it that was mesmerizing. I realized that I had heard it before. It was the same persuasive mojo that Robin had used on me in the lab, when he tried to get me to open the door to his cell. "However, I think we can all agree that is really not necessary in the case of my client, can't we?"

Jones and Rodgers stared at him for a moment. They were both still, their gazes unfocused as they struggled internally with the mental whammy that Robin was putting on them. I leaned forward in my chair, fascinated. I could believe that I had the same stupid look on my face when Robin had used his mojo on me.

Jones, the human mountain, broke first.

"There's really no need to hold him," he commented to no one in particular.

Rodgers was silent for another handful of seconds, still trying to retain her own agenda.

"You're free to go, Matt," she said in fits and starts, struggling over the words coming out of her own mouth.

"Excellent!" Robin clapped his hands and bounded up from his chair.

Both detectives blinked and seemed to come back to their senses. They looked a little confused, like a student in class when the teacher snaps them out of a deep daydream.

"You have my card," Robin told them with a brilliant smile. "If you feel the need to question my client further, please set up a meeting, and we will be happy to assist. In the meantime, I do hope you will continue to do everything to locate his sister." There was something sinister in the way he expressed his "hope" that was dangerous, like the cold steel of a threat wrapped in velvet.

"I... of course. That is our number one priority," Jones said indignantly.

"And we hope earnestly for Matt's sister to be returned home safely," Robin said. The golden-eyed stranger turned to the door, and I stood to follow him. The two detectives stared at us as we left. Rodgers's dark eyes were deep in thought as she studied us both. Jones looked mad. I'd be a lot more scared of him if there weren't bigger, scarier things already mad at me. That's not to say that it was the most pleasant thing to have a giant detective upset with you; he was just further down the food chain of predators after me than he would be for a normal human.

Robin opened the interrogation room door with a strong pull. I was a little surprised that it wasn't locked. The two detectives made no move to stop us from leaving. Robin led me back down the hall and past the mosh pit of police officers scurrying about without a word. I kept waiting for someone to stop us, for Rodgers to come to her senses and come flying out of the interrogation room screaming "Stop those men!" But she didn't. We walked right out the front door without a second glance from any of the cops.

I paused as the doors closed behind me, taking a moment to soak up the sun. I inhaled deeply and closed my eyes, smelling the sharp blend of city life and grass from the little bit of lawn in front of the building. I could feel the heat of the sun shining on my closed eyelids. I would never again take for granted the ability to go outside, I promised myself. Maybe I'd even take a hike when this was all over. You know, just to try something different.

"Are you coming or what?" Robin called, interrupting me celebrating my freedom.

I opened my eyes and looked ahead at him. He stood at the side of a bright gold (of course) Mustang convertible with the top down. It wasn't one of the classic Mustangs from the seventies, but it was also not one of the horrific ones from the late nineties and early two thousands. It was very sleek and modern. I wasn't completely sure if I had even seen that exact model on the streets before. "I think I'm your ride now," he said with an infectious grin.

Sure, why not? I had no way of getting back to my apartment. I didn't really want to go back in and ask the dumfounded detectives for that ride home. My mother always told me to not get into cars with strangers, but at this point, what else could possibly go wrong? Which was a dumb question, but after so much chaos, panic, and disorder in one sitting, your sense of fear starts to get a little numb.

I pulled my phone out and sent a quick message to Alex, asking him and Orion to meet me at my apartment. I also let him know that Golden Eyes from the lab had rescued me from the cops. There had been no response to my last message, which I found troubling. I hoped he was busy sleeping or something.

I trotted over to the passenger side of the 'stang and slid into the tan leather seat. The car smelled a little earthy to me, but the interior was immaculate. Robin keyed the ignition, and we were immediately blasted with some pop music. He quickly lowered the volume to a murmur with a flick of his hand on a dial. He shot me a quick embarrassed smile. His eyes were back to their solid-gold look instead of ones that could be mistaken for human.

I decided not to comment on either of these things and buckled my seatbelt instead. He did not buckle his, for the record. That's either because he's not as breakable as me or reckless. The engine turned over with a smooth purr, and we pulled out of the parking lot.

"I live—"

"I know where you live," Robin cut me off absently as he gunned the Mustang. I sat in tense silence for a moment as the golden-eyed lawyer began weaving us in and out of traffic. There seemed to be no pattern to his madness. Reckless drivers will squeeze their cars through gaps they shouldn't because they are in a hurry to get somewhere. Robin switched back and forth between lanes for no reason. When we got onto the interstate, he slid in between cars, moving at high speed simply because he could. And if he did so while not looking at the road, that seemed to be even better. All the while, I could faintly hear the radio playing music that I couldn't quite make out.

As he drove, he dug out a tin of Altoids and absently popped one into his mouth. Wordlessly, he offered me one of the chalky white tablets by extending his hand to me. I waved his offer away with a shake of my head. I'm more of a Tic-Tac guy myself.

"So," I said after a few moments. My left hand was grasping the seatbelt in a white-knuckle death grip. "What was that?"

Robin looked at me in surprise, choosing that moment to switch lanes and cut off a huge semitruck. The teamster driving it leaned into his horn. Its deep roar sounded more like it belonged on a cargo ship leaving harbor than any land vehicle.

"It seemed as though you could use a good lawyer. I thought I'd help out," he said.

"And your help is appreciated," I told him. "But why are you helping me?"

"Can't I help another soul in need out of the goodness of my heart?" he asked, sounding a tad wounded.

"Because even human beings rarely do anything for free. I may be new to this magical stuff, but so far I'd say that most supernatural beings make the average human look as generous as Mother Theresa."

Robin chuckled at my reply. It was a rich sound, and I felt something warm bloom in my chest, like the first sip of piping hot chocolate on a cold day. He was silent for a moment, his eyes solely focused on the road.

"There was a debt to be paid," he said finally.

"What debt?" I asked.

"You spoke on my behalf to the Hunter last night," he

replied. "I am certain without your intervention, I would still be a prisoner underneath that lab. You were also a prisoner. A debt was owed, and now it is paid."

"Oh," I said, thinking about that new information for a moment. Orion and Alex had talked to me a lot about free will, and the meager portions of it that were doled out to non-humans. From reading between the lines, my take on it was that it made inhuman individuals like Robin *particular* about things. That flash of insight also told me who or what Robin was.

"You're a fairy," I said with a ton of "duh" piled in my tone.

"Ugh, please, we much prefer to be called Fae." But he grinned as he said it. "What gave me away?"

"The obsession with paying a debt," I said. "That seemed very fairy – sorry, I mean 'Faerielike', compared to how your kind is often portrayed in mortal entertainment."

"Very good," he murmured. "You've learned quickly. There is always a nugget of truth hidden in the stories. The trick is finding it."

"The stories also say you are a crafty people, usually with more than one motive." Robin didn't respond to that with anything more than a smile. "So Shakespeare was telling the truth about the Fae?" I asked, glad to have my half-completed literature degree to fall back on. "Do you have a queen? Is her name Mab or Titania?"

"You're really asking a question of me, knowing I am one of the Sidhe?" He gave me an amused side glance as he changed lanes to pass someone on the left.

"Curiosity did kill the cat, I suppose." I sighed, willing to let the subject go. We rode in silence for a long moment. Now that I knew my lawyer was even trickier than a mortal lawyer, I wasn't eager to get into a conversation with him. I might end up mortgaging my soul again. I strained my ears to listen to the faint music as a distraction from the awkward silence. It also had the bonus of distracting me from the gut-wrenching weaving we were still doing through traffic.

"Ah, a deal, perhaps?" Robin said after a pop ballad had ended.

I glanced at him sideways. My distrust must have been obvious on my face because he laughed again. "Nothing sinister, my dear mortal, I assure you. A question for a question is what I propose. I will tell you about my liege if you will tell me how you came to lose your soul to Hell."

I thought about that for a second, like a jeweler examining the cut of a diamond from every angle, trying to catch a flaw in how it reflects the light. There was nothing obviously dangerous about it, but that didn't make me feel much better. But I was oh so curious.

"Very well, Sir Robin," I told him after a moment of hard thinking. "I agree to your terms: a question for a question. You go first, though."

"I must insist that you answer first, I'm afraid," he replied. "You mortals are much more likely to not follow through on a bargain, after all. Fool me once, shame on me; fool me four hundred and seventy-nine times and I'm not responsible for my actions any longer."

A lot of the stories said the Fae couldn't lie; others at least corroborated that they couldn't break their bargains. But of course, he knew that I knew those stories. That didn't mean they were true. Whatever, I was in for an inch already. I might as well go the mile. But I wasn't happy about it.

"Fine, Goldy," I grumbled. "What exactly do you want to know?"

"Tell me the story of how one such as you became indebted to the Darkness." That seemed like a very fancy way to say "sold your soul to Satan," but I didn't complain about his word choice. I told him the story of Dan the Demon and his act of soul fraud committed in the empty movie theater. I didn't go much further than that, though. He only asked for the how. He did not need all the details of the why. Not that I knew all of the answers to that myself. But I was a little proud of myself for not oversharing. Maybe I was cut out for talking to the Fae after all.

Robin was silent after my story ended. His cheerful face was furrowed in thought. We even drove like mortal beings for a few moments, observing the speed limit and sticking to a single lane of traffic. For a guy who seemed to always have something to say, he was very quiet.

"Gloriana," he said at last. "My liege's name is Gloriana. She is queen of all the Fae. And upon learning of my debt to you, she commanded me to render you such aid as I could, and to inform you that when you have time, she wishes to meet the human that has been so robbed."

"What interest does she have in me?" I asked with surprise, too caught off guard to even worry about asking another question, but Robin didn't seem to be in the mood to gouge me for asking questions. His manic cheerfulness was nowhere to be seen.

"Do you not know?" he asked me in surprise. "The only outcome of your story will be war."

"What do you mean there will be a war?"

"Perhaps I should say it will be *the* War. The War that is inevitable. Like the World Wars to you mortals, I suppose. One side has finally crossed a line that others will not ignore."

"Pretend for a moment," I said, rubbing a hand on my face, "that you are speaking to an idiot who has no idea what you are talking about. And try explaining it again using more specific pronouns and smaller words."

"You've met Nephilim, you've encountered demons, and you know I'm one of the Fae. Now replace that with your own nations: Americans, Russians, and whomever else you fancy. It is the same. And just like your nations, our peoples have rules too."

"So you're saying that Hell broke your equivalent of the Geneva Convention?" I asked, grasping the metaphor. "By stealing my soul, they've crossed some sort of line?"

"Ah! Yes, that fits with my analogy, thank you."

"But if I had willingly given them my soul, that wouldn't have broken the rules?"

"Correct, that is exactly the crux of the issue."

"Why should they be allowed to have my soul at all?" I asked irritably. "It's my soul. I don't want anyone to have their grubby hands on it."

"But that is an expression of your free will." Robin smiled a little as he said it. It wasn't a kind smile. It was small and twisted, sick with a strain of jealousy. "If you do not want to give up your soul, then you can choose to not do so."

"So the crime here is the violation of my free will," I mused. That was beginning to make sense to me. In some ways, that was how humans defined many crimes—it was the act of forcing your will on another to make them give you their wallet. They might do it, even if they didn't want to. Dan took my soul, but I didn't agree to it. Maybe I should have called it a soul mugging instead of soul fraud.

"Yes, the violation of a mortal's free will is a serious crime," Robin told me.

"Why do you guys care? What's all the fuss about claiming a human soul, and why respect our free will at all?"

"That is hardly an easy pair of questions to answer. There are many books written on the subject."

"I thought you guys couldn't create art," I accused him.

"Oh, trust me, they are far from *art*," he said, sticking out his tongue in disgust. "The simplest explanation to why your soul matters that I can give you is this: this is your world, not ours."

"That makes no sense," I said. "I've seen the things some supernaturals can do. We're nowhere near the top of the food chain compared to what's out there. How can this be our world?"

"And yet, you've never seen a demon before the other day," Robin remarked dryly. "Even my kind lives in the shadows, hidden from yours. We live in the shadows doing our best to be ignored. Demons stoop to preying on the lonely and helpless— no offense."

"None taken," I said automatically, thinking about his point. "So you're saying there's not some higher power that enforces 'the rules' on everyone? It's a fear of humans."

"There are two sides to the coin," Robin said. "On the one hand, this is your world. It belongs to the species with the free will to take it. On the other, humans are not as helpless as they used to be. There was a time when my kind was much more aggressive.

"But your species has grown up a lot since then. One of you wrote a book called *The Art of War,* by the Abyss! You have found a way to elevate violence to an art form." He shook his head. "Hiroshima and Nagasaki didn't only have humans living in them, you know."

That was a sobering thought. I wasn't alive during the World Wars, and I was very grateful that I'd never had to make a decision on the magnitude of melting two cities off the face of the earth. But it hadn't occurred to me that act of destruction might have made an impression on more than mortal nations.

"But the rest is certainly a bit of a cold war. Tempting a human into giving up their soul is fine. Stealing one is a violation that others will most likely not be willing to ignore."

"When does the war start?" I asked, feeling equal parts dread and excitement. Maybe if someone kicked Hell's teeth hard enough, they would give me my soul back.

"I think it already has," Robin said sadly. "Even if no one knows it."

"So I'm stuck in between a Heaven and Hell thing now?"

"The Heavenly Host will certainly be involved because they can't ignore their counterpart's blatant aggression. That would be like America ignoring China's and Russia's schemes. But this will be much bigger than just those two going at it. The demons love to drag everyone into their schemes. The only thing they love more than themselves is anarchy."

Now the look on everyone's face when I told them the story made so much more sense to me. Alex and Orion weren't only trying to help right some moral wrong. They were hoping to stop a war. I wondered, when we had called up Hell, if we hadn't gotten Lilith on the line, maybe this would have shaken out differently.

But she had seemed as surprised as everyone else. And she was sleeping with the Big Bad himself. If they even slept. Gross, whatever. I didn't want to know. The point is, she *should* know. But if she didn't know, then who was pulling the strings to start this war? Or maybe she did know and she was that good of an actress.

Then how did Lazarus and the lab figure into this? Why kidnap my sister, and why did Lilith want us to start a fight with them too? But Robin said that demons liked to pull everyone into schemes. A chill settled on the back of my neck. I was worried we were being played harder than a guitar in the hands of Santana.

"What do they even want with my soul?" I asked.

"Power," Robin replied without hesitation.

"What do you mean?"

"You are mortal, this is your world. If you give them your soul, you give them a piece of it."

"So, what, I'm like a jellybean in a jar at the fair?" I asked, not quite getting his meaning.

"It is more like you're in the stock market, and you own a share of all of this." He gestured expansively out of the speeding

Mustang. "Every non-mortal faction is trying to grab up a piece of the real estate while they still can."

That sounded a little ominous. "Is there some sort of time limit or endgame?" I asked him.

"What is it you mortals say? Ah, yes, time flies when you're having fun," he said with a twitch of his lips. "I've always liked that mental picture, time flying, when obviously it actually swims." He shook his head with a bemused smile, his shaggy black hair dancing in the wind as he floored his Mustang at a red light. I still had a headache.

"Basically, what you're telling me is that all the supernatural nations have an agreement to negotiate with humans for their souls instead of stealing them, and as long as everyone follows the rules, everyone sticks to their own lane?"

"You've got it!" he said with a wide grin. "We're much more corporate than militant these days. It's more profitable for all involved." His smile faded a little as he thought about that. "At least until now, I suppose," he said grimly.

I needed to talk to Alex and Orion. I was sure that they already knew a lot of this, but we needed to have a brainstorming session. Something wasn't adding up. The more I learned, the more I was convinced it wasn't more complicated than the fact that I was new and didn't know as much as everyone else.

Something here smelled fishy. We were going off half cocked all the time. And to be fair, after every curveball that had been thrown at us, I didn't think we had done half bad. When you're out of your comfort zone and under tremendous amounts of stress, it's hard to stop and objectively think through every step of the nefarious plot you are ensnared in.

I checked my phone again. Alex had responded. He and Orion would meet me back at my apartment shortly. There was also a warning to not accept any gifts from Robin.

That gave me a miniature heart attack. Had the offer of a

breath mint been a much more sinister move? I glanced out of the corner of my eye at my chauffeur. Our serious conversation over, he was back to his reckless driving ways, cutting cars off just because he could. A trail of irate car horns followed our progress down the freeway. Maybe I had been a little too rash agreeing to this car ride. Although, if he didn't get me killed in a car crash, I had gotten some valuable information out of him. I could only hope I hadn't given anything away that I would want back later.

CHAPTER 24

True to his offer, Robin dropped me off at the curb of my apartment. I was very creeped out that every supernatural thing I met seemed to know where I lived, but I guess that comes with the territory. Before he left, he opened his door and stood up on the lip of the floor to peer at me over the top of the golden Mustang.

"My queen knows that you have some urgent issues to attend to," he said. "But she hopes that the services rendered to you by me, her humblest of servants, will convince you to give her an audience."

"Sure," I said, thinking I didn't want to anger *another* leader of a supernatural nation. "How do I get in touch with her?"

He pointed over the car at a dandelion growing out of a crack on the sidewalk. Its fluffy round mane was full, like it used an exceptional volumizing shampoo. My inner child itched to blow on it and send those seeds dancing into the wind. I refrained somehow.

"Simply blow out one of her candles and speak her name three times. She will hear you and arrange your travel."

That seemed like a rather archaic method of communication.

Didn't she have an email address or phone number I could use instead? "What if I can't find a dandelion when I'm ready?" I asked.

He smirked at me. Apparently, that was a dumb question. "See you around," he called cheerfully, and dropped back into his sweet ride. With a roar and squeal of tires, he sped back out to terrorize the streets.

After he left, I stood out on the sidewalk for a while, staring at the dandelion growing in front of my house, cold fingers walking up and down my spine like spider legs.

Just when I thought my life could not get any weirder, something new proved me wrong. I'd have to get used to using flowers as a means of communication.

I turned to head to the relative safety of inside. Looking at the dump of an apartment that I lived in was something I did every day that I came home. But in this moment, I felt like I was seeing it for the first time. Discontent filled me to the brim. Why had I been okay with living in a place like this for so long? Why had I not even tried to pick up the pieces of my broken life and do something with it? I didn't want to be a failure anymore. I wanted to make something of myself. The great serpent of depression had caught me in its coils and slowly smothered me.

As terrible as it sounds, I realized that I had latched on to the events of the past few days. Yes, it was terrifying, and yes, horrible things were happening to people I cared about. But there was something about it that had shattered through my apathy like an icebreaker. I felt awake for the first time in years.

It's sad that it took such an extreme event to kick me out of my depression. Normal people go see a therapist or get some antidepressants. Maybe a little bit of both when the situation calls for it. I got my soul stolen and my undead sister kidnapped instead. Different strokes for different folks, I guess.

I stood on the sidewalk for a few moments, staring at my

apartment building and doing my best to feed the faint embers of ambition that I had found somewhere in my chest. Those little suckers like to flare up from time to time in everyone, I think. It's keeping them lit for any extended period that's the trick. But I didn't have the luxury of letting them die anymore. This time was going to be different. I was so focused on my new perspective that it took me a few minutes to realize what I was doing.

I was stalling.

I was afraid to go back into my apartment. The whole snuggly Violet situation had worried me. Not about what I would do, but the whole thing left me feeling gross and slimy. Even talking to her was hard for me now. If she kept upping the ante, I wasn't sure I could stop her. One way or another, it was going to eventually ruin her relationship with Connor, and that would be on me.

I'm not sure how long I stood outside my own home, afraid to take the first step in. I gathered strange looks from the occasional pedestrian who passed me by on the sidewalk. People don't usually hang out on the sidewalks, cooking under the Valley's desert sun. It was perhaps the first time in my life I'd ever wished that I smoked. It would at least give me a reason to loiter without looking so out of place. Everyone who passed me—the overwhelmed young mother pushing a stroller with twins or the construction worker with his orange hat pushed far back on his head—seemed to stare at me with building curiosity. It was as if each person was warning the next one that there was a young man standing outside in the middle of the afternoon for no apparent reason. Their stares felt like they had memory. But maybe that was me being self-conscious. What's the phrase? It's only paranoia if they're not out to get you. Something like that.

The cavalry saved me from having to make any further decisions. Alex and Orion swooped up to the curb in what I could only assume was Orion's car, a matte-gray Dodge Charger, because of course. This would be the second time today that I got in one of those. I guess Orion was some sort of magic cop. Sure, that could be the metaphor here.

I hopped into the back seat to a much different experience than I had earlier this morning. This time there were plush black leather seats instead of a laminated bench. No walls separated me from the front seat, and it didn't smell at all like bleach. All in all, I'd say it was a significant improvement over my first introduction to the vehicle class.

"Hello, friends," I said with a fake cheeriness.

Alex didn't look so good. Dark circles ringed his eyes, which made me think he hadn't slept at all since the last time I saw him. He and Orion were operating with superior hardware to me, but I assumed even they had limits. Orion looked much better. His granite face was smooth in the rearview mirror's reflection. I wasn't sure if that was because he had slept or if he still didn't need it. Maybe he was the Energizer Bunny, and Alex was more like an off-brand battery.

"So, uh, how are things?" I asked. It had been about twelve hours since we had last updated each other on the supernatural war that I was accidentally about to start. I figured there was a good chance that something else had gone horribly wrong since we last spoke.

"Pretty terrible," Alex grumbled from the passenger seat.

"That bad?" I asked.

"Worse," Orion murmured as he pulled the car back into the lane.

"I had a long talk with Robin," I began.

"Did you accept anything from him?" Orion asked sharply.

"No! I don't think so. He did offer me some breath mints, but I passed on them. He told me his queen wanted to meet with me when I had time or something."

From the back seat, I saw my compatriots exchange worried glances.

"Yeah, that sounded terrible to me too," I said, "but more importantly, he sort of filled in a lot of blanks for me about the scale of my, uh, 'soul situation,' let's call it."

Orion grunted noncommittally.

"What happens if a war starts?" I asked.

"Bad things," he replied.

"He's being vague," Alex chimed in with a sigh, "but he's also not wrong. Who knows what the different supernatural factions might throw at each other? What would happen if China, Russia, and the United States all decided to *really* throw down? Take that and then add a dash of the supernatural, and you should get the picture."

Terrifying visions of magical nuclear weapons that were somehow worse than regular nuclear weapons flashed before my mind's eye.

"That sounds pretty bad," I managed to choke out.

"But that is the next hopeless situation we need to deal with," Orion interjected, cutting off my inevitable barrage of questions about supernatural warfare. "For now, we have a meeting."

"Well, I hope it's casual attire," I quipped, looking down at the jeans and wrinkled band T-shirt I had worn through my police interview.

"Matt, it's with Lazarus," Alex said, turning around to face me. His face was somber, the playful confidence that always danced in his eyes nowhere to be seen. Seeing his inevitable cheer absent bothered me more than anything else had so far.

"Wait, Lazarus is a guy? I thought it was a company?" I asked in confusion.

"Lazarus founded the Lazarus Group," Orion explained. "It is also not his real name, but the one he is known by."

"Well, that's just bad branding," I complained. "Why do we have a meeting with the evil scientist guy? Also, *how* do we have a meeting with the evil scientist guy?"

"They sent an emissary," Orion grumbled.

"Like an ambassador?"

"More like a neutral third party," Alex offered.

"Can you stop using buzzwords and actually explain what is happening?" I snapped, my patience running thin.

"Lazarus's people reached out to someone who isn't scared of us but isn't mad at us either," Alex said. I knew that by "us" he meant "Orion," but it was nice to be included. "They requested a meeting to discuss our issues. We've gotta hurry—your interview with the cops ate into our window to get there."

"This is good, right?" I asked, feeling a little confused. "We can try to negotiate to get my sister back or something?"

"Why would things start going that easily now?" Orion asked softly.

I hated to admit it, but the killjoy had a point. Also, I was pretty sure that was supposed to be my line. I'm the sarcastic sidekick, after all. If Orion could do that too, what was I even doing here? But I let it slide. Everyone gets one good line. We rode the rest of the trip in silence. I can't speak for the two badass warriors in the front seat and where their minds were wandering, but mine didn't so much wander as it rolled to a stop. My life had been moving at a hundred miles an hour for the last few days, and my body was running on empty. In the warm embrace of the Charger's leather seats, I drifted into a semi-lucid dream where all I could see was Meg's face. I hoped I would see it again.

"Matt." Alex's voice pulled me out of my half sleep. "We're here."

I sat up from leaning on the car door and did my best to surreptitiously wipe a little bit of drool from the corner of my mouth. I was really tired, okay?

"Here" turned out to be the parking lot of an abandoned McDonald's on the south side of Los Angeles. The windows had all been smashed in, and it looked like anything not bolted down had been dragged off long ago. Three black SUVs waited, parked in a perfect line. Their tinted windows obscured the passengers within, but I guessed there would be a ghoul or two waiting inside, ready to be let off their leashes if something went down.

Orion eased his Charger into the lot opposite the vehicular phalanx. As soon as he shifted into park, the side door of the middle Suburban opened, and a man stepped down. My first glance of Lazarus was not what I expected.

Lazarus was an older gentleman, probably in his late sixties. He wore a tweed suit with a dark pocket square. He ambled toward us with a pronounced limp, aided by a wooden cane with some sort of gold topper that looked like either a gargoyle or a chicken. I couldn't tell. He was about average height, with thinning gray hair. His mustache clung tenaciously to his face. A pair of half-moon spectacles perched on his nose above his faded blue eyes.

His age didn't seem to slow him down too much. He reminded me of a bulldog or of Winston Churchill, which I guess is sort of the same thing. He looked more like a nerdy history professor than the leader of some evil scientific syndicate. But he approached our car alone and apparently unarmed, which spoke to a confidence I couldn't help but admire.

Seeing the man who had kidnapped my previously dead sister was weirdly anticlimactic for me. I expected to feel a burst of passion, of anger, of *something*. Instead, I felt the deadweight of yet another piece of the puzzle to solve settle on my shoulders.

"Here we go," Alex muttered as he popped the passenger door open. Orion slid smoothly out of his door, and I hurried to join them. The three of us trudged to the chewy center of the parking lot, the hot California sun having warmed the asphalt so that it felt more like rubber than road. I took the middle spot, with Orion and Alex flanking me on either side, which as far as backup dancers go, is about as tough as you can find. I hoped Lazarus would be suitably impressed.

"Well, aren't you three an unlikely band of hooligans and vandals?" Lazarus murmured as he looked us up and down. I guessed that was a "no" on the first impression striking fear into his heart. Watery blue eyes peeked above the half-moon lenses of his spectacles, and he gave us his full attention. It was academic in a way, I suppose. You could almost see his eyes cataloging and sorting everything he saw. Absently, he fished an honest-to-god pipe from his pocket and clenched the unlit stem between his teeth. Where did we keep finding these people?

"Master Hunter, your fame precedes you. But you other two—I was unfamiliar with either of you until my men started digging. An apprentice for you, Hunter, makes sense with this one." He gestured at Alex. "But for the life of me, I can't figure out how you fit into all this, Matthew Carver."

"What was I supposed to do, stay safe at home while they rescued my sister?" I shot back, feeling my body's temperature rising. Ah, there were my emotions. The red hand of anger massaged its way up the back of my neck quickly. I gritted my teeth, trying to force my body and mind to stay calm. Lazarus gave me a confused look, as if I had said something surprising. He pursed his lips around the stem of his pipe for a moment before pulling it out.

"What does torching my laboratory and ruining my research have to do with your sister?" he asked mildly.

"What did kidnapping my sister have to do with your research?" I shot back.

Lazarus's eyes narrowed. "Who kidnapped your sister?"

"Is he serious?" I turned to Orion. The human Greek god, or whatever he was, betrayed no emotion, which was as unhelpful, as usual. "He's really doing this bit?" I asked, turning to Alex, who at least looked as confused as I felt. My frustration was building to a new level, which the saner part of my brain knew was probably his tactic, but also, my brain agreed we didn't care. "You did, ya monster!" I snarled.

Lazarus gave a sort of embarrassed chuckle, like a grandfather does when his descendants embarrass him in public and he's not sure how to react. "Absolutely not! The Lazarus Group is a health research group. We seek to heal humanity, not to kidnap it," he protested.

"That's a lot of bodyguards for a philanthropist doctor," Alex said, nodding at the three SUVs behind Lazarus. "I've heard of a mob doctor before, but this seems a little ridiculous."

"The battle against Death is not always safe. The Reaper has many acolytes," he conceded. "But Matthew, we did not kidnap your sister. That's not what we do. Why would you even think we did?"

"What about all the people in cages in your research facility?" I demanded. "Did they all volunteer?"

"Monsters are not men," he said quietly, breaking eye contact to look down at the pipe in his left hand. There was an edge to his words that had not been present before. Like in a teacher's voice when he calls you to his office before giving you your test grades back. An involuntary shiver ran down my spine.

"We were told that you had Matthew's sister," Orion spoke, finally inserting himself into the conversation. Took him long enough.

"And who *is* Matthew's sister?" Lazarus asked, looking a little exasperated. "I came here to discuss reparations for the damages dealt to my facility. We have not kidnapped anyone's sister, let alone yours!"

"Megan Carver. Same last name, genius!" I said.

"This name means nothing to me." Lazarus sighed. "I asked you to meet me to see if we could negotiate some sort of truce between us. I begin to suspect you gentlemen are wasting my time…" He turned slightly as if he was going to go.

"She was previously deceased," Orion said softly.

Lazarus froze mid-stride and turned back to us with a fierce snap. "What did you say?" he hissed in surprise.

"My sister, until very recently, was dead," I said. It was obvious that had struck a chord in the mobster philanthropist, or whatever he was, and I felt a rush of excitement.

Lazarus hesitated for a moment, looking the three of us up and down, as if trying to spot a lie or figure out the truth.

"We do have a patient with a similar condition who was brought to us yesterday," he admitted slowly after he finished his thought. "She has been unconscious since before she was given into our care, and we have no identification for her. She's a Jane Doe."

"What do you mean *given into your care?*" I asked, feeling confused but still hopeful. "Who gave her to you?"

"The creature Lilith," Lazarus said with an uncomfortable twist of his mouth.

Orion let out a short hiss of surprise. My brain exploded. A thousand pieces of the puzzle fell onto the floor, mixed with five other new puzzles, and all the king's horses, despite being surprisingly avid puzzle players, could never hope to put them back together again.

"Wait…" Alex stammered after a second of silence. "If you didn't—"

"But she said…" I replied.

"Then…" Alex gasped.

"She lied," Orion said flatly.

"Who lied?" Lazarus asked.

"Lilith!" I cried. "When she told us your ghouls kidnapped my sister and demanded we burn your entire organization to the ground in response to the insult to her!"

"Ghouls?" Lazarus sounded insulted. "I would never employ

those monsters." He shook his head. "That's not even important. She said what?"

"My sister was brought back as part of a deal..." For a moment, I saw a genuine pang of sympathy in his crystal-blue eyes. The same look people gave me at Megan's funeral. I hated that look. But I didn't let it distract me. "She claimed that you had taken my sister as an act of aggression against her or something."

"So Lilith ordered Matt to get her back and make you pay to balance the scales between us and her," Alex finished, sounding almost in awe of the brilliance of the con that had been done to us.

Lazarus sighed softly and placed the pipe stem back between his teeth. His feet shuffled slightly as he leaned back on his cane and looked at us for a moment. Even though I knew this was a dangerous man—I had seen his monster dungeons, after all—he still looked like a tenured college professor to me. We sat in silence as he pondered this new information, absently puffing on his unlit pipe. I looked at Alex to see if his mind was as shattered as mine was. He nodded grimly. We had been played by a master.

We now knew Lilith had been lying to us. Well, I guess there was a chance that Lazarus could also be lying. But I didn't really see the point of that, and if you're placing bets on "Who told a lie?" between either A: Philanthropist Seeking Cure for Death or B: The Devil's Booty Call, I think the Vegas odds would be pretty skewed to one choice.

Assuming that Lilith had been lying to us, it cast all the events leading up to this parking lot meeting in quite a different tone. The ghouls that had broken into my apartment had most likely been working for Lilith. In fact, I realized with a sinking stomach, the ghoul that Orion had questioned for information had never given up any names. Lilith appeared out of nowhere— crazy how she knew how to do that, right?—and *told* us that the ghoul worked for Lazarus.

Meanwhile, she had taken my sister and dropped her right into Lazarus's lap. For a guy who was working to figure out how to cure death, a literal undead human would be something he could never resist. The real question, then, was why? Obviously, she hoped we'd get into some sort of conflict. But what was the point? Did she hope I'd die and get sent down to the Fiery Brad Pitts and then the whole soul fraud issue would be easily swept under the rug? But if that was all it was, weren't there like nine hundred easier ways to arrange my death?

"I think, gentlemen, that you are not my enemy," Lazarus said, intruding on my mental plotline examination. Apparently, he had already finished his own mental gymnastics much faster than me.

"We are not your enemy," Orion agreed solemnly.

"Matthew, your sister will not be harmed at all. You may see her anytime you like. I'll inform my security that they are to allow you on the premises. If we manage to wake her up, she will be free to leave." He hesitated for a moment. "Although if she is willing, we could learn so much…"

"So we're good?" I interrupted, feeling a little suspicious. Don't get me wrong, this was everything I wanted to hear. But if I had learned anything over the last few days, it was that anything too good to be true was actually a clever plot to ruin everything I had ever loved.

"*We* are, yes," Lazarus said slowly. "There may be some other complications that need sorting out."

"Why am I not surprised?" Alex asked no one in particular.

"What complications?" Orion asked.

"The damages to my lab are all repairable. That is what supernatural insurance is for, for God's sake. The… complication arises, gentlemen, in the form of our protection."

"I don't follow," I said.

"He's talking like mob stuff," Alex said, shooting me a glance.

He looked concerned all over again. "He pays someone to protect his place of business."

"Well, that clearly worked well," I said sarcastically.

"That is rather the issue, I'm afraid, young Matthew," Lazarus said with a sigh. "You see, reputation matters. You've made a statement about the capability of my protectors. In order to save face, they're going to have to respond."

"Whose territory are you in?" Orion asked softly.

"You don't know?" the professor asked in surprise. "The Dragon Dons, of course."

Alex buried his head in his hands. Orion went perfectly still, the same freakish tranquility that I had seen Lilith pull off in our first meeting. I, on the other hand, had a few teensy-weensy questions.

"Please tell me that's more a metaphorical name," I said, feeling a bit of true panic starting to rise in my guts. "Like the football team the Ravens aren't actually, you know... feathery."

This meeting had been going so well right up until the D word. In the past few days, I had seen some crazy things. Things I had never imagined to be real. But dragons? DRAGONS? Ever since I was a kid, I had always wanted them to be real. I had always imagined taming one or fighting one would be the ultimate end of my heroic journey. And now, after all those daydreams, it turned out they were real? How cool was that? But you know, also terrifying, because they probably wanted to eat my face.

"It is quite literal, I'm sorry to say," Lazarus told me with the sad smile of a principal forced to fail a dear student.

I made a hand motion that started as a fist pump of joy and turned into me banging my head into my fist several times. In case anyone was keeping score, this was now the fourth supernatural race that I had managed to start a beef with since, like, Tuesday, and some of them were doozies: Hell was actively out to get me, the Fae queen wanted to have a sit-down with me, I had burned down some sort of supernatural science lab, and then apparently started a war with actual dragons. Imagine that.

"I don't suppose you could have a quick chat with the 'dragons.'" I raised my hands to make scare quotes around the word. That way no one would know I was terrified. It was a foolproof plan, one I executed flawlessly. "Maybe let them know that we're cool and it's a sort of a 'no harm, no foul' kind of situation?" I asked.

Orion grunted dismissively to my left.

"I am not their master," Lazarus said with a sigh. "I wouldn't even say that I'm a customer. They allow me to reside in their territory. But they take any trespass on their turf rather personally. Plus"—he glanced at Orion—"there is a bit of a history there."

"What kind of history?" I asked, turning to my trump card in Nephilim form.

"The dragon-killing kind," Lazarus breathed.

Orion didn't look my way. His head was bowed, eyes fixed on a random spot of the pavement, but I could tell he was looking into the past, not the heat cracks. I wasn't even sure he was listening anymore.

That's when the next piece of the puzzle slammed into place. This was never about getting into a fight with Lazarus. I mean, maybe that was a side benefit. I can't imagine the big boss of Hell would be thrilled if humans stopped dying. What's the use of collecting someone's soul when they die if no one never died? So some random chaos and destruction tossed Lazarus's way was nice. But ultimately, that was a distraction.

Lilith wanted us so focused on Lazarus and his supposed kidnapping of my sister that we wouldn't stop to ask questions. We'd dive in headfirst and start something much worse. The Dragon Dons had been Lilith's real move. Judging by the look on Orion's face, it was a brutal counterstroke. Did it have a bigger implication for the interspecies war that my Faerie lawyer, Robin, had warned me about? I had no idea, but I'd be willing to bet all of my nonexistent savings that it did.

You had to take a moment to be impressed, really. How many layers did her plan have? How did she stay ahead of us at every turn? Because I was there. I heard the same speeches. Everything she said made sense. All her stories had been stitched together by a master surgeon. I had no idea the scope of the fallout that we were in for. All I knew was I never wanted to play chess against her. But I think I already had been, but with my life instead of bishops and rooks.

"What have we done?" Alex muttered. He sounded numb.

"She played us like a fiddle, didn't she, Orion?" I asked softly.

His head moved slightly in a short nod. Suddenly, I realized that Orion had shown a fatal flaw. A mighty and feared warrior he might be, but he was at the very least guilty of extreme hubris, if not right absolute gullibility.

True, I had fallen for her lies right alongside him. But I was new here. I came from a different school with different traditions and social groups. I didn't know dragons existed. I felt like it wasn't ridiculous to cut the intern on Team Badass a little slack. But Orion had confidently led the charge that Alex and I had been happy to follow.

I'm also willing to grant that Lilith, given her position and dating habits, was probably one of the trickiest creatures in the known universe. But shouldn't that have been our first clue? In that moment, I promised myself that I would never accept anything Lilith said at face value ever again. Which, given her mastery of manipulation, was probably something she expected and would use to exploit me in the future anyway, but we can't all be winners.

"Here's my card," Lazarus said after a long moment of silence. He handed me a business card he had fished out of his pocket. It read LAZARUS JAMES, CEO LAZARUS FOUNDATION and had a number. "I'll contact you the moment your sister's condition changes," he said. Then he spun on his heel and limped back to his waiting black SUVs. His caravan sped off and left us standing shell-shocked in the heat and the dust of the abandoned parking lot.

"Orion, say something." Alex looked at our champion, who was biting his lower lip, and I could see the stress rolling off him like a vivid mirage. There were no jokes now. His laugh lines had vanished.

"How bad is it?" I asked. "I mean, everything was already pretty freaking bad right? Like, is one more shovel of awful on the scale *really* going to make anything that different at this point?"

Orion looked up from the section of the pavement he had been trying to stare through. His black eyes locked on mine, and I saw something I had yet to see—uncertainty. Somehow, I knew what he was going to say even before he said it. Because at that point, it was consistent.

Things had gotten worse.

CHAPTER 25

No one spoke as we shambled back into Orion's personal police car and drove back toward town. That was fine with me, because my brain had been rendered into putty by yet another plot twist that seemed needlessly complex but brilliantly executed. Lilith was an MLB player beating kindergarteners at T-ball. Shouldn't there be some sort of equally clever cosmic force for good that kept her in check? Or at least one that showed up to counter her plans? Instead, all I got was Muscles McGee over here.

Bad as things were, I couldn't help but feel a little relieved. At least Megan was safe. The fact that she wasn't in some evil science lab being sliced up so her molecules could be peered at under microscopes was a plus. Granted, she was apparently never in danger, and we had made things an order of magnitude worse in an unnecessary rescue attempt, but peace of mind is priceless. Or something.

By silent agreement or pure instinct, we went to get food. Orion parked outside the Olympus Bar and Grille, the very same restaurant where I had met Alex and this whole roller-coaster had gotten started. The old, squat building still crouched defiantly between two tall modern office buildings like a tough stump that had no intention of being pulled out by man or beast. After the past few days, I found the stubbornness sort of encouraging. If this bar and grille could remain in the face of eminent domain and modernization, maybe I could survive the attention of Hell. Kind of different, I guess. But also... not.

Alex raised an eyebrow at Orion's back as he led the way to the front door. I trudged behind them, still trying to complete my flow chart of lies. Alex gave me a stressed look, but I was too defeated to even wonder why. Maybe he was scared of dragons too.

Orion pulled the door open and stepped to the side to let us enter. I glanced at the dirty green siding as we stepped in. Stubborn building or not, it could really use a fresh coat of paint. I had only been in the Olympus once before, but it seemed like it was some sort of a supernatural watering hole. Maybe I'd never noticed the bar and grille until recently because I had been one of the uninitiated. Or maybe it was the state of the paint. Seriously, a little upkeep never hurt anyone.

Once my eyes had been opened to the supernatural world, the restaurant popped in a way I couldn't ignore. Even now, there was something about it that drew my eye like it had a giant neon sign. Some sort of subconscious understanding or magical marketing? Who knew? Either way, there was something about the restaurant that called to me now. It could also be because I'd skipped breakfast.

Despite all these meta thoughts, I hadn't really considered what it would mean to walk into a room full of clued-in supernatural types with Orion. My one-man army was a big deal. People and things knew who he was. Right as Alex's stressed look started to process for me, Orion stepped in behind me and let the door swing shut.

The reaction was *immediate*. It was like when the hero walks into a bar in any Wild West flick. The low hum of conversation ground to an immediate halt with all the grace of a ten-car pileup. Heads snapped up and gazes ranging from curious to borderline violent focused through me and at Orion behind me. My butt clenched so hard under the onslaught of attention that I expected my next bowel movement to be diamonds.

Interspersed in the crowd, I saw the telltale sign of Nephilim genetics now that I knew what to look for: ears a tiny bit pointier than they should be, chins a bit sharper than I would expect, and there was something about the eyes that made them seem brighter. Their expressions ranged from openly impressed to wary. One table held three hirsute gentlemen in leather jackets who looked downright close to violence.

If everyone had been carrying six-shooters, hands would have been straying to hips all around the room. I half expected the barkeep with the white handlebar mustachio to pump a sawed-off shotgun to set the mood. For a few seconds, Mount Olympus was about two steps away from oblivion. Or at least a really wicked bar and grille fight.

Slowly, Orion raised both his hands, palms out. His face was expressionless, but I noticed his shoulders were slumped a little. With a shock, I realized this last turn with Lilith was weighing on him. Instead of a looming mountain, he was more of an aggressive foothill. Whatever diminished vibe he was giving off worked—one by one, heads turned back to their tables, and conversation growled back to life like a reluctant lawn mower engine.

The mustachioed barkeep nodded to Alex, and without a word, my friend led us down one of the aisles of booths. I followed his brisk pace and tried to get my eyebrows to come back down to their normal home on my forehead. The restaurant was packed with denizens seated at the bar or in the two rows of booths. There were a few empty booths at the back, and Alex led us to the farthest one.

This turned out to be one of those dumb booths where, instead of being square and designed for four people, it was a half-circle designed for three to get cozy. It's fine. I don't even like having personal space. Thanks, Timothy Booth, inventor of the booths, for this wonderful addition to the booth product lineup.

Out of the corner of my eye, I tried to drink up the characters in the bar and grille. The vibe was a lot further away from Mos Eisley Cantina than you might think. Everyone in the room looked like a human, for the most part. A couple characters were buried in trench coats with big hats, so I couldn't really see their faces. But it was all very normal looking. Which I guess was why the supernatural world was so good at blending in.

"I'll be right back," Alex said as he gestured at the booth. Orion and I slid in on opposite sides but sort of awkwardly met in the middle, leaving us both staring out at the booth across from us. The occupants—two short, squat men with impressive beards, who I hesitate to call dwarves—blanched under the weight of our stares and promptly left.

I say "our," but I'm willing to grant that Orion's did most of the work.

Orion and I sat in silence for a few moments as I idly studied the bar some more. Everyone seemed to have returned to their own conversations, but every once in a while, I caught a stray glance being thrown our way. People were doing their best to be cool, but when there is an apex predator in the corner, survival instincts demand you keep an eye on it. Or maybe it was the supernatural equivalent of a celebrity sitting down at a booth at your favorite bar. I eyed Orion out of the corner of my eye.

Maybe more of a war hero.

"They're trying to figure out where you fit in," Orion mused, breaking the silence.

"They should join the club," I muttered under my breath. I made eye contact with a tall brunette sitting in a group of completely normal-looking people by the bar. She gave me a small half smile and turned back to her drink. "Do I really stand out that much?"

"Like a sore thumb," Alex interjected as he slid into our little half-moon booth to my right, locking me into the creamy center of our team cookie. "Honestly, there has to be a treatment or something for your face. I'm kidding, by the way. I know there's no cure under the Stars for something like that." He gestured loosely at my whole face.

I shot him an annoyed glare. But one look at his blue eyes and I realized he was forcing the humor. Desperately trying to make things look up.

"I've been a regular here for years. Everyone knows Mr. Hunt over here. So that leaves—"

"That leaves me," I finished for him. "A plain old vanilla mortal running around with very established members of the supernatural community out of nowhere."

Alex and Orion exchanged a glance that I could *feel* connecting over the top of my head. That annoyed me. I'm not short, okay? At six feet in height, statistically speaking, I'm like four inches taller than the average American male. How do I always end up the short one? The odds for that seem ridiculous.

"You didn't tell him?" Orion asked Alex.

"I sort of assumed it was obvious," he replied. "Also, why is this my responsibility? You could have told him yourself."

"Told me what?" I asked.

"Why would you expect him to figure that out on his own when he already misses so much?"

"I... rude!" I protested.

"He usually figures it out eventually." Alex shrugged.

"That could be quite dangerous for—"

"I'm right here," I snarled.

Orion and Alex both glanced at me as if noticing me for the

first time. Which I found to be ridiculous since I was currently sitting hip to hip with both of them. I guess personal space really was something you got over as you got older. That explained a lot about wrinkly old men who liked to wander around gym locker rooms naked.

"Seriously, guys? I'm already playing against a stacked deck here. If there's something else I need to know, you have to tell me. No more secrets. No more lack of information. We've got to start making better decisions or we're gonna be dead before Tuesday."

"It's Wednesday," Orion said slowly, sounding confused.

"Yeah, so that's really not much time, is it?" I snapped. "Well, what? What else could possibly go wrong?"

My two comrades traded another look. After a moment, Alex shrugged and looked at me. His eyes met mine, and he gave me a twisted smile. I couldn't even find it in me to feel nervous. At this point, what else could go wrong?

"Do you remember the minotaur with the fiery head in Lazarus's lab?" he asked.

"Yeah, I seem to vaguely recall that," I said dryly. It had, after all, been only yesterday that the magical beast the size of a city bus had tried to run me over—several times.

"Well, wise guy, do you remember how you apparently stuck your hands on his flaming horns and sort of scooped up all of his fire?"

"Uh…" I faltered.

"And then your hands were on fire, but not burning?" he pressed.

I glanced over at Orion, who wore an expression I had never seen before: amusement. His lips were compressed into a tight line as he struggled to contain a laugh, and his dark eyes twinkled with something other than implacability. It was somehow still as intense as it was cheerful. But I guess that's par for the course.

"And *then* you proceeded to throw the fire from your hands like freaking fireballs and basically burnt the whole building down?"

I realized now that Alex's weird expression was also from holding in laughter.

"I'm willing to admit that my memory gets fuzzy right about then," I muttered, feeling a little flush. I hadn't had any time to properly sit down and process everything that had happened during our ill-advised raid on Lazarus's lab. A lot of it was a blur to me. But hearing the events from Alex's narration painted it in a certain light. "What, uh, what does it mean?" I asked, looking between their amused faces.

"My friend, I do not know what you did. But you are far from 'vanilla,' as you put it. If I tried to pull the stunt you did, the minotaur's fire would have burnt me to a crisp. He probably wouldn't want to admit it, but we'd have an equally charred Orion on our hands."

I glanced at the big Nephilim, who shrugged noncommittally. He almost seemed a little embarrassed. I guess it wasn't that often that Superman got shown up by Clark Kent. Wait, does that analogy even work? Whatever, you get it.

I was so used to getting bad news that I didn't even know how to respond to something positive. I had assumed my interaction with the fire was normal. Maybe the fire was a magical goo that didn't burn flesh? Kind of like a prop for stunt doubles. But then why did it burn the walls? And other people? Or was it real fire, and I was the magic? Was it possible to get a double migraine? If so, I think I had a triple.

"I need a drink," I muttered. Both of my demonic half-breed companions laughed, and that seemed unfair.

The booth fell silent again as each of us retreated to his own thoughts. A waitress who looked to be about my age, with a badge that read "Alice" and had long blonde hair to match, dropped a trio of waters at the table with a flash of a smile but was gone before we could order. I just wanted to eat, man. Then maybe the world would be better.

"Okay, the Magic Matt conversation can happen later," I said after a few moments of pregnant silence.

"Does it come with its own interpretive dance?" Alex asked.

"You're scaring me with these awful jokes, man," I shot back. "You're supposed to be the funny one."

"Good," Orion said softly.

That proclamation of doom killed the conversation for another few minutes. Alex drained his water and looked around the room like a dragon might be hiding behind the next booth.

"So… is dragon-slaying hard, or is there a crash course I can take?" I asked after getting annoyed. "I get this is another blow to Operation Live Past Tuesday, but they've got to have a weakness, right?"

"Imagine for a moment that you're swimming in the ocean and surrounded by great white sharks," Alex said, giving me a flat stare. "Then through some sort of magical gift, you learned to speak fluent shark. Your first words in this language were to insult every shark's mother and sister. Oh, also, you're bleeding while you do this."

Seriously, where was Alice? I needed to order my third drink, let alone my first one. I would say that I felt overwhelmed, but that felt like as much of an understatement as describing the California sun as "warm" instead of nuclear. I rubbed my face with my hands. Not for the first time, I swore to bring so very much pain to Dan the Demon for dragging me into this world.

"Well, don't you boys just look down in the dumps?" a woman's voice cut through my wallow session effortlessly. I knew without a shadow of a doubt that the voice did not belong to Alice the waitress. How did I know that? Because I wanted that drink, and I wasn't that lucky.

The woman who stood in front of our awkward little three-person booth looked like she had been carved by da Vinci on his best day. Tall and lean, her dark skin shone like it had been polished for a century. Midnight hair fell across her back in dark waves that danced in the light of the bar. She had sharp cheekbones that accentuated eyes so dark that I couldn't tell where her pupils ended and her irises began. The left side of her mouth was curled into a confident smirk as she looked at Orion. This immediately set her apart from everyone else in the room, who could barely make eye contact with my friend. Strength and confidence radiated from her like a warm breeze. It almost felt like Lady Liberty herself had smiled down on our little table.

Most telling, perhaps, was that the tips of her ears ended in sharp points. I had only ever seen ears with edges that pronounced on one other person before.

The bar abruptly began to empty. Several patrons stood up and walked out, waving apologies to the bar staff, who made no move to stop them. They didn't even look surprised. Apparently, there are times where dining and dashing is appropriate in the supernatural world.

I tried to catch Alex's eye for a clue on how nervous I should be, but he was staring at the woman with something approaching awe on his face. His lips were open at least an inch, but the woman ignored him completely. She only had eyes for the man with ears to match hers.

"Hello, Cassie," Orion said. "It's been quite a while."

"So, the rumors are true—the Hunter is assembling another Hunt." She glanced at me, and my insides twisted as I felt her measure me in my entirety. It felt like my soul had been wrung like a sponge so she could see what came out. "I don't suppose he told you how the last one died?" she asked archly, looking between me and Alex.

"It's not like that," Orion muttered darkly. I was shocked

to see him looking down at the table. I had never seen that expression on his face before. On anyone else, I would say he was intimidated by the woman standing next to us. But then I realized that his expression was one of shame.

"Of course it isn't," she said in a flat voice that made it clear she didn't believe a word he said. "But I can't wait to hear what exactly it *is*, since you've decided to tear much of the peace in half. You two, Soulless and Amateur, up, up." She snapped her fingers at Alex and me with the confidence of someone who was used to being obeyed. Without hesitation, we both leapt up, and she slid into my seat across from Orion. "Now scram, you two, Mom and Dad need to have a little chat."

Growing up, I had a friend who moved to the States from Mexico. His name was Anthony, and English was his second language. I had a sudden pang of sympathy for what his life must have been like growing up here. Life moves so fast on its own. But when you don't grow up with something, you are playing catchup for so long. The jokes, the implications, the idioms—they can't be taught, only learned. Everyone around me might be speaking English, but I never had any idea what anyone was talking about.

I followed Alex to the bar, a long wooden affair that ran the length of the room across from our booth. Several tall chairs were scattered in front of it, some turned sideways from when people had rushed out of the room. While it was wild that seeing Cassie and Orion together had made people leave swiftly and in an orderly fashion, what was more interesting to me was the folks who had stayed.

A few people were scattered around the bar, pointedly ignoring what I presumed was not one but two demigods catching up in a cozy booth only twenty feet behind them. A larger table had six or seven people lounging around it with an impressive amount of empty pint glasses on the table for the early afternoon. Their whole table struck me as nervous but trying to play it cool.

One of the few things I had noticed about this world was that a big part of it seemed to work like a food chain. Everyone was a predator. You either needed to be scary or quiet. I was unfortunately bad at both of those things. But also, if you want to live, you don't act like prey. Swagger is important. The men and women at that table weren't sure they belonged here, but they were willing to try faking it.

A quick glance around showed me some lightly curved ears that resembled Alex's.

"That's kind of rude, you know," Alex remarked as he led me to the bar.

"What is?" I asked, twisting my neck back to my friend.

"I can *feel* you measuring the point of my ears against the table over there." Alex leaned up on the bar in a gap of the chairs and waved at one of the bartenders. I tried to scoot another chair over to make room. It squeaked on the floor, causing half the room to jump and look at me. Blushing furiously, I joined Alex in leaning over the bar.

"It's like the locker room. You're not supposed to look."

The bartender looked expectantly at us, and Alex ordered some sort of IPA, so I ordered the same. I know absolutely nothing about beer, but I'd followed Alex's advice on much more important decisions before.

"Sorry," I said, turning back to Alex. "But that seems a lot harder because, you know... location."

Alex turned to look at me with a big grin. I sighed. The problem with having a supernatural world guide who is also a prankster is that I never knew how serious his information was. Like, *was* it rude to look at a Nephilim's ears to guess their heritage? Probably. Was it like breaking the sacred locker room code? Who knows? Alex would probably tell a joke to the Grim Reaper and laugh as his soul was taken off into the dark.

"Who is Cassie?" I asked. "Besides the obvious."

"And what is the 'obvious'?" Alex made air quotes to emphasize his sarcasm.

"She's at least as powerful as him."

"Oh, we're talking *super* obvious. Good job, you little ear-peeker."

I sighed. "What am I missing, Alex?"

"She's a Constellation too," a stranger down the bar to my left interjected with a cocky drawl. "Poor Cassiopeia, forgotten by the mortals already. I guess beauty is truly fading."

Surprised, I glanced over. An older gentleman was seated in a chair a few spaces down. He had a bottle of whiskey and was drinking some from the tumbler in front of him straight. As a person, he looked like he had seen better days. His old gray trench coat looked like it had been run over by a truck several times. He had light-brown hair that had gone gray at the temples to match his jacket, a rugged face with a strong jaw, and a face that looked eternally disappointed. Despite his slump, his shoulders looked broad and strong in that coat of his. The parts of his hands that I could see wrapped around the whiskey glass were scarred and beaten up. He wore a large gold ring with a round red stone the size of my knuckle on his right ring finger.

More importantly, he didn't radiate the same nervous energy that the table of younger Nephilim had behind me. He gave off real "I Belong Here" vibes. Alex narrowed his eyes at the man, but I couldn't tell if it was over being interrupted or suspicion.

I'm not a total idiot. I feel like I end up defending that statement an unfortunate number of times in a day, but here we are. I am aware of the constellation Orion. When I was a kid, my dad would always point out the brightest trio of stars in a line, which made up his belt. Once you found those, it was easy to spot the hunter in the sky.

I had assumed the name was a coincidence. I knew Orion

was *quite* old, and maybe that was what you named demigod babies back in the day. People still named their kids things like Leo and Noah. But a nasty thought wormed its way into my head at the stranger's tone. My knowledge of the stars and their tales ends about there. I know more about the Hollywood ones than the ones in the night sky. Outside of the Big Dipper, Orion was the only constellation I could name or identify.

"When you say Constellation..." I said slowly, looking between the stranger and Alex, "are we talking about the blinky lights in the sky at night? They were named after them?"

"Man, I keep forgetting how behind you are." Alex sighed.

"Let's just say the last time those two were in a room together, there was a war." The stranger emptied his glass in a shot. His face was as immovable as stone as he processed the shot and immediately began pouring another into his glass. I had consumed relatively little alcohol in my life, but after my tequila experience, I was impressed. This guy seemed tough.

"To answer your question," Alex said softly to me as we accepted our drinks from the bartender, "it's more of the other way around. The blinky lights are named after them."

Have you ever had an IPA? It's like an awful vegetarian smoothie. Like someone jammed a Christmas tree that was past its expiration date into a blender and then made you drink it after it had been juiced.

So when I say that I choked on my first sip of Alex's apparently terrible taste in beer, it was because of the awful taste and not because I was doing a spit-take in a bar full of immortals.

"Do humans even live here?" I complained to Alex after my coughing fit finished. "Like our ancestors *thought* that the constellations were stories in the sky and then as we supposedly got more 'advanced'"—I copied his air quotes from earlier—"we talked ourselves out of that theory."

"That's actually a very popular joke." Alex chuckled. "I'm

glad you can appreciate the irony. Mortals have learned to split atoms and harness lightning but lost so much of the wisdom of their ancestors."

"I guess it makes sense that the Constellations would hang out in the same city as the movie stars," I grumbled, trying to find some dignity for humanity.

"Don't mock the poor boy too much," the stranger said with a soft smile. The smile softened his features from angry drill sergeant to more of an old scoundrel. "It's not his fault he was born mortal. I would say a poor soul can only handle so much, but someone seems to have made off with his, haven't they?"

I suddenly regretted thinking he looked nice.

"Not a fan of mortals, huh?" I asked, feeling my neck flush. Growing up, I'd rarely experienced being singled out for my biology, but I was quickly realizing I didn't like it.

"On the contrary, I think humans are quite useful. They're like minnows, they make excellent bait."

I was about to tell the gentleman that I had excelled at Sharks and Minnows at my neighborhood pool growing up, but a strong hand on my shoulder stopped me. I turned and looked into the narrowed eyes of Orion.

"I thought I saw you inhaling whiskey at the bar," Orion said.

"Oh, calm down, Hunter. Now's not the time. I was merely engaging a few strangers at the bar over some drinks." The small smile hit the older man's lips again. "I come in Peace."

I noticed the waitress who had never come for our drinks, Alice, standing behind the man down the bar. She and the rest of the staff hadn't batted an eye when Cassie had shown up and most of their customers had abruptly left. But as she watched Orion and the stranger interact, she looked definitively nervous, which was in turn making me nervous.

"Come back to the booth," Orion said softly. "My friend would like to meet you." The game was apparently over. The stranger ignored us, and we left the bar with our beers in hand and my pride trailing on the floor behind me like a line of toilet paper stuck to my shoe. Orion led us back to the little three-man booth that Cassie now stood next to.

"Let me get a look at you," she said, turning to me and leaning down slightly. I'm a solid six feet in my socks, but she was at least six two or I would drink more of that IPA. I certainly wasn't going to for any other reasons. She reached up a hand with long, pointed nails painted a dark ebony to match her skin. It made them look more like claws than fashion. She gripped my chin and turned my face side to side like a grandmother, but her dark eyes bored into mine, and I was certain she now knew my Social Security number and all of my passwords.

"My, my," she said after reading the tea leaves of my heart for an uncomfortable amount of time. "They really did take your soul, didn't they?"

"Well, it was really just the one guy," I said. "His name is Dan. Dan the, uh, Demon."

"You really going to go to war over him?" she asked, arching an eyebrow at Orion.

"I already have."

CHAPTER 26

Cassie left after Orion's answer. She didn't seem the type to drag out her goodbyes. She inclined her head to her equal in a gracious nod and then turned and walked out the front door. When I looked back at the bar, the man in the gray coat was gone too, but that didn't bother me much. He didn't seem like a fun guy.

We ate a late lunch. I had an Olympic burger. I don't know what sort of training or trials burgers must go through to compete in the Olympics, but this one didn't have much chance of medaling in its future. I didn't drink any more of the IPA.

We ate in silence. I don't know what the other two were thinking about. My thoughts were a cocktail of dragons and fire and death, which were shaking me. After lunch, Orion and Alex gave me a ride back to the apartment. The sun was setting into the California desert as they dropped me off at the curb. Its golden light turned a blood red as it bounced off the clouds. Alex rolled down the passenger window.

"Stay inside tonight," he urged. "Things only get worse from here."

"Don't worry, that should be easy," I promised. "There's monsters out there!"

As I trooped up the stairs to our third-story apartment, I chuckled to myself. As if there was *anything* that could get me to leave my house tonight. I had had enough of the outside to last me a few weeks. Every time I went outside, I made things worse for myself.

I stood outside the door of my own apartment for five minutes before I even reached for the keys in my pockets. I was willing to admit that it might be a little harder than it should have been. What was waiting for me on the other side of the door? My best friend, Connor, who I wasn't sure I could look in the eyes, was certainly home at this hour. His fiancée, who was now voodooed into being obsessed with me in the creepiest of ways, would probably be there. The last time I saw her she had climbed into bed with me, and that was not something I was eager to repeat. Once upon a time, it would have been something that I would have loved to do repeatedly. But while getting what I wanted, I had managed to ruin it. There's probably a lesson buried in there somewhere.

I was supposed to hunker down for the night to use its threshold to protect me, though it hadn't seemed to do a lot to stop the ghouls from breaking in. Come to think of it, I wasn't convinced my home was that much safer than the outside.

I took a deep breath and slid the key into the lock. Slowly, I eased the door open and peeked in. The apartment was empty but surprisingly clean. A few dishes waited in the sink, and the living room had the edges of a blue tarp peeking through the drawn curtains of our big window.

If you didn't look too closely, everything seemed almost normal. Which seemed to be the supernatural community's specialty. The lights were off, and I could tell by the feel that my apartment was empty. Nothing magical about that. Everyone knows how to listen to their home. You can tell when it's empty or full. The silence sounds different.

I let out a relieved sigh from the big breath I hadn't realized I was still holding. Maybe they were at Violet's. I wouldn't want to stay in an apartment that had been the site of a kidnapping and still had a broken window if I had another option. Or I probably wouldn't have wanted that a week ago. A slight draft was so low on my list of complaints that it barely even registered. I was pretty confident a dragon couldn't fit through the hole in my wall, so what was the point of even worrying about it?

As soon as I was inside and safe, I felt the last of my energy evaporate like water on a hot sidewalk. I stumbled over to the couch, and after giving it a quick sweep with my hand to check for glass shards, I practically dove onto the cushions.

I grabbed the remote and fired up the TV. The first channel was a news station discussing the strange fire at the Lazarus lab. No thank you. I skipped around until I found some cartoons and leaned back into the couch's warm embrace. At least the demon deal hadn't affected the couch. I could still trust its love to be real.

That was the most insidious part of this demonic "gift." The thing that was so gross about Violet suddenly throwing herself at me. When I had dreamed of being with her, it wasn't in a gross, possessive way. A little selfish, sure, but I wasn't a monster. I wanted *her* to want *me*. But the real Violet wanted *Connor*, and that was okay. I had been (mostly) okay with that. A mild dash of heartbreak, like a dash of Tapatío hot sauce. It's tangy but not enough to stop you from living your life.

But now, whatever made Violet want me, I could tell it wasn't something inside of her. She acted completely different. Seeing what Violet had to become in order to want me hurt me more than if she had never wanted me. It was just like Megan being alive again. Of course I wanted my sister back, but not like this.

Frustrated, I stood up from the couch. Without even realizing it, I began pacing around the couch, circling it like a shark on the hunt. A few days ago, my life had been terrible. But it had been a normal sort of terrible. Everyone understood the sad (basically) orphan with motivation issues who took a lot of depression naps and was angsty. My character arc was relatable. Now who the crap was I supposed to talk to? The stuff I needed to say to process would land me in an insane asylum.

Alex and Orion were great. I appreciated their guidance and friendship. But they weren't fully human. They had lived in this world for a long time. To me it was new and overwhelming, as if I had been deaf, and after being healed, I decided to attend an EDM show on my first day of hearing. I needed someone to connect with. But who could possibly understand what I had been through?

My pacing was interrupted as the bolt in the front door popped into the unlocked position like a gunshot. I twitched, turning to face the door and dropping into an automatic crouch. My heart belly-flopped into my stomach as the door opened and Connor walked in with Violet, both carrying brown paper bags from the grocery story.

Honestly, I think I would have rather gone another round with the ghouls than have the two of them walk through the door.

Connor looked worn out. He was wearing a rumpled red polo and a pair of dark wash jeans. The wrinkles were out of character for him. He liked dressing well. I guessed that the bags under his eyes might have something to do with it. Violet, on the other hand, was bursting with energy. Her blonde hair was pulled back into a ponytail, and she wore a gray crop top over a pair of light-green sweats.

"Matt, you're back!" Violet said with a bright smile over the top of her bag as they came in. She promptly dropped her load on the table and rushed over to give me a hug. I stood as woodenly as I could as she leapt onto me, wrapping arms around me in a fierce hug.

Noble intentions aside, she still smelled amazing. Like heaven and lilacs or something. I barely know what lilacs look like, but according to the labels of most shampoos, they're essential to the magic that makes girls great.

"I was so worried," she breathed into my ear.

Heat rushed up my neck as I blushed. Terrified, I looked to Connor to see if Violet's actions were bothering him, but he had his back to us both as he put some groceries in the fridge.

"Did everything go okay at the station?" he called from the kitchen. "Any news on Megan?"

"Ah, no, they're still looking," I managed to gasp out as I tried to pry Violet off me as she tried to snuggle even closer. It was *very* distracting. I was a little proud of myself for juggling my lies while also under physical and emotional attack. I couldn't very well tell them that a supernatural billionaire had her in his science lab because a demon princess had given her to him, could I?

"I'm sure they will find her soon." Connor turned back right as I managed to extricate myself from Violet's grip and take a few steps away from her. He treated me to a whole eyeful of sympathy. At six two, my friend was just enough taller than me for it to almost seem condescending. It wasn't, but it almost seemed so. It's the curse of taller, aristocratic people, I think. They look a certain way, even when they're not trying to.

"Thanks, man," I said. I actually meant it too. Connor had no idea what was going on. In his world, kidnappers had taken my sister, who had been alive this whole time, for unknown reasons. What else was he supposed to say? I appreciated the attempt, even if he was in the dark.

"Are you doing okay? Do you need anything?" he asked.

"No, I'm trying to unwind from… everything."

"Okay, I was going to crash early. I'm running on fumes. I didn't sleep at all last night." He glanced at the edge of the tarp visible behind the drawn curtains. "Unless you need company?" Connor is a ride-or-die friend. I knew if I said I needed him to sit on the couch with me until six a.m., he would do it. But he didn't deserve that. This was my mess, and I was going to clean it up.

"Nah, man, I appreciate it. But I'm just gonna sit here. You guys go get some sleep."

He looked at me for a moment with his brooding brown eyes, then nodded and headed for his room. I couldn't help but notice that Violet hadn't moved from my side.

"Don't worry!" she called to him as he headed to his bedroom. "I'll keep an eye on him." She slipped an arm around my waist, which caused panic to run up and down my spine like pins and needles on crack.

"Even better!" Connor turned to give both of us a smile. "I'd stay up and keep you both company, but I am about to fall asleep on my feet. If I wake up, I'll come back out." He yawned as he opened the door. "Or maybe not."

A Bad Feeling™ settled over me as I watched him leave. Well, a second bad feeling, maybe. A flock of bad feelings came to roost inside of me as my brain began to connect the dots. I glanced at the clock on the kitchen oven. It said 7:43 p.m. Connor may not have gotten much sleep recently, but all through college, I had *never* seen him go to bed before nine p.m.

Was this Dan's meddling curse at work? It had to be. It wasn't enough that it had cast a love spell on Violet, but it made Connor oblivious as well? I flicked my eyes over to meet her green ones. They were much too close, less than a foot away. I jumped. When had she gotten that close? *Calm down,* I snapped at myself. I'd literally pole-vaulted over a fiery minotaur yesterday. She was only a human girl. What was I afraid of?

It was just that her eyes were so very green, and I really liked the color green. In fact, the longer I looked into her eyes, which were so awfully close to mine, the more I thought green might be my favorite color in the entire world…

"Ack!" I said as I slammed my eyelids closed, cutting my traitorous eyes off from the mesmerizing green my world had become.

"What's the matter?" Violet asked, concern flooding her tone. It was really nice that she cared so much. I couldn't help but feel touched knowing that someone cared.

"Uh, nothing!" I yelled, turning away from her and stumbling toward the living room with one hand extended in front of my blind self to keep me from running into any walls. "I think a bug flew into my eye or something. I'm totally fine, no need to panic. How are you?"

"You're so dumb sometimes," she said, laughing. My wrist suddenly was alive with sensation as she grabbed it and pulled me back toward her. "Open up, genius, let me see."

"No, no, I think I need to keep them shut," I wheezed. "I read that, uh, keeping them closed after something runs into them for a bit is good for your… sclera."

I'm not pathetic. But there's something magical about when the girl you like touches you. Not like that. I mean in general. When a girl touches a boy who likes her, it creates something like a feedback loop that will short-circuit every single intelligent brain cell in a male's body. And if we're being honest, I didn't start with that many to begin with.

"Honestly, if you're worried about your… 'sclera,' was it? You should probably keep them shut forever." She laughed, letting go of my wrist and giving me a swat on my arm. Slowly, I opened my eyes and looked at her. She beamed at me and turned to head into the kitchen. I did *not*, and I cannot stress this enough, watch her leave even though her seafoam joggers practically demanded my attention with smoke signals and a twenty-one-gun salute.

"Sit on the couch. We picked up some ice cream, and I think today requires dessert," she called as she went back to the kitchen.

Maybe I was being paranoid. What had Violet done that was wrong? She was always a bright, outgoing individual. It was one of the things I had always liked about her. Her presence always added a little pizzazz to the room. And while she had been extra outgoing to me over the last few days, maybe it was only because it was my birthday and my ghost sister got kidnapped. A little tension worked its way out of my gut. Maybe just this once, it wasn't going to get that bad, I told myself. I dropped onto the couch and kicked my feet up on the coffee table.

"What kind of dessert are we talking about?" I asked over my shoulder. I hoped it was cookie dough. I like cookie dough.

Something soft that smelled nice landed on my head.

"See for yourself," came the giggly reply.

I reached up and pulled a gray crop top into my vision. The same gray crop top that... My subconscious about broke my own neck whipping us around. I'd like to be able to claim that there was a logical reason to turn around. But that decision was handled by the instinctual part of my brain, which only thought about two things: food and... other food.

Violet stood in the kitchen, looking at me with a smirk. She was in killer shape. The crop top had been covering a black lace bra that was incredibly distracting and only added to her allure. The girl who had been the girl of my dreams was more than dream worthy. The back lighting from the kitchen played along her silhouette, highlighting the flare of her waist as it led to her hips. Her arms were behind her back, and she was shifting like she was nervous or trying to escape from a pair of handcuffs, like Houdini.

A faint pop sounded from behind her back, and her arms started to relax and come back to the front of her body. The black bra shifted, its lace straps sliding freely down her shoulders. My stomach lurched with enough force that I was sure it was going to tear out of me and smash through the floor to the neighbors' living room below. She hadn't been trying to escape restraints on her hands.

"I just remembered!" I said in a panicked squeak. "I'm so late. I have an appointment."

Violet paused her sensual movements at my squeak and frowned. "What kind of appointment could you possibly have on a Wednesday night?"

Desperate, I cast around the apartment for inspiration. On the coffee table amongst several Chinese takeout menus was a flyer for St. Sebastian's Wednesday night Mass, which could not have been more convenient.

"Church!" I yelled triumphantly, snatching up the flyer. "I'm going to church tonight." We stood across from each other for a few seconds. She, a quarter naked, frozen in the act of becoming half naked, and me thrusting a church pamphlet with General Tso's sauce on it toward her like it was a shield.

"Okay," she said with big pouting lips. "We can have dessert after church."

CHAPTER 27

So here's the thing, and it's going to sound stupid: I went to church. I realized as I grabbed my jacket and raced out of my own home into the quickly cooling desert night that I didn't have to go to church. But I still went to church.

I don't have the best relationship with churches. The last time I was in one, it was to bury three-fifths of my family. And yes, even if one of them was now in some sort of undead situation, we did still technically bury her, so I figured it still counted.

But on the other hand, it was sort of dumb that I hadn't gone to one yet. When something goes wrong in life, there's usually an expert that people go to first. Got an ant infestation? Call an exterminator. Got a toothache? Call the dentist. Got a demon thing? Team up with a bunch of lunatics who aren't fully human isn't usually the first choice.

St. Sebastian's was a couple blocks north, according to my delicious-smelling flier. The sun had set during the latest episode of the soap opera that was my life, and the temperature was rapidly cooling down, as deserts tend to do. I hunched my shoulders and started to walk in the direction of the church, mind racing. I didn't really have a plan. When I was a kid, my grandmother had taken me to church a lot. I had heard a good amount of the sales pitch, but I'd never heard anything about Nephilim, Faeries, or dragons (oh my!). So if I walked in spewing tales of a demon stealing my soul, I was as likely to end up in a medical facility as I was getting any liturgical help.

But at this point, what exactly did I have left to lose? Maybe this was all going on in my head. I'd finally had a break from reality and imagined the whole thing on my birthday. My sister was still dead, I still had my soul, and my roommate's fiancée wasn't trying to play two naked peas in a pod with me. Honestly, a part of me thought that scenario didn't sound so bad.

St. Sebastian's turned out to be somewhere I had been before: It was the church I had decided not to go into at the beginning of my adventure. Catholic churches often remind me of castles, which I suppose is by design. However, instead of a tall steeple and sweeping sandstone walls, there was a squat one-story stone building with peeling white paint and a roof that rose like a bursting bubble and a small cross in the center. Instead of sweeping stained-glass windows, there was a small sign that backlit those plastic letters you could slide in and out to make your own custom text. The sign currently read:

WEDN SDAY MASS

CANC L D

SEE YOU SUNDAY!

Technically, I was a little early for Mass, even if it wasn't happening. But that sounded about right for how my life had been going. There were narrow arrow-slit style windows on either side of the doors that showed that the lights inside were still on. I figured since I had walked all the way there, I might as well poke my head inside. It wasn't like I could go home. The front doors of the church were two thick wooden doors that curved together to make a half circle. Without really thinking about it, my feet stopped moving on the sidewalk, right before

I stepped onto St. Sebastian's property.

I had no idea what the rules for churches are for someone like me who had their soul taken by the Big Downstairs. I know vampires aren't supposed to be able to cross into someone's home without an invite. I wasn't super clear on if or how that applied to churches. I know they didn't like crosses, so I was assuming they weren't on the guest list. I made eye contact with the cross on the roof and held it for a few nervous seconds. My eyes itched and the palms of my hands felt sweaty, but I chalked that up to stupid nerves. I was pretty sure that I wouldn't burst into flames if I went into the church.

Pretty sure.

"This is it," I muttered to no one in particular. I took a step and... felt nothing. I didn't burst into flames. Shaking my head, I wiped my sweaty palms on my pants and tried to start breathing at a regular pace again as I walked to the front of the church.

Tentatively, I grasped the brass ring knocker on the one on the right and pulled, half expecting to find it locked. But to my surprise, the door swung open smoothly on well-maintained hinges. I stuck my head the door and found an empty foyer that had seen better days. A blue carpet, once a rich royal but now faded to a lighter blue, showed wear and tear from many footsteps. Dark wood paneling ran the length of the room, with a table to my immediate right stacked high with the same flier that had been on my coffee table.

Beyond, through a set of doors that were open, I could see the sanctuary, with rows of pews and a gated-off table stacked with candles and a large golden crucifix. A long red carpet ran down the middle all the way to the center. There were a surprising number of people for a Wednesday night, given the cancelation sign. While the foyer looked a little worn, the sanctuary was well taken care of. The stone floors gleamed, and golden candles on the walls shone bright with polish. St. Sebastian's might not have been a famous cathedral, but there was a sense of pride that radiated from its upkeep.

I crept into the foyer slowly, like a little church mouse, afraid to break the heavy silence that always occupies churches that aren't in session. My grandmother always told me when I was a kid that was how you felt in the house of God.

A woman was to my left as I walked into the main sanctuary. She stood with her head bowed over a row of candles that were freshly lit. She held a long match in her hands, which gave off a small trail of smoke, spiraling its way to Heaven—or at least the ceiling.

A few other folks were spread amongst the pews in various poses of solitude. It had been a very long time since I had prayed, but I was already here. I had literally placed a phone call to Hell this week. Might as well go for broke.

I didn't go more than a few rows up from the back. I was never a front-of-the-classroom kind of kid. I slid into an empty hardwood pew on my right and scooted in a few feet toward the center of the row. It was kind of silly. All I was going to do was close my eyes and talk in my head, but I felt nervous. What was I supposed to say? *Hey, sorry I haven't called in a while, hope things are going well. Listen, I was wondering if you had a spare soul lying around that I could borrow? Just for a little bit until I figure some things out?* I sounded like an alcoholic nephew, and I didn't even like drinking that much.

I glanced around the pews, looking for someone's homework to copy. Most people were hunched forward, head down. One lady all the way at the front was kneeling, but I wasn't sure I was looking for that much extra credit.

"Here goes nothing," I muttered to myself as I knitted my fingers together and bowed my head. I stared at the scuffed toes of my sneakers for a moment before remembering to close my eyes. I squished them closed extra hard to make up for lost time.

"I'm sorry to bother you," a man's voice said softly from over my shoulder, "but I can't help but notice that you're new."

Startled, I jumped in my seat, popping upright and turning to face the man sitting in the pew behind me. An older priest or minister—I'm a bit fuzzy on the difference—sat behind me. He was dressed in a black button-down shirt and black slacks, with the high white collar that you see on TV at his throat. He was older, maybe in his late sixties, with what little hair he had left long turned into gray wisps like clouds. He gave me a warm smile with blue eyes that seemed to sparkle with something I couldn't quite put my finger on.

Well, that was fast, I thought with a suspicious glance to the ceiling.

"Uh, yes, sir?" I replied, my tone rising on *sir* to show that I wasn't really sure how to address him.

"Usually folks call me Father Bryant. Sir was my father," he told me with a cheerful wink. "What do they call you?"

"Matt, mostly."

"Well, Matt Mostly, I'm glad to meet you. What brings you to our humble sanctuary even when service is canceled?"

"I didn't know it was canceled before I got here," I muttered weakly. Now that I had a real-life priest in front of me, I didn't exactly know what to say. I wasn't really ready to get the Emily Rose exorcism treatment, but also, I was pretty desperate.

"Looking for a Wednesday night Mass, then?" he asked in a gentle voice.

I grumbled in my head about wise old men and their ability to see beyond simple explanations. I was a better liar than this. But lying to a priest while I could literally see a life-size crucifix did not seem like the smartest of life choices. Especially since my eternal soul was missing. I wasn't trying to find a tenth ring to Dante's Inferno.

"I'm not sure," I admitted. Why did I suddenly feel like a

teenager caught sneaking out after curfew? "I think I'm in some trouble, and I don't really know who can help."

"If you are looking for help, you've come to a house that specializes in it, Mostly Matt. What sort of trouble are you in?"

I couldn't help but appreciate Father Bryant. He had spotted me, a kid in his sanctuary who he didn't recognize, and gone out of his way to check to see if I needed help. That wasn't how most people were. But now I had to figure out how to answer his well-meaning question.

"I met a demon about a week ago, and he tried to buy my soul. I turned him down! But then he sort of had a breakdown and forged my signature, and now I think... Uh, the Devil thinks he owns my soul, but he does not! And I don't know what to do." I opted for a panicked thousand-mile-an-hour explanation.

With each word, the grandfatherly smile faded from the corners of his mouth, and the sparkle in his eye turned to something else.

"You sell your soul to the Devil and come here for shelter?" he hissed. "You spit upon the Lamb of God and come crawling here for aid?" His voice, which had been a polite whisper, grew to an enraged shout. Red flush began to creep up his neck as he worked himself into a fury.

I am not sure what I expected.

Heads started to pop up from silent prayer and turn our way like a bunch of religious prairie dogs. I stared at the father in shock, my mouth agape. Despite my misgivings, I had been expecting a more excited, prodigal-son sort of reception from the warm welcome I had been given.

"You reject the cornerstone and dare to enter the house it was built upon?" He was full-on yelling now, and the acoustics of the sanctuary magnified his rage magnificently.

I was caught off guard, but my own irritation bubbled to meet his energy. I had been taken advantage of, beaten up, and threatened enough for one week. My patience had reached its boiling point. Instead of help, all there was here was more disappointment and snap judgment.

"Oh, that's my mistake, then," I snapped. "I was looking for a magic castle and got confused." Not my best work, but I promised myself after I came up with a better comeback in the shower tomorrow morning, I would come back and tell him that. If I wasn't dead by then.

I slid along my pew back into the middle aisle and stormed back to the entrance. I could feel the eyes of the entire room on me as I stomped. It was like a great judgmental weight, a spiritual squat bar settling on my shoulders. All of this, I thought, was incredibly unfair. The tear that worked its way free of my left eye and started to run down my cheek agreed with me too. I asked it.

I made my way out of the sanctuary and back into the antechamber room with the deep-blue carpet. I intended to blow my way through the big wooden doors and back out into the night where I seemed to belong, but a firm hand grabbed my upper arm.

A week of violence, lack of sleep, and bursting frustration did not leave me in a mental place to react to surprising physical contact well. I spun, and my hands balled into fists of their own accord. I was so ready to let that sanctimonious father have a piece of my frustration, frail old man or not. My flight-or-fright reaction was all out of flight.

But the man who grabbed me by the arm wasn't Father Bryant. For a second, I thought he might be, as he wore the same black on black with the fancy collar. But that was where the similarities ended. This man was probably half the old man's age. Tall, dark, and whipcord lean, his shaved head had to be waxed with how much light was reflecting off it. He had thick horn-rimmed glasses with circular lenses and a severe face like he had just eaten something sour.

Oh great, I thought. They sent the younger, more mobile priest for round two.

Despite my assumption, the tall priest immediately released my arm as I turned, and for a moment, his sourpuss expression lightened.

"I'm sorry. I didn't mean to startle you," he said, his voice thick with an almost British accent. Only then did I realize that he was staring at my balled-up fists. "I couldn't help but overhear—"

"I don't want any trouble," I said as I tried to step around him toward the door. "I'll leave, and you can skip the lecture."

"Forgive me," he said, scooting to block my path. "But I think I might be a better audience than Father Bryant." He pointed down a side hall, away from the sanctuary. "My office is right there. Talk to me for five minutes. No lecture, I promise."

I hesitated. My emotions were pretty riled up. I had been skeptical about coming to church for help. Father Bryant's reaction had basically confirmed my bias. But I'd be an idiot to walk away from anyone offering help at this point.

"Five minutes," I grumbled.

The tall priest smiled, and his severe face relaxed a little, like wax melting or the first thaw of spring. Maybe he wasn't sour, I realized, just nervous.

"Come with me," he said and led me down the hallway.

True to his word, his office was three doors down. The sign outside the door said REV. GERALD PIKE, and the next thing I knew, I was sitting in an oversized leather chair across from its twin on the other side of a thick wooden desk. The room looked like it had been hit by some sort of literary tornado, but instead of destruction, it scattered books and papers everywhere. The cramped office had the pleasant musk of an old library, a smell of disintegrating binding glue and fading knowledge. Each of the four walls had as many bookshelves as could be crammed on it, and each bookshelf was stuffed to the brim with books, even though I vaguely remembered my grandmother telling me gluttony was a major sin.

There was even a pile of books at my feet, which the reverend directed me to stack there to make room on the guest chair to sit. Gerald shifted some papers from his desk and leaned forward with his hands clasped. He focused his dark eyes on me from behind his circular lenses and smiled again.

"It would probably be best if you started from the beginning," he said.

"Father Pike, are you sure that you—"

"Please, call me Father Gerald," he interrupted, waving away my formality with an off-handed gesture. "Not that different, I know, but still less formal." He laughed, seeing the confused look on my face.

Well, shoot, this seemed like the best clerical audience I was ever going to get, so I decided to swing for the rafters. I told him everything: from Dan the Demon defrauding my soul to Megan coming back from the dead to accidentally prank-calling Lilith, to my fairy—sorry, Fae—lawyer, the dragons, and everything in between.

As I talked, his eyebrows rose, but he never interrupted or spoke. He just listened. He didn't look at me like I was crazy or dirty. He just listened.

"So in conclusion, uh, forgive me, Father, for I have sinned?" I said uncertainly as I finished my summary.

Father Gerald gave a short laugh, which was the first sound he had made since I started talking. "I'm grateful that you're aware of that." He chuckled. "But that's not as relevant to this particular story."

He reached over his shoulder to the shelf behind him and produced a silver canteen that he poured into a pair of glasses that were sitting on another shelf a level up.

"It's only water, I'm afraid, but the canteen keeps it nice and cool." He finished pouring and passed me a glass. "Cheers," he said, and we both sipped some in silence. The water was indeed cool and refreshing after talking my head off for the last fifteen minutes.

After finishing his drink, Gerald pulled his glasses off his face with deliberate movements and folded them on his desk. He rubbed his face with both hands, and a quiet sigh emerged from behind his hands. After a few seconds, he pulled his glasses back on and peered into my eyes with a dark-brown stare.

"I don't suppose there's any chance you're insane, that you hallucinated the whole thing?"

"I don't think so," I replied.

"Yeah, I don't think so either," he muttered.

"So you believe me?" I demanded. My head felt like it was spinning. Father Gerald's and Father Bryant's responses to my story were so different that I couldn't believe I was in the same place. How was it possible that two men could have such different responses while wearing the same uniform?

"I do," he said with a firm nod.

"Why?" I blurted. I meant to ask him something more along the line of "What do I do?" but my heart needed to know some things more than my head did, I guess.

"You mean, why do I believe you when one of my peers practically cast you out into darkness?" he asked in a dry voice. "The funny thing about faith, Matt, is that it is supposed to be the belief in things unseen. But it turns out, that is an awfully hard thing."

"I'm not following."

"Don't judge Father Bryant too harshly," Father Gerald said in a soft tone. "Remember what it was like before you saw some of the things that are waiting in the dark."

I thought I understood what he was saying. If you had told

me a fraction of my own story a week ago, I would have thought you were a raving lunatic. But I didn't understand why the priest's reaction had been so poor.

"I'm confused. Aren't you guys supposed to believe in Satan and demons and stuff?" I asked. "Seems like part of the requirements from what I know."

Father Gerald chuckled again and nodded. "Did you know the Catholic Church has ceremonies for exorcisms of people, animals, and places?" he asked. "Do you know how rarely a priest is ever asked to perform one and how rarely one of those results in something you can see? Father Bryant has been serving the Church his whole life, and I promise you that he has never come face-to-face with a real demon. Until you do, demons are almost more of an idea than a monster. Do you know what the best strategy to defeat humanity is for Hell?"

"Hold us down and eat our faces off?" I guessed.

"That's way too much work. All they have to do is wait until we forget. Father Time fights their battles for them." He waved a hand to his dusty library. "These books are full of things we've already mostly forgotten. I only read them because I've caught a glimpse of the fangs lurking just outside our common knowledge."

"Have you performed an exorcism that was real?" I asked, feeling a burst of hope. "Can you exorcise me?"

"I have never performed one," he said while giving me a sad smile. "But you can probably tell by my accent that I was not born here." He gave me a small smile. "I grew up in Uganda. Before I came to the States to pursue seminary, I saw many things my peers would not believe.

"But for you, I'm afraid an exorcism would be worthless. You're not possessed. You could probably not bear to come into this building if you were, let alone drink that." He pointed at the water he had served me moments ago.

"Holy water?" I guessed.

"That is real, by the way." He gave me a slightly sheepish grin. "Never hurts to be too careful."

"So I'm not possessed. I guess that makes sense. Is there like a reverse-exorcism vacuum-cleaner spell where I can suck my soul back into my body?"

"I... don't know," he admitted with a sigh, leaning back in his seat. "I haven't read all these books yet. I only recently inherited this office when my mentor retired. I've never heard a story even a little like yours."

We were both quiet for a moment. My initial optimism from meeting Father Gerald was fading quickly. While I appreciated a sympathetic ear, I had a bad feeling that this trip wasn't going to get me any closer to finding a solution.

"Then what am I supposed to do?" I asked quietly.

"I... don't know," he admitted with a gentle sigh. "I wish I could give you an easy answer. But you're definitely outside of what little knowledge I have." His eyes moved from me to look around the room almost wistfully. "I'll start researching right away. There might be something here; I just need to find it."

Once again "mights" and "could-bes" were the best I was going to get. I washed down the bitter taste of disappointment with another swig of holy water, which honestly was a better chaser than I expected.

"Don't despair, Matt," he said, noticing my disappointment. "I won't forget you. Have a little faith and wait."

I didn't want to be a cynic, but it sort of felt like I had a friend who worked at the DMV who had a lot more trust in the system than I did. No matter how many promises you made me, I knew it was going to take longer and cost more than I wanted it to.

CHAPTER 28

After exchanging phone numbers with Father Gerald and escaping his endless waves of promises to scour his library, I snuck back out to the front of the church. I appreciated the enthusiasm of the young priest, but the undertow of false hope was not something I was trying to swim in too much. I'd just dangle a toe or two and see if anything nibbled. Father Bryant gave me a glare from the safety of the sanctuary, and I gave him a cheery wave, because I'm a people person.

The sun was completely down behind the ridge of the mountains, and the dark desert night had settled on the city. I mean sort of. LA's light pollution is a robust wall keeping the night at bay. Growing up, I had always heard people complain about not being able to see the stars at night in the city. Now that I knew more about constellations, I wasn't so sure that was a bad thing. In some ways, it made me appreciate light pollution in a new way. Man's defiant stance against the outer darkness or something.

Besides, the stars weren't all impossible to see, I realized as I squinted at the night sky. I could barely make out the three stars in a line that made up Orion's belt. I'm not sure I had ever seen

Orion even wear a belt, come to think of it.

I chuckled, thinking about how insane it was that I was now sort-of friends, or at least comrade-in-arms with the guy the stars were aligned for. Everyone claims to know a celebrity with a star on the Walk of Fame in Hollywood. My guy had a whole constellation.

Despite that, he was still pretty easy to have a conversation with. Sure, he was a little intense. But earlier today, he had tried to tell me a joke. It wasn't a good one, but lots of intense people weren't funny. Humor is for weak and scared people like me. In fact, now that I was thinking about "Things Orion Had Told Me" earlier tonight, he clearly said to me: "Stay inside."

It was right about then, as I stared at the night's sky—the sky that was currently happening tonight—that I suddenly got another Bad Feeling™. One of those bad feelings that starts at the back of your skull and floods down your whole body like an avalanche of fear. The hairs on the back of my neck stood at attention like privates on parade. I couldn't shake the feeling I was being watched.

I had been so reactionary, running out of my home chased by a problem that was unavoidable. Orion's command hadn't even crossed my mind as my feet crossed the doorstep. And here I was—outside at night. But I would berate myself later. Realizing my mistake wasn't the same as coming up with a solution to my problem. I needed to be proactive.

Violet had threatened me with "dessert" after church, and I was quite sure that she had a different sort of use for ladyfingers in mind than tiramisu. My home was not safe, even if it was physically safer for my body. Even though it was a bad idea, I didn't have any better ones, so I started walking home at a brisk trot.

This whole situation stunk to me. After several days of chaos, I felt like I was starting to develop a tiny amount of instinct. So far, every time I was in a bad situation, it turned out that someone was manipulating the circumstances. Odds seemed high that this was a continuing trend.

I did the only smart thing I'd done in a week and called for backup.

"Matt, what's wrong?" Alex panted into the phone before the first ring of the phone even finished. He sounded like he had just woken up. I could practically picture him shooting bolt upright.

"I think I've been played," I said, not wanting to waste time. I felt like a boogeyman was going to jump out and nab me at any second. "I'm outside, a few blocks from home. But I don't think I'm going to make it back if I try."

"Falling Stars!" he swore. "I'll call Orion. Where are you now?" I shared my location with him, and he told me not to move before hanging up. I felt a little relief knowing my own big bad wolf was going to come get me. Now all I had to do was survive the next fifteen minutes or so. I stopped my power walk and lounged against a light pole, trying to catch my breath.

I looked up and down the sidewalks of the four-way intersection in the city suburb that I was stranded in. Everything looked normal. A fair number of homes had their lights still on, though we had entered the hours where schoolchildren and people with early jobs were already in bed.

As my heart rate slowed to normal levels, I continued to look up and down the intersection to make sure no one was approaching. After each check, I would whip out my phone to see if time had magically started running faster and my backup was almost here. I even started to feel a little foolish. I was going to look so stupid if this was a false alarm.

I glanced up and down the street once again and saw no one. It was a perfectly quiet, empty street in a perfectly quiet, safe neighborhood.

So naturally, that's where the attack happened.

I looked up from my phone and saw a figure walking down the street from the direction I had come, and my heart fell. The distant silhouette was walking slowly and showed no signs of aggression, but every instinct in my body was screaming to run.

My feet didn't even ask for permission, they turned, and my whole body gladly went with them. We didn't go far. I took fewer than five steps before I realized there was another silhouetted figure waiting for me in that direction. I spun again, looking down each of the streets of the intersection, and each had an approaching figure in the unnatural dusk created by night and light pollution's battle for dominance.

Helplessly, I stood in the center of the intersection in a pool of light from the streetlights and turned to face my pursuers. I was boxed in from every side. There was nowhere to run. Why did I not ask for a gun? Would I ever see boobs again? That last question was either the most or least relevant but only by a little.

Picking a direction arbitrarily, I turned and stared at one of the approaching figures. They seemed to be taking their time, closing in on me. Maybe they enjoyed the hunt. As my stalkers drew closer, I realized I recognized the form of these hounds. Each of them wore a billowing black cloak like the ghoul who kidnapped Meg had been wearing. As they drew closer, I realized they were tall enough to be ghouls. The first cloaked figure came to the edge of the pool of light I was standing in and stopped. The wet corn chip scent smelled like a ghoul too. I could barely make out the tip of its snout inside the black hood. Slowly, so I looked as little like prey as possible, I turned to see if the other ghouls were getting closer. I thought I did a surprisingly good job of looking cool, calm, and collected, considering my stomach was about ready to leap out of my mouth and run off on its own.

One by one, the ghouls approached my little light circle and stood impassively on the edge, like they were waiting for something. A couple puzzle pieces clicked together real fast. This song and dance was familiar. I had been manipulated with ghouls before. I didn't bother looking around; I knew she could hear me.

"Hello, Lilith," I said into the night.

"So, the puppy does learn eventually," she said right behind me, I *knew* she was going to do that, but I still twitched. I turned to face the woman who had apparently literally seduced the master of seduction himself.

The Valley is hot. Volcanoes are allegedly even hotter. Lilith is… another level of heat entirely. The first time I had encountered her, she had been mostly restrained inside a summoning circle. It had helped to dampen her pheromones or something. But tonight, she was out in the wild, and I got a full blast of her.

Lilith's on-the-nose red hair was pulled back into a casual ponytail that swayed behind her as she shook her head with a bemused smile at me. Tonight, she wore black on black on black: combat boots, what I wanted to call tactical booty shorts, and a long-sleeved crop top. She looked like a sexier Lara Croft, and that was not supposed to be possible. Her eyes were unsettling— they were black, from sclera to pupil there was no other color but the abyss. She was at least my height if not a little taller, and those black orbs bored into my eyes with a predatory hunger.

"So, good news," I said after a moment of staring. "We definitely punished that Lazarus guy for you. Burned his whole building down. Thought you'd be thrilled."

Lilith stared at me in silence. I think she was trying to decide if I was stalling or an idiot. The secret was that I was both. I'd like to pretend that I had a master plan, but the truth was that I figured as long as we were talking, she wasn't plucking my eyeballs to eat like grapes. Oh, and eventually Alex and Orion might show up and kick her ass.

"It seems even the dragons get mild mannered in their old age," she said dryly. "I'm surprised you're not a pile of ash right now. They've been begging for an excuse to go after your friend for centuries."

It seemed we were laying our cards on the table. If she was admitting that she sent us to die to dragons, then the game was over.

"I guess if you want something done right, you do have to do it yourself," Lilith said with a dramatic sigh. She took a step toward me and began to raise her right hand.

All of this was bad. But that last part sounded *especially* bad. Maybe I should have stayed inside and looked at Violet's boobs. At least I wouldn't have been murdered by Satan's old lady.

"I can't believe I'm about to say this," a woman's voice cut into the night, "but step away from the soulless mortal, Lilith."

My head whipped around as another woman stepped into the light. When I realized who it was, my heart soared. She was a tall woman with skin the color of night. Unlike the last time I saw her, she wore a bronze crown that was set with a series of large diamonds, and she carried a tall bronze staff with a crescent moon at its head.

She, too, had gotten the dark clothing memo. She wore a pair of dark jeans and a gray turtleneck that made her bronze necklace even more noticeable.

"Cassiopeia, darling, surely you didn't mean to tell *me* what to do," Lilith purred. Her eyelids were half closed over her black eyes as she tracked the Constellation's approach.

"I prefer to think of it as a friendly piece of advice," Cassiopeia replied with a nonchalant shrug, "but if you feel the need to get all twisted about it, be my guest."

Lilith's wicked smile grew even wider, and she raised her left hand and snapped. Four more ghouls stepped out of the darkness to join the cloaked figures standing outside the ring. I turned to stand back to back with my rescuer. She had come to help me, the least I could do was watch her rear. Well, not *her* rear—you know what I mean. I dropped into what I hoped was a fighter's crouch, hands open wide, ready to grapple the first inhuman monster who made a move.

While technically I was undefeated against ghouls, I wasn't eager to go a second round with them. Cassie was a Constellation, but I wasn't sure if that meant she was on the same level of violence-as-art as Orion.

"What's the plan?" I whispered over my shoulder, but the statuesque woman ignored me.

"Last chance, Pretty Girl," Lilith taunted.

I looked from hood to hood, trying to spot which one would make the first move. Not that I could do much about it if they did, but it made me feel better.

"Orion is going to owe me so bad," I heard Cassie mutter to herself. I turned to see if she was looking at me, but she was already moving. Her staff twirled in her left hand like a living thing. Her right hand dropped to her waist, and she produced a mean-looking pistol faster than a Wild West gunslinger from... somewhere.

Before a single ghoul had even twitched, she fired once. The gun roared in the Los Angeles suburb and shattered the peace of the night. I was dimly aware of a ghoul slumping to the ground to her right, as she carelessly tossed the gun back to me without looking.

"Catch," she said calmly, as if she executed ghouls every day.

"Gah!" I yelled back as I dove to my knees on the asphalt and managed to catch the pistol in my arms like a dangerous football. I juggled the weapon in my hands like a hot potato as I rose from my crouch, looking at a ghoul that was still taking its first few steps.

I managed to pull the gun up as the black-cloaked monster barreled at me like the Death Express. My first shot winged the beast. He twisted to the side from the force of the impact but kept on chugging toward me. My second shot hit a leg. He went down in a faceplant on the pavement. My third and fourth shots went into his back in case he felt like getting back up.

I spun from my first target to check my back. I could almost *feel* the claws of another ghoul about to rip into my back as I was distracted. But it turned out I was not the only one distracted.

Cassiopeia danced among the ghouls like a miniature hurricane. Her staff spun and lashed out, striking as no less than five different ghouls jockeyed around her, trying to get their claws in her. She twisted to one side, dodging a tackle from one beast. At the same time, she lashed out with her staff, the crescent moon slicing the snout of another one of the monsters. I briefly felt bad for doubting her ability to live up to Orion's skill. They clearly did not hand out Constellations to just anyone.

Lilith stood on the other side of the melee with an amused smile. But it wasn't at the battle between her minions and Cassie. She was smiling at me.

Right about then, my subconscious finished doing some basic addition: one dead ghoul plus a second dead ghoul plus five ghouls battling equals seven ghouls. Eight ghouls minus seven ghouls almost equaled one dead Matthew Carver.

I caught the blur of movement in the corner of my eye. A dark shape against one of the streetlights. I dropped to the ground sideways and let out what I can only describe as a very manly scream as a ghoul sailed over me in a tackle attempt that any NFL linebacker would be proud of.

The beast and I scrambled to our feet. He was faster, but I had a gun. My world was panic, fear, and adrenaline. Time seemed to move at a crawl, but compared to my ability to form coherent thoughts, it might as well have been light speed. My hands moved up at a glacial pace as the beast lumbered toward me. As soon as my eyes saw his chest through the sights, I pulled the trigger as fast as I could. I emptied the remaining bullets into its dark robe until the dry clicks snapped me out of my panicked perception of slow time.

Cassie was still beating the crap out of the rest of the ghoul platoon. Several were down for the count with arms and legs twisted in hideous directions from their cloaks. The last two were on the retreat from her brutal staff strikes. Cassiopeia, on the other hand, looked every inch the royal that her crown proclaimed her to be. Her long black hair streamed behind her like a model's flowing in a fake breeze during a photoshoot. She could have run a business meeting immediately after this and not looked an inch out of place.

Lilith wasn't smiling anymore.

I think I knew in that moment as I watched her face transform from sex icon to devourer that I was going to die. Up until now, we had been playing with kid gloves. Orion and Lilith had done a staredown, but no one had really let loose yet. But now, in Lilith's crumbling expression, I saw the collapse of restraint. She raised her hands. Her black nails had grown into black-tipped claws. My gulp was probably audible even over the battle raging between us.

With an audible snarl, Lilith dashed around Cassie and her two remaining opponents and headed straight for me, and I was out of bullets. I don't actually think that it would have mattered. Immortality would be pretty stupid if your one weakness was bullets. That would be like if Superman were allergic to oxygen.

Out of options and ammo, I threw the pistol at Lilith like a baseball and turned tail. During the first few seconds of flight, my adrenaline thought we had a shot. I was *flying*. Why did I never try out for track? I was a natural-born runner!

Then the whole world shook, and when it stopped, I was on the ground looking up at the furious face of Lilith as she bore down on top of me. There was no more beauty in her face, only rage. Somehow the contrast between her normal beauty made this snarling visage even more disturbing. Her solid black eyes now had a deep red leaking in from the edges, and she had apparently grown a pair of fangs in the last few minutes.

She straddled me, holding me down against the pavement. I could feel the day's heat bleeding into my back. Normally my testosterone would be quite excited about this pose. But for once in my life, both of my heads were in agreement that this was terrifying.

"I'll reunite you with your soul right now," she snarled, slashing down with her clawed hands across my chest. I screamed as her nails burned their way through my shirt and chest. I flailed without any effect as she pressed me into the pavement.

"All you had to do was *die*," she hissed, slashing me again. I think I screamed, but I don't know. My everything was fire and pain. For one eternal second, I got a slight taste of what Hell might be like before I was slammed back into consciousness and had to stare into the raving abyss of Lilith's eyes.

"I'm going to enjoy watching you suffer for an eternity, fool," she hissed, drawing back her claws for one final strike.

Dimly, I was aware of the sound of an approaching vehicle.

A matte-gray Charger slid past, a long arm trailing out of the driver's seat in an almost relaxed manner. As it cruised by, the hand darted like a striking snake and buried itself deep in the red mane of Lilith.

One moment she was straddling me, holding me down to the unforgiving pavement. Then she was gone, pulled up by her roots like a furious carrot. The Charger squealed to a drifting stop, and Orion apparently let go, letting the momentum send Lilith flying down the street, where she bounced several times before sliding to a stop.

I let out a little cheer from my back on the pavement.

Orion flowed smoothly out of the driver's-side door. In his right hand, he gripped the middle of his scabbarded sword with the ruby hilt. He wore a gray jacket that was open over a white shirt and a pair of faded blue jeans. His hair was immaculately combed and slicked back. Between him and Cassiopeia, I wondered if there was some sort of Constellation dress code. He began walking toward where he had thrown Lilith without any hesitation, his shoulders squared for a fight. And as badass as that was, it wasn't what caught my attention. His normally stoic face was twisted into a mask of rage. The Hunter was furious.

Alex burst out of the passenger door and ran to me. His blond hair was spiked in every direction, and he wore a light-blue bathrobe over a white sleeveless shirt and a pair of bright-red pajama bottoms. I felt better that he had also missed the dress code memo. He dropped to a crouch by me and looked me over.

"You okay, bud?"

"Never better," I managed to wheeze. "Thanks for making your entrance dramatic. I wouldn't want to be saved too soon. That would be boring."

"Okay, I think you're fine," Alex said, standing up and offering me his hand. "If you have the strength to be sarcastic, you're probably not dying."

"Also, thanks for dressing up." I grunted as I let him pull me to my feet. My chest stung and my shirt was in tatters, but I thought he was right. I suppressed a shudder as I stood up. If Lilith had just gutted me, I would be a cooling carcass on the street. Maybe this was why parents told their kids not to play with their food.

Lilith was already back on her feet, facing Orion. She had a couple nasty tears in her Lara Croft outfit, but otherwise, she looked fine. Even her hair seemed fine, which was a testament to whatever shampoo company had partnered with Hell.

"Took you long enough," Cassie remarked, stepping next to us. A quick glance behind her showed a pile of cloaked bodies, which almost made me feel bad for the ghouls. Almost.

"Fine," Lilith snarled into the night as the four of us lined up to face her. "We can do this the hard way."

Despite her threats, I couldn't help but feel a lot better about the situation than I had even a few moments ago. We outnumbered her, *and* two of my teammates were on the varsity squad. What could possibly go wrong?

Lilith threw her head back and let out a horrendous shriek. It started high and shrill but quickly dropped into a bass octave that I could feel vibrating in my chest. Her black fingernail claws began to glow with a black light. Her head snapped down, and she slashed her hands in front of her, her glowing fingernails seeming to carve a rent in reality itself as they moved. It was like seeing a tiger tear up a piece of paper, but the paper was the veil between our world and a bad, bad place. I could feel heat pouring out of the portal. Even from twenty feet away, it made a California summer day feel cool and relaxing.

"Come, my children!" she shrieked. "Mama needs your rending teeth and crushing jaws. Come forth and devour my enemies and drink their marrow!"

"Balls," Alex breathed as the first creature emerged from the Hell Gate. It looked like it had started life as a dog. Or had been put together by someone who had heard about dogs from a friend. But that friend was high on hallucinogens and having a nightmare the only time they ever saw a dog.

The "dog" had an exoskeleton of yellow bone plates that locked together like the world's biggest and most damned armadillo. It had a long tail that ended in a set of spikes that looked like they had been stolen from a stegosaurus. What flesh was visible between the ridges of its armor looked like exposed red muscle tissue. Viscous liquid dripped from its exposed tissue and landed on the pavement where it sizzled like a frying egg. Also, this thing was big. It was easily five feet tall on all fours. Most troubling to me was the fact that its eyes glowed red with an infernal fire that matched Lilith's.

"Okay, that's pretty intimidating," I stage-whispered to Alex, still feeling confident. "But there's four of us—"

The first creature finished exiting the portal and was immediately followed by a second, then a third, and finally a fourth. They took aggressive positions between Lilith and us, walking forward one slow step at a time. A symphony of growls rolled toward us like the beginning of an earthquake.

Lilith's laughter rose above their growls. She was panting from the exertion of summoning the beasts, but her wicked grin was maniacal.

"Do you like my hounds?" she asked. "They love to eat new friends."

"Lilith, we do not need to fight," Cassie said gravely.

"Silence, tramp," Lilith snapped. "You've always been jealous of me. The Constellation of Beauty, outshone by my own star." Her eyes danced madly with the flames of Hell. "Give me the boy, and I will let you pretend that you were never here." Her gaze fixed on me in a *most* predatory manner. "You know why he must die."

"You cannot have him." Orion's voice rang out clear and strong against the night. "Take your hounds and go, or you may collect their pieces later."

I'm not going to lie, the Hunter is not the most emotive individual, but he excels at threats. I shivered a little.

"Oh, poor Hunter, can you not bear to see another pack torn to shreds? We both know you won't draw your sword. You haven't for centuries." She cackled, and the hairs on the back of my neck rose. "I call your bluff." She threw back her head and let out a howl. Her pack immediately picked it up and began loping toward us.

"Get behind me!" Cassie yelled, stepping in front of Alex and me and extending her staff like a spear.

"There's weapons in the car," Alex called to me, turning and sprinting back to Orion's Charger. I was too absorbed by the scene unfolding in front of me to follow.

The lead hound bore down on Orion with an inevitable trot, and he moved to meet it. True to Lilith's prediction, the Constellation didn't draw the sheathed blade. Instead, he seemed content to use it like a staff.

Holding it in the middle of the red scabbard, he thrust it forward like a giant stick for a dog to play with. The hound bit down with its infernal jaws, barely missing his hand. But that proved to be a mistake. In one smooth move, Orion planted his feet and pushed down, then out and up.

With a surprised whine, the demon dog found its own momentum turned against itself. With a grunt, Orion flipped it over him in an arc and spun, slamming the dog down into the pavement with a sickening crunch. I felt the force of the impact in the soles of my feet.

Quick as a snake, the Hunter stomped his foot on the beast's neck with so much force that it looked like he was trying to nail the beast to the ground with his own leg. Orion spun, turning to face the rest of the pack as they bore down on him.

As I watched, Orion met the lunge of another hound with a fierce roundhouse kick that knocked the beast off its paws. His hand flashed to his back waistband, and he pulled out a comically large pistol that roared like a cannon as he fired it at the dog he had kicked.

Cassiopeia flowed into the battle beside him like deadly silk, her staff spinning in a bronze blur once again. She took up a position behind his back, holding two of the dogs at bay with aggressive stabs of her staff.

A grating sound drew my attention back to the first hound, the one that Orion had suplexed into the street. It had rolled onto its side and was slowly getting its feet under itself. Its bony exoskeleton scratched against the ground like stone on stone.

"Alex..." I called to my friend who was still rooting through the Charger. The hound surged to its feet and shook itself like it was trying to clear its head. Given the cosmic smackdown it had just received, I really couldn't blame it. As it finished having the wiggles, its burning red eyes didn't turn toward Orion and Cassie fighting the rest of its pack. They locked immediately on me.

Hoping to stall the hellhound for a few moments, I looked down at my inert, flameless hands. "Now would be a really great time for you guys to light back up," I yelled at my palms.

They did not deign to respond.

Desperate, I held both of my hands out toward the approaching pack and tried to summon the flames. "*Burn*," I commanded.

The hound cocked its head and looked at me, like a pup trying to understand a new game. After a moment of confusion, it took another menacing step toward me.

"Alex! We're gonna need those weapons!" I yelled, turning to run to the Charger. Alex had the trunk open and was scrambling around inside, his back to me. Breaking eye contact and showing fear is rule number one of things that you aren't supposed to do with an angry dog. As I turned and ran, the hound let out a howl and came after me.

"ALEX!" I screamed.

My pajamaed friend's head popped out of the trunk, and he pulled out a long-handled sledgehammer. In his other hand, he held some sort of compact automatic gun.

"Catch!" he yelled, and suddenly I was trying to catch the second gun thrown at me in the span of ten minutes. How had I gone my whole life without ever having a gun thrown to me like a baseball? Apparently, in the supernatural world, it happened nonstop.

I caught the gun—practice makes perfect—but I didn't slow

down as I raced past Alex and the tail end of the Charger. As I ran toward him, Alex squared up, swinging the sledgehammer back like he was Babe Ruth.

"Batter, batter, batter," I wheezed as I ran past him. As I passed the swing zone, I ground to a stop and turned, raising my gun. The hound completely ignored Alex, its red eyes still focused on me. Alex waited until the beast got close and swung the head of the hammer up over his right shoulder, both hands firmly placed on the shaft.

The dull gray head slammed into the bony chest of the hound with a sound like stone breaking. The beast's legs tripped on the hammer, and it went down, flipping end over end with a series of horrendous breaking sounds. The hound slid within a few feet of me, totally broken. Even with its body ruined, its eyes were still focused on me, and it bit angrily at the air, trying to get to me.

Alex stepped up beside me and slammed the hammer down in an overhead smash on the beast's head, which burst with a horrific sound like a rotten pumpkin. Alex and I both turned away coughing as the smell of sulfur and evil wafted off its carcass. We both stared at it for a few moments, chests heaving. I fired a few rounds of the gun into it. It seemed like something Arnold Schwarzenegger would do. Besides, better safe than sorry.

"Home run," I said to Alex.

"Badass," he said. We high-fived. It was sick.

A heartbeat later, all the air left my body in an explosive burst as my back slammed into the side of the Charger. Lilith had reentered the fray, sending me flying with a kick while I was distracted with awesome high-fives. Her red hair shot in every direction, like she had been caught in a wind tunnel. Her eyes were completely red, dancing with rage. Alex ducked a swipe from her glowing black claws, letting his sledgehammer drop from his hands. Another hound leapt from beside Lilith and chased Alex, driving him even farther away.

Orion's pistol barked, and Lilith twitched to the side from the impact. She looked over my head to the other side of the car at something I couldn't see and laughed scornfully.

"You'll have to be rougher than that," she called.

This is it, I thought to myself as I gasped for air like a goldfish that jumped out of its bowl. *This is how I die.*

But Orion was there.

The Hunter leapt over the car and landed between Lilith and me with his dancer's grace. His jacket was torn in a few places, but he seemed otherwise unscathed in the battle. He still held the sword in the red sheath in his right hand, gripped firmly in the middle, far away from the hilt. Behind me, I could hear Cassie continuing her dance with the hounds, keeping them off Orion.

"Okay, Hunter, let's see what you've got," Lilith sneered and leapt forward.

Maybe it was because I was oxygen deprived and gasping for air, but I struggled to keep up with their movements. Lilith surged forward with slashing aggression. Orion danced aside from her strikes, occasionally using his sheathed sword to turn a blow or swing it like a bat.

Orion seemed like he was at an extreme disadvantage. He didn't have magical claws, and he had to keep himself in between Lilith and me. Each time she shifted him to the side, she'd steal another step closer to me. Also, he had a sword that he literally wasn't using. Despite that, as the fight continued, I got the sense he was in total control. Every step he took was deliberate. He'd dodge, step to block her movement, strike to drive her back and repeat like a simple waltz.

Lilith's face was on fire with frustration. Her red-eyed gaze kept turning to me with the same fanatical obsession that her hounds had shown a few moments earlier. Every bone in my body was urging me to get up and run. The spirit was willing, but the oxygen was still absent. So I sat and watched my friend battle for my life.

Orion certainly lived up to his reputation. There was no way that Lilith was going to beat him in one-on-one combat, and a look at both of their faces showed that they both knew it. But Lilith was a scion of Hell, so of course, she cheated.

The hound that Alex and I had killed suddenly blazed to life. What trick does every dog know? How to play dead. Its body was still damaged, but it seemed like it still had some gas in the tank as it lunged from the ground at Orion's heels at the same moment Lilith went on the attack.

I tried to call a warning to Orion, but my lungs were still recovering. All I managed was a wheeze and a cough. The hound hit Orion from behind, tripping him as Lilith lunged forward. Orion went down, but he pulled Lilith with him. They ended up in a pile, wrestling for a hold on each other.

Orion's sword flew from his grip in the struggle and slid to my feet, its ruby pommel pointed directly at me. Slowly, I reached out and placed my hand on the hilt of the sword. Nothing exciting happened. It didn't shock me or have a magical voice that spoke inside my head. It just felt like a sword.

The wrestling match continued to rage on. The hound had one of Orion's boots in its mouth, preventing him from rolling effectively. Lilith was using her advantage and had climbed on top of him, straddling him like she had me. Orion had both of her wrists grasped in his hands, but I could tell he was fighting a losing battle.

My lungs were on fire, but Orion was here because of me. I wasn't going to sit there and gasp for air while my friend was murdered. I dug the tip of the sword sheath into the ground and levered it like a cane to stand. My legs felt like they were full of Jell-O and not bones, but the struggling immortals were only a few feet away.

Lilith managed to get her left hand free of Orion's grip and swiped at his face, cutting his cheek as she tried to gouge out one of his eyes. I took two steps and knew what I had to do. I didn't know why exactly Orion never used the sword, but Lilith had made it clear that she was scared of it. Maybe it was something that could hurt a demon. Bullets sure didn't do much.

I gripped the hilt of the sword in my right hand and the sheath in my left. The ruby in the pommel seemed to dance with an excited light as I drew the sword free. The blade itself was a simple thing. It wasn't a super long sword, less than three feet of straight steel with no crossguard, and a simple pommel that could be held with one hand or two. I was almost disappointed in how normal the sword seemed—until it burst into flame.

It wasn't a dark flame like I had seen Lilith use, but a bright, cheerful fire that cast back the darkness like a bonfire on the beach.

Lilith's hands were both free, and she was slashing at Orion with wild abandon. But at the light from my blade, she stopped, turning to look at me, her mouth hanging open in shock.

I could see the flames mirrored in her demonic eyes as I swung the sword. I swung for Meg. I swung for Violet and Connor. I swung for Alex and Orion. I swung for me because I was super pissed off.

The flaming blade passed through her neck like scissors through tissue paper. Her head went flying as her body collapsed to the ground on top of Orion.

The broken hound that was biting Orion's leg froze, then burst into a thousand stony pellets like a rain of gravel. Distantly, I heard the other hounds following in the footsteps of their alpha.

My hand suddenly felt like it was on fire. With a shout, I dropped the flaming sword to the ground. The moment I let go of the hilt, the fire went out, and it clattered to the ground, looking for all the world like a normal blade. The palm of my right hand was pink and ridged with a burn that matched the pattern of the hilt.

The headless body of Lilith, Queen of Lies, Lover of the Devil, began decomposing at my feet.

CHAPTER 29

Everything that happened after I chopped off Lilith's head was a blur. Someone got me into the back seat of the car and my hand wrapped in gauze. At some point, Cassie left. I didn't get to thank her for coming to my rescue, but I knew I would have been dead without her.

I spent the night on Alex's couch. I had to move the mountain of comic books and paperbacks to the floor to make room for my body. My only blanket was a *Star Wars* beach towel.

When I woke up at noon the next day, there was a glass of water on the coffee table with a pair of extra-strength Tylenols. I almost forgot why I might need them until my whole body began to ache. I knocked back the painkillers and groaned as I sat up. I felt like I had been run over by several cement mixers. I made it as far as sitting up with my feet on the floor and put my head in my hands.

"I told you that you'd probably live," Alex's voice called from a room over. He sounded bright and cheery. Despite his heroics in saving my life the night before, I suddenly remembered he was my mortal enemy: a morning person.

There are two types of people: people who need at least

twenty minutes of silence after waking up and savages. If you're smiling before nine a.m., there's something wrong with you.

"Hnng," I grunted back to him.

"Here," a softer, less cheerful voice said. I looked up to find a bedraggled Orion still wearing the same gray coat and jeans he had worn last night. He was holding out a *Fellowship of the Ring* coffee mug in his hand. It was full of a steaming brown liquid that was either coffee or gasoline. At this point, I'd take my chances. I took the mug and held it in my left hand. My right wasn't interested in any more heat for a while.

"Mind if I sit?" he asked, gesturing at the couch.

"Please," I said, choking on a sip of the bitterest coffee I had ever tasted. I guess that whole thing about Nephilim not being able to make art included coffee. Orion sat and steepled his hands with a sigh. We sat like this for a moment. I was grateful for the silence as I ingested the "coffee" and tried to wake up. I could only assume this was going to be another conversation that didn't make me happy. Boy, was I getting tired of these.

"We need to talk about last night," he said after a pregnant pause.

"Why didn't you draw the sword?" I interrupted him.

"It's complicated," he said, looking away.

"I don't think that it is," I said quietly.

"You should tell him," Alex said, entering the room. "As always, he's the only one who doesn't know how bad this is." The lesser Nephilim leaned back against the wall across from us and crossed his arms. For once there was no happy smile on his face. He was still in his battle-scarred pajamas and bathrobe. My friend didn't make eye contact with either of us but tried to stare a hole in the gray shag rug.

Orion was silent for so long that I began to worry that he had finally turned into a statue. But after what felt like forever, he started to speak.

"Because I knew if I drew the sword, there was no going back."

"Why would the sword do that?" I asked. "It's just a sword. A cool fiery sword, but what's the big deal?"

"It's quite a famous sword." Alex laughed with an edge.

"More importantly, it's an escalation. It is very hard to kill an immortal. But the sword is something that can."

"So, she is *dead* dead?" I squeaked. I don't know if I really thought that I had actually killed Lilith. In the back of my mind, I had assumed she probably got sent back downstairs to Hell in a puff of smoke or something like that. After licking her wounds, she could possess another body and return to plague me again. I had thought my solution was temporary.

"As a doornail," Alex chimed in from where he leaned on the wall.

"It is complicated to explain," Orion said slowly. "We were trying to stop her, but we were not threatening her. I could have put her head through the engine block of the car without causing insult. To someone like her, that's fair play."

"But if you drew the sword you go from shooting hoops and playing the game to pulling a gun in the endzone?"

"I don't know how you think sports work, but I think you get the idea," Alex said.

"At least I can make coffee that doesn't taste like a tar pit," I muttered into my mug as I took another sip. "So let me get this straight: you were not drawing the sword to... not be rude?"

"It is important to respect your elders," Alex replied sagely.

"Threatening Lilith's life would have given a lot of my enemies all the excuse they needed," Orion answered. "There are many who have been waiting for the moment to come after me again."

"You're talking about the dragons and stuff, aren't you?" I guessed.

"More than just them. I used to hunt them all."

"In the old days," Alex said, "Orion was like a pro-human vigilante. He'd prowl around and jump all kinds of monsters that preyed on humans."

"What happened to the rest of your Hunt?" I asked quietly.

"Most of them died," Orion croaked, his voice going raw. "I agreed to stop hunting if they let the rest live."

"So, you killed some of their friends, they killed some of yours, and there was a truce. Lots of big scary things wanted to break the truce, but they needed an excuse, and killing Lilith is a giant excuse?" I guessed.

A whole bunch of conversations clicked into place. The way that everyone seemed to be afraid of Orion. The snide comments about the last people who had worked with him. Robin's shock that Orion would threaten him. Cassie's question about going to war over me wasn't idle chitchat. Orion was warning her. I think for the first time, I understood what it meant to have Orion the Hunter on my side.

"Much worse," Alex agreed.

Orion said nothing, only looked at his hands.

"So, you're telling me that instead of saving Orion's life from the literal girlfriend from Hell, I screwed us?"

"Yes," Alex immediately replied. He pulled a shiny red apple from one of his bathrobe pockets and bit into it with a juicy crunch. I winced at the sound of that bite. It seemed thematically the wrong time to be eating red apples.

"But also, no," Orion said with a nod to me. "She could have and would have killed me easily. Despite the circumstances, I owe you my life."

My respect for Orion skyrocketed once again. He had willingly stepped into the ring against an opponent who could have killed him, but he wasn't allowed to try to kill in return. Holy crap.

"Yeah, well, put it on the tab," I said, not sure how to respond to the situation. "I'm sure I'll owe you another five times by the end of next week."

"Ain't that the truth," Alex groaned as he took another bite of his apple. "The last time he went on the Hunt, blood flowed like water."

"You did well." Orion turned to Alex and held out his hand. "I was... dismissive of you when you brought me to Matthew. That was wrong of me. You've proven yourself in multiple battles. You are worthy of your bloodline. If you will accept it, it would be my honor to have you as my squire."

Alex froze partway through accepting the handshake, doing a respectable imitation of the stillness Lilith and Orion showed when they were surprised.

"Falling Stars," he swore in disbelief.

Orion gave him something of a pained look, one eyebrow arched.

"Sorry, no offense," Alex said, holding up his free hand. "You sure you want me to join the Hunt?"

"You've earned it several times over," Orion said, pumping his hand in the shake a final time. "You both have." He turned his black eyes on me. A terrified thrill ran down my spine. "Squire" had never come up during career counseling in college, but after the last few days, it felt right.

"I should never have gone over and said hello to the soulless human," Alex muttered, finally shaking Orion's hand.

"You wanted a chance to prove yourself," I said. "Isn't that why you helped me in the first place? Now we have to stop an apocalyptic war and survive it being open season on Orion and the boys."

"I was hoping to prove myself in a situation that was like a seven out of ten." Alex sighed dramatically. "This is like a forty-five out of ten."

"More like a forty-six," Orion replied.

That was when I got really scared. If *Orion*, of all people, was cracking jokes, we were for sure dead.

After our depressing powwow, they took me to see Meg. The place where Lazarus's people had taken my sister was much more subtle than the one that I had burned down. From the outside, it looked like a generic four-story office building. There were no logos or signs announcing who or what worked in the building. The parking lot was busy with folks coming and going, most of whom wore scrubs. It looked like a totally normal medical building.

Lazarus, the mobster philanthropist, met us at the doors to the facility. He was still rocking the tweed suit and the cane topped with a mysterious golden animal, but today his pocket square was a vivid purple. Positively wild, I tell you. He still had his half-moon spectacles perched on his nose like he was a modern-day Benjamin Franklin.

He was flanked on either side by two men who looked like they ate NFL linebackers for breakfast followed by seventeen protein shakes for a snack. They wore black tactical outfits, and each of them openly carried a submachine gun in their hands.

"Gentlemen," he said with his reedy voice as we approached. "As you can see, I am a man of my word. Please do not disappoint me, and keep yours."

"A deal is a deal," I said, raising my hands in an open gesture. "I just want to see my sister. We don't want any trouble."

Lazarus harrumphed once but nodded.

"Then if you would be so good as to follow me," he said, turning around. His two guard dogs didn't move. Their eyes locked on the three of us. I sighed but followed. Alex and Orion followed me, and the two giant slabs of meat followed them. We made a nice little parade through the lobby.

The interior was anything but generic like the exterior implied. Everything was sleek and modern like it had been at the Galahad lab. We walked across a marble floor that had the Lazarus logo: two scrolls crossed behind the image of an old cup or goblet, stamped on the floor in bronze. More mountains of meat stood guard at regular intervals around the room. Men and women in scrubs moved at brisk clips, seemingly unbothered by the presence of the armed guards. I wondered if they were a new feature or if this more incognito facility was better defended. Alex had said we would only get one freebie. I guess he was right.

Lazarus limped his way to an elevator that promptly slid open for us. It was an extra-large elevator, big enough to fit all six of us. I couldn't imagine if they were moving minotaurs and other massive creatures around they'd want to use the stairs.

"Has she woken up?" I asked Lazarus as he pressed the button for the fourth floor.

"There's been no change," he said, turning to look at me. His watery blue eyes looked almost compassionate. "She's stable and comfortable. We've been running tests, but so far nothing physical seems to be wrong."

The elevator dinged, and the whole gang filed out into the hallway. This floor looked like every hospital hallway I had ever seen. The wall was a two-tone variation of beige, and the white linoleum floor was speckled with colored flakes like the pattern on paper Dixie cups. More nurses and doctors in scrubs walked up and down the hallway, going into patient rooms. Like the first floor, the staff moving around paid us no mind. We might as well have been invisible.

Lazarus stopped at the room marked 411. A sign next to the door read "Carver, M."

"She's in there," he said. "Your friends should wait with us here in the hall. We don't allow too many visitors in the room at once." He glanced at a golden wristwatch. "Fifteen minutes?"

I nodded. I wanted to protest all the restrictions, but I didn't have a lot of bargaining power in this situation. My sister was in some sort of undead coma and needed help. I had burned this guy's research lab to the ground, so he didn't owe me any favors. Alex and Orion must have understood because neither of them protested when I agreed to the terms.

I slipped into my sister's hospital room, and for a few moments, all I could do was stare at her body lying in the bed.

This was my worst nightmare come to life. She had already died once before. Seeing her as still as a corpse for a second time threatened to break my heart all over again.

Her short brown hair was splayed out on her pillow like a dingy halo. Her face was at peace. She could have been asleep for a short nap—except for the breathing device that was hooked up to her mouth and the sound of pumping air filling the room as the machine sent oxygen in and out of her lungs. I wasn't even sure she needed to breathe anymore, but it was still an unsettling sight to see a loved one have a machine breathe for them.

I dragged a chair from next to the window and pulled it up to the side of her bed. Hesitantly, I reached out and took her hand. It still felt cold and clammy to my touch. My brain knew the truth of what she was, even if normal people couldn't see it. I forced my hand to hold hers, even though it made my skin crawl. So far, the only perk out of this soul fraud was getting to see my sister again. I wasn't going to waste it.

"Hey, sis," I said quietly after a few moments. "I'd really appreciate it if you would wake up. I could really use your help."

Nothing answered me but the rise and fall of the oxygen pump and the beeping of the machines.

As I sat there with Megan, I began to process the events of last night. I had killed someone. Yes, I had killed in the fight at Lazarus' lab. But Lilith was far more human than the faceless guards had been to me. Maybe it was because I knew her. But it was more than that. Lilith had been someone important. She was like the second-in-command of Hell. And supposedly the Devil's girlfriend.

All I'm trying to say is: I felt different.

I was a killer now.

I had enemies that were going to come for me. They had tried to use me as a pawn to start a cosmic war, but despite some incredibly powerful being's best attempts, I was still on the board, and despite having no idea how to really play supernatural chess, I had taken the enemy's queen.

For the first time in a long time, I didn't feel helpless anymore. My perspective shifted to appreciate what I had survived so far.

If they wanted me to be in their game, fine. I'd turn myself into a knight. They had shown me the cracks in my reality. My sister was dead, but also wasn't. Determination flooded through me in a way I don't think I had ever experienced before. I didn't have to wait to die. I could beat this. I could get my soul back. I could get my sister back. And if I couldn't, then I was going to go down swinging.

"Hey," I said to my sister's unconscious form. "I'm going to finish what they started. I'm going to bring you back for good." I squeezed her disgusting hand that felt a little too mushy to be right.

A knock sounded behind me, and the door opened slightly.

"Mr. Carver, I'm afraid that's time," Lazarus said gently into the room.

"That's all right," I said, letting go of my sister's hand. "I've got things to do."

COMING SOON

Thank you for reading Soul Fraud! Matt, Alex, and Orion's adventures will continue in *Dandelion Audit,* which will be available for pre-order in late 2022! (I hope.)

If you enjoyed the book, please remember to leave a rating on Amazon. Rent is coming up.

ACKNOWLEDGMENTS

I've always wanted to write a book. Ever since I could read one. Maybe even before, who knows. But wanting to write a book and actually publishing a book are two very different things.

I did not do this one my own, and I want to make sure everyone knows it. A huge thank you to the alpha readers who read something far worse and less coherent than what you just did: Molly, Aki, Caleb, and Kate crawled so this novel could walk. Or something like that.

To the tireless beta readers who helped me bring this in for a landing and encouraged me when I doubted it: Jeremy, Daniel, Casey, Ryan, Erica, Lauren, Cris, Galen, Katie, Elias, Aaron, and SM. (And a whole host more.)

To Taylor, who gave fantastic feedback and gave it a much-needed editing pass. (I don't actually know how commas work; I just put them where I feel like they should go.)

To Crystal, for her tireless edits and advice as I continually ran into a part of the process I didn't know how to do.

To my manager, Amber, and Ryan, who helped me plot the course of success for this book, without whom it might not be edited or available in audiobook form.

And finally, to all of you. Thanks for reading this far. Thanks for joining me on this journey. I hope you had as much fun as I did.

Let's do it again.

ABOUT THE AUTHOR

When he's not frantically trying to figure out how to steal Matt's soul back, Andrew is also a gaming YouTuber known as Sigils. He loves making people laugh, video games, and food. (Not always in that order.) He lives in LA.

To learn more about him you can go to his website: andrewgivler.com

Printed in Great Britain
by Amazon